PRAISE FOR MARK MORRIS

TOADY

"A strikingly imaginative mixture of horror and fantasy, with a real sense of supernatural terror and with scenes of horror so strange they border on surrealism"

— Ramsey Campbell

STITCH

"A sizzling banquet of the bizarre that simply demands to be read"
— Julian Lloyd Webber, *Sunday Express*

"A big, blusteringly red-faced, glowering novel of neo-religious cults, bizarre sex and rarely plumbed levels of almost impenetrable blackness... the essence of true horror"

— Peter Crowther, *Fear Magazine*

THE SECRET OF ANATOMY

"Finely crafted and powerfully written, The Secret of Anatomy is an apocalyptic journey into dark and forbidden territory"

— Clive Barker

"Morris orchestrates the non-stop occult action with fearsome intensity"

— Christopher Fowler, *Time Out*

THE OBSIDIAN HEART TRILOGY

"The writing is great: knowledgeable, intelligent, thoughtful, echoing the deceptively literate poetry of the mundane in such work as that of Stephen King"

- SFFWORLD.com

"A wild, scary, exhilarating ride."

—Kit Power, *Ginger Nuts of Horror*

FIDDLEBACK

"Eerie, assured and utterly compelling, this is a novel you will not forget"

— Michael Marshall Smith

"Nightmarish... Morris writes superbly about a small town's gathering of menacing forces"

— *Time Out*

IT SUSTAINS

"Morris weaves together a boy's troubled adolescence and inexplicable supernatural doings in this subtle, elusive, and unforgettable tale."

— *Publishers Weekly*

THE IMMACULATE

"Easily Mark Morris's best novel so far... A real contribution to the literature of the ghostly"

— Ramsey Campbell

ALSO BY MARK MORRIS

Novels

Toady (1989)
Stitch (1991)
The Immaculate (1992)
The Secret of Anatomy (1994)
Mr. Bad Face (1996)
Longbarrow (1997)
Genesis (1999)
Fiddleback (2002)
Nowhere Near An Angel (2005)
The Deluge (2007)
Dead Island (2011)
Vampire Circus (2012)
It Sustains (2013)
The Black (2014)
Zombie Apocalypse: Horror Hospital (2014)
The Wolves of London (Obsidian Heart Book 1) (2014)
The Society of Blood (Obsidian Heart Book 2) (2015)
The Wraiths of War (Obsidian Heart Book 3) (2016)
The Great Wall (2017)
Indigo (2017)
(with Charlaine Harris, Christopher Golden,
Jonathan Maberry, Kelley Armstrong,
Kat Richardson, Seanan McGuire, Tim Lebbon,
Cherie Priest and James A. Moore)
The Predator (2018)
(with Christopher Golden)

Anthologies

The Spectral Book of Horror Stories (2014)
The 2nd Spectral Book of Horror Stories (2015)
New Fears: New Horror Stories by
Masters of the Genre (2017)
New Fears 2 - More New Horror Stories by
Masters of the Macabre (2018)

Collections

Close to the Bone (1995)
Long Shadows, Nightmare Light (2011)
Wrapped in Skin (2016)

Chapbooks

Birthday (1992)
The Dogs (2001)
The Uglimen (2002)
Stumps (2009)
Albion Fay (2014)

Nonfiction

Cinema Macabre (2006)
Cinema Futura (2010)

THE
WINTER
TREE

by Mark Morris

READ UNTIL YOU BLEED!

THE
WINTER
TREE

MARK MORRIS

CONTENTS

INTRODUCTION:

PLEASE READ THIS BIT FIRST!

Look, I know the temptation is often to skip the introduction to a book, or maybe, for fear of spoilers, to read it after you've read the book itself. But on this occasion, can I politely ask that you resist that temptation? Because the thing is, before reading this book I think you really ought to know what you're letting yourself in for.

Okay, firstly, and most importantly, there's this: what you're holding in your hand is not a new novel.

In fact, in many ways *The Winter Tree* is as much a historical document, or even a curio, as it is a novel. I wrote it the year after I graduated in 1984 at the tender age of 21. What I want to do over the next few pages – what I *need* to do over the next few pages – is put *The Winter Tree* into some kind of context. I need to explain why it's being published now, after all these years, and to... well... I guess, to make excuses for it, really.

First of all, though, a bit of history.

As I say, I started *The Winter Tree* in the autumn of 1984, not long after turning 21, and I finished it in the summer of 1985, give or take a month either side of my 22nd birthday. Aside from a couple of *Doctor Who* novels I wrote when I was 12 (longhand in ring-binder notepads), this was the first full-length novel I'd attempted. When it was finished I sent Xeroxed hard copies out to several editors, including, as I recall, Jo Fletcher, who I think was then at Sphere Books, Nigel Robinson at W.H. Allen, and

Judy Piatkus at Piatkus Books.

The Winter Tree was never published (looking back it's not difficult to see why, but more of that later), but it came pretty close – perhaps closer than it deserved. More importantly for me, though, it generated interest in my work, received some really positive feedback, from these three editors and others, and ultimately paved the way for *Toady*, my second much better, and far more ambitious, novel. I wrote *Toady* between 1985-88 (it was a *loooong* book), and it was subsequently bought by Judy Piatkus at Piatkus Books, who had seen and liked *The Winter Tree*. Piatkus Books released *Toady* in UK hardback in 1989, then sold the paperback rights to Corgi/Transworld, who not only released the mass market paperback edition in 1990, but gave it enough marketing *oomph* to turn it into a Top Ten Bestseller, and US paperback rights were then sold to Bantam, who released *Toady*, under the (bland) title *The Horror Club*, in 1991.

While *Toady* was receiving the plaudits, its older sibling *The Winter Tree* was gathering dust in a filing cabinet in what we call the back workshop, where we keep things like tools, tins of paint, ladders and walking boots. And there the manuscript stayed for over thirty years, until a casual remark about it by me on Facebook prompted Pete Kahle of Bloodshot Books to drop me a line. Pete told me he'd be interested in publishing *The Winter Tree*, if only as a curiosity piece, as a literary equivalent of one of those 'Before They Were Famous' TV shows, in which a celebrity's past is put on display like dirty washing for all the world to see. Or, to put it in musical terms, like one of those rough demos of a band's early songs, recorded in someone's garage.

I was interested in the idea, and so for the first time in three decades I dug the book out to give it a read. It was an *interesting* experience, and afterwards I advised Pete not to commit to anything until he'd had a chance to look at the manuscript himself.

Several weeks later – the book didn't exist in digital form, so I had to package it up in a box and snail-mail it to the US – Pete got back in touch to say he'd still like to go ahead. I agreed on the proviso that I could write this introduction. Which is why you're now reading these words.

So what kind of book is *The Winter Tree*? Well, I guess the best way to describe it would be as a 1980s style horror potboiler. It's certainly influenced by my genre reading at the time, which back then was a haphazard mish-mash of Pan and Fontana horror anthologies, a small amount of good stuff like King and Herbert, and a vast amount of – yes – 1980s horror potboilers about Satanists, axe murderers, giant man-eating insects, and demonic entities rising from the swamps of Hell and feasting on the flesh of the living.

A quick aside: between finishing *The Winter Tree* and starting *Toady*, I read Stephen King's *Danse Macabre*, which for the next couple of years acted as my genre Bible. It was thanks to that book that I became more selective about my reading, discarding the trash (fun though much of it was – and occasionally still is), and discovering writers such as Robert Bloch, Fritz Leiber, Ramsey Campbell, Anne Rivers Siddons, Shirley Jackson, Ray Bradbury, Peter Straub, Charles L. Grant and others. *Toady*, I think, certainly benefits from these more... shall we say, *upmarket* influences, whilst still retaining something of the gung-ho freneticism of youth. 1980s horror was often big, brash and unashamedly melodramatic, and *Toady* very much embraces the Zeitgeist of the era. Compared to *The Winter Tree*, though, it's a model of maturity and restraint.

Look, before I go any further, let me just say that I'm

not here simply to tear my own work apart. All I really want to do, before you read the book, is to let you know that I'm acutely aware of its faults. Any writer worth his salt is his own fiercest critic, and revisiting early work is invariably a tortuous process. Whenever someone tells me they've read one of my early books, my immediate instinct is to apologize for it. Writers see nothing but the frayed edges, the loose ends, the unfinished corners in their own work that readers often either miss or disregard. It just so happens that *The Winter Tree* has more frayed edges and loose ends than you'd normally find in a published novel. But it does have good things in it too. So let's concentrate on those first, shall we?

It has atmosphere and a decent sense of place, I'll give it that. The woodland scenes in particular, I think, although a bit ragged around the edges, are pleasingly effective. When, in 1986, I sent Ramsey Campbell some of my early stories, after he had kindly agreed to read and criticize them, he wrote back to say that he found some of the scenes of terror 'very effective, helped by your sense of timing and your ability to slow down at these points – writers often rush them and spoil them.'

Although *The Winter Tree* was written a couple of years before the batch of stories that Ramsey read, I feel his comments could equally have applied to certain scenes in my first novel. I've always been aware, I think, of the importance of building atmosphere, of timing a scene so that it's neither dragged down by being too slow or rendered ineffective by being too rushed. With that in mind, the two main protagonists' initial foray into the woods, the courting couple in the car at night (an outrageous horror cliché, but effective nonetheless), the two cops on night patrol, and sections of the climactic manhunt are, therefore, all scenes that I think I can be justifiably proud of writing at the age of 21. All but the first of those scenes take place in the dark, but there are a couple of daytime scenes too, elsewhere in the book (primarily involving characters who are uneasy in their own homes), which I think come pretty close to the level of creepiness I was striving for – a creepiness heavily influenced by 70s TV shows such as Brian Clemens' *Thriller*, and by low budget British movies such as *Blind Terror*, *Fright* and *Fear in the Night*, which as an adolescent I'd watch in a state of rigid, seat-gripping tension.

Where the book falls down is primarily in its – and my – naiveté. I'm astonished, looking back, at how ill-informed I was at the age of 21. My worst offence is, without doubt, my sloppy handling of the police investigation into the series of murders that take place in and around the village of Limefield, and the various incidents associated with that – not least, the breakout and subsequent disappearance of over fifty inmates from the local prison, which seems to raise no more than the barest flicker of alarm among the local constabulary!

It's embarrassing, in these far more enlightened and informed times, to detail the book's many failings in its depiction of police procedure, but I'm going to lay my cards on the table. Without going into specifics, or trying to give too much away, here is pretty much how police handle things in *The Winter Tree*:

After a horrific double-murder is committed in the local wood, the police turn up and immediately transport the remains to a nearby morgue 'for forensic examination'. Once the bodies have been removed from the scene, the police simply leave the area - *without* cordoning off the crime scene, and *without* scouring the area for forensic evidence. When, a day or two later, another murder takes place in the wood, the police respond by putting up a fence (as if there's only one point of access) and posting a patrol car, manned by a couple of officers, whose job it is to warn people away from the area 'for their own safety'. Astoundingly the local Chief Inspector (who, ironically, is criticized by various characters for being too much of a stickler for the rules) then calls a meeting in the village hall to generate ideas and opinions from the local people as to how he and his officers should proceed with the investigation (!!!). As a result of this meeting, he is cajoled and bullied into agreeing to a barely-organized manhunt, in the woods, in the dead of night, involving a mob made up of police officers, armed with guns, and men from the village (many of who have been drinking), armed with an assortment of makeshift weapons, in the hope of stumbling across (and presumably bludgeoning to death) the murderer...

Yes. Quite.

As I say, I'm shocked, looking back, to discover quite how little I knew about the workings of the world at the age of 21, and certainly I now find it impossible to imagine how I could ever have thought that such an account of a police investigation would be considered even remotely acceptable and convincing to readers. I can only assume that at the time I thought a British 1980s police force would operate in much the same way as one from a 1930s Universal Frankenstein movie. Certainly, the parallels are there: the manhunt at the end of *The Winter Tree* is not a million miles from the villagers, armed with pitchforks and flaming torches, marching on Castle Frankenstein, with the Burgomaster at their head.

If I'm being generous, I could argue that the naiveté prevalent throughout this novel is kind of charming. If you're of a forgiving disposition, you may even find it amusing – not to mention an interesting example of a writer who is still breaking out of the cocoon of childhood and taking his first faltering steps as an adult.

Because, when it comes down to it, that's what *The Winter Tree* feels like – it's a book full of juvenilia that aspires to be taken seriously; an immature book that is trying very, very hard to be grown-up and serious.

I tried hard to populate the book with vibrant, believable characters – and unwittingly ended up, for the most part, with caricatures and ciphers – particularly in the aforementioned village hall meeting scene. I tried hard to show characters *in extremis*, to depict their heightened emotions as honestly and accurately as I could – but all too often their arguments and responses come across as hysterical, ill considered, and – yes – curiously child-like (not to mention their wildly over the top responses to their encounters with the supernatural, which invariably either render them catatonic with shock or reduce them to gibbering wrecks).

Child-like too is my own weird assumption that country folk would all own guns. And when I say 'all', I mean not just the farmers, who in *The Winter Tree* seem to carry their weapons around with them as a matter of course, but 'ordinary' folk too, like the parents of our two teenage protagonists, Kevin Truscott and Martin Mason.

Mr. Truscott, of whom admittedly little is known, but who is depicted as a typical 'dad' type figure – middle-aged, balding, vaguely ineffectual – even owns a sawn-off shotgun, for God's sake! Perhaps he's a bank robber on the sly. Or perhaps (and this is more likely) I was not entirely sure at the age of 21 what a sawn-off shotgun was, or what it was used for, but just thought it sounded cool.

What else? Well, resisting the temptation to nit-pick my way through the book's many clichés and plot holes, I'd like to talk briefly about the Old Man. The Old Man – let's call him Deus X. Machina, because he's never named – is a prime example of the somewhat cavalier manner in which magic and mysticism is portrayed in *The Winter*

Tree. When you read this, be prepared for the fact that there are certain 'mystical' elements in the novel, which simply *exist*, but whose origins and workings are never explained. At the time I'm sure this was because I was striving for a sense of awe, of other-worldliness, but reading the book again now, all these years later, these elements simply come across as a) unfocused, b) irritating, and c) damned convenient when they need to be, particularly during the novel's denouement (of which I'll say no more).

So, all in all, what do we have here? We have a novel written by a still immature and fairly unworldly young man, who – thankfully – was destined to become a much better writer, and (though I say it myself) fairly quickly too. There is a big leap, both in terms of quality and maturity, between *The Winter Tree* and *Toady* – although it's worth bearing in mind that because *Toady* took me three years to write (during which time my dad died suddenly from a heart attack, which I think made me grow up very quickly), I was in my mid-20s when I completed it, added to which the book then underwent a professional editing process, which would have further ironed out any rough patches – a process which *The Winter Tree* never benefitted from.

As is obvious from the rest of this introduction, there is a lot wrong with *The Winter Tree* – and yet at the same time it was considered good enough by a number of highly respected professional editors to generate interest in my future work. Evidently, they saw *something* in this often unfocused, unbalanced, naïve collection of ideas and set pieces which made them sit up and take notice – and I hope you will too. If nothing else, for those of you who have followed my career over the past three decades, *The Winter Tree* will serve, as I said at the top of this introduction, as an interesting historical document, and perhaps as a kind of warts and all example of the standard you should expect to be striving for at the start of your career, producing work which is far, far from perfect, but which nevertheless contains just enough nuggets of gold to produce a glitter that catches the eye.

Mark Morris,
Sunday 15th April, 2018

PART ONE

SUN

CHAPTER ONE

SWANEY (SPRING 1978)

Russell Swaney took the carving knife from the kitchen drawer and wrapped it carefully in a plastic bag. He shut the drawer and slipped the package neatly inside his denim jacket, looking around with furtive eyes. He tiptoed down the hall, opened the front door, and crept out.

The spring air was fresh and spicy with new hope. Nature had crawled from its annual depression of winter and was looking ahead with the glimmerings of a smile. Russell Swaney noticed none of this. A day was just a day to him — they were all the same. He strode purposefully, a small figure in denims and scuffed trainers with lank black hair. His mouth was pert, the nose snubbed and freckly just like any other small boy, but the pale, dead eyes were disturbing in the ten-year-old face.

It was 6:45 a.m., and the sky was still only half-awake, swirling with confused colours. The houses were dim, not quite in silhouette except for the rooftops, and the pavements were an even, dark blue-grey.

Russell knew his mum would hit the roof when she discovered he'd run off, but he didn't care. Why should he have to wait around to talk to that bloody social worker again? He hated her. She was a stupid, ugly bitch with her little round glasses, her posh voice and her trendy haircut. All she could do was ask questions. Questions, questions, questions. One after the other, in a stupid soft voice that never changed. What makes you so destructive? What makes you so bitter? Why do you kill animals? Why did you bash in that dog's skull with a hammer? Why did you throw that rabbit off a motorway bridge? Is everything all right at home? Is everything all right at school? Do you have many friends? Do you have many problems? Just questions all the time.

But he wouldn't answer. Why should he? She wasn't interested. She pretended she was his friend, she pretended to like him, but really, she hated him, Russell could tell. He used to look forward to her visits just so he could swear at her and spit at her and know she wasn't allowed to get him back, but even that was boring now. She just sat there like a lump of shit and took it all, a sickly smile on her face, and her head nodding like one of those stupid dogs in car back-windows.

Russell crossed the main road, hurried along a side street, and took the rough, almost unnoticeable path that led off towards Redheath Woods and the farms at Moor Cross. The path was uneven and narrow, little more than a passageway hemmed in by bushes and trees. Sagging wire-netting on both sides barely held off the encroaching vegetation. It was very still and quiet. There were no cars around yet, and Russell felt peaceful. He wished it could be like this all the time; nobody but him in the world so he could live as he liked and do exactly as he wanted.

A bush had fingered its way through the netting and was growing across the path ahead in a rebellious attempt to block the way. Russell picked his way carefully through it, feeling the weight of the knife in his jacket. He pressed it against himself through the material and the plastic bag crackled slightly. Russell felt a thrill fizz up through him like tiny bubbles. He smiled. A thorny branch snagged at the bottom of his trousers as though it knew his intentions and was trying to hold him back. Russell wrenched it loose and continued on his way.

The sky was brightening now, the darker layers peeling away to reveal the light beneath. As if on cue, the sun began to deal out columns of white-yellow to the waiting clouds.

After half a mile Russell stopped. He peered through the wire-netting. Beyond a patch of marshy scrubland was a wooden fence, embraced with shrubs and bushes, which bordered a field full of sheep. The sun sparkled on the dew, making the sheep look like cotton wool balls in a sea of green glitter.

Russell struggled through a hole in the netting and circled the marsh. Although grass sprouted from the scum-flecked water there was no telling how deep he might sink if he tried to walk across it. He paused when he reached the fence and looked over at the grazing sheep. Many of them had been recently lambing, and their bellies sagged and swayed with milk. The lambs tottered unsteadily, staying close to their mothers, Russell reached into his jacket and took out the knife. He unwrapped it from its plastic covering and held it in front of him. He turned it back and forth in his hand almost reverently. The sun glinted on the polished metal, hypnotising him with a flashing, lighthouse rhythm. Gripping the knife tightly, he climbed over the fence into the field.

Thomas Bates looked at his watch. Only 7:20 and the morning already felt old. Mind you, the lambing season was always busy. Cows and pigs and hens had no sympathy; they still expected just as much attention. Thomas had been up at 5:00 that morning, well before anyone else. He'd done his rounds on the farm in the dark and had even managed to bag a rabbit for the supper table in the woods: not bad going considering how poor the light had been. Now he had only the sheep and their young 'uns to check up on in the top field, and then he could go back home and get some breakfast inside him. Petra, his wife, would be putting the eggs and bacon in the pan now, and the kids would be fetching in some firewood and doing the milking before getting ready for school. Thomas felt contented. The winter was often a treacherous time for farmers, but that year it had been kind to him.

Business had slowed, but not struggled, and at least he had lost none of his stock. As he trudged up the rise which sheltered the top field from all but the most ruthless winds, Thomas thought of the bacon and fresh bread smells which would be filling the farmhouse at this moment.

But his appetite disappeared like a falling brick when he topped the rise and saw the carnage before him.

Sheep and lambs lay sprawled in the grass in grotesque

positions, their fleeces spattered with blood. Some of them were still alive, twitching horribly, their eyes glaring like mad orbs of clouded glass as their life gushed away from them.

Thomas' immediate thought was that a dog had been at them. But then he noticed that their throats had not been torn and mangled, but slashed open—sliced cleanly with a blade. He dropped to his knees by a dead lamb and picked it up gently. It lolled in his arms like an empty sack of skin.

The head spun on a thread of muscle and fell to the ground. He felt sick with loathing and disgust. Who could have done such a thing?

Then he saw the boy.

Russell was finding it more difficult to catch the sheep now. The first few had been easy. He had chased them, dived on them, and held them down while he cut their throats. But the smell of their blood, hot and rich and steamy on the air, had startled the others, and they'd started to run round and round the field, fleeing blindly to nowhere. The lambs had been easier to catch than the sheep, but the sheep were better to kill. They struggled more and their bleating seemed to hold a note of real terror whilst the lambs just sounded confused.

The knife was happy in Russell's hands, and Russell was happy that the knife was happy. He grinned through a maskful of blood. His hair, his face, his clothes, the knife— all were red. The handle was so slippery he could barely grip it.

Russell breathed in the smell of the blood, relishing its sickly odour. He felt powerful. He was a king, a ruler, the master of all things. Anything that lived was Russell's enemy, but once he had conquered it, once he had killed it, then it became his subject. Pain and killing were his watchword. Blood and death were his strength.

He was creeping up on a transfixed sheep, like a hunter through the grass, when the first shot exploded behind him. Russell jumped and whirled, red-streaked knife held high in hateful defiance. A man was striding across the field towards him, shotgun pointed straight up, smoke furling from the barrel and trailing away like a battle flag. The man's face was red, and his eyes were bulging like boiled eggs. His lips were moving, but Russell couldn't hear any words. All he could hear was the roaring in his ears, and his temples booming like war drums

For a moment the rage inside Russell almost took over. He was the king, and killing was his pleasure: who was this peasant to tell him otherwise? He was about to run at the man, to slice him up as he had done with the sheep, but then something approaching sanity asserted itself and he turned and ran. As the second shotgun blast tore the spring morning in two, Russell ducked, but the man was only firing into the air again. The roaring died away in Russell's head as he scaled the fence and pelted across a fallow field. He could hear the pounding footsteps of the man behind him, and fancied he could feel a harsh, rapid breath on his neck.

His hair itched with drying blood, and the blood glued the knife to his hand, making it part of him. He felt light-headed, ecstatic. His young legs, pumping with adrenalin, blurred beneath him, carrying him easily away from the lumbering farmer. Up ahead was another fence, bristling barbed wire attached to a line of wooden stakes, and beyond that the banking sloped down at a steep angle into a tight valley and then came up just as steeply on the other side. For a moment, Russell was puzzled. Then he noticed the top of a red brick structure with a huge arched opening leading into blackness, and realised where he was. The railway line! That peasant with the gun wouldn't catch him now. He vaulted over the fence, nimbly avoiding the barbed wire, and began to lower himself backwards down the steep banking towards the railway track. He used the knife, stabbing it deep into the sloping ground as he descended.

Thomas Bates clambered over the barbed wire fence with difficulty, tearing his trousers. He swore, hurried to the banking, and peered over the edge,

Russell was well below him, only ten or fifteen feet from the track. The thickset farmer stomped about impotently like a bull who has just seen a potential victim leap to safety over a gate.

"You come back here, you murdering little bastard," he screamed. The boy looked up at him, gore-streaked face twisted in a devil-mask.

"Fuck off," he shouted savagely.

"I'll have the police on you!" threatened the farmer.

Russell thought of the sheep, lying in bloody heaps about the field, and a giggle of pleasure danced in his throat. He was about to reply when he heard an approaching rumble from the tunnel mouth. A train was coming!

The boy twisted his head and stared stupidly, his smile fading and his eyes widening into white ping pong balls in his red face. He clung to the hillside as the rumble increased ominously.

Up above, Thomas felt a faint vibration beneath his feet as the train roared into the tunnel. To Russell, it seemed as though the whole hillside was being shaken in an immense fist. He felt his feet slipping and sliding, and the earth crumbling away beneath his fingers. He clawed desperately for a handhold but found himself being jerked nearer and nearer to the grinning teeth of the railway track.

"Help me!" he screamed, his childish voice piercing in the crisp morning air. Thomas could only stand and watch as the boy slid ever closer to the guillotine-clean sleepers.

With a sudden flurry of dust and rubble, Russell fell. He rolled down the last ten feet onto the railway track and came to rest on his back, gravel clinging to the sticky blood on his face and clothes. He barely had time to raise his head before the train thundered out of the tunnel.

It swept over the small body like a charging silver dragon, severing limbs with barely a murmur to its progress. Thomas Bates turned his head away, bile rasping in his throat. He took a few steps backwards, dropped his shotgun, and vomited into the grass. He was still retching when the swooping thunder of straining metal had faded into the distance. Then, his innards a curdled mass of sour fear, he turned and ran. He didn't stop until he was back home.

CHAPTER TWO

THE SWING (SUMMER 1986)

By the time Kevin Truscott left the house just after breakfast, the earth had been baked into a hard, dusty submission. This summer was turning out to be a real scorcher, he thought, as he walked the familiar route to Martin Mason's house. Most of the time it was too hot to do anything but lie in the grass and fry. You could almost feel the sweat sizzling on your brow as it evaporated in the heat.

Yesterday had been the hottest day so far. The boys had seen a paving stone expand so much in the heat that it had split in half with a loud, echoing crack, and the section of tarmacked road directly in front of Kevin's driveway was spongey and yielding where the sun had partly melted it. Kevin clenched his hand and winced. His palm was still blistered where he had rested it on a car bonnet that had been hot as an iron.

He reached Martin's house, number one Bawley Lane, and rang the bell. The door swung wide and there was Martin, grinning his lopsided grin.

"Come in," he invited, "I'm just having breakfast."
Kevin followed Martin through into the kitchen, envious of him as always for living in Bawley Cottage. It was a tiny, low-ceilinged house, inset with beams and glowing with character. Everywhere was dark wood and handsome stone. A large fireplace smiled out at a three-piece suite you could just sink into, a grandfather clock demanded respect in the hall.

"Mind your head," Martin said, as he always did when they entered the kitchen. Kevin ducked through the doorway and sat down, watching as Martin wolfed a bowl of Rice Krispies.

"What's on the agenda for today, then?" Martin said,

forcing two hunks of bread into the toaster.

Kevin shrugged. "Same as usual, I suppose."

Same as usual meant lying around in the field behind Martin's house, shoes off, jeans rolled up to their knees, and t-shirts tied in a sweaty knot around their waists. Martin wrinkled his nose.

"I'm fed up of doing nothing. I fancy doing something today."

"Like what?" said Kevin. "It's too hot for sport."

"Oh, I don't know." Martin was silent for a moment, contemplating his toast as he bit into it. Then his face brightened. "Why don't we go for a walk up into Redheath Woods?"

"What for?" It sounded too energetic for Kevin.

"It'll be a lot cooler there. And we could walk through to Moor Cross village and have a few pints in The Rams."

This suggestion appealed to Kevin. "Good idea," he said.

Immediately after breakfast they set off, money jangling in their pockets, content in the knowledge that four weeks of freedom still stretched ahead before the grindstone of schoolwork began to turn again.

The woods were about two miles from Martin's house, just beyond the golf course. It was a stifling walk over the back fields with no shelter from the blazing sun, and the boys took it slowly. The fields gleamed, and a meadow, plump with buttercups, strained upwards, paying homage to the Sun God. The lazy buzz of summer sounds caressed their ears like a lullaby.

The two boys panted to the top of a rise. Martin shielded his eyes and pointed across to the landscape undulating far below them.

"Look at that view," he said in admiration. Kevin nodded, peeling off his t-shirt and tying it round his waist.

It seemed as though the whole of West Yorkshire was spread out below them, the white and grey buildings like seeds scattered over the land. The valley floor shimmered slightly behind a heat haze, but the brightness of the colours glared through as though everything had been scrubbed and freshly painted.

The boys climbed the stone wall which bordered the golf course and began to trudge leisurely over the clipped green towards a belt of dark trees at the top. This marked the perimeter of Redheath Woods. The trees had been cut back rather severely to allow for the golf course, and the contrast between velvet smoothness and rough foliage was striking, like the hairline of some huge giant made from vegetation.

Kevin looked across at his friend as they made their way up towards the line of trees. Martin was tall and gangly with uncombable blond hair swept carelessly to one side, and a long, toothy grin. He moved easily with a loose-limbed stride, arms swinging, t-shirt draped over one shoulder.

Kevin often thought how different he and his friend were. He was short, stocky and dark-haired, but it was not only physical differences that identified them apart. Martin was boisterous, witty and spontaneous, whereas Kevin was quiet, plodding and a methodical thinker. Kevin often wondered what it was that made them such good friends. No, more than friends. They were inseparable—blood brothers for life. He couldn't even recall how their friendship had started; it just had, that was all. It had grown from dimly remembered and unremarkable roots as many lasting friendships are apt to do. He supposed the attraction was that they played off one another, providing qualities which the other didn't possess. Martin caught Kevin's eye and his face eased itself into the familiar rubber-band grin.

"This is great, Kev," he enthused. "I love the summer."

Kevin smiled secretly to himself. He knew that six months from now, Martin would be wallowing, clothes-muffled, through three-foot snowdrifts telling him how much he loved the winter.

They reached the trees and slipped through into a velvet shadow-world. It was cooler here, a drowsy, sun-warmed breeze ruffling their hair and kissing them lightly on the cheeks. The branches and leaves of the trees caught much of the sun, throwing a dappled, swaying pattern of light and shadow onto the leafy ground. It was a randomly idyllic setting, a jumble of nature that was still somehow whole and perfect. A path of sorts led along the side of a gently sloping valley from which trees and bushes sprouted at strange angles, and a stream manfully forced its way along the bottom. The sight opened a box of childhood memories for both of them.

Kevin remembered one summer, five or six years before, when they had raced paper boats from one end of the stream to the other. They had discovered, with the delicious excitement of childhood, that the water ran above ground for over a mile before finally disappearing into the hillside. In some parts the water had been little more than a trickle, forcing its way through partially collapsed dams of rock and bracken, whereas in other less congested areas it had been almost two feet deep.

"Hey, look up there," Martin said. "Our old den. Remember how we used to sit up there and make ghost noises to frighten away little kids?"

Kevin laughed. "Yes, and I'll never forget dropping conkers on the head of that bloke when he was taking his dog for a walk." They both chuckled at the memory. The woods seemed to welcome their laughter, the leaves rustling gently in approval.

The den was nothing more than an uprooted tree trunk set high on the opposite side of the valley. It had fallen across the stream one winter, and the smooth, salmon-coloured circle where the tree had been cut away to make it safe had appealed to the boys' explorer instincts. They had scrabbled down the side of the valley, over the stream and up the other side. What they had found there had amazed and delighted them.

The toppling tree, an enormous oak, had gouged huge chunks of earth from the ground to form a hole into which, as thirteen-year-olds, they could snugly fit. The tree stump clung to the hillside by a number of thick roots which were still buried deep in the earth. This meant that the bottom of the tree, from which grotesquely-twisted roots reached out like petrified tentacles, served as a hiding place from anyone who happened to be walking along the edge of the stream down below. The boys had been able to watch the comings and goings in the woods without being seen themselves.

"Come on, Kev, let's go up and have a look at that old den," Martin said. He hopped over the remnants of the stone wall that bordered the edge of the valley and half slid, half ran, down the hill to the stream. Kevin followed. The water was normally around eight inches deep at this point, but the heat had taken its toll and there was barely enough now to keep the ground wet. The two of them padded across the stream and climbed up the other side of the valley to the tree stump.

It had been five or six years since they had last been here, but with a peculiar sensation of déjà vu, Kevin found himself reaching out and grabbing hold of the root he had always used to heave himself up those last few feet—the root that was shaped like an ear trumpet and which had a little nick in it where Martin had once demonstrated the sharpness of his boy scout penknife.

"Hey, look at this," Martin exclaimed, eyes widening with delight. Kevin peered into the hollow beneath the tree roots. Martin reached in and brought out a shabby bundle of paper, wrinkled and faded by the elements.

"Our old comics!" Kevin cried. It was somehow reassuring to know that they had been nestling there for the past five years, waiting for the boys to return and rediscover them.

Martin snapped the rotten string holding them together, and began to browse through the pile, eyes sparkling as though he had unearthed a chestful of treasure.

"There's something else here," Kevin said. He reached into the hollow and lifted out a thermos flask, cracked down the middle and covered with grime.

"God, I remember that," Martin said. "We used to bring coffee and sandwiches when we came here for the day sometimes."

"My Mum was hunting for this all over the place not so long ago to take camping. I'd forgotten we used to bring it here with us."

Martin took it and began to unscrew the lid. "I wonder if it's still got anything inside it," he said.

"I wouldn't," Kevin warned, "not if it's coffee. Think of the smell after all this time."

Nevertheless, Martin unscrewed the lid and put his nose to the opening. "Urggh!" He recoiled in disgust, holding the flask away from him at arm's length. "What a stink! You don't still want this flask, do you?"

"No, not now," Kevin replied, "not if it smells as bad as

that. Besides it's got a massive crack in it."

"Hold on, then." Martin put the flask down on top of the tree stump, resting it against a root. He fished around in the surrounding undergrowth until he found a large slab of stone.

"Stand back." Martin raised the slab above his head and hurled it down at the flask. The flask shattered, sending jagged shards tearing into the air. They both jumped back at the impact, instinctively shielding their faces. Bits of silvery glass and plastic were everywhere, the largest pieces still resting on the tree stump, gaping open like a burst egg shell. Martin jabbed the largest piece with a stick, "Look at this mould," he said. The inside of the flask was coated with a foul-smelling dust speckled with green, congealed blobs of mould.

"That used to be coffee," Kevin said, a little sick at the smell.

"Fancy drinking that," said Martin, screwing up his face. He suddenly scraped a little of the cobwebby mould onto the end of his stick and thrust it under Kevin's nose. Kevin jumped back, almost slipping down the slope, and swiped his hand away.

"Don't be so stupid, Mart," he stormed as the taller boy melted into laughter, "that wasn't very funny."

"Your face," Martin gasped. "You should have seen your face."

"Piss off, you wouldn't like it!" Kevin hated Martin's messing about sometimes. He stood there, seething, while Martin giggled breathlessly.

"Oh, come on, it wasn't all that funny," Kevin said haughtily.

"Yes it was. It was really funny. Your face..." Martin collapsed again. Kevin gave him a v-sign and wandered further along the top of the valley, trying to look unconcerned. He noticed a strangely shaped tree, and another childhood memory stirred.

"Martin," he shouted, "come here and have a look at this." Martin came, still grinning, but Kevin was too preoccupied and excited to worry about him now. The incident with the mould wasn't really that funny anyway. Martin always tried to spin the joke out for as long as possible; it was an old and infuriating habit he had. He forgot his mockery immediately, though, when he saw what Kevin had discovered.

"Wow," he breathed, "it's our tree."

The tree hooked over in a ragged quarter-circle, looking like a bent old woman nervously peering into the stream below. It wasn't just the tree, though, that excited them. It was also the rope that dangled from it.

The boys had tied it there some years ago and used to take turns swinging out over the stream. It was a good twenty to thirty feet drop, and below was a rocky section of banking, but they had never had any accidents. Looking at it now, Kevin was appalled. He supposed they had been cushioned by that special spell of innocence that is cast over childhood.

Martin took the rope in his hands and tugged it hard. It looked damp and partially frayed, but it held. He began to wind it round his hand and wrist.

"Mart, you're not going to swing on that are you?" said Kevin with a thrill of horror.

Martin looked up. "Why not? We always used to."

"But that was years back. That rope will have rotted away by now. It won't take your weight."

"Aw, course it will," said Martin and turned away. Kevin watched anxiously as Martin clenched the rope with both hands, went a few steps back from the edge of the valley to gather impetus, ran down, and launched himself into space. Kevin closed his eyes as he heard the tree moan and creak under Martin's weight. The branch bounced alarmingly as he swung back and forth. The rocks below were like a pool of motionless crocodiles, waiting for the rope to snap and their victim to come plunging down into their stone jaws.

But the rope held.

Martin swung out over the valley time and again, whooping with delight, blond hair flapping in the wind. As Kevin watched, a smile crept up on him unawares and planted itself on his face. With a slight shock he realised he was waiting for Martin to tire so that he could have his go. *No,* the Adult inside him said frantically, *No, it's too dangerous.* The Child elbowed the Adult aside, *Just one little go, it'll be all right.*

But still Kevin hung back.

Martin finally came to rest, letting himself slow down until he could gain a foothold on the sloping hillside. He was flushed with excitement, his eyes sparkling. He unwound the rope from his hand and held it out to Kevin.

"Have a go," he challenged. "It's brilliant."

"I'm not stupid," Kevin heard the Adult inside him reply.

"Oh, go on, it's perfectly safe," Martin said irritably.

Kevin shook his head. "Knowing my luck, it'll probably break when I swing on it, and I'll be right out over those rocks at the time."

"Rubbish. Feel how strong the rope is." Martin handed the end of the rope to his friend. Kevin took it and pulled as hard as he could. The tree creaked and swayed slightly, but only through the springiness of summer sap. The rope held firm.

"I don't know," Kevin said doubtfully, but as soon as he had taken hold of the rope he knew the Child was going to win. He was toying with the rope when Martin said, "Go on. I dare you to."

This was the ultimate challenge. Even now they often played *Dares*. It was one game that had stayed with them and proved useful in providing them with an extra push in certain situations. Kevin often found Martin's dares outrageous and reckless, but he usually ended up rising to the challenge. However, it was easier this time. Kevin wanted to swing on the rope. The dare just helped to push him over the edge.

"All right," he said. "I will." He wound the rope round his hand, gripping the end tightly with a sweaty palm. He backed up the hill a few paces, then ran down and launched himself into space.

He felt a wild, free sensation, and a wonderful, stomach-curling terror as the ground whooshed away below him. The branch jerked and swayed like the arm of a conductor leading his orchestra through a frenetic piece of music. This, though, only added to the thrill of it all. Kevin felt breathless and dizzy, but so alive as he looked down. The rocks and the stream lurched and cavorted far below. He looked up at the rope attached to the tree branch, both surfaces moving against one another. The rope was so sharply in focus that he could see each yellow fibre. Above that the grey tree branch looked blurred, and way above that, in another world, was the bluest sky he had ever seen.

He let himself slow down and looked keenly around with a new and refreshing perspective. Martin waved as Kevin looked across at him sitting on the bank. Kevin took one hand from the rope and waved back. He swung back and forth, back and forth, a human pendulum. At last, reluctantly, he let the rope slow to a stop. As the tree branch settled he reached out with his foot and placed it on the sloping, but very solid earth.

Martin had wandered a little further up, and was sitting, studying the ground. Kevin walked up to him. He noticed Martin was holding something small and sparkling, and curiously looked over his shoulder.

"Mart, what—"

"Oh, get out of the way, Kev," Martin said, waving his hand impatiently. "You're in the light."

Kevin stepped to one side, able to see now what his friend was doing. Martin held a tiny magnifying glass, angling it so that a minute dot of white sunlight was pinpointed onto the dry grass. The grass had already started to smoulder. Kevin walked round and sat down on the other side of Martin, out of the sun's light.

Martin positioned the magnifying glass again and directed it onto the grass. They both sat engrossed, looking down, their heads almost touching. Immediately the grass started to smoulder once more, and a few seconds later the boys were rewarded with a tiny lance of flame. Martin sat back, satisfied, as the flames spread, shriveling blades of grass into black embers. Dusty smoke spiraled upwards, and as the fire gained momentum it began to crackle quietly.

Martin stood up and stamped his foot down on the little fire, blotting it out. The patch of charred grass looked peculiar in contrast to the greenness around it.

"Come on, let's go and use this magnifying glass on some other stuff," Martin said. He looked around for a more interesting target.

"You're a bloody pyromaniac, you are," Kevin said, laughing.

"Yeah, I know," admitted Martin. "It's good fun though,

isn't it?" They wandered back down the banking.

"Let's see if it'll burn the rope," Kevin suggested, pointing at the swing. Martin looked doubtful.

"It probably won't. It's a bit too shady in here, I think, with all these trees around."

"It's worth a try, though," Kevin persisted. Martin shrugged and walked over to the crooked tree.

"Hold it up a bit, then, so we can get it into a bit of sunlight." The rope was in the shadow of the tree and Kevin held it out so that it was touched by the dappled sunlight that filtered through from above. Martin delicately held the magnifying glass between thumb and forefinger and positioned it so that a spot of light was directed through the lens and onto the rope.

Nothing happened for quite a while, and Martin began to turn the magnifying glass round in his hand in an attempt to find a sharper light point. When he was satisfied, they settled down to wait again.

The seconds stretched into minutes as they waited, concentrating on the tiny dot of heat, urging a flame to burst from it.

"This is no good," Martin said at last. "It's not going to work, and my arm's getting tired."

Kevin was about to agree when he saw a tiny spiral of smoke curl almost invisibly into the air.

"No, wait," he said, "look!" Martin looked. The smoke was becoming a little denser now. It was black and oily, and in the humid atmosphere it smelled acrid.

"At last!" Martin cried in triumph, his fatigue forgotten. He trained the glass on the rope again. The smoke gradually became blacker and more plentiful. Just when they thought smoke was all they were going to get, flame sparked from the rope. They both cheered as the flame grew and began to explore the rope, lapping round the edges and creeping upwards.

"We'd better put it out," Kevin said after a moment. The fire was increasing with alarming speed. It was climbing the rope, devouring as it went. Martin and Kevin picked up handfuls of dust and dirt and threw them at the rope to smother the fire. However, the fire refused to be smothered. Most of the dust particles were instantly frazzled, producing a choking cloud of embers. As the cloud settled it became obvious that the fire had lost none of its voracity.

"Shit!" spat Martin. He began to slither down the slope towards the stream. "You keep chucking dust at it, and I'll see if I can get some water."

Kevin picked up handfuls of dirt and threw them onto the fire, one after another. His efforts became more and more frantic as the fire increased.

"Hurry up, Martin," he screamed, his eyes streaming from the billowing dust and heat.

Martin appeared as a hunched silhouette through the swirling heat vapours. In his hands he carried a rusty tin tray in which thick, muddy water sloshed.

The fire roared in triumph as it touched the tree. The rope was a pitiful shriveled tendon, black and dangling like stringy charcoal. The dry wood of the tree began to burn quickly, turning from ash-grey to ember-orange to cinder-black as the fire swept over it.

"Quickly," urged Kevin. He took one end of the tray, Martin the other, and together they hurled the sluggish contents over the fire. Immediately the wood began to sizzle, the fire to die; for a moment it looked as though they had won. Then, slowly, the fire reasserted itself, turning the water to steam and breaking into new life until it was almost as strong as before.

"It's not enough," babbled Kevin hysterically. "We need more water."

Martin slid back down the bank, clutching the tray, knowing it was probably useless. Kevin felt greasy with smoke dust and sick with heat.

The sweat sprang from him, making his arms shine and his hair itch with damp. The smoke was choking grey and thick, enveloping the tree like a shroud before curling into the air. Kevin felt it whirling about him, catching at his throat and blurring his vision.

Suddenly, unexpectedly, the tree split. An enormous crack of rage from the bark had Kevin leaping backwards, covering his face protectively. He half expected a fireball to come splintering out at him, or for the ground to burst open beneath his feet. The tree was a burning face, its hair a thrashing nest of orange and yellow vipers spitting black sparks.

As he watched, Kevin thought he could see the tree swelling and bursting, like a pod unable to hold the bloated flesh of its fruit within. But, of course, that was impossible. Trees didn't swell. It was a trick, played by his streaming vision and the writhing heat haze.

Yet the sound was unmistakable; a cracking and crunching as the enflamed wood split. He saw a black line appear in the bark, cleaving its middle. And through the smoke and the gloom of embers he thought he could see the tree begin to open like a hinged door. And... surely not. Something inside it seemed to stir.

Kevin jumped as a hand touched his shoulder. It was Martin. He was grimy, his hair plastered over his forehead.

"I've got some more water," he croaked.

"Too late." The words struggled through with difficulty. Kevin pointed at the tree. "Look."

Martin looked. The flames and smoke were swirling about the tree like a demon cloak, allowing only an occasional glimpse of the seared trunk. Martin suddenly raked in breath and slammed it out again. The action was so intense and violent that Kevin felt fear tingle his nerve ends like an electric shock.

"What was that?" said Martin. He gripped Kevin's arm painfully.

"What?" Kevin said. Martin turned slowly, his eyes glaring. He stared into Kevin's face as though some dark secret were etched there.

"Something moved," he hissed. The boys were drawn to the tree again.

Something hideous seemed to be happening to it. It appeared, through the smoke and flame, to be swelling and growing, to be reproducing itself. It appeared to be giving birth.

Something was turning sluggishly in the trunk, something gnarled and black. Strips of bark were splitting and falling away as though the thing inside was ripping through the womb of its mother to get out.

As the smoke cleared once more, the boys caught another tantalising glimpse. A huge branch, shaped vaguely like an arm, seemed to be growing from the centre of the mother-tree, prodding and searching the ground. Then, once again, the smoke screen smothered their view.

It was a grotesque game of peek-a-boo. Now you see it, now you don't.

As well as the smoke screen, the stifling heat haze distorted shapes like a crumpled film of polythene. Perhaps it was this that stretched the tree-shape into illusionary angles and gave the impression of swelling and movement.

Or perhaps not.

Can heat make a tree crack and split and burst open? The boys weren't sure. But as they watched they heard more sounds coming from the tree; small, cautious, calculated sounds. And then the smoke suddenly cleared like a curtain swishing back from a stage.

And they saw it.

Something unbelievable and obscene was pulsing into a world that was never meant for it. It had a gnarled, blackened appearance and was glistening with the birth-sap of its tortured mother. It was roughly man-shaped. Two arms, like twisted branches, sprang from deformed shoulders, root-like tendrils squeezed into charred points served as fingers.

Kevin felt terror sweeping over him as the huge thing slowly waved its head from side to side. It was crouched low as though scanning the ground, tottering and swaying as it became acclimatized to its new surroundings. The great body heaved and trembled, breathing in strength and relishing the freedom it was never meant to have. Suddenly it became motionless and the 'head' cocked as though sensing the boys' presence. Slowly, slowly, the monstrous frame straightened, and the head creaked torturously up.

For the first time the boys could see the face...

They ran...

CHAPTER THREE

THE FIREFIGHTERS

The fire raged long into the night. It used the dry summer air as an ally and extended its influence with amazing speed. Around noon, Thomas Bates, the farmer, saw thick black smoke invading the sky like a distress signal and telephoned the fire brigade. When the gleaming engines arrived, the fire had become a vast, gluttonous beast, gorging itself in all directions. And by the time the fire was eventually vanquished, almost twelve hours later, two square miles of surrounding woodland and farmland had been laid to waste. The ground had been reduced to an even carpet of scorched earth that crunched underfoot, and the trees were a forest of spiders' legs, black and spindly.

Three fire engines and two hundred enthusiastic villagers, using thousands of gallons of water, had worked long and arduously to keep the blaze within acceptable limits. In the end, the beast had been slain. But the price had been high.

Ken Rackman slowly rolled up the hose with screaming muscles. His flesh felt roasted, his eyeballs poached in their sockets. He looked around wearily, thinking it was tragic that such beauty could be plucked away with such ease. Only a blasted skeleton of nature was left, stripped of dignity, shunned by light. He had seen it so many times. It was the devastation he and his colleagues lived with. It was part of the job.

He finished rolling up the hose and heaved himself onto the engine. His heavy clothes and helmet tried to drag him back. Rackman pulled off his helmet and swept an arm across his brow, wiping away the sweat. Steam rose from his hair and mingled with the clouds of smoke that drifted eerily through the night like gloating phantoms.

"All ready?" said the driver. The men grunted assent and the engine turned over and roared into life. Slowly, jolting over the rutted land, the last of the firefighters moved away.

Kevin lay on his bed, staring up at the ceiling. His body felt numb, but his mind turned over and over, a whirlwind that used fear as energy.

He had run all the way home; two and a half miles in sweltering heat. No wonder he had felt so tired. Martin must have run home too—Kevin couldn't remember. As soon as he'd seen the face, all else had faded into nothingness, the single most important thing in the world being to put as much distance as possible between himself and it. *The face*. It glared into his even now. It swam before him wherever he looked. Even when he closed his eyes he could see it. It lived in his vision, engraved there like a tattoo.

Kevin was scared; so scared that nothing else mattered. It was as though the lid of the world had been removed to reveal the darkness beneath. He felt marked, tainted, touched by that darkness. Martin, too, must've...

Martin? Where was he? Kevin shivered, feeling suddenly very vulnerable. He had to see Martin. They had to talk. They had to stick together. He didn't know if it would help much, but at least it would be reassuring.

He struggled out of bed and began to pull on his shoes before he even realized how dark it was. He had been so preoccupied he hadn't noticed it was nightfall. So that was it then; he would have to wait until morning. Nothing in the world would persuade him to venture out into the dark alone.

Kevin looked at his clock. It was just past twelve. He felt a stab of superstitious fear. Never before had that hour meant so much to him. The Witching Hour. If anything was going to happen to him, it would happen now. He padded across the room and switched on the light.

He waited. Silent, absolutely motionless he waited, hunched up on his bed, squeezed tight into a ball with his knees up under his chin and his arms curled round his body. It was safer that way. He felt smaller, less conspicuous. He squeezed himself tighter. Perhaps he could squeeze himself so tightly that he'd disappear for an hour.

He tried to close his eyes and clear his mind and think of everyday things, but it was no use. His mind was racing madly on its own tracks, a carriage of thoughts on a Ghost Train ride.

He'd slept all afternoon. As soon as he had reached home he'd come upstairs, pulled off his shoes, flopped onto his bed and slept. He remembered reading somewhere that sleep could act as a defence mechanism if the mind was under stress. He supposed that was what had happened. His mind had been clogged with fear, and it had needed him inactive for a while so it could filter some of that fear away. Kevin hoped Martin had slept too. If not he might well be a gibbering heap by now.

If he was still alive.

Kevin tried to push that thought from his mind. He considered phoning Martin, but the prospect of moving terrified him. His room was a haven, and if he stayed perfectly still until one o' clock, then perhaps he might—just might—be okay. He looked at the clock. Twelve o' nine. He had survived for nine minutes; only another fifty-one to go.

Kevin suddenly realized how quiet it was. Where was everybody? Where was the banging of doors, the muted murmur of the television, the whispered arguments of his younger brother and sister in the next bedroom, the creak of beds, the hammering of the cistern whenever someone turned on the tap in the downstairs toilet—where was it all?

It worried him that he hadn't noticed the silence before, just as he hadn't noticed the darkness, and he cursed his mind for its slow reactions. It seemed to be piecing his world together bit by painstaking bit, allowing just a little to seep through at a time. It was as though he was going along a corridor, inset with many doors; rather than flinging all the doors wide and allowing his mind to sort the random thoughts out naturally, he was being made to open one door and familiarise himself with the room beyond before moving onto the next one. It was a disturbing and frustrating process. He needed to consider, to organise, to plan, to build up his defences, but what chance did the thinking mind have when the instinctive one was only just beginning to emerge from its shell?

The stillness troubled Kevin. All he could hear was a fraught, intense silence, like the crystal whine of a tuning fork reaching its highest pitch. He longed to hear familiar sounds. House-sounds. Sounds that used to annoy him so much before but would be so eagerly welcomed now. What had happened to the television: the magic box that usually managed to produce a scream or the blare of a car chase when he was within a hair's breadth of slipping into sleep? To be kept awake by 'The Streets of San Francisco' tonight would be a godsend.

And where were his brother and sister? Surely not asleep. They usually argued in heated whispers about whose turn it was to switch off the light, or who had been responsible for leaving toys on the stairs and putting Mum into such a bad mood. But now—silence. Not even the muffle of blankets or the shifting of bedsprings. Surely Mum and dad hadn't kept them out anywhere this late at night? And even if they had, why hadn't they let him know?

Kevin could feel the panic and the fear simmering up inside him. His senses might have been slow, but his imagination was tripping on speed. He closed his eyes and rubbed his temples with the tips of his fingers as though sanity and reason could be massaged through into his skull. There were a hundred possible explanations. Maybe they had gone to Uncle Harry's and had broken down on the way home. Or maybe the twins were stopping at one of their schoolfriend's for the night and Mum and Dad had taken the opportunity to go for a drink. Or maybe—

A door slammed.

Kevin felt a juicy sickness in his mouth, and his heart began to yammer in his chest, *He's here, he's here, come and get him, he's here*.

Footsteps sounded in the hallway below and then began to climb the stairs. They were stealthy, as though something was trying to conceal its movements. Kevin counted the footsteps breathlessly. He knew when they had reached the top of the stairs. There were thirteen in all and the eleventh one creaked.

There was a pause, and then the footsteps began to approach along the landing— slow and measured like the ticking of his bedside clock. It was twelve sixteen.

The footsteps stopped right outside his door. Kevin's body was rigid. His hands were clutching at the bed covers so tightly he could see his bones glaring white beneath the skin. The handle turned, and the door sighed open. A head appeared.

"You all right, Kevin?"

"Dad!" Kevin felt his body collapse, the fierce tension dissolving into a heady relief.

"Who did you think it was?" The head was balding, bespectacled and amiable. It was the most wonderful thing Kevin had ever seen.

"Where is everybody?"

"We've been helping to put out the fire. I'm surprised you and Martin weren't there. Jamie and Sam are over at the Salters."

"What do you mean? What fire?"

"In the woods."

"The woods?" Kevin repeated stupidly. He felt a tiny muscle in his neck begin to throb.

"Half of Redheath Woods has burned down. Where've you been?"

"Martin and me went over to Moor Cross. To the Rams."

"What time was this?"

The tremor in Kevin's neck became more insistent. "Late morning. About eleven."

"That's about when they reckon the fire started. You didn't see anything did you?"

"No." Kevin felt an urge to justify himself. "It was really hot and dry in there, though. I'm not surprised it went up in flames."

"Why didn't you see anything on the way back? The path through the woods is the quickest way home."

Kevin bit his lip. A desperate lie saved him. "We got a lift back from one of Kevin's mates. He was in the pub when we went in."

"Didn't you see the smoke?"

The questions just kept coming, one after another, buffeting him.

"No. I suppose I had a bit too much to drink. I've been asleep all afternoon." Kevin felt relieved that his lies had dovetailed neatly into truth.

"You shouldn't drink so much," said Mr. Truscott. "Especially at dinnertimes and in this heat. It's not good for you."

"I know, Dad. I didn't mean to, but Martin's mate's working and he kept buying them for us."

Mr. Truscott smiled and ruffled his son's hair, something he did less and less frequently these days. "I was just the same when I was your age," he said. "Once you've had a couple you don't feel like stopping, do you? Especially on such a dry day."

Kevin forced a smile.

"Do you fancy a coffee, son? You look a bit white."

Kevin realised he had had nothing to eat or drink since breakfast time. He swallowed; his throat felt shriveled and dry. He fancied he could taste burning wood. "Yes, I'd love one," he said. "I'll make it." He jumped up and followed his father downstairs, anxious to keep him in sight. He was worried that if he didn't his father might be spirited away by some malevolent force. Kevin was jittery, but he tried to keep his voice light.

"Where's Mum?"

"Collecting the twins."

"Has she gone in the car?"

"Yes, why?"

"Nothing. Just wondered."

The kitchen was warm and cozy. Kevin pulled the curtains, blotting out the night. He avoided looking outside, thinking that if he did he might catch a glimpse of something in the bushes, watching him.

"I'm going to have a bath," Mr. Truscott announced. "I stink of smoke."

Kevin stole a glance at the kitchen clock. It was twelve twenty-six. Still the Witching Hour, but Kevin felt normality setting around him now like a jelly.

"Okay, Dad," he said. "Have they any idea how the fire started?" He hoped it sounded like a throw-away question.

"Not really. As you say, it was dry and hot. Probably just

built up."

"Yeah." Kevin busied himself putting the kettle on, taking five cups down from the shelf, and scooping coffee into each cup. His father went upstairs. Kevin heard him moving about and then the sound of water splashing into the bath. He jumped suddenly as two eyes, shining bright yellow, pierced the curtains, but they were only the headlights of the car as it pulled into the drive. Kevin hurriedly made the coffee, snatched up two of the cups, and trotted upstairs.

"Can you tell Mum and the twins there's a drink waiting for them in the kitchen. I'm off to bed," he said to his father, handing him a coffee.

"Yes, all right. Night, Kev."

"Goodnight, Dad."

He closed his bedroom door just as his mother's key turned in the lock downstairs. He wanted to avoid her that night. He didn't want to have to lie to her as well. He heard his brother Jamie's insistent voice, shrill with excitement, asking about the fire engines, and his mother's subdued, tired answers. The sound of the house, the mushy hum of human activity, comforted him.

It was twelve thirty-five now. Kevin switched off his bedroom light and turned on his torch. That way a line of tell-tale light would not show below his door and he wouldn't be disturbed. He pulled open the bottom drawer in his chest of drawers. It contained comics, music magazines, photographs, football cards, old school exercise books — stuff he was loathe to throw out. He delved in the drawer, sifting through the contents like sand. Eventually he found what he was looking for — a stiff rectangle of card wrapped in brown paper. He withdrew it and unwrapped the paper, wincing as it crackled, hoping no one outside would hear. He extracted the card and shone his torch onto it.

It was an old school photograph from 1977. The girls were wearing long white socks, grey skirts and blazers, and thickly-heeled platform shoes.

The boys had shorts, fat ties and hair almost as long as the girls. Kevin was standing on the middle row, Martin a row above him with an expression on his face like a startled rabbit. They had howled with shame-faced laughter at themselves many times.

But this time Kevin didn't laugh. This time he was not interested in himself, or in Martin. He was interested in the face. He had recognised the face straight away. The features had been gnarled bark, the mouth hanging cavernously open in a silent scream of misery and torment, blank eye-sockets staring hopelessly out into nowhere. But despite the loathsome, horribly distorted expression, the face had been unmistakable. Kevin stared at that face now — the face as it used to be. The high cheekbones, the sneering mouth, the lank hair, and most of all the eyes. Eyes that could chill even when deadened by celluloid.

The eyes of Russell Swaney.

The woods were still and eerie, the trees standing like black-clad mourners at their own funeral. Pockets of grey smoke skulked between the branches. Ash floundered over the earth, tormented by the wind. Every so often a tree would creak and sigh, and a sooty limb would snap and tumble down to the ground. There was no life here. Teeming colonies of insects and animals had been trapped and roasted underground, their homes becoming their tombs.

The crooked tree still perched on the hillside, a charcoal-stick hybrid of its former self. This was the centre of it all, the Heart of Death. The tree was splintered, strips of bark splayed out like arthritic fingers. The thing moved in the bark, gathering strength in the womb, turning over sluggishly in a parody of sleep. It had no name. It had planted itself like a seed within the human child. It had grown, it had flourished, fed by the child's life energy. It had moulded the puny flesh, controlled it, and in the end, it had destroyed it, seeking release.

But release had meant only confinement. Release was a sham, an empty promise, a warped longing. Release was true death. But at last they had come, as it knew they would. And now it was free.

It was a dark soul. And it was hungry...

Kevin was up and dressed much earlier than usual the next morning. He had slept little, his mind too full to rest. When he had finally managed to doze, the sleep had been fitful and exhaustive, washed with screaming faces carved in bark and tapering branches that reached out like claws. He dreamed a spiky, gnarled hand was pushing a candle into his face. He tried to run, but his body was paralysed, unable to move. The hand came closer and closer. The fingers opened, releasing the candle, and the flame came roaring into his eyes...

Kevin awoke. The light was the sun, prodding through a gap in the curtains directly onto his face. It was rising over the horizon in a welter of red fury, turning the sky crimson, the clouds pink. Kevin blinked, still seeing the image like a negative behind his eyelids, except that now the sky was brown, the clouds orange, and the sun green. He stretched his stiff limbs and moaned. His clock said six twenty-one. He couldn't have been asleep very long because he remembered looking at his clock at five ten. Just over an hour. Kevin washed and changed slowly and quietly. He knew there would be no point in going to see Martin just yet; his parents didn't leave for work until eight thirty, and Kevin would have to make up some excuse for being there so early.

He sloped downstairs into the kitchen, preferring to switch on the light rather than open the curtains. He made cereal, toast and coffee and took it upstairs to his room. As soon as he put the Weetabix in his mouth, he realized how hungry he was. He wolfed the rest down and went for more toast.

He was out walking by seven twenty. The house was too stifling and claustrophobic, lingering with yesterday's memories. He gulped the clean air gratefully, allowing it to flood through him like a panacea. Yesterday he had felt timid, vulnerable, as though something was bearing down upon him, crushing him under a weight of fear. But today he felt different; his mind had coped. He felt a resolve, a determination, almost an eagerness to face this unknown and do battle. He walked the streets feeling fresh and alive, his mind rampant with plans and possibilities.

He wandered aimlessly for a while before making his way towards Martin's house. He always enjoyed the walk to the cottage. Although officially he lived in Limefield village, Kevin didn't feel as though he and his family were strictly part of village life. Living on the estate on the other side of the green they were regarded as outsiders.

As he walked, the dull, square twentieth century housing, packed together in identical rows, gradually faded away to be replaced with clusters of tiny sleeping cottages (the homes of the real villagers), and the carefully tended village green. As he walked further still, this gave way to green fields and trees heavy with bud. The housing became sparser and more archaic, farming cottages of rough stone with bountiful gardens. Tethered goats nibbled grass, snorts and neighs issued from barns and outhouses, and the pungent aroma of manure hung on the air like an ancient country recipe.

He sat on a bench where he could see Martin's house. The car was still there, a gleaming fawn Cavalier, this year's model. It looked keen and powerful, incongruous next to the dozing cottage. Old and new; an ancient battle; a sour mixture.

Kevin read the neat plaque screwed to the bench, polished by the backs of overcoats and sweaters, while he waited.

'Presented to the citizens of the borough of Limefield by Alderman George Mellor to commemorate the accession to the throne of England of King Edward VII, April 16th, 1901.'

Underneath someone had scrawled *'NF Pakis Out'* with a red marker pen. Kevin shielded his eyes. A white glare of sunlight from the windscreen of the Cavalier was blinding him. He began to fidget on the bench. Surely it had gone half past eight by now. Everyone in Martin's house must have overslept. Unless...the thought struck him like a dash of ice cubes on his hot flesh. What if the thing had come for Martin last night? This possibility dissolved his resolve and his determination, and fear set in once more. But he had to find out. He had to see.

He had always envied Martin's quiet life in the countryside, but now he desperately wished there were cars and people and houses around him. The tiny cottage windows under the over-hanging thatched roof were like blind eyes. They could be concealing so much.

He quelled his panic with difficulty, swallowing again and again as bile rose in his throat. He must stay calm, he must be reasonable. Maybe it wasn't even half past eight yet, maybe the heat had slowed time, dragging it into a crawl.

Kevin began walking away from Martin's house, back up the lane. He knew that just over the rise was a stone wall, and if you stood on the wall and craned upwards you could just see the church clock in Limefield. He came to the wall and climbed up onto it. The time was eight forty-nine. Kevin felt the pulse in his neck burst into life again. As he watched, the minute hand on the clock hovered and clicked on another minute. Ten to nine. Surely Martin's parents would have gone by now?

He began to run back up the lane, panic spurring his gelatine legs. After twenty yards he stopped. Running in the heat was like wallowing through sludge. A humid vice gripped his lungs, making him struggle for breath. He bent over double, a stitch jabbing his side, breathing deeply in and out. After a few moments, he straightened up and carried on.

The cottage was still basking innocently in the sunshine, the Cavalier still parked in the driveway. Kevin approached cautiously. All seemed quiet and peaceful, as normal as ever. He walked up the drive on wobbly legs, his senses tuned by apprehension, ready to turn and run at the slightest noise. But he heard no sound coming from the house. He raised his hand to knock at the front door and then paused. Perhaps it would be better not to announce his presence. He might walk in on a family breakfast and have some embarrassed explaining to do, but that would be so much better than the alternative.

He tried the door, pulling it towards him so the handle wouldn't grate. It was unlocked. He entered warily, leaving the door open in case a quick escape was needed. His body felt tense and awkward, nerve ends scrunched tightly together. He stood in the hall and held his breath. All he could hear was the ponderous tick-tick of the grandfather clock. The usually sedate sound seemed to have become ominous.

The sitting room, however, looked as it always did; the furniture in place, last night's ashes clustered in the grate. Nothing had been disturbed here.

He went through to the kitchen, painfully aware of the pad of his feet on the carpet. The kitchen looked okay too. There was the usual early morning clutter of coffee cups, toast crumbs, cereal packets and lidless jam jars; nothing to suggest that anything unusual had taken place. Kevin had once seen a film where this loony had killed people and put the heads in the fridge. He crossed the room and reluctantly opened the fridge. No heads.

The back garden gleamed in the sunshine through the window, the grass pale and wheaty and in need of a cut. Kevin stared at it and sighed, putting off the moment when he would have to look upstairs. The front door was a long, long way from the landing, and there were too many comers he could be hounded into up there.

He suddenly heard a sharp, dry *ker-chunk* behind him. Something had entered the kitchen. He whirled to face it as a scream forced its way up into his shrinking throat...

CHAPTER FOUR

LOVERS LANE

The deadly snout of a double-barreled shotgun was pointing directly at his chest. Behind the barrel, Martin looked almost as scared as Kevin.

"Bloody Hell, Mart," Kevin gasped, grabbing hold of the sink to stop his legs from collapsing beneath him, "you gave me a right bloody shock."

Martin lowered the weapon. His hands were trembling which made the gun look nervous. He sank onto a chair and grinned uncertainly.

"I'm glad you're here," he said. He looked terrible. His face was sickly pale except for his eyes which were bloodshot and heavily ringed with red. His clothes were crumpled and grimy, and his hair still looked sweaty from yesterday's fire. Kevin lowered himself into a chair, the shock in his belly subsiding. He gripped his friend's arm reassuringly.

"You all right, Mart?" he asked, afraid that the loudness of his voice might crack his friend to pieces. He certainly looked fragile enough.

"I will be in a minute," Martin replied.

"Did anything... happen here last night?" Kevin asked tentatively.

"Happen? What do you mean?" Martin's voice was almost threatening and Kevin realised his friend was close to breaking point. He tried to keep his voice calm.

"You know... anything unusual? After yesterday?" He felt reluctant to voice his fears in case the spoken word might somehow magic them to life.

"No, no, of course not. I was just taking precautions, that's all."

"Where are your mum and dad?"

"In London for a few days with some friends." It was becoming a struggle for Martin to talk. He spread his arms out on the breakfast table and sank his head between them. He sprawled there amongst the breakfast things like a shot cowboy in a western.

"You were here on your own, then, last night?" said Kevin.

The head on the table nodded slightly. Kevin felt a wash of sympathy. He put his hand awkwardly on his friend's back. Alone all night in a spooky old cottage in the middle of nowhere with something stalking the woods. It was no wonder his friend was so shattered. In fact, he was surprised Martin wasn't crouched, gibbering, in a corner by now.

"I spent the night in the bathroom," Martin said faintly. "It's the only door inside the house with a lock on it. I sat in the corner with the light on, holding the shotgun all night. I couldn't sleep. I never noticed before how much this bloody place creaks. I kept thinking something was moving around outside."

"Don't worry, Mart, you're all right now," Kevin said soothingly. "I'll make us a cuppa and then you can have a kip on the settee. I'll stay here. We'll be okay."

Martin nodded again and raised his head, making an effort to pull himself together. Kevin put the kettle on and began clearing away the pots in the kitchen. It felt strange to be taking charge. Martin was usually the leader, the one with the ideas. It alarmed Kevin to see his friend so drained, so lacking in invention. Kevin wondered how he would have felt if he had had to spend the night alone in the cottage.

He cleared the kitchen up, forced Martin to drink a cup of tea, and then went upstairs to fetch a pillow. When he came back down, Martin was fast asleep over the kitchen table. He seemed barely to be breathing.

Only his eyelids, flickering minutely, convinced Kevin his friend was still alive. He dragged Martin to his feet with great difficulty. Martin was so much taller, and his feet trailed uselessly behind him. Eventually Kevin maneuvered him into the sitting room and deposited him onto the settee. Martin landed without a sound and immediately plummeted into a deep sleep.

Kevin sat in an armchair, the gun propped against the wall next to him Later he and Martin would talk. But for now, all he could do was sit and wait and listen to the clock, which ticked away the precious seconds to nightfall.

Nightfall wasn't quite so threatening to Macky Cooper. In fact, it was his favourite time. The darker and more out of the way the better as far as he was concerned.

The dark and his new car were an irresistible combination. Or so it had proved in the three weeks since he'd bought it. Of course he'd told everyone he'd bought a 'new' car. Well, he wasn't really lying. It was new to him. The fact that the thing had an acute case of indigestion and more dents than a baked bean tin used for shooting practice was of little consequence. The crooked front light, cracked side mirror, and bald tyres could easily be overlooked. The important thing was that it went. And it did. *Vrooom!* Or rather *gurgle, gurgle, chunk, chunk, shudder*. But that could be overlooked too.

Macky leaned back and looked out at the stars through his windscreen. They winked at him knowingly, unashamed voyeurs. The moon perched in the wings, commanding the best seat in the house. It lit up the glade, throwing the shadows of the trees into sharp relief. They criss-crossed the roof of the car, giving it the appearance of a mechanical zebra.

"Have you finished yet?" Macky said to the girl sitting next to him. She was putting on lipstick, guided by the reflection in the driving mirror.

"I won't be a minute. Don't be so impatient," she said teasingly.

Macky sighed and leaned back further. Why did birds bother about such fucking dumb things at times like this? Here he was, ready and available, and she was putting on bloody make-up. For Christ's sake, it wasn't going to make any difference. He was going to screw her whatever she looked like. And all that bloody stuff she was so carefully applying would come off as soon as they got down to it—all over his face probably.

A joke came into his head. This bloke goes to the doctor's and says, 'Doctor I'm a bit worried. I've got this bright red ring around my prick', and the doctor says, 'Come on, then, get your trousers down and let's have a look'. So this bloke drops his trousers and sure enough he's got a bright red ring all round his prick. The doctor examines it for a minute and then straightens up. 'What is it?' asks the bloke, 'is it an infection?' and the doctor looks at him and says, 'No, it's lipstick.'

Macky looked across at Sharon carefully applying her own lipstick and he sniggered—a nasal, primitive sound. Sharon looked across at him, the lipstick poised in mid-air.

"What's the matter with you?" she said.

"Nothin'," replied Macky. "I was just thinking about somethin' one of me mates did, that's all."

She tutted and tossed her head to show she was above it all and continued applying her lipstick. At last she was done, completing the ceremony by pouting her lips into a white handkerchief, leaving a sensual autograph.

"Right," she said, smoothing her skirt and swiveling round to face him, "I'm ready."

He restrained himself from retorting 'About bloody time too', knowing it would send her into a sulk. Instead, he curled his arm around her shoulder and pulled her towards him. They started kissing. Heady, breathless kisses. Wrestling with their tongues. Her lipstick tasted good, female and slightly perfumed. He began to explore her body with his hand, running it down over her thin blouse, feeling the swell of her breasts and the dip into her stomach. He moved his hand lower, stroking her thigh all the way up to the top of her short skirt. His hand slowly rose higher and higher with each stroke, pushing her skirt up almost to her waist. He slipped his hand into the warmth between her thighs and she opened her legs slightly to assist him. As his rhythm continued, languid but intense, she began to moan and gasp quietly. She stopped kissing his mouth and instead bent her head slightly and showered his chin and throat with light, moist touches of her lips.

She began to manoeuver her body downwards. At first, Macky felt a buzz of irritation, thinking she was doing it to evade his exploring fingers, but as she pulled up his t-shirt, he relaxed again.

She squirmed lower. Macky felt hands deftly undoing his belt and sliding down the zip on his trousers. His erection enjoyed glorious relief. He gasped as her head dipped between his thighs like a viper striking at its prey. His hands gripped the steering wheel tightly as she began to lap at him. His head snapped back involuntarily, his back arched, and he began a natural pumping motion with his hips, thrusting in and out of her warm oral embrace. She moved against him expertly, making little wet guttural sounds.

Macky looked out of the window, eyes dewy with ecstasy. The woods crouched around them, sheltering them, shrinking the world into this tiny darkened glade, the heart of which was the rapture of the bobbing head between his thighs. Suddenly, he started and lunged forward, as though shaken from a dream. Sharon released him and looked up angrily, coughing and spluttering.

"What the fuck do you think you're doing?" she stormed. "You nearly choked me then."

"Ssshhh," Macky urged her, placing a hand lightly over her mouth. She shrugged her head away viciously.

"What is it?"

"I saw something moving. Between those trees over there." Macky pointed towards a dense patch of trees and shrubs, a ghostly skeleton of shape picked out by the moonlight.

"So what?" Sharon said. She was not impressed. She liked her efforts to be appreciated. "It was probably just an animal or something."

"No, it was too big. I think it was a man," replied Macky. His voice was low and struck a chord of chill within her. She struggled up from her knees, hair awry, and looked wildly out into the darkness.

"Don't talk like that," she said in a wheedling voice, "you're scaring me."

"Perhaps some twat's come to spy on us," said Macky, the old aggression returning to his voice.

Sharon's passion had evaporated like morning mist to be replaced by an unpleasant sense of crawling apprehension. The trees, which before had been allies to their secret games, now seemed to have changed. Their friendly guises had been peeled away to reveal threatening Mister Hyde personas. The embracing branches had become grasping fingers, the intimate closeness a brooding claustrophobia, and the smiling moon a glaring murderous eye. It was as though an evil spell had been cast over the land.

"I can't see anything," Sharon said, hoping her words would break the spell and dissolve the murky aura of menace.

"I did see something," Macky persisted.

"Maybe it was just the moon going behind a cloud or something," suggested Sharon, silently pleading with Macky to relax and grin and say, 'Yes, of course, that's what it was. Stupid me, I should've realised.'

Instead he shook his head and looked at her.

"No, I definitely saw something. Something big. I'm sure it was a man."

"Oh, Macky, let's go home. I'm scared," wailed Sharon.

She was thinking of a story they used to tell as kids. It was called The Hook and was about a young couple, just like themselves, out in the woods. The young couple are in this car in the woods and the radio is on. Suddenly the music stops and this news bulletin comes over the radio saying that a lunatic has escaped from a nearby mental home just the other side of the woods. The news bulletin warns people not to venture out of their houses until the lunatic is caught and says that he is easily recognised because he has a huge hook in place of his right hand with which he butchers his victims.

Anyway, the couple are sitting in the car and it's all dark, and the girl begins to think she can see something moving about in the trees, and she can hear noises outside the car. She pleads with her boyfriend to take her home, but he tells her not to be silly and that it's only her imagination. As time goes on, she gets more and more scared, certain there is something moving around in the blackness. She begs her boyfriend to take her home and eventually he concedes. They drive out of the woods and back into town. She begins to relax as they drive once more among streetlights and noise and people. Eventually they arrive back at her house. The boy gets out of the ear and walks round to the passenger's side to open the door for her. When he reaches it a look of horror passes over his face and he faints. Wondering what has frightened him, the girl opens the door herself. As she does so she hears a clattering sound. She looks. And there, hanging on the door handle, is an enormous metal hook...

That story used to frighten Sharon when she was ten, but it had been a comfortable fear, like climbing to the top of the stairs in the dark. Now, sitting here in this car, with swaying blackness all around them, the story seemed to adopt a new and poignant perspective. She couldn't rid herself of the image of the hook, deadly and gleaming, hanging from the door handle. Macky was saying nothing. His head was cocked and his eyes, brilliant white in the moonlight, stared out into the woods. She touched his arm, breaking his trance.

"Come on, Macky," she pleaded. "Let's go home." Just like the girl in The Hook; the gleaming, flashing hook hanging from the door handle. Macky put his arm around her shoulders and smiled reassuringly.

"It was probably nothing, Sharon," he said. "I was probably wrong. We don't want to go home just yet." He cursed himself for opening his big mouth. He should have left that to Sharon. Things had been heating up nicely.

But Sharon was inconsolable. Every breeze that ruffled the leaves now was in reality a huge hook parting the bushes, and every gleam of moonlight on tree bark was the glint of metal in the night.

"I want to go home," she whimpered. "You can come in if

my parents are out."

The big *if*. Macky wasn't prepared to take the chance. "Oh, come on, Shar," he said in the gentlest, most persuasive tone he could muster, "we'll be all right. I'll protect you."

"No, Macky. I want to go home."

Macky cursed under his breath. Fucking prick-teaser, that's all she was, he thought unfairly. Letting a bloke think he was onto a good thing and then stopping just like that and demanding to be taken home. Well, he'd show her. She wasn't going to make a fool of him that easily.

"We're not going home yet," he said quietly, "not until we've done what we came here to do. You're not going to make a cunt out of me."

"Please, Macky," Sharon begged in a tiny, tear-stained voice, "please take me home. I'm so scared."

"You go home if you want," sneered Macky. "You know the way. It's a bit of a long walk, though, and it's dark in these woods at night. You might get lost. Or perhaps the peeping tom'll get you first."

Sharon's face crumbled into tears. She wailed loudly, broken words of pleading carried along in the flood. Her tears were clear on her face, glistening, turned black by mascara.

Macky felt uncomfortable, and a little ashamed of his outburst, though he wouldn't show it. How was he to know that she really had been scared? He'd thought she was using it as an excuse, that she'd just been leading him on.

"Shut that bloody noise up," he said gruffly. "I'll fucking take you home, then."

This took the edge of panic from her tears, though she continued to weep into a handkerchief grubby with mascara. *Bloody women*, thought Macky. Here he was, seventeen years of age, and already disillusioned with them. He reluctantly stretched out a hand to the ignition key.

As he did so, the car gave a violent lurch like a boat tossed by a strong wave. The two of them were jolted from their seats. Sharon screamed, and then as the car settled, subsided into tears again.

"What the fuck's going on?" Macky yelled, furious. It was bad enough that some joker had completely wrecked his evening; now the cunt was trying to knacker his car as well. As if in response, the car gave another violent lurch. Macky saw red.

"I'll have you, you fucking bastard!" he roared, eyes bulging, spittle flying from his mouth. "You just fucking wait!"

He shoved the door open. Sharon clutched at him desperately.

"Don't go out, Macky, please," she begged, "just drive off. Don't go out."

But there was no stopping him. He shrugged off her grasp savagely.

"No twat's going to fucking mess about with my car," he spat. And then he was gone.

Sharon began to weep afresh, her hands clutching at empty air. The summer breeze swept into the car, bringing a warning with it. She yanked the door closed and locked it. It would probably irritate Macky, but she could live with that. As she pulled the door handle, she thought for a moment she could hear a clatter as the hook swung against the car door. But it was only the click of the door closing and Macky's footfall on the grass.

She heard his voice, angry, aggressive, shouting into the night. She couldn't make out the words because there was a boiling in her head. Her body felt bloated with terror, her brain discharging gory images, conjuring up creatures from her deepest imagination like some demon register. She squeezed her eyes tightly shut and hunched her body into a ball, whimpering like a wounded animal.

She was trapped in a nightmare, in a horror film; The Hook had come alive. A sound suddenly sliced through the stifling air, cutting deep into her senses. It was a high, shrill sound and it caused terror to burn into her chest like fire. It was the sound of Macky screaming.

Kevin jabbed at the embers with the poker, stirring them

into fiery life. Orange sparks flew in protest up the chimney.

Martin came through from the kitchen with a tray bearing two steaming mugs and half a loaf of bread. "Here, get this down you," he said. He still looked drawn and pale, but some of the old jauntiness had returned to his voice.

"Great Mart, thanks." Kevin took the mug and sipped after blowing furiously on the steaming soup. He still burnt his mouth.

"We can have some bacon and eggs later if we get hungry," said Martin. He gave Kevin a sidelong look. "You will stay tonight, won't you, Kev?"

"Yeah, course I will," promised Kevin. "You don't think I'm going home now, do you? Not in the dark."

After ten hours of sitting still and quiet in an armchair watching over Martin, Kevin felt in need of noise and activity. Martin had finally awoke at seven-thirty that evening, and Kevin had chatted unceasingly ever since to rid himself of the tension that had been slowly mounting inside.

"After we've eaten this," he said, munching bread, "we'll have to decide what we're going to do. We need a plan."

Martin nodded, his mouth full. "I'll tell you," he said, spraying bread crumbs, "that bloody thing that came out of that tree scared me shitless. I thought I was going to have a heart attack."

Kevin smiled without humour. "Did…did you see its face?" he asked hesitantly.

Martin stared down into the mug, eyes haunted by the memory. "Yeah," he said quietly. He looked up. "It was Swaney, wasn't it? That kid from school who got run over by a train?"

Kevin nodded. They were both silent as the name hung in the air like a dark threat.

"I still can't believe it," said Martin. "What exactly was that thing?"

Kevin shrugged. "Swaney's ghost?" The words were ludicrous on his lips, but Martin didn't laugh. In fact, Kevin had never seen him look so serious.

"But why did it come out of a bloody tree? And why did it

look like... like it did?"

Impossible questions. Kevin had no answer.

"And another thing," Martin continued, voicing the thoughts that had been pounding in his head for over a day. "If it is a ghost, if it is Swaney, can it be killed? I mean, Swaney's already dead. How can he be killed again?"

There was a frantic, desperate note in his voice now, and just a touch of hysteria. Kevin knew he had to be the calming influence. He spoke with a confidence he did not feel.

"I don't know. We'll just have to do what we can. Maybe the thing has gone, maybe we'll never see or hear from it again. We've just got to play it by ear, Mart. If it comes tonight..." (Martin shuddered, Kevin's voice became firm) "...we use the shotgun. If that doesn't work, we run like hell. I don't know what else we can do. Tomorrow we'll go and see Keith Francis, tell him about this. Maybe he can tell us what to do."

Kevin tailed off. Now that his thoughts had been put into words, they sounded tame, useless, ill-considered. He expected Martin to reject his suggestions, to come up with something of his own. Surprisingly, however, Martin said, "Yes, that's probably the best thing to do. Keith might know a bit about this. He's into this sort of stuff isn't he."

Kevin nodded. "Yes, he's got a roomful of books on occult and folklore and things. I spent the afternoon there once - you remember, when I did that project on witchcraft at school? I reckon if anyone can help us, Keith can."

Keith Francis was a tutor at the boys' school, a controversial character who was often at loggerheads with the authorities. A conviction for possessing cannabis, and an arrest for threatening behaviour at a student demo whilst at university, had almost destroyed his chances of undertaking a teaching career. His fascination with folklore and the occult had resulted in another major storm when he once related his paranormal experiences to a group of students who'd said they were interested in the study of parapsychology. The stories he told were reported in the local rag as being 'so terrifying that a girl student was severely emotionally disturbed for weeks afterwards.' As a result, the local vicar had accused Keith of 'heretical teachings', and the education authorities charged him with breaking the unspoken code of morality within teaching, and on a more concrete basis, of not sticking to the requirements of the 'A' level curriculum. The message was clear: Conform or you're out.

It went without saying that his students loved him.

The boys took it in turns to sit on guard throughout that night, Martin from one until four, Kevin from four until seven. They spent the night downstairs in the sitting room, and kept the fire burning despite the humid weather. After some discussion they decided to douse the lights and use torches. The ghostly beams and shifting shadows gave them the jitters, but at least they didn't feel they were drawing attention to themselves.

As Kevin settled down for his three hours sleep, he thought this must have been what it was like in the trenches. A warm cottage was far removed from a muddy hole in the ground, but the situation was the same: one man always on guard, not knowing if and when the enemy would attack. The night was not for sleeping; it was for watching, and for waiting until the morning. But for Kevin and Martin, waiting was all they did that night.

For them at least, the night was uneventful.

CHAPTER FIVE

THE DISCOVERY

The man in the shabby overcoat and the frayed, wide-brimmed hat stood and looked around him. The sun shone down through the trees in spears of light, piercing the woods with heat, but the man seemed not to notice.

His overcoat he kept buttoned to the neck, and the wide brim of his hat kept his face hidden in shadow.

After a moment's contemplation of his surroundings, he began walking again. He trod lightly, making hardly any sound at all. As he walked, he sighed. There was much he had to do.

Suddenly he stopped. He heard voices, and movement coming towards him. He looked along the path and saw an old man and a large red setter dog approaching. They posed no threat to him, but it was important that he was not seen just yet. He stepped to one side, off the path, melting into the trees as if he had never been there at all...

❧

"Here, boy! Come on, Rags, come on."

Where the hell was that bloody dog? It was too hot to go chasing after him today.

Arthur Willis coughed, the dry smoky air catching at the back of his throat. It was still a mile or so from where the woods had burnt down, but the ashes seemed to linger all around, a ghostly reminder of tragedy. He had even noticed a hint of smoke in the air in the village that morning. Not car fumes and pollution, but wood smoke. It was a pleasant enough smell, but it played havoc with his bronchials.

Him and his chest. His mother had always warned him about smoking them Woodbines, but forty years ago, with an image to keep up and a body as sound as a bell, he'd paid little heed.

"Rags! Hey, come on Rags. Where are you?" Arthur called, looking around. He didn't mind the dog bounding away over the fields and lanes, but he liked him to stay close in the woods. He caught a streak of red out of the corner of his eye and the next minute Rags was there, feathery tail waving, long pink tongue hanging from his grinning mouth. Arthur laughed and stroked the sleek head.

"Now you stay close in the woods, d'you hear?" he said. "I don't want you getting lost." Rags wagged his assent and was off again like a bolt of rusty lightning.

Arthur strolled through the woods, stopping every now and then to catch his breath. It was a terrible thing about that fire. He hadn't been able to help because of his chest, but he'd heard all about it in the pub, and had read about it in the paper.

The consolation was that it could have been much worse than it was. They'd done a marvelous job to contain it. There was no telling where it might have spread to if everyone hadn't mucked in. It would almost certainly have destroyed the entire woodland, and thus put paid to his and Rags' early morning walk. It might even have reached the village and his cottage. He paled at the thought.

"Rags, stay close. Don't go too far," shouted Arthur, seeing his dog disappear along the path ahead. Rags stayed still, looking back, saliva drooling from his mouth. When Arthur had almost caught up, he bounded away up the path ahead. Arthur breathed deeply, enjoying the sunshine and the lazy chorus of bird song in his ears. He followed the winding path through the woods, pushing aside nettles and overhanging foliage with his walking stick. The path rose gradually along a gently sloping valley parallel with the golf course, to eventually emerge onto a dirt track that led to the main road back to the village. An hour's walk; just right. He wondered what the golf club would do about the greens that had been destroyed by fire. Most of them were all right, but the far ones looked like giant pieces of burnt toast, completely unplayable. He supposed they would just have to cordon them off and reduce the number of holes.

His thoughts were interrupted by a sudden flash of light that blinded him. He blinked, rubbed his eyes, and looked across to where he thought the light had come from. There it was again, something catching the light of the sun and reflecting it through the trees. Curious, he took a few steps up the path, hoping for a clear view.

He saw a car parked in a clearing in the woods a couple of hundred yards away across the valley. It was the windscreen that had bounced the sunlight into his eyes. It looked like an old car, quite battered, though from this distance it was difficult to tell. Arthur decided to investigate.

"Rags. Here, Rags. Come on, boy. This way," he called. The setter appeared, quite unperturbed by his master's unusual change of direction. Arthur retraced his steps and took the right-hand path where the two sides of the valley joined. Rags took the more direct approach, scrabbling recklessly down one side of the valley and back up the other. Five minutes later, Arthur reached the little clearing.

The car was a white Ford Cortina, M registration. The body was dented, the tyres bald, and the front lights askew, giving the car a peculiarly drunken stare. However, despite its dilapidated state of repair, it still looked roadworthy, and Arthur found it hard to accept that it had just been dumped. The spare parts alone would have fetched a hundred pounds or more.

Perhaps joy riders had stolen the car, driven it into the woods, and abandoned it, thought Arthur. But if so, why bring it here, so far away from the village? It was a bloody long walk back in the dark. He scratched his head, puzzled. Then he noticed the door.

It was the one on the passenger's side, which is why he hadn't seen it at first glance. It had been ripped forcibly from its hinges and lay on the grass about ten yards away. It must have been joy riders, he thought. They had driven into the woods, perhaps had a crash, knocked the door off on a tree, and then hadn't been able to get the car started again.

It seemed the most feasible explanation, but still Arthur

was troubled. Somehow it didn't ring true. The car looked too neatly parked, there were no skid marks, and none of the surrounding trees looked to have been hit. Furthermore, there was no other damage done to the car, or at least none that he could see. True, the bodywork was dented, but they were clearly all old dents, amateurishly patched up with cement and paint that didn't quite match.

He looked inside the car. On the back seat was a handbag. It contained make-up, pills, money and a comb, but no clue to the identity of its owner. He left the handbag where it was and turned away, his mind spent of possibilities. He decided to inform the police and leave the matter in their hands. They'd know what to do.

"Come on, Rags. Home, boy," he called. The dog was scrabbling about on the other side of the glade, intent on something on the ground.

At his master's voice, his head rose and he trotted obediently across. Arthur was just about to turn and start walking when he noticed Rags' muzzle.

It was smeared with dirt and grit and something else. Something dark and sticky that looked like blood. Arthur called the dog over and examined him. Yes, it was blood, and it didn't seem to be Rags' either. The blood covered the dog's snout, dripping from his chin and frothing from his jowls. Arthur opened Rags' mouth and began to clear the blood away with some tissue paper he had in his pocket. Rags, reveling in the attention, stood patiently, his tail waving lazily. Arthur expected to see a laceration inside the dog's mouth, perhaps made from a sharp stick or stone, but there was nothing.

Intrigued, he crossed to the other side of the clearing. Had someone had an accident after all? Perhaps they had staggered, dazed and bleeding, from the car only to collapse deeper in the woods. He reached the spot where Rags had been clawing and nuzzling at the ground, and the sight almost stopped the breath in his throat.

Blood was everywhere. It covered the ground like a dirty red blanket, tacky and obscene. Arthur felt a dizziness and a nausea sweep over him. It had no right to be here, all this blood, it didn't belong. There looked to be bucketfuls of the stuff, all splattered in this one little area. Perhaps two animals had met here in the night and had fought it out to the death under this oak tree. But what animal sheds so much blood?

And where was the carcass? Dragged away by the victor?

Arthur's mind reeled. The possibilities were endless, ranging from unpleasant to downright unthinkable. A trail of blood led from the main area deeper into the woods. Whoever or whatever had been injured had leaked that way.

He followed the trail tentatively. Rags went ahead, his nose to the ground. Arthur was beginning to heave and struggle for breath. This was all getting a bit too much for him. He looked at his watch. His wife would be expecting him back in twenty minutes. Maybe he should leave it. He didn't want her to worry. But the cat murderer, Curiosity, drove him onward. He couldn't give up now. If he did, he would wonder forever what the bleeding thing had been.

Rags was up ahead out of sight. Suddenly he began barking. Arthur detected a strange note of urgency in the bark and quickened his pace. He tried to ignore his wheezing chest. The trail of blood was still strong, like a grisly path of discovery stretching before him.

He circled a clump of dense bushes and saw Rags ahead, standing by a shallow dip in the ground, legs stiff, barking. The trail of blood stopped there and accumulated into something hunched and dark upon the ground. Arthur crept closer. He felt dread squeeze his heart. He wanted to go away from here. There was something wrong, something evil about the place.

But his eyes were held by the dip in the ground and the bundle that crouched within it.

Was it rags? Old clothes strewn on the ground? He moved closer, and still he didn't see.

And then he saw.

There were two bodies bunched into the ground. One was male, the other female—that much was obvious. But the rest was hidden by mutilation.

They had no faces; just red, tattered holes where faces had once been. They had been bludgeoned, twisted, cut apart by a demonic shredding machine. They were gory morsels, barely humanity.

Arthur felt pain and terror roar through his head. His chest closed up and stifled him. He fell to his knees and was sick on his dog.

CHAPTER SIX

INFLUENCES

Silas Revelle locked up his shop, sat down, and wondered what was happening to him. For two days now, he had had this headache, and it was becoming increasingly worse. It had come to him on Sunday around noon—a small, tight spark of pain that clicked on like a lightbulb in his skull. Since then the pain had expanded, become more insistent, until now Silas felt as though his whole head was beating like a heart.

He sat there for a long time in his dingy shop, surrounded by the smell of damp and the rows of shabby, second-hand books. The window onto the street was coated with grime, making the world outside looked choked; discoloured wallpaper peeled from the walls to reveal soggy, grey brick beneath; years of dust and filth encrusted the wooden floor. Silas closed his eyes. To think he had come to this!

At school he had always been regarded as a brilliant and imaginative pupil. His violent, often sadistic, temper had aroused some concern but, because of his academic prowess, had largely been explained away as the frustrated yearnings of a young and enquiring mind. At university his dabblings in Satanism and extreme political activism had again been largely overlooked due to the excellence of his academic work. Silas had come away from university with a first class honours degree in psychology, and a hatred of the establishment.

He had had only one real friend in his life, a young man called Peter Boorman. Silas and Peter had met at a rally organised by the extreme political group, The Platoon of Saint George. Peter was a heroin user with an Adolf Hitler fixation, and it was the mutual scorn of all they saw around them rather than real friendship that had brought the two together. They had pooled their resources and rented this pit of a shop in Cranbydale, intending to use it as a base from which to spread their political gospel. It was Silas who had had the idea of using the downstairs room as a second-hand bookshop. Peter had scoured the local jumble sales, buying up books at five or ten pence each and then re-selling them at a five hundred to one thousand per cent profit.

For a while, things had worked well. The bookshop had raised enough money to pay the rent and to provide funds for their political ventures. They had managed to run off some copies of their own magazine, *The New Revolution*, which had sold well at political meetings. Gradually they had built up support for their ideas, mainly from extremists who had thought their own parties not extreme enough. For the first time in his life Silas had been happy.

And then disaster had struck.

One day, just over six months ago, there had been a knock at the door. Silas had opened it to find two policemen standing outside. His first thought had been to slam the door in their faces, but then he had noticed their expressions, their looks of bland compassion, and something between curiosity and dread had made him keep the door open.

Peter, they told him calmly, was dead, killed by a heroin overdose. He had been found in an alleyway that morning, slumped between two dustbins like a bag of rubbish.

Silas had slammed the door in their faces then. He had run upstairs, whimpering like an animal, where he had slumped onto his cold, damp bed with the stained sheets and cried for his lost love. For three days he had kept himself locked away, eating nothing, seeing no one.

Since then, things had gone from bad to worse.

Silas had neglected his politics so much that gradually his supporters drifted away. He had neglected the shop too, opening only one, two, occasionally three days a week instead of the six days he had opened before. Business had slumped dramatically. Debts and bills had piled up. Now Silas was two months in arrears with the rent and had received a final demand from the

Electricity Board only that morning. Was there any wonder he was having a brain haemorrhage?

He opened his eyes. The shop was so squalid it seemed to mock him. The sun was trying to struggle through the grime-slick windows, but the yellow slats of light only served to show the shop up for the dump it was. Silas pushed himself up from his chair. The pain clung to the inside of his skull like a passenger, tightening its grip when he moved his head. He staggered up the stairs, which themselves seemed to stagger. The pain in his head was now so intense that the open doorway to his room was like a drop into nothingness, a blurred rectangle of white cut into the wall. Silas fell through the doorway and flung himself onto the bed. He lay with his face buried in the pillow while something burrowed into his mind. He felt sick and dizzy, his fingers and toes tingling as they went numb. After a while he drifted into sleep.

Something was calling him. Silas was unable to resist the cries, but at the same time he felt warm and happy; it was good to feel wanted again. In his dream he rocked and caressed and comforted the thing that needed him. He was made to feel responsible and paternal. Baby needed feeding, baby needed feeding, but first he had to....

Wake.

Silas blinked his eyes. Had he been asleep or just thinking? He sat up, and a sudden wave, almost of ecstasy, came over him. It was as though he had a friend again, as though Peter had come back. He sprang up from the bed and rushed downstairs. The pain in his head had gone now, had been replaced by a comforting weight that seemed to balance his mind. Silas felt a sudden resolve, a flash of inspiration.

He had to go to Limefield.

⁕⁖ೲ⁖⁖

Pamela Chesney strutted into school, large buttocks swaying from side to side like footballs in her tight track-suit bottoms. It was the first time she had been back since term had ended three weeks ago, and immediately the slightly chemical smell of wood varnish and chalk dust depressed her. She strolled along the corridor towards the staff room. On her left, the cloakroom looked unnaturally empty, rows of stubby metal hooks beckoning like crooked fingers. Her footsteps seemed to boom in the hollow corridor; the school without children was like a shell.

But despite its lonely feel, Pamela preferred the school this way. She disliked most children and hated the rest. She had been cornered into becoming a teacher because her mother and father had been teachers themselves. A number of times she had tried to get out of the profession, but pressure from her parents had always prevented her from doing so. Whenever she brought up the question of resignation her mother would become suddenly ill, saying that Pamela was making her sick with worry, or her father would glare and tut and shake his head in disapproval until she changed her mind. Discipline and authority had been drummed mercilessly into Pamela from an early age, and she had never quite managed to pluck up enough courage to defy her parents' wishes.

She reached the staff room and went inside. Everything was arranged neatly for once; waste bins and ashtrays emptied and polished, magazines piled into neat stacks, coffee things cleared up and put away in the cupboard. The order depressed Pamela; it reminded her that the school was poised for another long term. Even the knowledge that there were still four weeks to go before it started did little to cheer her spirits. She took a glass from the cupboard and filled it with water. After one sip she grimaced; it tasted metallic and reminded her of school coffee. She poured the water away and went to look in her pigeonhole. There was only one letter, and a periodical that she never read but had not got around to cancelling.

She opened the letter. It was from Edith Mulhally's father, complaining about her 'bullying' and demanding a showdown. Pamela screwed it up and flung it angrily at the waste bin. It bounced on the lip and came to rest under a chair, but she didn't bother to pick it up. On the way out of the staffroom she met Trevor Hoyle, the caretaker.

"Morning, Miss Chesney," Hoyle said, his white moustache

bristling like a toothbrush. Pamela grunted a reply. "Come in to do some work before school starts again have you?" Hoyle continued.

"Yes," said Pamela.

"Ah, well, you'll be needing the key to your office then."

Hoyle drew a huge bunch of keys from his pocket and began to flick through them, muttering to himself.

"I've got my own, thanks," Pamela said and moved away.

"Ah, right you are, Miss Chesney, right you are," Hoyle said to her retreating back. Pamela ignored him. She went down a flight of steps which led to the changing rooms, unlocked the door at the bottom and went inside.

She sighed at the familiar smell of showers and talc. The smell was only faint, but it was there, and no amount of scrubbing or airing would get rid of it. Her own office was tiny, tucked away to the right of the gymnasium doors. It contained a desk, a chair, a miniscule filing cabinet, and a jumble of broken hockey sticks propped in a corner. She squeezed between the desk and the wall and sat down, noting with resentment that they hadn't bothered to clean her office. Clumps of dried mud were still dotted about the floor, punched with small, round stud-marks, and her waste bin had not been emptied.

She sorted through a pile of papers on her desk: letters to be answered, sports fixtures to arrange, a curriculum to finalise. Where to begin? She stared blankly at the top sheet on her pile. She really didn't feel like working today. All weekend she had had a nagging pain in her head, and this morning it seemed worse than ever. She started reading, but the pain slowly intensified until at last it seemed the words on the page were banging into her skull like nails. She closed her eyes and the pain seemed to scratch and probe at the back of her eyeballs. In the darkness behind her lids a shape began to form...

༺ ༒ ༻

Trevor Hoyle pushed the changing room door open with his backside, his hands occupied with holding the tea tray. Miss Chesney was a bit of a sourpuss, but surely even she couldn't refuse a nice cup of tea, and Hoyle liked a bit of company with his elevens. He whistled as he strode through the changing room. Work was so much easier during the holidays, without all the kids about. Mind you, he did like the kids. They were a good bunch, most of 'em, and they certainly livened the place up a bit.

He came to Miss Chesney's office and, adjusting the tray so he could balance it with one hand, rapped on the door. There was no response.

"Miss Chesney?" he called. After a few moments of silence, he tried again. "Miss Chesney?" Still no reply.

Hoyle felt disappointed. Perhaps she had gone home. Deciding to check, he pushed the office door open.

Miss Chesney was slumped over the desk, her head in her hands. Papers were strewn about her, some having fluttered to the floor.

"Miss Chesney?" Hoyle said, thinking she had fallen asleep. He saw the fingers of her left hand begin to stretch out slowly on the desk like the legs of a waking spider.

"Miss Chesney?" Hoyle repeated. "Are you all right?"

Miss Chesney stirred. Slowly she raised her head.

"My God!" Hoyle exclaimed. The tea tray slipped from his fingers and crashed to the floor.

Miss Chesney's pupils were gone. Her eyes were pure white and seemed to bulge from their sockets. As Hoyle watched, her lips curled back in a jerky snarl and a thread of saliva drooled from her mouth.

"Miss Chesney... you... I..." Hoyle stuttered, and pushed himself away from the doorway with trembling hands.

Pamela Chesney stood up slowly, her sightless eyes fixed on Hoyle. She crouched low, like an animal preparing to spring, and advanced towards him, pushing aside the heavy desk with frightening ease.

Hoyle backed away, capable only of small, stuttering steps. There was a thick, pulsating boom in his head like a heartbeat magnified underwater. The walls seemed to close in. The stocky, track-suited figure of Pamela Chesney stretched out stubby fingers that had hooked into talons. Then the figure and the walls rushed upwards out of Hoyle's vision, and an out-of-focus floor came to meet him.

Pamela Chesney stepped over the caretaker's sprawled body and stood, swaying, for a moment. Her pupils suddenly came back into her eyes, clunking down like the reel on a fruit machine; they were large and very dark.

Slowly she walked from the room.

❦

"I'm sick of shootin' at trees," said Spud Campbell, hefting the airgun in his hand. "Let's go over the other side. I know where there's some rabbit burrows."

Nicky King looked doubtful. "I dunno, Spud," he said. "I'd like to stay this side of the woods. They reckon there's somethin' funny about the place since the fire."

"Who reckon?" Spud said scornfully.

"Well my mum for a start. She says—"

"Your mum?" Spud snorted. "Christ, Nicky, what's the matter with you? Goin' soft or somethin'? You're just like a fuckin' old woman."

Nicky looked embarrassed. "Well, what about Macky then?" he said. "He told us he was comin' in here last night, an' he ain't been seen since."

"Aw, he'll show up. He'll be fuckin' that slag Stewart somewhere."

This raised a smile from Nicky, but still he looked doubtful.

"Come on," said Spud. "What can happen to us? We're armed, remember. We've got this." He squinted through the sights of the air rifle. Nicky tutted, but nodded reluctantly.

"Okay, but if we don't find any rabbits, we're comin' back. And we keep to the main path, we don't go wanderin' off anywhere."

"Yeah, yeah. Just relax, Nicky-boy. Tonight, you and me'll be eatin' rabbit stew."

They set off along the top of the valley, Spud first, Nicky following. Spud was large for seventeen. His hair was shaved into a bristling skinhead cut. He wore a white t-shirt which sweat caused to cling to his back, tight jeans and black Doc Marten boots. A panther holding a Union Jack was tattooed on his left arm, a Yorkshire rose on his right.

Nicky was smaller and skinnier. He was dressed all in black and had spiky orange hair. His studded wristbands looked too heavy for his fragile wrists. His face was sharp and weasly, his eyes in a permanent squint. His skin was white, greasy-looking and peppered with spots.

Spud lit a cigarette and tossed the match into the undergrowth.

"Watch it," said Nicky. "You'll be setting the rest of the bloody place on fire."

Spud snorted a laugh. "Yeah, that'd be really funny," he said. "That'd really give the pigs something to think about." He stuffed the cigarette packet back into his jeans pocket.

"Well, aren't you gonna offer me one?" Nicky said.

"Nope," said Spud.

"Bastard," said Nicky.

"Yep," said Spud.

They walked in silence for a few more minutes. At last Nicky said, "I don't think we ought to go much further now, Spud. I can smell the smoke from the fire."

Spud suddenly dropped to his knees and ducked behind a tree. "Shhh," he said. "Get down."

Nicky looked around. "What for, Spud? I don't see—"

"Just fuckin' shut up!" Spud hissed. He dragged Nicky down beside him. They crouched behind the tree, heads together, looking at the opposite side of the valley through the foliage.

"What we lookin' at, Spud?" said Nicky.

"Just wait and you'll see. They're just out of sight at the moment."

"Who are?"

Spud eased the air rifle into firing position. "There, look now," he said.

Nicky looked. Three boys, about nine or ten years old, were walking along the opposite side of the valley. The boy at the front had a stick which he was using to thrash the undergrowth aside.

"Just kids," Nicky said, disappointed. "I thought it was

rabbits."

"They'll make good targets," Spud said, raising the rifle.

Nicky's voice held a note of horrified awe. "You can't kill kids! Spud, you can't."

"I'm not gonna kill 'em, pillock," Spud said irritably. "I'll aim low, for their legs. Or their arses." He laughed. "Yeah, that's what I'll do. I'll make their arses sting."

Nicky sniggered into his hand. "Yeah, that's it. Make the little buggers run."

Spud squinted through the rifle's sights and pressed the trigger. The rifle jerked slightly in his hands and emitted a sharp *Phut* sound. The boys on the other side of the valley turned and stared.

"You missed 'em, Spud," Nicky said, never one to avoid stating the obvious. "You missed 'em."

"Shut up, shithead. I'll get 'em this time." The air rifle reloaded, Spud raised it again to his shoulder. The boys had begun walking once more, though now they were huddled closer together which made them easier targets. They kept looking back nervously, wondering where the sound had come from.

Nicky watched them moving away, kept his eye on them for a good fifteen seconds. At last he said, "Hurry up and fire, Spud. They'll be out of range soon."

There was no reply. Nicky glanced to his left. Something was wrong with Spud. The rifle was in his right hand, pointing at the ground. His left hand was spread over his face, cradling his head.

"What's up, Spud?" Nicky said. Spud didn't answer. Nicky tapped him on the shoulder. "Spud, what's up?"

Spud removed the hand from in front of his face, and Nicky leaped up in horror, banging his head on a tree branch. Spud's eyeballs were white and moving slowly in his sockets like slugs. As Nicky watched, they seemed to strain outwards, stretching his lids wide.

"Spud, Spud," Nicky whimpered. "What's the matter? Are you on somethin'? Answer me, Spud, answer me."

But Spud's only answer was to raise the air rifle and point it at Nicky's face.

Nicky backed away, hands held up. "No, Spud, put the gun down," he stammered. "You don't know what you're doing."

Spud stood up, his face stretching into a hideous smile. It was that smile that broke Nicky; he turned and ran. The grass seemed slippery beneath his feet, and his body was awkward, a weight that refused to be coordinated. Behind him he heard nothing. He was not sure whether Spud was chasing him or not.

Then he heard the familiar loud *phut*, and something whacked into his hand, instantly numbing it. Nicky yelped and put on an extra spurt of speed. His orange hair blazed like fire in the sunshine as he sprinted down the valley path.

Spud made no effort to give chase. He was needed elsewhere. He tossed the air rifle into the muddy stream at the bottom of the valley, turned and walked away.

Baby needed feeding.

⌒⌒⌒⌒⌒

"Mike, are you going to wash that car or are you just going to sit on your arse all day?"

There was no reply, and Cynthia Hargreaves glowered at the back of the red and white striped deckchair. It was not fair that she should be stuck in the kitchen whilst her lazy husband lounged around in the sun all afternoon. She opened the window wider.

"Mike!" she shouted, not caring whether the neighbours heard or not. "Will you answer me?"

There was a murmur of voices, but only from the cricket commentators on the radio who sounded as drowsy as the weather.

"Mike!" she yelled. The commentators droned on. The weight in the deckchair didn't move. Cynthia dried her hands and marched out of the open back door. "Mike, will you—" she began as she reached the deck chair, but then stopped. Mike wasn't here. It was only a couple of library books that caused the seat to sag. Cynthia chewed her lip, puzzled. Where could he have gone? She shrugged and strolled back towards the house.

"Mummy!" The voice of her daughter shocked her. It

seemed so full of terror. She looked around wildly, half-expecting Cassie to swoop out of the sky and into her arms. A moment later Cassie came tearing around the side of the house.

"Mummy!" Cassie screamed again and headed for the back door.

"Cassie, Cassie, I'm here!" Cynthia said, hurrying down the lawn towards the house.

Cassie stopped, turned, and came running towards her. She flung herself at Cynthia and wrapped her arms around her waist.

Cynthia stroked Cassie's head, gently parting her blond fringe which felt damp with sweat. She took Cassie's arms from around her waist and crouched down, holding the little girl's hands.

"Cassie, love, whatever's the matter? Has that nasty dog been chasing you again?"

Cassie shook her head. "No, no, it was Daddy. He frightened me."

Cynthia frowned. "Daddy frightened you? What do you mean? Where is he?"

Cassie looked fearfully over her shoulder. "He was on the road, Mummy. I saw him walking. I ran to him, but he pushed me away. And then he looked at me and his eyes were all white. I said 'Daddy' and then his eyes came back again, but he still didn't smile. Mummy, what's wrong with him? Why did he make his eyes go like that? It was scary."

"Shh... shh..." Cynthia said as Cassie began to cry. She pulled her daughter towards her. Cassie clung tightly to her neck. "I'm sure daddy didn't mean to frighten you. When he comes back, we'll ask him why he did it. Okay?"

Cassie nodded.

But Daddy didn't come back.

⁂

Cranbydale Prison was situated halfway between Cranbydale and Limefield, on a lonely stretch of moorland. It was a bleak, forbidding place of dark brick, high walls and tiny barred windows. In the evenings, it loured at the sky—a great, black, eyeless mass which seemed to sway and shift as the clouds drifted along behind. It looked lost and empty, but appearances were deceptive. To fourteen hundred and seventy-nine men, it was home.

Greg Trenchard sat reading his paper and drinking coffee from a flask. To his right, a flight of metal steps led to a catwalk which ran all the way round the room. This pattern was repeated three times, and from the ground floor, it looked like an image reproducing itself in a mirror. Above Greg's head, a net had been stretched to prevent suicides.

Greg liked the night shift best of all. Some of his mates found it too quiet, too creepy, but Greg didn't mind. He had no family to go home to, and there was never any trouble, not like in the daytime. At first, he had been unnerved by the echoing coughs and groans, and the troubled cries of men in nightmare, but now he hardly noticed. Indeed, the noises reassured him; silence in a prison was a suspicious sound.

The page crackled as he turned it over. Here she was, Busty Belinda from Brighton who claimed to have had lusty nights of kinky sex with some pop star or other. Greg read the article slowly, his eyes constantly flickering to the photograph that accompanied it. So mesmerised was he by Belinda's boobs that he didn't realise anyone had come up behind him until a hand touched his shoulder. He spun round, reaching for the stave inside his jacket, but when he saw who it was, he relaxed.

"Bob, don't do that! You scared the life out of me. What are you doing back here?"

Bob Tickner rubbed a hand over his face. "I... I came back for something."

Greg pulled up a chair. "Here, you'd better sit down. You look knackered. Fancy some coffee?"

"Please," said Bob, and sat down gratefully.

Greg poured fresh coffee into the plastic cup and glanced sidelong at the beefy, grey-haired man sitting beside him. Bob Tickner always made him nervous. In Greg's opinion, he was a vicious bastard who would probably have been in prison himself if he hadn't found a job that gave him an outlet for his aggression. It was said that he ran a protection racket in the prison with the help of some of the more violent inmates, and that he frequently accepted bribes. Of course, there was never any evidence to support these rumours. Bob was too cunning to get caught.

"Careful, it's hot," warned Greg as Bob took a swig of coffee. The big man put the cup down and wiped a hand across his mouth.

"That's better," he said, and belched loudly.

"What was it you said you came back for?" Greg asked.

Bob opened his mouth, then closed it again, looking bewildered. "I don't know," he admitted. "I was in the locker room getting ready to go home when I suddenly thought there was something I had to do back here. But I'm damned if I can remember what it was."

"Oh well, I suppose it'll come back to you," said Greg. To mask his nervousness, he picked up his newspaper and began reading again.

"Yeah, I suppose it will." Bob finished the coffee, then slumped forward over the table with a groan.

"You okay?" asked Greg, tearing himself away from Busty Belinda once more.

"Splitting headache," Bob explained. "I've had it all weekend."

"Too much of the hard stuff on Friday night, was it?"

"I dunno. It doesn't usually affect me like this."

Greg reluctantly put aside his newspaper. "Shall I get you a couple of aspirins?"

Bob gave a slight nod. "Yeah, thanks."

Greg got up and went over to the first aid box. He unlocked it and sorted through the contents until he found what he was looking for. "Here we are," he said. But when he turned back to the table, Bob was gone.

"Bob?" Greg looked around. He crossed to the door that led to the locker room and tried the handle. It was locked, so Bob couldn't have gone out that way. He wouldn't have had time, and besides, Greg would have heard the key in the lock.

Greg sighed, exasperated, and tossed the box of aspirin onto the table. Where the hell could Bob have got to? He heard a sudden creak above his head and looked up. Bob was strolling nonchalantly along the catwalk.

"Bob," Greg hissed, "what are you doing?"

Bob stopped dead, but not because Greg had called him. He took a metal keyring from his belt and began to unlock one of the cell doors.

"Bob," Greg called again. "Bob, stop that!" He raced up the stairs, feet clanging on the metal steps.

Like a great beast, the prison began to wake. Men murmured and groaned. Some began to bang on their cell doors. Bob took the key from the lock and tugged the heavy door open.

"Bob!" Greg yelled. Men were shouting and swearing now, thumping their cell doors like zoo animals hurling themselves at the bars of their cage. Amid the clamour, Bob turned to face him. Greg recoiled. Bob's eyes were white and crawling in their sockets.

"Bob," he croaked, his mouth suddenly very dry. "Bob, what's wrong?"

Bob's face was expressionless, though his white eyes seemed to glare coldly. After a moment he turned away.

Through the open cell door, Greg saw a shape sit up and swing its feet over the side of the bunk bed. He drew his stave and advanced.

"Lock that door, Bob," he said quietly. "I don't know what's wrong with you, but you can't do this. Do you understand me?"

Bob said nothing. The figure in the cell stood up, and Greg rushed forward to slam the door, attempting to elbow Bob aside as he did so. But Bob was as immoveable as a rock. As Greg jarred his arm on Bob's chest, he thought he might just as well have tried to push down a wall.

Bob turned his head jerkily, fixed Greg with those slithering white eyes. He stretched out a long, muscular arm, plucked the stave from Greg's hand, and casually whacked him over the head with it. Greg staggered back against the railings as the floor, walls, doors and ceiling became a blurred carousel of shape and colour. He watched stupidly as Bob tossed the stave over the railings where it bounced on the net below.

The man came out of the cell. It was Wilkins, eight years for armed robbery. He wore dull blue prison clothes but, like Bob, his eyes were white and bulging.

Greg was too dazed to defend himself as Bob picked him up and flung him into the cell. He crashed into the opposite wall and was just in time to see Bob close and lock the door before he blacked out.

"What's up, Sarge?" said Atkins, coming through the door. "You look a bit put upon."

"Put upon? You're not joking," replied desk sergeant Cyril Prothwell. "The number of times I've answered that phone today I'm surprised I haven't got biceps like Rocky."

"Been busy, has it?"

Before Prothwell could reply, the phone rang again. Prothwell glared at it. Atkins skipped neatly round the desk and picked it up. "Hello, Limefield police station. Can I help you?" He listened for a moment, then pulled a face. "Really, Mrs. Parker, and when was this?... I see, yes... Well, I'm afraid we've got our hands full at the moment, but we'll try to get someone out to you in the morning... yes, yes I know, Mrs. Parker... No, it's no trouble at all. Goodbye." He put the receiver down gently. "Mrs. Parker," he explained to the sergeant. "She says there were some prowlers around her house earlier."

Prothwell tutted and raised his eyes heavenwards. "God, that's all we need. I don't know what's going on today, I really don't."

"Why, what's up?"

"What's up? Everything's bloody up! Do you know how many missing persons reports I've had today?"

"No, sarge."

"Nineteen. Nineteen! In one bloody day! We only had about three or four the whole of last year."

Atkins whistled. "Maybe it's a reaction to the murders," he said. "People getting edgy."

Prothwell shook his head. "No, most of the reports came in

during the day, before the paper came out."

"Yeah, but you know how word gets around in the village. You don't need a newspaper to know what's going on."

Prothwell sank into a chair. "I hope you're right, John, but the thing is, we haven't been able to trace any of these people so far. They're not at work, not at friends' houses, nowhere. You'd think we'd be able to find at least one or two of them to allay the fears a bit. All day long it's been, 'Sorry, madam. No, I'm afraid we've not found your husband yet', or 'Sorry, sir. No, I'm afraid your wife has still not turned up.' I feel like a bloody parrot. I might as well record a standard message and go home."

Atkins smiled. "I think you need a cuppa, Sarge."

"I need something stronger than tea, but I expect it will have to do for now."

Atkins rounded the desk and went into the kitchenette. A few minutes later, he came out with two mugs and handed one to the sergeant.

"Two sugars. That's right, isn't it, sir?"

"Yes. Thanks, John." Prothwell sipped the tea gratefully.

"How's the bloke who found the bodies?" asked Atkins.

Prothwell put his tea down and stretched back on his chair. "Still unconscious, but the doctors reckon he'll pull through. It was lucky he had that dog with him or we'd have three corpses on our hands now, not two."

"A proper little Lassie by all accounts," said Atkins.

"Yes, the dog stood over the old man's body, whimpering and barking until someone came. Mind you, we were still lucky. Most people would have ignored a barking dog. It was fortunate that Paul Timmis, the vet, was walking his own dog at that time. He heard the old man's dog barking and went to have a look. There's been a lot of people setting traps in the woods just recently, and he was worried the dog might have been caught in one."

At that moment the phone rang again. Prothwell looked as though he would have liked to crush it to pulp with his bare fists. Atkins snatched it up quickly.

"Hello, Limefield police station. Can I help you?"

Prothwell heard a tinny voice jabbering faintly. He sighed

and closed his eyes.

"Jesus," Atkins said suddenly, "when did this happen?"

Prothwell opened his eyes. Atkins looked shocked, his hand gripping the receiver tightly. Prothwell raised his eyebrows, questioning.

"Hang on a minute, sir," Atkins said into the receiver. "Perhaps you'd better talk to the sergeant." He cupped his hand over the mouthpiece.

"What's up?" said Prothwell.

"It's Inspector Carside, sir, Cranbydale CID. There's been a breakout from the prison—about fifty men gone. It happened an hour ago."

"Bloody hell!" exclaimed Prothwell. He put out a hand for the receiver. "Just what is going on around here today? It's like all Hell's broken loose!"

CHAPTER SEVEN

A PRISON OF SOULS

Kevin and Martin had spent most of that day out of Limefield. In the afternoon, they had taken the long and sweaty bus ride into Cranbydale, eleven miles away, to see Keith Francis.

"This is the place isn't it?" Martin said, strolling up the drive.

"Yes, number sixteen," confirmed Kevin. Martin rang the doorbell, and the two boys stood self-consciously, thinking over what they were going to say. After a moment the door opened. A woman stood there. She was small and vaguely pretty, dressed in a sweatshirt, jeans and a headscarf. She held a paintbrush in her hand.

"Hello," she said brightly before either of the boys could say anything. "Have you come about the plumbing?"

"Er... no. We've come to see Keith. Is he in?" replied Kevin, a little thrown by the question.

"Oh yes, of course. Come in." She held the door wide and yelled up the stairs, "Keith, there's two boys to see you."

They stepped into a narrow hallway. The house was dingy after the brightness outside, and the smell of paint was everywhere.

"He'll be down in a minute. Would you like some coffee?"

"Yes, please," they said simultaneously. She bustled away, full of cheerful energy.

"Hey, Kevin and Martin. What brings you here?" said Keith Francis, wiping his hands on a rag as he came down the stairs. Kevin always found it difficult to think of Keith as their English Literature tutor. Like Martin, he was tall and gangly. His hair was long (he allowed it to grow over summer and then had it cut again in time for school), and his straggle of beard untidy. He wore small, round spectacles which had a habit of slithering to the end of his nose, a 'Kiss My Ass' t-shirt, and jeans so ragged that only faded CND patches held them together.

"We... er... we'd like to talk to you about something," said Martin.

Keith looked from one to the other, noting their unease. "Okay, fine. Look, we'll go in my study. It's about the only place unaffected by all this decorating. We're having a complete overhaul. Mags was getting sick of the vermilion walls." He gestured down at the grey, paint-splattered sheets covering the bare floor-boards. "Don't think these are our usual carpets." The boys smiled at the joke.

Keith led them to his study, a converted bedroom on the floor above. The walls were lined with bookcases, nearly all of which were crammed full. Despite his scruffy appearance and laid-back attitude, he was something of an academic.

"Can I get you boys a beer?" he said.

"Well, I think your wife's making coffee actually," replied Kevin.

"That's no problem. Would you prefer a beer?"

The boys nodded gratefully. Keith grinned and went downstairs to fetch the beers.

"Have you seen this place?" Martin breathed as soon as the door had closed. "It's like a library."

"Yeah I know. I spent the whole afternoon here once. He's got some brilliant books. Some of them are hundreds of years old. If Keith can't shed some light on this, I don't know who can."

They sat patiently, the smell of paint and turpentine still lingering in their nostrils. There was something about being surrounded by books, Kevin thought, something warm and cosy and peaceful. The study door opened, bringing a fresh waft of chemical stink into the room. Keith handed round cans of beer. He perched himself on the vast oak desk and ripped the ring pull off his can.

"Now then, what's it all about?" he said. His tone was easy, but as the boys knew, he liked to get to the point with uncomfortable suddenness.

Hesitantly, awkwardly, Kevin told him the whole story. As he told it, he was painfully aware of how it sounded—ridiculous, laughable, idiotic—but he continued doggedly. He told the tale as a monologous account of events, Martin chipping in with colour and description. He kept glancing anxiously up at Keith's face, trying to judge his reaction. If he had seen a trace of disbelief or derision, he would have dried up immediately, unable to continue. But Keith just sat and listened, sipping his beer, face impassive. He frowned slightly when the boys admitted responsibility for the fire, but apart from that— nothing. Not even when they told him about Swaney and showed him the photograph did he change expression. He just took it and gazed at it with cool, grey eyes.

When the telling was over he leaned back and looked at the boys. He took a Marlboro from a crumpled packet in his jeans pocket, straightened it out, lit up, and took a long pull. Finally, he murmured, "It's quite a story."

"Do you believe it?" Martin forced himself to ask.

Keith massaged the straggle of beard on his chin. "Why should you come all this way just to lie to me?" he said. Kevin could have cried with relief.

"Will you help us?" he asked eagerly.

Keith shrugged. "If I can."

"We were thinking you might be able to shed some light on what happened," prompted Martin.

Keith exhaled smoke. He leaned forward, looking thoughtful; his spectacles slid to the end of his nose. "Just a minute," he said, "I think I might have something..." His voice tailed off. He crossed to the bookcase and lifted down a heavy volume bound in scratched, faded leather. "Here we are," he said, and carried the book over to the desk, cradling it in his arms like a baby. He set it down and the two boys pressed in eagerly.

"Now then, where is it?" he muttered. He flicked through the dry pages swiftly but reverently, fingers deft from years of practice.

"Aha!" he cried in triumph. He pushed the book to one side and indicated a small illustration. The boys craned their necks forward to see.

It was a faded drawing, the figures possessing the stylised stiffness and simplicity of medieval art. It depicted a peasant man, complete with smock and hat, standing before a tree. The bark of the tree was gaping open and stepping out of it was a horned demon with scaly skin, pointed tail, and hooves instead of feet. The two boys stared at the drawing, fascinated.

Martin felt a strange numbness, and a deep, dark fear flowered inside him. The drawing seemed to leer out of the page to mock him. He felt like an unimportant scrap in time, a pawn in a game. The thing that had come out of the tree was Russell Swaney, but at the same time it was something else; something older and much more powerful. He tore his gaze away from the page. "What is this book?" he said. His voice sounded wild and hollow, not part of him at all.

"It has no title," said Keith. "It's not printed, it's handwritten. I suspect it's simply a collection of notes. You know... folklore, ancient beliefs, that sort of thing. There are some herbal remedies in there and what I guess to be spells or incantations of some sort. I mean, to someone like myself, a book like this is virtually priceless. Promise me you won't tell a soul you've seen it."

"We promise," Kevin said solemnly. The pages of the book were yellow and dust-dry, the lettering strange, the leather that bound it cracked and peeling. Kevin felt it was like the magic journal of some remote necromancer, passed down through the centuries for this moment.

Martin was still studying the book. "What language is this?" he said.

"It's no language really," Keith replied, and laughed at the boys' bemused expressions. "To be more specific, it's actually a sort of mish-mash of Olde English, whatever form of French the Normans spoke, and just to make things a bit more complicated there's a smattering of Latin and what I think is Italian in there too."

"A real easy reader huh?" said Martin dryly. Keith laughed again.

"It's a monster, all right," he replied passionately. "A huge

Frankenstein's monster of language."

"Do you understand any of it?" Kevin said.

"Quite a bit of it now," answered Keith. "It's been an obsession of mine over the past year. I've sat for hours in this room, staring and staring at the pages, trying to make sense of them. I've tried permutation after permutation in an attempt to discover the alphabet used. At long last, I feel I'm finally getting somewhere." He shook his head and murmured almost affectionately, "What a bastard it's been."

Kevin pushed the book over to him. "You don't know what this bit means do you?" he said, indicating the block of delicate lettering that related to the illustration.

"Wait a minute," Keith said. "I'll just find my translation." He rooted through the drawers of his oak desk, lifting out wads of paper and flicking through them. At last he found what he was looking for. "Ah, yes," he said, "The Prison of Souls."

"The what?" said Martin.

"This heading here is translated as The Prison of Souls," Keith explained. "It's one of the more obscure medieval beliefs. In some parts of the British Isles, largely on the Western coast and in parts of Ireland, it was thought that when a man died he had either a light soul or a dark soul. If he had a light soul, then all was well and good. He went up to Heaven or wherever. But if a man had a dark soul, it would be imprisoned, trapped within some natural element on God's earth. Often it was a tree or a bush, but it could just as easily be a stone or even a drop of water. There the dark soul would remain until the time came for it to be reborn and given another chance. It could stay imprisoned for tens, hundreds, even thousands of years."

"But what are these dark souls supposed to look like?" Kevin wanted to know. "I mean the thing that came out of that tree didn't look like that demon-thing in the drawing."

Keith shrugged. "I don't suppose shape is particularly important. The medieval artists nearly always depicted the Devil or a demon in this way—all had the standard hooves, horns and tail. Remember it was a time of virtually one hundred per cent illiteracy. Symbols were all-important, not words."

"But what's it doing here? How did it get out of the tree?"

Martin demanded. He couldn't believe they were really having this conversation. Keith shrugged again.

"I don't know. Maybe we'll find some answers in here, maybe not. There are parts of the text I haven't managed to translate yet."

For a few moments, nobody said anything. Keith finished his cigarette and looked around for an ashtray. Unable to find one, he drained his beer and dropped the cigarette stub into the empty can.

"Does the book give any indication of how to get rid of these 'dark souls'?" said Martin, breaking the silence. "I mean, can it be banished by a few choice words from a priest or anything?"

"Not that I know of," replied Keith.

"Then we're more or less back where we started," said Kevin gloomily.

"No, we're not," said Martin. "At least we know what this thing is now. And Keith says there's some of the text he still hasn't translated. So, he can start on that whilst we... well, whilst we wait I suppose."

"Yeah, and concentrate on staying alive," muttered Kevin.

"Oh, don't be so pessimistic, Kev. We can't just give up. We don't even know if this thing harms people."

"It does. I know it does. I can feel it. It's evil, Mart. And there's no use pretending. You know it too."

This seemed to knock some of the stuffing out of Martin. For a moment, his eyes flickered with the fear that had been evident at the cottage the day before. "Yeah, well... But I still don't see why we should just give up," he said. "With Keith's help, we've got a chance."

"Don't put too much faith in me," said Keith. "I'll do my best, but I can't promise anything."

"No, we know, Keith. I don't suppose anyone is used to this sort of thing. You hear about the odd vicar driving demons out of people and all that, but I don't suppose there's many people around who've seen what me and Kev have seen."

Kevin looked at his watch. "I think we'd better get off, Mart," he said. "It's nearly five. My mum's expecting me back."

"You can stay here if you want, you know," said Keith. He

waved his hand vaguely. “I’m sure we can find room for you somewhere.”

“No, no. We’ll be all right,” Martin mumbled.

“Okay, well I’ll phone you as soon as I come up with something. You’d better give me your telephone numbers.”

They told him, and Keith scribbled them down on a scrap of paper. As they were about to leave, there was a knock on the study door. It opened to reveal Keith’s wife, Margaret. She held a newspaper in her hands, the evening edition of the *Cranbydale Observer*. Her face was ashen.

“Hey, Mags, what’s wrong?” Keith asked.

“Look at this,” Margaret said in a voice shot through with disgust and disbelief. She handed him the paper. “They were pupils at your school. It only happened a few miles away. In Redheath Woods.”

“What are you talking about?” Keith said. He took the paper and opened it out.

The headline on the front page assaulted them in huge, bold, black capitals: **KILLER IN THE WOODS**.

Below, in smaller capitals, it said **POLICE HUNT MANIAC AS COURTING COUPLE ARE FOUND MUTILATED**. There was a photograph of the spot in which they were found, and two small passport photographs of the dead couple.

“Shit,” Keith said quietly.

Kevin felt numb and sick, and somehow responsible. “Oh no, oh no...” was all he could whisper before his throat clogged with fear. He closed his eyes and wished he could wake from the nightmare.

But, when he opened them again, the first things he saw were Macky and Sharon staring up at him.

Nightfall.

The crooked tree stood in the twilight, a jagged silhouette against the murky sky. Its stumps were twisted and blackened, its trunk gaping open in a frozen scream. It looked dead and alone, cloaked in shadow.

But it was not dead. Not yet. And it was not alone. Swaney was there.

Breathing.

Far away, over the land, the white lights of police cars penetrated the blackness like lost fireflies. They were searching for clues, but they would find nothing; there were no clues.

The tree creaked as Swaney shifted again, and the trunk seemed to bulge and swell. The dark soul was restless—hungry. Last night it had killed once, twice, and with each scream of pain, with each welter of blood, it had grown stronger. Its power had increased. But that power was still exposed, formless, a raw nerve, a mouth that needed feeding. The dark soul was now too weary, too vulnerable, to feed itself again. It needed others.

It had used last night's power to extend its influence. To reach out icy tendrils. It had groped and grabbed at minds, forced them to bend to its will. Soon it would be fed. Soon.

Feet crunched suddenly on the black ground. Out of the gloom, three figures emerged. The first was Silas, his eyeballs white, his black, pointed beard like a shadow that was swallowing his face. Behind him came Mike Hargreaves, sightless eyes gleaming and jerking in their sockets, Hawaiian shirt black and sooty, bare feet striped with cuts from the teeth of dead wood. The third figure was crouched low, shuffling along. In the twilight, he appeared to be a hunchback. Then he swung round his arms, straightened up, and heaved the weight from his shoulders and onto the ground.

The sheep landed heavily in a puff of ashes. The three figures stood over it for a moment, heads lolling on their shoulders, arms hanging loosely, eerily silent as the fog of smoke shifted between the black trees.

Then Silas's arm came up and he gestured at the dead sheep. The black-haired man in prison clothes picked the sheep up and carried it over to the crooked tree. He held it against the trunk, offering it to the tree like some grisly sacrifice. Mike Hargreaves came forward. From his belt, he took a hammer and a long metal spike, and as Wilkins held the sheep against the tree, hammered the spike through its neck. When it was done, Wilkins let go. The sheep sagged, its weight dragging down on the spike, but it did not fall. It hung there, blood dripping steadily into the ashen ground and becoming lost in the dust. The three figures turned and walked away. For a moment all was silent, except for the steady *drip-drip-drip* of the sheep's blood on the ground.

Suddenly, the crooked tree seemed to shiver and tremble, its branches began to sway and creak. Its trunk yawned open. A long, black, gnarled branch that might have been an arm emerged slowly from the wound. A cluster of twigs unfurled like a hand and reached out to cup the blood.

It was feeding time.

That night was the hottest for many years. Throughout West Yorkshire buildings became kilns, and cars became ovens in which leather seats gave out stifling fumes. Radio stations proudly announced record-breaking temperatures as though the achievement was theirs. Chimneys became redundant. Sunstroke was more common than indigestion.

Limefield, like the rest of West Yorkshire, basked in the heat wave. But the difference here was that the people were afraid. Despite the warmth, doors remained closed and locked. Deck-chairs leaned, folded, against garage walls; deflated paddling pools and barbecues collected dust in sheds. The humid summer air seemed to hang like a dense, deadening blanket over the village.

Pubs became meeting-places, their bright lights attracting people like moths. Here gossip was used as a means to share fears, and alcohol as a means to forget them. Beer and spirits were swigged like water. By closing time many pub-goers spilled, laughing, into the streets under the illusion that their drunkenness would protect them.

The air was still, and the moon was high and bright in a clear, cloudless sky. It was a summer sky. A sky for lovers. But no lovers went into the woods that night.

Something had happened there, something strange and unnatural. The dark soul had feasted on death, had tasted power once again. Now it had gone, leaving the crooked tree forever, needing its security no more.

And, with Swaney's passing, the tree mourned and died, and its dying chilled the air. The sheep's carcass, drained of blood, stiffened with the chill that emanated from the dead bark. A frost began to collect on the tree like an array of sparkling, bitter dewdrops.

By morning the tree was white with frost. The sheep's eyes were glassed over with ice. It hung, solid and frozen, welded to the metal spike that skewered it. Winter lay upon the tree whilst all around there was summer.

But little by little, the winter began to spread....

PART TWO

RAIN

CHAPTER EIGHT

DONAHUE

Ramsay Bosfeedy sat back and enjoyed his second cigar of the day. As editor of the *Cranbydale Observer*, he felt he was entitled to it.

The newspaper's sales had doubled over the last week, and if he could sustain the interest it would mean big times ahead. The *Observer* was only a local paper which usually dealt with such devastating topics as market prices, gardening tips, and visits by local celebrities to open fêtes, but the events of the last week had transformed his modest little rag into a vital source of information and hard news.

Bosfeedy was an enormously fat man with a red face and bald head. He thought he had outwitted everybody by growing his hair long on one side and combing it carefully over the bald patch. He puffed on his cigar and allowed himself a blissful smile, well satisfied with the more than competent way in which his small team of journalists and backroom boys had handled the challenge of some real reporting. Coverage of the murders had been a first-rate piece of journalism and had attracted the attention of the biggies in Fleet Street. Suddenly Bosfeedy was an important man. He had been chatting to the editor of *The Daily Mirror* on the telephone just this morning, and this afternoon he was due to meet a delegation from *The Star* who were making the journey from London to see him.

Bosfeedy was ambitious, bubbling with plans and ideas. The murders would provide good copy for another week or so yet—the police angle, the distraught relatives, the funerals, my discovery of the bodies by Arthur Willis, etc... and maybe by the time all those possibilities had been exhausted some new developments in the investigation will have come to light. The errant thought that a couple more murders would be good for business seeped through before Bosfeedy could squash it. The guilt he momentarily felt was swept aside by indignation.

Well, why shouldn't he feel satisfied, he reasoned to himself. Naturally he was as shocked as everyone else by the murders, but it didn't do to confuse one's personal and professional views did it? A good journalist remains clinical and objective and has two main priorities. One is to report the news in a precise and accurate way, and the other is to think in terms of readership—it is always important to bear the economic considerations in mind. Those had been his golden rules at journalism college and he had stuck by them ever since.

It couldn't be denied that the double murder was the biggest news story to be covered by the *Observer* since he had become its editor six years ago. And he had dealt with the matter tactfully and sympathetically, hadn't he? He had been accused by the dead girl's uncle of heartless sensationalism, but that was only to be expected from distraught relatives. They just resented his professional manner—it happened to hundreds of journalists and editors. Relatives aside, the rest of the public had responded by buying up the newspaper within two hours of its distribution. Printers had worked late to get a thousand more into the shops before they closed for the night, and they had sold out too.

He felt he had a duty to the public, a duty to dig deep and discover the true facts. Maybe a few people would get hurt, but many more would benefit. Maybe the coverage would even help to catch the murderer. He could see it now: **POLICE PRAISE NEWS EDITOR FOR VITAL HELP IN MURDER INQUIRY**. He could get his own picture on his own front page. If he did, it would have to be the one taken at the formal dinner to celebrate the visit of Princess Margaret in 1981. That had been before his hair had begun to fall out, and the angle had flattered him by blotting out all trace of his double chins.

He finished his cigar and killed it in the ashtray. He decided to ring the hospital again to see if the old bloke who had found the bodies had recovered from his heart attack and was ready to talk yet. If he was, he would get Donahue over there right away. He was flicking through the Yellow Pages when the telephone rang. Bosfeedy picked it up.

"Hello." The preoccupied expression on his face changed and he reached for a notepad and pen. "Really, sir... that's most interesting," he said, suppressed excitement in his voice. "If you'll just hang on a minute, sir, I'll get this down... Now, what did you say your name was?... I see... and how do you spell that?... and the address?..." Bosfeedy scribbled the information on his pad and underlined it with a self-satisfied flourish. "Right," he said briskly, "I'll get someone over there right away. Thank you very much, Mr. Bussey. Goodbye."

Bosfeedy put the phone down and went to the door of his office. He opened it and said to Miss Taylor, his secretary, "Is Philip Donahue around?"

"Yes, Mr. Bosfeedy," said Miss Taylor. "He was talking on the phone in here a few minutes ago."

"Well get him for me, will you? Tell him I want to see him immediately."

"Yes, Mr. Bosfeedy."

Bosfeedy went back into his office and sat behind his desk. A few minutes later there was a knock on the door.

"Come in," shouted Bosfeedy.

A thin man in his late thirties with pinched, sallow features entered. He wore a zip-up sports jacket and faded jeans. "You wanted to see me, Ramsay?"

"Yes, come in, Philip. Sit down."

Philip Donahue pushed the door shut and sprawled in the leather swivel chair before Bosfeedy's desk. It was warm and gave an unpleasant sensation of stickiness, like sitting on liquorice. Philip smiled across the desk at Bosfeedy; an equal's smile. He was, after all, the journalist of the moment. All the major dailies were showing interest in his coverage of the murder and the fire.

Bosfeedy leaned forward over the desk, crossing his pudgy hands in front of him. His double chins wobbled.

"I've got another big story for you," he said. Donahue regarded Bosfeedy's eagerness with slight disgust.

"What is it this time?" he said dryly. "Earthquakes? Vampires?"

Bosfeedy frowned. "Now don't start getting facetious, Philip. I can easily give this assignment to somebody else."

Turd, thought Donahue. "Sorry, Ramsay, just a joke," he said, smiling.

"I should hope so. I am still the boss you know."

"Yes, I know, Ramsay, sorry."

Bosfeedy regarded Donahue for a moment as though to ascertain whether his apology was genuine or not. Apparently deciding that it was, Bosfeedy said, "One of the Limefield farmers just rang me. A Mr..." he consulted his pad "...Bussey. Said he found one of his sheep hanging from a tree in Redheath Woods with a tent peg through its neck. He also mentioned frost or ice on the tree or some such nonsense. I didn't quite catch that bit."

Donahue whistled. "The woods again! What the hell's happening over there? Is the heat affecting people's brains or something?"

Bosfeedy said, "I want you to get out there straight away. Talk to this Bussey. See if you can maybe bring in a link with the murders. It doesn't matter how obscure it is as long as we can work it into a headline."

Donahue nodded and smiled, though Bosfeedy's lack of sensitivity and compassion disgusted him. *Maybe that's why he's an editor and I'm just a lowly journalist*, he thought wryly. He stood up to go.

"Oh, and Philip?"

"Yeah?"

"You'd better take Anton with you. Get some nice, clear pictures to put on the front page."

"Okay, will do." Donahue left.

❧

Kevin and Martin were having one of their not infrequent arguments. Kevin was pushing a shopping trolley up and down the aisles of Limefield's only supermarket, whilst Martin consulted the shopping list and selected the goods. They were working as quickly as possible, anxious to finish and get back home in case Keith rang them.

"Next time don't make so much bloody noise," Kevin was saying.

"I wasn't," replied Martin defensively. "Don't blame me."

"Course you were. You always do when you play with our Jamie's Subbuteo. Shouting your head off every time you score a goal. You're like a big kid."

"I was shouting quietly," said Martin indignantly.

"Quietly? You?" scorned Kevin. "You couldn't be quiet if you tried."

"It was you running to the phone every time it rang that got us chucked out," said Martin, changing tact.

"Yeah, but you were never far behind me," said Kevin, "and you're the one with elephant's feet."

"Oh shut up, Kev," said Martin. "You really piss me off sometimes."

The shopping was completed in a smouldering silence.

The boys had slept at Kevin's house the night before, and had been there all morning, waiting nervously for the phone to ring. Kevin's mother could tell they were excited about something, despite their obvious efforts to behave naturally. Martin's excitement was particularly tiring, shown by ceaseless fidgeting and an increase in decibels of his already loud voice. At breakfast, she thought he was going to set his chair on fire he was squirming about in it so much. At first, she had sent them upstairs, but this had only resulted in floor-thumping and shouting which, combined with the heat, was giving her a headache. Unable to stand it any longer, she had sent them, protesting, into the village to do some shopping.

Now they were queueing at one of three checkout tills. Kevin wondered whether he could add a couple of Mars Bars to the rest of the shopping without his mum noticing the change was down. He decided he could.

Martin, as usual, was the first to break their silence. "I hope Keith doesn't ring while we're out," he said.

"Relax, Mart. If he does, we can ring him back. I'd rather he rang while we were out shopping than not ring at all."

"Yeah, I suppose so."

The two boys packed the groceries inexpertly into plastic bags and went outside. The brightness caused them to screw up their eyes, and the plastic bags soon became unpleasant to carry.

Martin crammed most of his Mars Bar into his mouth in one go, then stopped to steady the bag on his thigh. He wiped his sweating hands on the back of his jeans.

"God, this is bloody hard work," he said.

"Have you seen all the coppers around?" said Kevin, shifting his bag from one hand to the other.

"Yeah, there's loads of them isn't there? I wonder if they'll find anything in the woods."

Kevin shook his head. "I doubt it."

"Have they been round to your house yet?"

"No, I think they're doing the estate this afternoon."

The police, the majority of which had been called in from outside, were involved in a door-to-door investigation of the village. The journalists, on the other hand, who had started swarming into the village the day before, seemed more interested in a door-to-door investigation of the pubs.

Kevin and Martin decided at this moment to follow their example. The plastic bags were becoming slippery with sweat, and the goods inside seemed to have defied gravity and increased to twice their natural weight. Martin pushed open the door of The Plumber's Arms and they slipped gratefully into the welcoming coolness of the pub.

At this hour, it was usually quiet and peaceful with no more than a few of the elderly locals at the bar. Most of them were retired, and the calming drone of conversation and soft clink of beer glasses could almost lull you to sleep.

Not so today, though.

In the corner were a rowdy group of press reporters and photographers. Glasses and empty plates were strewn about the three tables they had shoved together. They eyed the boys briefly as they came in, then went back to their drinking and talking. They seemed to be playing a game called "Who Can Talk The Loudest?"

Martin dumped his bag by a table situated as far away as possible from the invaders and went to the bar. Ron Brabier, the landlord, greeted him amiably.

"'Ello, young Martin. It's good to see a familiar face. There aren't many o' them in 'ere today."

Martin nodded towards the crowd in the corner. "Who're that lot? Reporters?"

"Aye, that's right. Come up from London. Bloody rowdy buggers. Mind you, I'm not saying I don't welcome the trade, but they go about as though they own t'bloody place."

Ron was a middle-aged man, running to fat on his own beer. He had short white hair and a grizzled moustache. He was also a dreadful gossip. He leaned forward confidentially.

"It were terrible about them murders, weren't it?" he said.

"Yeah," said Martin, feeling uncomfortable.

"Did you know 'em, them two who were killed?"

"Not very well," said Martin. "I've seen them around. They went to our school."

Ron lowered his voice until he was almost whispering in Martin's ear.

"I 'eard the bodies were so mangled they could only identify 'em from dental records."

He was imparting information that the reporters from London would never glean from the lips of any villager. Martin should have felt privileged, but all he did feel was an ugly, churning fear in his stomach. "Really?" he said, trying to look interested.

"Oh aye. Of course the police knew who they were anyway 'cos they found the lad's car, and the lass's mam had rung 'em the night before to say their lass were missing. They still 'ad to check though, you know. It was bitter wasn't it?"

"What? Oh yes," said Martin. Ron scooped two glasses down from the shelf and began to fill them.

"I'll tell you somethin' else an' all," he said. He looked furtively to left and right, then leaned forward again. "They reckon t'car door had been ripped off its hinges. Pulled right off by somethin'. Now what sort o' thing's got strength to do that, d'you think?"

"I don't know," said Martin.

"Aye," said Ron, nodding his head sagely, "there's

somethin' weird goin' on in them woods. What with the fire the other day and now this. That's £1. 60 please, Martin."

Martin fished in his pocket, produced two pound coins and handed them across. The hand-pulled beer settling in the glass didn't seem quite so appealing now. Ron gave him the change and, to Martin's relief, was called away immediately to serve an inebriated photographer. Martin took the beers back to the table.

"You all right, Mart? You look a bit pale," said Kevin.

"It's this bloody thing in the woods, Kev. It scares me shitless. Ron's just been giving me some nasty little details about the murder, stuff he's probably picked up from the pissed-up coppers on a night."

"Like what?" said Kevin, then immediately changed his mind. "No, no, don't tell me. I don't think I really want to know."

Martin began to drain his glass quickly. The beer didn't taste as good as usual. There was a burst of ragged laughter from across the room. A young woman with heavy make-up and a pale blue trouser suit was waving her arms in the air. "And then they hit Roger as well," they heard her squeal which was followed by another burst of laughter. Martin finished his beer and put his glass down on the table.

"I think we ought to be getting back," he said. "Keith might have been trying to ring us, and besides these Cranbydale coppers are a bit keen. I don't want to get done for underage drinking again."

Kevin didn't argue. He finished his beer and the two boys heaved their bags up and left, calling goodbye to Ron on the way out.

"Cheerio, lads," called Ron, "and take care."

"We will," said Martin, and closed the pub door.

⸙

Philip Donahue drove with mechanical efficiency towards his destination, paying only limited attention to the road ahead. His mind was wandering, sifting through the jigsaw puzzle events of the last few days, trying to fit some of the pieces together.

Beside him, slouched on the passenger seat, was Anton Brabier, brother to Ron of The Plumber's Arms. Like his brother he was running to fat. He was sleeping off a liquid lunch, his Olympus cradled in his arms like a pet poodle.

In Donahue's opinion, the Redheath Woods murderer was not a man, it was something else; a large animal perhaps, like a lion or a bear. A bear would be the more likely because Donahue had seen the bodies and the boy's car, had seen the way the door had been ripped off its hinges and flung casually aside. He shuddered as he recalled the state of the bodies. He couldn't believe that a man had the strength to inflict such injuries. The bones had been twisted and snapped like cardboard, the flesh gouged out in lumps, the faces—he swallowed. He had never seen anything like it.

But if it was a bear—and Donahue was not sure whether even a bear would have the strength to rip a car door from its hinges—where had it come from? If it had escaped from a zoo or a circus, it would surely have been reported. His only thought was that some private zoo owner had let it free for whatever reason. Maybe he couldn't afford to keep it any longer and didn't want it to be destroyed? Donahue smiled; it seemed a highly unlikely explanation. The sheep killing, for instance, didn't fit. If the sheep had been found simply mutilated in a field, he might have found his own theory a little more convincing, but hadn't Bosfeedy said that the sheep was found hanging from a tree with a tent peg through its neck?

Donahue sighed. The trouble was he had a journalist's mind. Asking questions was his forte, and it was frustrating when they fizzled out, unanswered. He resigned himself to the fact that he would just have to be patient and take things step by step. First, he would go into the woods, talk to this farmer, and have a poke around by this tree. Then he would go into the village and look through the inn registers. Any names in there who weren't press he would follow up. It occurred to him that the police had probably thought of this already, but it was worth a try. Maybe he would find something they had missed.

He stopped the car and jabbed Anton Brabier in his vast

stomach.

"Come on, you fat slob, we're here," he said.

The photographer opened his eyes and looked wildly around for a second, completely disorientated. "Huh, wha? Wassmatter?"

"I said we're here. Get ready to take some nice pictures for Mr. Bosfeedy."

Brabier groaned and rubbed the muggy haze of sleep from his face. "Oh, Donahue," he moaned, "I was having a brilliant dream. I'd just been picked to play in the FA Cup final for Leeds against Tottenham. I was just being interviewed by David Coleman on the team coach on the way to Wembley."

Donahue chuckled and patted Brabier's fat stomach. "Never mind, Anton," he said, "with all this flab the kit would probably have been too small for you anyway."

"Ha ha, very funny," replied Anton. His mouth was dry and his head was beginning to throb thickly. He was not in the best of moods. He put a hand to his forehead and closed his eyes.

"The perils of dinnertime drinking," remarked Donahue with wicked glee. "Come on, we've got a job to do."

"You take the photos, Philip. I'm just going to lie down here and die."

"Oh no," said Donahue. "Dying you can save till later. Right now, you're coming with me."

Brabier hissed wearily through his teeth. "You're a first-rate bastard," he said with feeling.

"That's me," said Donahue.

Brabier pushed open the car door and dragged his bulk into the steaming afternoon. He winced as the full force of the sun danced on his hangover.

Donahue set off through the shattered, smoky woods at a brisk pace.

His feet crunched on the blasted earth and clouds of dusty ashes puffed up round his ankles. Brabier struggled after him, wheezing and panting. The camera strap around his neck chafed his skin and his trousers felt like wallpaper pasted to the backs of his legs. He looked around. Everywhere was black, desolate and emaciated. He shivered. It was a hopeless place. The trees seemed to watch them.

"Come on, Anton," called Donahue.

"Just a bloody minute, I'm coming," gasped Anton. Donahue waited impatiently for the photographer to catch up, noting with distaste the sweat that stained the armpits of Brabier's shirt and dripped from his chin.

Brabier reached Donahue at last and put out a hand to a tree branch to steady himself. The branch immediately crumbled away into black dust beneath his fingers.

"Just over there," Donahue said, shielding his eyes and pointing across an acre of land that was patched yellow, black and green from the effects of the fire. Anton, too, shielded his eyes and followed Donahue's pointing finger. He made out a small, grey farmhouse and a couple of large barns.

"That's where he lives, is it?" he said. His tone suggested the farmer had no right to inhabit such a remote wilderness.

"That's right," said Donahue. "Just a nice little stroll away." He set off across the fields. Anton groaned and stumbled after him.

They were both sweating by the time they reached the farmhouse, and Anton's breath was rattling alarmingly in his throat. Donahue led him over to a dry stone wall which bordered the farmer's cottage.

"You just sit here and have a rest," he said. "I'll go and see if our Mr. Bussey is in."

Anton sank gratefully onto the wall and watched as Donahue went through a rickety gate and crossed the muddy yard to the front door. Donahue's knock was answered almost immediately by an elderly bulbous-nosed man dressed in shapeless trousers, collarless shirt, ancient trilby and Wellingtons. Donahue and the man shook hands, talked for a few moments, and then set off down the path back to the waiting photographer. Mr. Bussey stopped briefly to pick up a shovel that was leaning against the gatepost.

"This is Mr. Tom Bussey, this is Anton Brabier, our photographer," said Donahue, making the introductions.

"Oh aye, pleased to meet yer," said the farmer. They shook hands briefly.

"Now if you'll show us where you found your sheep, Mr. Bussey."

"Aye. This way." The farmer led the way back across the patchwork landscape. When he reached the black trees, he veered away to the left and followed the path that ran along the top of the valley deeper into the woods. He trudged steadily, but with a deceptive speed, and the two newspaper men had difficulty keeping up in the heat.

"How... how far is it?" gasped Donahue.

"Oh, nobbut a mile," replied the farmer. He pulled a scratched and battered tin of Old Holborn from one pocket and a packet of Rizlas from another and rolled a cigarette as he walked.

"What time did you find your sheep?" asked Donahue.

"It were about eight o' clock this mornin'. I noticed I were one down and thought she'd escaped and wandered off into t'woods. I never expected to find the poor lass hangin' from a tree, though. If I catch the buggers who did that, I'll take a bloody shotgun to 'em."

"Is the sheep still there?"

"Aye, she's still there. She wouldn't be, but there's somethin' not right about these woods."

"Not right?" said Donahue. "How do you mean?"

Bussey gave Donahue a peculiar sidelong look. He popped the slim roll-up into his mouth and lit it before answering, "When I found 'er this mornin', the tree she was hangin' from was white with frost. And the poor lass was 'ard as a rock, just like she'd been in deep freeze. There were a layer o' thick ice all round the tree and on the peg that were through 'er neck. That's why I've brought this." He held up the shovel. "It's to chip the ice away so I can get 'er down."

Donahue frowned. "What do you mean—ice? How can there be ice? This is the height of summer. There were record breaking temperatures last night."

"Aye, well I know that as well as anyone. But I'm tellin' you, that tree and all the land round about were covered wi' ice and frost this mornin'. I can't explain it. All I know is that tree were cold, as cold as winter, and all round about it were warm."

Donahue was bewildered. He knew the farmer would not deliberately lie to him, but his mind could not accept what he had just been told. There must be some reasonable explanation, he decided.

But there was not. And ten minutes later Donahue and Anton Brabier were staring at a sight that turned their sweat cold and clammy on their skin, and tipped logic and reason on its head.

"It's not possible," Anton said, trying to deny the evidence of his own eyes. "It's just not possible."

The crooked tree stood on the hillside, cloaked in a white, glittering layer of ice and frost. It looked like an evil witch-queen flanked on all sides by hordes of black demons. The sheep hung from its jagged spike like some ghastly ice-sculpture, and a veil of frost lay on the ashes all around the base of the tree like the hem of a flowing gown.

"It must be some sort of joke," Donahue said at last. "You can buy false snow in shops. They use it in the theatre. It comes in an aerosol can."

"That ain't no joke," the old farmer said calmly. "Look here." He walked up to the tree and stopped astride the rough line of frost that surrounded it. He bent down and put his arms out by his sides. One hand he placed on the frosty earth, the other he placed on the black, flaky ashes. "Come and feel," he said.

Donahue went to join him, feeling an odd reluctance to approach the crooked tree. It disquieted him, gave him an indefinable feeling of hollowness and despair. He bent down by the side of the farmer and positioned his hands as the old man had done, one on the frosty ground, the other on the black ashes. It was an unpleasant sensation. His right hand lay on a knobbly sheet of slippery, hard earth, freezing cold to the touch, whereas his left lay on a crumbling bed of warm ashes.

"I don't understand it. It's not possible," was all he could say.

"Aye, I know," said the farmer, nodding his head.

"Do the police know about this?" Donahue asked.

"Nay, not yet. You were the first people I rang." The farmer looked steadily at Donahue, who smiled. He had been a journalist long enough to know that when someone informed the press before the police in matters such as this, their motives were usually financial.

"Hmm, well I suppose they'd better be informed," he said. "Look, Mr. Bussey, I'll tell them about this myself if you like, though they may still want to speak to you."

The farmer nodded. "Aye, all right young man." He seemed about to say more, but then closed his mouth.

"Yes?" prompted Donahue.

"I were just wonderin'. If I'd told the police about this before I told you, you wouldn't 'ave 'ad much of a story to print would you?"

Donahue considered. "No, no, you're probably right, Mr. Bussey."

"Aye," said Bussey. "That's what I thought." He looked meaningfully at Donahue again.

Donahue appeared to be lost in thought. At last he said, "I... er, I wonder whether you would accept a little something from the newspaper, Mr. Bussey, as a gesture of appreciation for your time and trouble?"

Bussey had the courtesy to look pleasantly surprised. "That's right kind of you, young man. Thank you," he said.

"Don't mention it," said Donahue. "It's the least we can do."

Bussey nodded, satisfied, and touched the brim of his old trilby. He approached the crooked tree, hefting the shovel he held in his hand and swinging it back behind his head.

"Hey, what are you doing?" cried Anton. The farmer looked round, surprised by the sudden outburst.

"I'm gettin' me sheep down," he said. "I'm not leaving the poor lass up there."

"Do you think I could just take a couple of photographs first? For the newspaper?"

The farmer lowered the spade slowly. "Aye, get on wi' it then," he muttered. Anton sprang into action. He whipped the lens cap off his camera and took a series of photographs from different angles. He looked almost agile as he circled the tree, clicking away. When he had taken around a dozen photographs, he stood back.

"Okay, Mr. Bussey, thanks," he said.

The old farmer lumbered forward again.

"Would you mind if I took a few shots of you actually getting the sheep down?" asked Anton. The farmer gave him a long, piercing look, obviously resentful of Anton's eagerness to record what he considered an ugly and distasteful event. However, a picture in the paper might be worth a few extra quid, he thought shrewdly.

"I reckon that'd be all right," he said.

He began to hack at the tree with the shovel, sending chunks of ice flying in all directions. Donahue stepped back hastily as a tiny splinter hit him just above the eyebrow. But Anton seemed oblivious to the danger. He hovered around like a dog hungry for scraps, recording the gruesome task for posterity.

Eventually Bussey stepped back, a light sheen of sweat on his face. The spike, loosened from the ice, released itself from the bark as the dead weight of the sheep pulled down on it. The sheep hit the ground with a sound like rock striking rock.

Bussey heaved the sheep up onto his shoulders. "Have you done 'ere?" he said.

Donahue nodded. "Yes, I think so."

As the farmer started off back to his farm, Donahue looked around. He had planned to stay and have a poke round by himself, but it was obvious there was nothing else to find. He hadn't realised the place was quite so desolate.

"You ready, Anton?"

"Yes, yes," the photographer said, putting the lens cap back onto his camera. He gave the crooked tree a last look, and Donahue noticed him shiver.

"You all right?" he said.

Anton turned to him. His eyes held a troubled, haunted look. "Yes, it's just this place. It's like the old man said—there's something not right here. This is a bad place, Philip, evil. You might think I'm just being daft, but... well, it scares me." He looked away, embarrassed.

Donahue patted Anton's shoulder. "It scares me, too," he said quietly.

CHAPTER NINE

INTRUDERS

Keith Francis pulled off his spectacles and rubbed his aching eyes. He was weary and frustrated. All day he had been shut up in his study and what had he achieved? Nothing. He looked at his watch and was shocked to see it was coming up to two in the morning. He had had a vague idea that it was somewhere around midnight. No wonder he was so exhausted.

He had been up at seven thirty that morning and in his study by eight with toast and tea. Margaret had brought him cheese sandwiches around noon, and only for nut roast at six had he left his study and made a brief pilgrimage to the dining room. That meant he had been looking at this page for—he made a swift calculation—Seventeen hours! Seventeen fucking hours!

He looked with disgust at the heaps of notes spread on the desk and floor around him, and at the numerous scrunched-up balls of paper that lay in and around the wastepaper basket.

"Shit, shit, shit," he said viciously, and swiped his hand across the desk, scattering the notes. They fluttered to the floor like startled seagulls. He sat back, ran his fingers through his hair, yawned hugely and closed his eyes. He could still see the layout of the page clearly, like a brand on the inside of his eyelids. He was sure he could take up his pen and reproduce the illustration of the demon coming out of the tree line for line. He yawned again and began to massage some life back into his neck.

Why did the old git have to have a different code for every bloody section, he thought to himself, *and why the hell doesn't he use a conventional alphabet?*

"Oh well, sod it. Time for bed," he said aloud.

Mags had been in bed for a couple of hours and would be sound asleep by now. She was pissed off at him for shutting himself in his study all day and leaving her to do the decorating. He guessed half of it was because he wouldn't tell her exactly what he was doing.

"Important work for the school," he'd said.

"What do you mean, important work? School's still three weeks away, what about our decorating?" she'd replied. He'd merely shrugged, a habit that infuriated her. It meant he was keeping his secret, the matter was closed. At dinnertime she had tried again.

"Are you going to be much longer?"

"I don't know."

"Well, what is it you're doing exactly?"

"I've told you. Important work for the school."

"Yes, but what important work? Maybe I could help."

"No, I don't think so."

"Why the hell not? I'd appreciate some help with the decorating, you know."

"I know, Mags, I'm sorry, but I just have to get this finished."

"Well, why won't you tell me what you're doing?"

"I just can't. It's a bit confidential, that's all."

"Surely you can tell me! You don't think I'm going to shout it from the rooftops, do you?"

"No, of course not. Don't be stupid."

"Well why won't you tell me? And don't call me stupid."

"I just can't, that's all. Just trust me, will you?"

"If you won't tell me, it obviously means you've got something to hide."

"What's that supposed to mean?"

"It means you're probably up there reading your stupid ghost books just to get out of helping with the decorating."

"Oh, come on, Mags. Don't be so bloody stupid."

"I've told you, don't call me stupid!"

And it hadn't ended there. He had heard doors banging all evening and washing up clattered about in temper, and at eleven thirty she had poked her head round the door, said a curt 'goodnight' and stomped out again.

Keith sighed. Normally when they had been arguing they made it up in bed in the morning, but Keith knew the lack of results today meant he would have to go through the same palaver again tomorrow. Maybe it would be easier just to tell her the truth. But what could he say?

"Look, Mags, the fact is these two students of mine, Kevin and Martin, saw a monster crawl out of a tree the other day. Now it looks a bit like the tree it came out of, and it's got the face of this boy they knew at school who got run over by a train eight years ago. Except it's not really him. It's his soul, and it goes around killing people. Now, I've got this book you see—let's just call it *The Observer's Book of Tree Monsters*—only the trouble is it's written in gobbledygook, and my job is to translate it and find the magic solution. Only I've got to do it pretty quick before this nasty monster comes along and eats my two friends and lots of other people besides. So, you see, darling, that's the reason why I can't help you with the decorating right now."

Oh well, forget it, Keith thought, *deal with it in the morning*. He was about to open the study door and go to the bathroom when he heard a sound. It came from downstairs and sounded as though someone was furtively moving furniture around. He opened the door silently and stepped out onto the landing, listening. There it was again—a small, stealthy movement, and wasn't that a footstep just then? Maybe Mags had gone downstairs for a drink or something. It would be sensible to check before jumping to any conclusions.

He tiptoed to the bedroom door and pushed it open. The house had a hollow, echoey feel without carpets down to stifle the sound. He looked into the room, but his eyes could make out little in the darkness. He forced himself to stand motionless in the doorway whilst his eyes became accustomed to the gloom. After a few moments he was able to make out hazy shapes. There was the wardrobe, the dressing table, the chair, and that bulky thing in the corner was a cane stool brought back from a holiday in Hong Kong four years ago. He could make out the bed, too, and a motionless mound in the bedclothes. Was that Mags or had she just pushed the covers back when she got out? He jumped as the stillness was broken by a heavy breath and the soft crumple of bedclothes. So, Mags was in bed. He closed the door.

From downstairs he could still hear phantom sounds of movement as though someone was familiarising himself with the layout of the rooms. Keith realised he was trembling. He had never tackled burglars before. How many would there be? He would look a right idiot if he went downstairs with a challenge on his lips only to discover four or five enormous shotgun-carrying thugs. The thought reminded him that a weapon would not come amiss. He crossed to a door further along the hall and pulled it open.

It was a cubbyhole full of paraphernalia—the jumble sale room as Mags called it. There were lengths of old material, out-of-favour paintings and ornaments, a tin trunk full of children's books, a deformed plastic Christmas tree, out-of-fashion clothes, a peeling ironing board, and dozens of other knick-knacks collected over the years that they had been reluctant to throw out.

Keith searched through the rubbish for a weapon. He had almost decided on a hideous bronze statuette of a Chinese man curling a long moustache around his finger when he noticed the broken half of a snooker cue propped in the corner. He had only kept it because it was the cue with which he had once achieved a break of thirty-one as a student. He hefted the cue in his hand. It was the heavy end and it felt good.

He crept downstairs, wincing every time the bare stairs creaked a warning to the intruder (or intruders) below. He stopped at the bottom and listened. Silence stretched before him like a blanket. Had he been heard coming downstairs? Was there someone behind the door waiting to pounce on him at this very moment? He stood for what seemed like minutes deciding on the best policy. Would it be better to creep around in the dark looking for the intruder or would it be more desirable to lose that element of surprise and turn on all the lights? He decided on the latter. Light would be more welcome. He stretched out a hand and pressed down the switch. The downstairs hall was solidly and dependably normal. There was no sign of a break-in, no indication that anything had been rearranged or tampered with.

He was breathing heavily, his nerves stretched taut like piano wire. His heart knocked impatiently on the door of his chest, and pulses fluttered like moths beneath his skin. He swallowed. Where next? It would be logical to start with the nearest door and work round. That meant the kitchen first, which lay to the left of the stairs.

He moved quietly to the door. The snooker cue seemed greased in his palm. He wiped it briefly with his sleeve then, taking a deep breath, shoved the door open. His hand immediately went to his left, scrabbling for the light switch. He found it and clicked it down. The kitchen was empty and tidy. He stood, panting, trying to keep his breathing as quiet as possible. Eventually he calmed down and psyched himself up for the next door. It was the sitting room directly opposite the kitchen. To his right was the staircase, and not quite parallel with that, to his left, was the front door. He crossed the hall and put his hand on the door handle. *Okay, let's go for it*, he thought, and pushed the door open.

Again, his hand searched for the light switch. For a panicky few moments he couldn't find it, and he realised how much of a sitting duck he was, framed in the doorway. Then his fingers found the square of plastic around the switch and a moment later the room was bathed in light. It, too, was empty. He walked in. There was nowhere to hide, and nothing had been moved. The furniture slept beneath white sheets dotted with paint. Keith looked behind the shrouded suite, but it was more of a nervous gesture than based on any real conviction that something was lurking there.

He stopped dead as he heard a small creak on the staircase. He darted from the room, half-expecting to see a dark figure creeping upstairs. There was nothing. He smiled uncertainly at his own nervousness. He was not usually the nervous type.

He checked the other two possible hiding places on the lower landing, the toilet and the boot cupboard under the stairs. Not surprisingly they, too, were empty and untouched.

He decided to go to bed. The adrenalin steaming through his body had stimulated him into wakefulness for the few minutes he had spent in his foolish search, but now sleep was reclaiming him. He became aware once more of his heavy eyes and limbs. He put a hand on the banister and lifted his foot to place it on the first step, and it was in that position that he froze.

He could hear it again; scrunching, creaky movement, this time from upstairs. If it had been an old house he would have put it down to the natural settling of the building onto its foundations, but this was not an old house. It was modern, sturdy and compact and he had never known it to creak. Besides, this was subtly different. He had been in enough haunted houses (or supposedly haunted houses) to distinguish between the natural movement of the building and the pressure of human weight on yielding floorboards, and this was definitely the latter. Someone was upstairs. Upstairs while his wife was asleep in bed!

He took the stairs two at a time, fear for himself now replaced by fear for Mags' safety. He reached the top landing and stood, breathing heavily, the broken snooker cue clenched in his hand. There was silence again. He opened the bedroom door and looked inside. It was too dark to see anything. He crossed the room, instinctively avoided banging into the bed, and switched on his bedside lamp.

The light was dim, but enough for him to be able to make out the room clearly. His wife was sleeping peacefully, her dark hair spread over the pillow. He stroked it gently for a second. She moaned and turned her head slightly before settling again. Keith checked the room thoroughly. He looked in and behind the wardrobe, under the bed, and even pulled back the curtains to ensure nothing was perched on the windowsill. When he was satisfied, he left the room and pulled the door closed quietly behind him, leaving the bedside lamp on.

Now, he thought with a weary impatience, a quick check of the upstairs rooms just to put his mind at rest, and then bed. First, he checked the bathroom and the airing cupboard, and then the spare bedroom which was empty of furniture but contained a set of fitted wardrobes along one wall. He opened each in turn, heart fluttering, expecting a stocking-masked thug to leap out of every door. But it was bare of everything but dust.

He stepped back out onto the landing. Now there only remained the jumble sale room and his study to check. He knew the cubbyhole was too small and cluttered to conceal anyone, but he opened the door anyway. An ancient teddy bear stared at him with one glassy eye, spewing stuffing from its mouth, and the Chinese man grinned and twirled his moustache. He shuddered and closed the door.

Now there was only his study left. He was about to push the door open when a minute sound touched his eardrums. It was so brief and indistinct that he couldn't even swear he had heard it at all. But it gave him the uncomfortable idea that something was moving behind the study door. Taking a deep, shivering breath he pushed the door open and turned on the light.

He got a fleeting impression of movement, heard the fluttering of pages turning rapidly in a book, and then silence. He also thought for a confused second that there had been a figure standing at his desk, peering at the book on the table. But the figure resolved itself into the outline of the long curtain across the room, and the bulb-headed shape of his desk lamp. He stood in the doorway for a moment looking around. The impression that he had just disturbed some presence was strong. He crossed to the desk and looked at the ancient, leather-bound volume that rested there. He frowned, troubled. The book was open on the page of the illustration, and Keith was sure he had closed it before leaving the study. He closed the book now and looked around the room again. A sudden certainty that he was not alone came over him. He shook it off with an effort and went out, switching off the light and closing the door behind him.

In the airless summer night, the study was still and empty. There was no breeze, but the curtain by the window suddenly stirred and then became still again, as though something had just left the room.

⁓

Though the lounge was full, no one spoke. They were as motionless as waxwork models, eyes glazed over, barely breathing.

The cottage they were in was small and pretty and remote, situated at the end of a lane about a mile from Redheath Woods.

The owner of the cottage, a sixty-one-year-old widow called Edith Pumphrey, was in the cellar, lying beneath a pile of sacking, her throat slit from ear to ear.

Silas was sitting cross-legged on the floor with his eyes closed, like a holy man in a state of trance. Around him, people lolled like drunks, many of them wearing prison-clothes. A frumpy, track-suited woman sat next to a young man with a soiled Hawaiian shirt; a skinhead leaned against a traffic warden who was drooling like a baby.

Silas's mind was linked to Swaney's, their thoughts locked like two writhing black snakes in a deadly embrace. He was snarling and moaning, his lips curling in a parody of speech, eyeballs squirming nightmarishly behind closed lids. His hands were clenching and unclenching, clenching and unclenching, as though they had a restless life of their own.

Suddenly his head arched back and his eyelids rolled open to reveal white, sightless orbs flecked with yellow. Spittle bubbled from his mouth. He began to rock and shudder, vibrant with frenzied, malefic energy. It seemed for a moment as though the fabric of his body would burst apart. His eyeballs bulged grotesquely, a bloated tongue seethed from his lips, blood began to trickle from an ear and from beneath his fingernails.

Then Swaney released him, and he fell limply to the floor like a rag doll dropped from a great height. He lay gasping where he was for a few minutes, his black hair hanging over his forehead in greasy strands. At last he straightened up and opened his mouth. Sweat dripped from the point of his beard.

"Wake," he said, but the voice that grated through his vocal cords was not his own. It was harsh, animalistic, inhuman, and it seemed to slither from his mouth like something thick and alive.

Slowly the people in the room began to stir. Bodies straightened, heads were raised, eyelids slid open to reveal eyes that were either pure white or had dark, blank pupils.

"There are two boys," the Silas-thing grated. His head seemed to creak slowly round as though made of wood. His voice dropped to a hideous whisper. "Two boys."

The man strolled along the top of the valley, pausing only once to take his hands from the pockets of his shabby overcoat and pull his wide-brimmed hat down low over his face. His footsteps were light and airy and, despite the glaring sun, he appeared to cast no shadow onto the ash-choked ground. He may have been muttering to himself, but the sound was indistinct, like a barely heard murmur of wind.

At last he stopped and raised his head slightly. The tree was before him, beautiful in death but so, so cold. The man sighed and seemed to shiver inside his bulky overcoat. He approached the tree slowly, holding out a hand as though to calm a wild animal. Gently he laid the hand on the slippery, ice-white tree trunk. Immediately there was a slight sizzling sound and the ice began to melt.

At last the man lowered his arm and stepped back, leaving a hand-shaped depression in the ice, black with the tree trunk beneath. As he watched the hand-shape filled in again, becoming speckled with points of frost that seemed to ooze from the bark. The frost bloomed like mould, and continued to form, layer upon layer, until the handprint had been completely obliterated.

The man shook his head. "My poor, poor sister," he whispered in a gentle voice. "My poor, poor sister."

Angela Truscott wiped pastry from her hands and began to mop the mess from the kitchen surface. Now there was just the onions, mushrooms and tomatoes to chop and fry, the cheese to grate and the salad to prepare and tea would be out of the way. All she had to do was cover the pizza base with topping, sprinkle on the grated cheese and pop it into the oven. What could be simpler?

She hummed as she worked, feeling satisfied and contented. The sun threw plenty of light into the kitchen and even the dreary street outside looked nice in the sunshine. A bird fluttered onto the windowsill and began to peck delicately at the breadcrumbs she had put there. Mrs. Truscott watched it until the bird, appearing to sense her presence, puffed out its little chest and launched itself towards the nearest rooftop.

She smiled and went back to her work. Normally in this weather she would have had the kitchen door (which was also the back door) open to take full advantage of the sun's warmth and light, but since those horrible murders a few days ago she hadn't felt safe unless every outside door was tightly shut. The policeman who had called the day before had stressed the importance of keeping all doors shut and locked and the children safely indoors. He had meant well but had only succeeded in making her even more nervous than she already was. She had gone straight out and bought a chain for the front door so that she could see who was there before opening it.

Mind you, it wasn't so bad living on the estate. At least there were plenty of people around and street lamps up every road. The ones she felt sorry for were the farmers and their families who lived right up on the edge of the woods where there were no street lamps and the nearest neighbour a mile or so away. The police were checking up on everyone, but they couldn't be there all the time, could they?

She took mushrooms from the fridge, washed them in the sink, and carried them in cupped hands over to the chopping surface. Then she selected a knife from the cutlery drawer and set to work. The knife made tidy little *chip-chip-chip* sounds and she soon found herself chopping to a beat as she hummed. She could hear a radio somewhere, Diana Ross singing 'Chain Reaction', and the low grinding chomp of a lawnmower.

The harsh ring of the doorbell zig-zagged through the dreamy summer atmosphere, making her jump. She cursed and wiped her hands on her apron as she went through to the front door. She could see the blurred outline of a figure through the patterned glass. It appeared to be a young man, slim with blond hair. Martin? She opened the door to the length of its chain and peered through the gap.

"Yes?" She could see now that it wasn't Martin at all. This boy was a little older, maybe twenty-two or twenty-three. His face was gaunt, his eyes wide and dark, and his hair had a tinge of red. He was dressed in t-shirt, denim shorts and hiking boots, and he had a rucksack on his back.

"Sorry to bother you," he said in a soft, strangely flat voice, "but could you tell me where I can catch a bus into Cranbydale? I'm afraid I got a bit lost and I'm supposed to meet someone there this afternoon."

"Yes, certainly. The best place to get a bus would be the green in the village. Do you know how to get there?"

"No, I'm afraid I don't."

Mrs. Truscott gave him directions and drew a vague map on a scrap of paper. She closed the door, hoping the boy wouldn't get lost. She wasn't very good at giving directions. She wondered whether she ought to have warned him about the murders but decided against it. It would probably only alarm him. He had obviously hiked through the local farming country without coming to any harm, and it seemed silly to tell him what could have happened now that he was in the relative safety of Limefield.

She strained her ears for any sound that the twins might be making upstairs. She could hear nothing and was relieved. They were evidently playing quietly now after all the tantrums which had followed her announcement that they were not to play outside until the murderer had been caught. It was frustratingly difficult trying to impress the danger of the situation onto eight-year-old children. She often thought that maybe it had been a mistake to have children again after a ten-year interval. Of course, Alan and herself had always planned to have two or three children, but after Kevin's birth in 1968 they hadn't reckoned on the car crash. Her injuries had not been particularly serious— one broken leg, two broken arms, a trace of internal bleeding and the usual cuts and bruises (although nothing serious enough to scar), but the shock of the accident had sterilised her.

At the time it hadn't seemed particularly important. They had one fine son and the fact that they were all still alive was enough. But as time wore on, she realised she was beginning to get broody again. It was a feeling that depressed her greatly, but she couldn't seem to shake it off. Eventually she mentioned it to

Alan, and they talked over the various possibilities—adoption, fostering, various artificial means of conception, but these alternatives to her had seemed unnatural or unfulfilling. Eventually they decided to try out fertility drugs and after a couple of hopeful but fruitless years the drugs had suddenly done their stuff. She would never forget her joy when at the age of thirty-three she had been told she was not just pregnant, but pregnant with twins!

She smiled, remembering that confused, stressful time and how far it was behind her now. She remembered the crushingly horrific post-natal depression she had suffered only as snatches from a bad dream, and how dirty nappies and teething had coincided with Kevin's first problematic steps into puberty. There had been times in those months following the birth of the twins when she honestly believed children were a curse on humanity, and she had wondered whether the answer would be to drown her children or herself. She stood now at the bottom of the stairs, looking up.

"Jamie? Samantha?" she called. Silence. She frowned and tried again. "Do you two want any lemonade?" She felt irritated and a little worried in case they had defied her orders and sneaked out to play with their friends.

"Jamie, Sam, are you up there?" she shouted again, and again there was no reply. "If you're playing a stupid game and not answering me I'm going to get very cross," she called, hoping that that, in fact, was what they were doing.

Letting out an exasperated sigh, she climbed the stairs. There were no sounds of children playing coming from behind the closed bedroom door, but of course if they were pretending not to hear her there wouldn't be. They would be crouched on the other side, trying to conceal their sniggers. She called them once more just to give them a last chance, then opened the door and went inside.

The sight was so unexpected that for a moment all she could do was stand and gape. Two figures held her gagged and bound children in mercilessly tight grips. Mrs. Truscott could see the redness of tears in Samantha's eyes. Both children were limp as though any resistance had been shaken out of them. She was about to scream when a large, sweaty hand closed tightly over her mouth and a sharp crack on the back of her head sent her spinning into blackness.

⁙

Twenty minutes later Kevin and Martin arrived at the house. Because of the murders and the fact that Martin's parents would be away until the weekend, Mrs. Truscott had insisted that Martin stay with them for a few days. The two boys had been over to Martin's house to pick up some things—clean clothes and toiletries mainly—and to make sure the house was in order. They felt aimless and nervous. Keith hadn't yet rung, and they didn't dare strike out on their own.

Kevin pushed open the front door. It rattled to the end of its short chain and then stopped.

"Oh shit," he said, "I'd forgotten about that." He pushed as much of his face as he could into the gap between door and frame and shouted, "Mum, Mum, it's me! Can you let us in?"

There was no response. He tried again, as loud as he could, and Martin helped by banging on the door with one hand and ringing on the doorbell with the other. Still Mrs. Truscott failed to appear.

"She must be out," said Kevin. "We'll have to go around the back."

They did so, expecting the back door to be locked and the key to be in its usual hiding place under the flowerpot on the garage window sill. However, the back door and back window were both wide open.

"Hey, look here," said Martin.

"What the hell's she playing at?" said Kevin, annoyed. The two boys went into the kitchen. Kevin noticed the half-chopped vegetables on the side and the oven busily heating itself to the right temperature. For the first time he felt a squirm of unease.

"There's something not right here," he said to Martin. "She wouldn't go out and leave the oven on, she's really paranoid when it comes to electrical things."

"She's probably upstairs or something. She just hasn't

heard us," said Martin. Kevin went and stood at the foot of the stairs.

"Mum! Mum!" he called. The house was silent. He ran upstairs, looking in every room, but it was obvious that the place was empty.

"No luck?" said Martin. Kevin looked worried.

"There's nobody in at all. I don't like it, Mart, something's wrong."

"Don't worry, Kev, she's probably just popped out somewhere and forgot to lock the back door. It'll be all right."

Kevin was about to reply, but at that moment the telephone in the hall began to ring. He went to pick it up, his thoughts elsewhere.

"Hello," he said vacantly.

"We've got your mother, your brother and your sister," said a flat, somehow dead voice. Martin saw the look of horror pass over Kevin's face and his optimism took a dive.

"Who... who are you?" Kevin's voice was little more than a shocked whisper. "'What do you want?"

"You and the other boy. Be at the deserted farmhouse on the Moor Cross Road through Redheath Woods in one hour, otherwise your mother, brother and sister will be killed. Come alone!" Abruptly the caller rang off. The fading *ching* at the other end was as sharp and final as the fall of an executioner's axe. Kevin didn't move. He stood crouched in shock, the telephone receiver gripped tightly in his hand, eyes staring at the wall as though something repulsive was forming there.

"Kev, what is it? What's happened?" cried Martin.

"They've got Mum and Jamie and Sam," Kevin said in a half-sob, half-whisper. "We've got to go to the old farmhouse. If we're not there in an hour they'll kill them."

"Oh God," said Martin quietly. He sank onto a chair. "Oh, fucking hell fire."

The two boys sat as though turned to stone for a moment, and then Martin came to a decision. "I'll ring Keith," he said. Kevin's response was panicky and vehement.

"No! He said we had to go alone. If anyone else is with us they'll kill them."

"We've got to let someone know what's going on," said Martin. Kevin clasped his arm in a painful grip.

"No!" he shouted.

"Kev, look," said Martin gently, "Keith'll understand. If your family's lives are in danger he won't be stupid enough to be seen with us. But someone's got to know, Kev, we can't go there without letting anyone know."

Kevin released his grip uncertainly and Martin picked up the phone. He flicked through the telephone book for Keith's number, dialed it and waited, listening to the *burr-burr* at the other end.

"Hello?"

"Hello, Mrs. Francis. Is Keith there?"

"Yes, he is, who's calling please?"

"It's Martin Mason."

"Okay, Martin, if you'll just hang on a minute."

Martin waited nervously, listening to the tinny silence. After a few moments he heard the clatter of the phone being picked up.

"Hi, Martin. Look, I know why you're ringing and I'm sorry to have to disappoint you, but—"

"Keith, Keith," interrupted Martin, "it's not about that at all. It's something else. Something has happened at this end." He told Keith about the phone call and the conditions set by the caller.

"Oh, shit," said Keith, appalled.

"Keith, what can we do?" said Martin, aware that he sounded like a lost child. Keith let out a long, heartfelt sigh.

"All I can suggest," he said at last, "is that you play along for a while. Go to this farmhouse, but be very, very careful. I'll make my own way there. I'll park the car on the edge of the woods and go the rest of the way on foot. I think it would be best if Kevin didn't know I was coming. I'll make my presence known if I think I can do anything."

"Okay... Keith?"

"Yeah?"

"Who do you think it is who've got Kev's mum and the kids? Do you think it's anything to do with... with Swaney?"

Martin thought for a moment that Keith wasn't going to answer. Then he said, "I'm afraid that's the way it looks to me. It seems as though Swaney has cast his net a bit further afield."

"You don't think these people will kill Kev's family do you?" Martin's voice was strained.

"I don't know," said Keith evasively, "not if we can help it. Look, let's save the talking until later, shall we? You two had better get moving."

"Yeah, okay. See you later, Keith."

Keith restrained himself from saying that he hoped so. "Yeah, see you soon. Good luck," he said, and put the phone down.

CHAPTER TEN

THE FARMHOUSE

The cup of tea Donahue had bought was bitter and lukewarm, and he couldn't bring himself to drink more than half of it. He chewed on a plastic cheese sandwich and watched the passersby in the street outside. There had been a tension in the air this week, a fear that manifested itself as hushed gossip in the streets and a hurrying home before the dark set in. He could sense the atmosphere as clearly as in some old Hammer vampire movie where the Transylvanian village cowers beneath the shadow of the Count's castle on the mountainside. Donahue thought with grim humour that if he walked into a Limefield pub and asked the way to Redheath Woods, the locals would fall silent and regard him with wide, fearful eyes. Perhaps one would come forward and deliver some doom-laden cryptic warning.

Donahue yawned. He was feeling low. His investigations had led him nowhere, and his room last night had been too hot to sleep in. He put his elbows on the cafe table and leaned his chin on his hands. He felt more comfortable here than he had in his muggy bed with the clinging sheets. He closed his eyes. He would just have five minutes.

What had really drained him was writing the story the day before and musing over its possible implications. He had written and re-written that story, wondering how best to explain the unbelievable state of the tree.

In the end he had written in icy, factual prose—an unusual, often unacceptable style for newspaper work. It was the only way the story appeared to have any credibility at all. The paper would reach the streets in little over an hour. He was dreading the impact it would arouse. There was bound to be controversy. There would be cries of hoax, there would be ridicule and disbelief, there would be chaos and hostility in the village itself. He knew also that the story would attract a fresh swarm of visitors to Limefield who would come to witness this miraculous sight with their own eyes. This, in turn, would incense the villagers and the police who would get onto the newspaper about it. He knew even before the paper reached the streets that he had stirred up a very angry hornets' nest with a very big stick.

At midnight last night, round about his lowest ebb, he had considered not writing the story at all, had even half-considered resigning and telling that pig, Bosfeedy, to shove his newspaper up his arse. But, in the end, what would have been achieved? Bosfeedy still had Anton's incredible photographs and all he would have done would have been to dispatch another journalist to cover the story, and probably one of the younger, less-experienced ones who tended to possess the sensitivity and tact of a bulldozer.

So, Donahue had written the story. He had set it down exactly as it was and had dropped it round at the offices before he could change his mind. Bosfeedy had taken one look at it and called Donahue into his office.

Donahue recalled the uncomfortable ten minutes he had spent with his editor. Bosfeedy was sitting behind his desk, banana fingers drumming on the wood, looking like an enraged warthog about to do battle.

"Hello, Ramsay," Donahue said, pleasantly enough.

Bosfeedy failed to respond and his accusing glare was unnerving. Finally, in the quietest and mildest of voices, he said, "What the fuck is this?" and gestured at the evidence on the desk before him.

"Have you read it?" Donahue asked bleakly.

"Of course I've read it. That's why I'm asking. Just what sort of shit is this?"

"It's not shit," Donahue said, struggling to keep his voice steady. "It's all true, Ramsay, every word of it. Don't Anton's photographs prove it?"

Bosfeedy stood up—an awesome sight, like a human

volcano about to erupt. Donahue stepped back nervously, but Bosfeedy merely lit a cigar with slightly trembling fingers and took a puff at it before replying.

"How can it be true?" he said.

"I don't know how it can be true, Ramsay. I don't understand it any more than you do. All I know is what I saw. My story explains it all as it is. No frills, no colourful language, just facts."

Bosfeedy was silent for a long moment, regarding Donahue levelly through expressionless eyes.

"You realise I can't print any of this," he said finally.

"Can't print? What do you mean?"

"People wouldn't believe us, Philip! We'd be a laughing stock!"

"But the photos prove it too, don't they? And the evidence is up there for anyone who cares to go and see for themselves."

There was another long pause whilst Bosfeedy considered.

"I don't know, Philip," he said. "It's fantastic, it's unbelievable!"

"It's true," cut in Donahue. "Just print it, Ramsay. Print it as it is and put in as many of those photographs as possible; nice and big and clear. Sure, there'll be cries of hoax at first, but as soon as people realise that it is true, as soon as they see for themselves, then think of the reputation this newspaper will have. This could be the story of the decade, Ramsay. That tree could become famous throughout the world, as famous as... as... I dunno... as The Shroud of Turin. You've got to print."

And put like that, Bosfeedy had not been able to resist. In an hour from now the story would appear.

Donahue's stubbled cheek rasped on his hand as he slumped lower in his chair. All day he had been on his feet and he was exhausted.

He had taken a light breakfast that morning and had started early, feeling strangely refreshed despite his lack of sleep. After his encounter with Bosfeedy, he had driven over to Cranbydale Hospital to talk to Arthur Willis about the discovery of the bodies, and to a prison officer called Greg Trenchard about the prison breakout. Unfortunately, Trenchard was still in a light coma, a state he had been in since Tuesday evening, and Arthur Willis was a sad and confused figure, badly affected by his experience. At last, under Donahue's questioning, the old man had burst into frightened tears, and Donahue had left under the stormy gaze of Willis's nurse, feeling like shit for trying to force Willis to remember. He had spent the rest of that morning in the local library, reading up on strange phenomena, trying to find some explanation for the ice on the tree. Again, he had drawn a blank; nothing he could find was even vaguely similar. At last he had given up and driven into Limefield where he had had some lunch, hoping that the afternoon would fare better.

However, his afternoon had been almost as frustrating as his morning. He had spent it on a tour of Limefield's hotels, though they could hardly be called that. They were really little more than pubs which offered overnight accommodation for a dozen or so guests. There were six in all in Limefield, and Donahue had checked over each in turn, swiftly flashing his press card and claiming he was a police officer when the landlords threatened to get difficult. But once again he had found nothing.

Apart from press, there were precious few paying guests, and those that he had talked to had struck him as being very un-murderer like. The clientele included a number of businessmen and sales reps, a few students on overnight stops between one day of hiking or cycling and the next, a private investigator named Hutchins called in by the local butcher's wife to monitor the movements of her amorous husband, and the manager and coach of a Second Division football team who had travelled to the area from the Midlands with the intention of signing a centre-forward from a local non-league side. They wanted him, explained the manager, in time for the start of the season which was two weeks away.

All in all, thought Donahue, a very above-board group of people. He had at least hoped for a religious crank, or some sick-minded individual who kept a scrapbook full of newspaper clippings about the Yorkshire Ripper or the Moors Murderers.

But his day's work had led him to a dead end, both physically and metaphorically, and now here he was, snoozing in a cafe, his lack of sleep finally having caught up with him. He decided to ring through to Bosfeedy and ask for permission to stay in Limefield for a few days on the paper's expense. He was sure there would be no complications or arguments, especially if he assured his greedy editor he was onto something really big. Donahue felt he needed to be nearby, to be right here where everything was going on. He was as sure as he would ever be that things weren't over yet.

Margaret Francis was seething. Keith had been so vague and uncooperative these last couple of days, shutting himself away in his study and refusing to tell her what he was working on. Normally, she wouldn't have minded, but this was supposed to be his holiday and they had vowed to set aside these two weeks for decorating the house. Together they had taken up the carpets, covered the furniture, chosen the paint and wallpaper, bought the materials, and set to work. It had been a combined effort, and even though it was only decorating, it had been enjoyable because it had been something they had done together. She liked it so much when they worked together; it gave her a feeling of oneness, of unity.

But then, without a word, Keith had washed his hands of the whole thing and retired to his little den, and she had been unable to get through to him since. Now, it seemed, he had just driven off somewhere without a word. One minute she had heard him on the phone and the next he was slamming the front door and starting up the car engine.

Well, she thought not unreasonably, *if he's going to keep secrets from me I'm just going to go up there and see for myself what he's been doing that's so important.* She felt a little guilty at her intentions. She had never snooped on her husband before, but this time she felt she was justified. They had always agreed that a man and wife shouldn't keep secrets from one another; in fact it had been one of their private vows—to always tell each other everything. She couldn't be blamed, therefore, for prying into his affairs. Keith should be the one who was feeling guilty.

Having justified her actions in her own mind, she went upstairs.

The study door was open. At least Keith didn't lock it up. As she walked in, she had a sudden strange impression, as though something had darted away from the desk and she had caught the movement only with the corner of her eye. She spun round with a little gasp, half-expecting to see some small animal, but there was nothing. She smiled shakily and approached the desk which was piled high with papers and notes. More sheets of paper were piled up haphazardly on the floor, and the wastepaper basket was littered with screwed-up balls of yet more paper. The book resting in the centre of this white landscape looked incredibly old and incredibly heavy. She leaned and tried to read the print, but it made no sense to her. There was a drawing on the page which showed a little devil coming out of a tree. *Stupid,* she thought.

She straightened up. "Schoolwork, my arse," she murmured to herself.

She would give him a right going over when he got home, wasting his time on this stuff when he was meant to be working on the house. She remembered another vow she had made—never to be the nagging housewife—and smiled grimly. Well, if Keith was a little more thoughtful and reasonable, she wouldn't have need to be, would she?

There was another sudden flash of movement just beyond her field of vision, and again she whirled, startled. Once more there was nothing there, but this time she had been almost certain. It had looked like a man just flickering away out of sight. She shivered and looked round uneasily. The rows and rows of books sat calmly, permanently, each supporting the other, worlds concealed within their pages. The room was obviously empty. Millions of tiny dust particles swirled and spun in a shaft of light that reached like a golden rod from the window to the floor. She looked back down at the book. The little devil was poised, its scaly arms reaching out for the eternally terrified peasant man. Margaret began to read the text that accompanied the drawing, but she soon stopped, irritated. What sort of language was that? She looked at the front of the book but could find no title. She took one more look around the silent room and then left, closing the door firmly behind her.

While Margaret was walking across the landing of their home, trying to shake off a feeling of unease, Keith was thrashing the hell out of the engine of their 1975 Mini. He hoped to make it to the old farmhouse in time to be of some help. The journey was only some fourteen or fifteen miles in all, but Cranbydale's one-way system and the dreadful state of the roads between Limefield and Redheath Woods put a time of between thirty and forty minutes on the journey.

Keith looked at his watch. Martin had called him fifteen, maybe twenty minutes ago, which gave him another forty minutes to park the car, look for the farmhouse on foot and, once there, find a hiding place. So far, he had managed to manoeuvre his way through the fairly busy late afternoon traffic in Cranbydale and was now zipping along the relatively free road towards Limefield, keeping a wary eye out for the police. He couldn't afford to be pulled up for speeding now.

Fifteen minutes later he parked his car in a layby near to the woods and got out. The air was close and muggy, like it is before a thunderstorm, and Keith felt sure that the weather would break soon. The air in the woods was particularly bad, smoke dust hanging in the atmosphere like an invisible gauze. He looked around to get his bearings. Where was this bloody farmhouse? He didn't know the woods very well. Although he had been here for Sunday afternoon walks with Mags on a couple of occasions, everything looked so much different now. The woods had lost their colour and beauty, and all landmarks had been obliterated. The trees formed a forest of polluted corpses which stretched endlessly before him. Making an educated guess, he took the left-hand path, the nearest of three that led into the woods. He walked steadily, the ashy ground snapping and crackling underfoot. It was a peculiar and unpleasant sensation, like walking on a carpet of small bones.

After a while he began to breathe heavily. The smoky air rasped at the back of his throat, and the crumbling ground made the going strenuous. He felt as though he had been wading for hours without getting anywhere. He stopped and looked around him. It was a depressing landscape, black, twisted shapes writhing from the ground like a graveyard of Guy Fawkes dummies. He took off his spectacles and wiped away the pockets of sweat that had collected beneath his eyes. His shirt clung to his back like a second skin, and his feet felt as though they were smeared with grease inside his Hush Puppies. His watch informed him there were fifteen minutes of the hour left. Oh well, even if he was going the wrong way it was too late to turn back now. He walked on...

 ...And was rewarded a little over five minutes later by the solid shape of the farmhouse bobbing into view behind a curtain of trees. This was where he would have to be careful. He left the main path and approached the house in a roundabout way, moving from tree to tree. He winced at the sharp sounds made by his feet on the brittle ground, but of course that couldn't be helped. He manoeuvred into position behind the blackened ghost of a wild gooseberry bush and slumped down, irrespective of the mess he was making of his clothes. From here, he had a clear view of the farmhouse.

It was sturdy and very old, made of grey brick blackened by fire, and it possessed what had once been a thatched roof. Now all that remained were a few shriveled wooden beams that criss-crossed drunkenly in a vague semblance of an arched shape. It was so dark inside the house that the glassless ground floor windows looked as though they had been covered over with black paper. What remained of the door was ajar.

Keith ducked his head down as he glimpsed movement to his left. But he raised it again as he recognised the two figures cautiously approaching. Kevin and Martin had arrived.

❦

"Well, this is the place," said Martin, trying to keep his voice light.

"I can't see anyone around," said Kevin.

Martin looked at his friend worriedly. His shock and fear

seemed to have been replaced by a grim-faced *let me at 'em* attitude. It was a case of Kevin's heart ruling his head, which, as well as being unusual, was also dangerous in a situation like this. Before coming out, Kevin had taken a carving knife from the kitchen drawer and tucked it into his jacket. Reflecting that that wasn't such a bad idea, Martin selected a meat skewer and tucked it into his.

"We've got to be careful," said Martin, "don't do anything stupid."

"Do you think we ought to go inside?" said Kevin.

Martin hesitated. Should they? He didn't expect the kidnappers to come marching out and introduce themselves, but all the same it was not an appealing prospect. He stood, undecided, looking at the house. It appeared to be deserted. He wondered if Keith were here, hiding in the bushes somewhere, watching them. The thought that Keith could be watching them reminded Martin that others could be watching them too. He looked around him uneasily, but all he could see were black, twisted shapes.

"I think we'd better go inside," he said at last.

"Come on, then," said Kevin. They made their way over the shattered garden fence and up the path to the front door. It opened with a raucous creak on blistered hinges.

"The place is gutted," said Martin, peering into the gloom. And, indeed, all the wooden fittings in the house had burned away, leaving only the stone framework.

They crunched inside over a floor of charred wood. The air was stale as though the house was dying from the inside.

"How many rooms are there in this place?" whispered Martin.

Kevin shrugged. "Dunno. Seven or eight?"

"Well this one's obviously empty," said Martin. "Let's try the others."

"Do you think we're supposed to go looking for them?"

"I don't know. I suppose so," said Martin.

They moved out of the room, conscious of the echoing crunch of their feet on the dead floor. The ground floor had two more rooms. One was a large kitchen which also served as a dining room. The kitchen amenities such as stove, sink and chopping surfaces were at one side of the room, the remains of a dining table and chair in the centre, and at the other side was an open hearth with black melted lumps that had once been leather armchairs clustered around it. Everything was covered in a thick layer of ashes.

"This one's empty too," said Martin, standing in the doorway. Kevin curiously tugged at the door of the ancient cast-iron stove. The hinges screeched in protest. A small black animal darted from the interior and scuttled over the floor, making them jump.

"What was that?" said Martin.

"Just a mouse or something," replied Kevin.

The last room on the ground floor was tiny and windowless. Martin guessed it had probably been used as a storeroom or a laundry. The boys took one brief look and withdrew, wrinkling their noses at the harsh, acrid smell.

"It looks like we'll have to go upstairs," said Kevin. His voice was quiet and emotionless.

"Those stairs don't look safe to me," said Martin doubtfully. Like the rest of the wood in the house, they were black and fragile-looking.

"We'll just have to be careful," said Kevin and started up.

It soon became obvious, however, that the staircase was useless. The first step cracked and crumbled away beneath Kevin's weight, as did the second.

"It's hopeless," said Martin. "No one's been using those stairs."

"But they were supposed to meet us here. They've got my mum and the twins. Where are they?" Kevin's voice cracked, and he slumped to the floor, the resolve draining from him.

Martin was suddenly aware of three things all happening in rapid succession. The first was that the light coming in through the front entrance was obscured by the appearance of a bulky shape; the second was a tremendous blast like an explosion which hurt his ears; and the third was the appearance of a large hole in the stairs just a few inches above Kevin's head.

"Fucking hell! Run!" he screamed, dragging Kevin to his

feet and propelling him through the doorway and into the kitchen. Behind him, he heard the dry click of a shotgun being primed for another shot. Martin dived through the doorway after his friend and looked around desperately.

The only possible escape was through the window, but they would never make it in time. Luckily Kevin had recovered his wits enough to be able to help.

He picked up the remnants of a stool from the floor and tossed it across to Martin.

"Use this," he shouted. Martin caught the puny weapon cleanly and scurried into position behind the door. A moment later, their attacker entered, shotgun swaying from side to side in his hands like a divining rod. Martin briefly had time to register the fact that he was a young man with reddish-blond hair before he brought the stool crashing down. The wood spat black splinters across the man's knuckles and he dropped the gun. Kevin made a dive for it, but the man, moving like an automaton, kicked him away and pounced on the weapon himself. Martin made ready to leap on the man's back and bear down on him so that he was unable to use the weapon, but the man was too quick. In one movement he snatched up the gun, rolled over on his back, and brought up the barrel, pointing it squarely at Martin's chest. Martin backed off nervously, expecting his innards to decorate the kitchen at any second. The man climbed to his feet and for the first time the boys could see his eyes. They were wide and dark and staring as though drugged. Martin shivered; there was nothing human about them at all.

"Where's my mum?" sobbed Kevin. The shotgun swung round to cover him, but the man made no reply.

"Look, we made a deal," said Martin, trying to keep his voice calm. The gun swung back. The man looked from Kevin to Martin to Kevin again as though unsure which to kill first. His face was as bland as a tailor's dummy's.

"Look," Martin continued, "you're only getting yourself into more trouble you know."

The man made no response.

Kevin was close to tears. "Please let my mum and the kids

go," he sobbed. "They've not done you any harm. Please let them go."

Surprisingly the man spoke, though his voice was as flat and as dead as his eyes. "We can't do that."

"Why not?" said Martin. "What are you going to do to them?"

To his horror, the man's pupils suddenly rolled backwards into his head, leaving white, glutinous eyeballs. As he watched a change seemed to come over the man's face. His bones became sharper, tighter, his brow heavier. His white eyeballs receded and narrowed into slits. When the transformation was complete, Martin found that he was looking at the lean and brutal features of Russell Swaney.

The Swaney-thing opened its mouth to speak. Martin could see that its tongue was purply-black and swelling like a balloon.

"They will feed me," the Swaney-thing grated. "Their deaths will feed me." The voice became suddenly high, sing-song, like a mad child's. "I'll cut them into little pieces. Bit by bit by bit by bit."

"No!" screamed Kevin, so hard that Martin jumped, "no, no!"

Martin saw Kevin's hand go to the carving knife in his jacket. He grabbed his arms and pinned them to his sides. "No, Kev," he hissed in his friend's ear. "You've got no chance. Look at him. It's Swaney."

"Poor little boy, upset about his mummy," piped the Swaney-thing. The eyelids opened wide and the white eyeballs seemed to slide out like snails from their shells. The voice became deep and guttural again. "'Don't worry. We'll look after her. We'll chop her up. Bit by bit. And when she's dead we'll start on the little girl. Bit by bit by bit."

This time there was no stopping Kevin. He tore himself free from Martin's grip and leaped towards the Swaney-thing with a scream of hatred. He whipped the knife from his jacket and held it high above his head.

The Swaney-thing grinned hideously, stretching the young man's face like a rubber mask. It stepped back, took aim, and pulled the trigger.

Fortunately for Kevin, Keith chose just that moment to enter the room. He came up behind the Swaney-thing and gave it a vicious shove. The blast from the gun gouged huge chunks of black masonry from the ceiling.

Perhaps the dark soul did not have the control it thought it had; perhaps it felt clumsy and constricted using this human body as a glove, as an extension of its influence; or perhaps it had simply underestimated the resourcefulness of the two boys. Whatever the reason, the body of the young man was caught completely off-balance and fell heavily to the floor with the weapon beneath it. The Swaney-thing twisted round onto its back and clawed for the gun. But at that moment Kevin landed heavily on its chest, his face twisted with hate. Before anyone could stop him, he brought the knife down, burying it deep in the young man's brain. Immediately the body went limp. The Swaney-mask slipped from the young man's face. He became human once more.

He lay, looking up at the knife handle projecting from his forehead with an expression of mild surprise. It seemed to take a long time before blood began to pulse from the wound and run into his staring eyes.

Kevin, suddenly realising what he had done, fell away from the body. He curled up into the foetal position on the floor and began to make small, anguished sounds, heaving like a beached whale.

Martin crawled over to his friend on jelly limbs. He tried to say something, but the incident had shocked away his power of speech. He spread his arms protectively around his friend's huddled form and shared his anguish.

CHAPTER ELEVEN

THE NIGHT-COMERS

The weather broke an hour later. Grey clouds, like the grizzled beards of old men clustered in conversation, crept in from nowhere. The rain they held was both surprising and welcome.

The parched countryside soaked up the moisture gratefully, whilst cows and sheep stood out in the fields, content to let the rain wash away the heat and sweat from their bodies. In the village a group of young men stripped to the waist and improvised a primitive rain dance on the green whilst older people, sheltered beneath umbrellas and plastic hoods, looked on, shaking their heads.

But the rain was not welcome everywhere. Its falling was a dismal sound in the woods. It turned the ashy ground to black slush and succeeded only in transforming the trees into things of sinister beauty, like black marble sculptures of emaciated people.

The crooked tree collected the raindrops and spat them out as jewels of ice. The hard frost that had formed on the ground was spreading, beginning to touch the trees around it. One or two had patches of frost already on their bark, cradled in the dips and crevices like a feathery white infection. The ground was knobbly and crystallized, and the rain that fell onto it was immediately captured and frozen, and as it froze it spread even further.

Like some self-destructive urge of nature, or some freakish wasting disease, the winter was eating the ground.

As Donahue had expected, the story caused an uproar. As soon as the paper reached the streets, he left the cafe and slipped back through the rain-lashed streets to the doubtful sanctuary of a room in The Shoulder of Mutton. Once there he locked himself in and refused to accept any calls. The journalists from the major dailies, on the other hand, emerged like rats from their hotel rooms—sniffing, demanding, disrupting, causing a wide and hostile rift to appear between themselves and the villagers. The farmer, Tom Bussey, chased hordes of reporters from his land with a shotgun after he had seen them in his garden, uncaringly trampling his wife's flower beds to pulp, and the landlord of The Shoulder of Mutton, Reginald Carter, thumped a reporter and broke his jaw after the journalist had turned nasty over Donahue's refusal to see any visitors.

The *Cranbydale Observer* was inundated with phone calls from villagers incensed at this latest violation of their privacy. Many of them demanded compensation from the newspaper, whilst others threatened to exact terrible revenges on Donahue, Bosfeedy, Anton Brabier and anyone else who was found to have been connected with the story. Other calls came from religious men, some concerned, some interested, some outraged, and from the police who demanded to know why the newspaper had published the story without first informing them of the situation.

Even between the villagers there was conflict. A brick came sailing through the window of The Plumber's Arms, with a note tied to it which read, 'That's for having a bastard as a brother', whereupon Ron Brabier ran out into the street, caught the man responsible, bashed his head against a wall, and was arrested and charged with assault.

By midnight the initial furor had died down, though hostility still seethed beneath the surface. The landlords did a roaring, if resentful, trade, easily packing the few rooms for visitors with the influx of the amazed and curious sightseers who flocked to the village.

The roads into Limefield became so crammed with cars that the police were forced to set up roadblocks and turn them back, one after another. Many of the sightseers, unable to wait until the morning, ignored the warnings and ventured out into the woods in the dark, intent upon seeing the miraculous sight for themselves. More police were drafted in to deal with this. Patrols were posted in the woods, lanes leading into the woods were closed off, and farmers were asked to report the presence of any strangers on their land.

But not everyone who came to Limefield that night were sightseers. The next day, an already baffled police force would find dozens of abandoned cars in the area—parked in fields, in laybys, at the sides of roads—and enquiries would reveal that the occupants of those cars had mysteriously disappeared...

⸎

The cottage stood still and silent in the moonlight, unaffected by the chaos just a mile or two away. In a downstairs window, a lamp burned like a single, watchful eye. All around the countryside was stirring—rain bobbed the heads of flowers and muttered in the grass, insects chirruped softly, a lone owl hooted as it searched for food.

The new arrivals came like an army of phantoms, in ones and twos, skulking through the darkness, keeping to the shadows. They avoided the police patrols and the watchful farmers with ease, guided by the power of the dark soul, which monitored their movements and drew them, unscathed and unchallenged, to their destination. By morning there were close on two hundred people packed into the tiny cottage, though from outside not a soul could be seen.

⸎

Kevin stared blankly at the cup of tea before him on the table. His gaze didn't shift even when Martin took the cup and poured its contents down the sink.

"How is he?" asked Mr. Truscott, himself looking haggard and much older than his forty-six years.

"No change," said Martin gently. "He won't speak or respond to anyone. He just sits there, staring into space like a zombie."

"He's still in shock," said Keith. "The only thing we can do is keep talking to him and keep him warm. If he's not out of it in another couple of hours, we'll have to give him a couple of sleeping pills. He's got to relax."

Martin drew Keith to one side. "I'm really worried about Kev. He's taking this really bad."

"Yeah, I know," said Keith, "but you've got to admit, it's hardly surprising. You'd probably be the same if you were in his situation. Worrying about his family is bad enough, but now on top of that he's got to cope with the guilt of murder."

"It wasn't murder," protested Martin. "You heard what that... that thing said to him. He was provoked."

Keith held up a hand. "Hey, whoa, don't snap my head off. I'm not accusing Kevin. All I mean is that the police will probably see it as murder."

Martin sat down and ran a hand through his hair. "What a fucking mess this is," he said miserably. "I wish there was something we could do."

Keith pulled a chair around and sat with his elbows resting on the back, his long legs splayed out either side. "I know how you feel," he said, "but we can't go rushing into things. All we can do at the moment is sit tight, play it by ear."

"Do you think these people will... well, y'know... do anything to Kev's mum and the kids?"

Keith frowned and shook his head. "I honestly don't know, Martin. I suppose it all depends on how much of a threat you and Kevin are to Swaney."

Martin snorted. "A threat? How could we be a threat to something like that?"

"Again, I don't know. Maybe just because you've seen it and it's afraid you might tell someone. Maybe it's not pumping on all cylinders just yet."

Martin sighed. "So, what do we do? Tell someone now and put Kev's family in danger, or wait and see what happens and give Swaney the chance to get stronger?"

"Tough decision," said Keith sympathetically, "but remember your silence can only be guaranteed while Kev's family are alive. Once they're dead, you've got nothing to lose."

"Huh, big deal," said Martin.

"No, think about it, Mart. It means that, at the moment, Kevin's family are more useful alive than dead."

Martin nodded. "Yeah, I suppose so." He thought for a moment. "There was something that that... thing said at the cottage. It said 'Their deaths will feed me'. What do you think it meant by that?"

Keith shook his head. "Maybe Swaney uses death as energy, as a lifeforce, or maybe... No, I don't know."

"What were you going to say?" Martin prompted.

Keith looked grim. "Or maybe it feeds on pain rather than death."

Martin shuddered. "Horrible."

"I'm only guessing," said Keith. He shrugged apologetically. "I mean, well, dead is dead, isn't it? But pain... pain releases a lot of energy. It's like carrying sadism to an extreme. Something that not only enjoys giving pain but uses it... harnesses it in some way."

"But if pain makes it stronger, why doesn't it kill its followers, feed on them?"

"I assume it needs them," said Keith. "Once it's strong enough, perhaps it will."

Martin was about to say more, but at that moment Mr. Truscott wandered across. "I still think the best thing would be to call the police," he said, resuming a past argument.

"No," said Keith firmly. "Honestly, Mr. Truscott, that would be the worst thing to do. If the people who have your wife and children find out you've contacted the police they'll kill them straight away."

"But how will they find out? The police can be discreet. They know how to deal with these things."

Keith was adamant. "The kidnappers may have someone watching us at this very moment. Or your phone may be tapped. They've been in the house, remember."

Mr. Truscott looked around and shuddered at the reminder.

"Besides," Keith continued, "look at Kevin. He's in no state to answer questions the way he is at the moment."

Mr. Truscott looked unhappy, but his face sagged in resignation. "No, I suppose you're right. I just wish there was something I could do." His voice became desperate. "I feel so hopeless."

Keith patted his shoulder and smiled what he hoped was a reassuring smile. "Patience is a virtue," he said. The words sounded inadequate, but he couldn't think of anything better. Mr. Truscott nodded vaguely and wandered away again,

"I'm worried about him too," Martin said. "He's acting like a forgetful old man, just wandering around like that."

"I suppose it's his way of trying to cope," said Keith. "His mind is keeping his body active, trying to stop him dwelling on what's happened."

There was silence between them for a few moments while Keith lit a cigarette, then Martin said, "Why do you think Swaney only sent one person to kill us?"

Keith shook his head. "I don't know. I suppose he thought a shotgun would be enough. Or perhaps he didn't want to risk too much in one go. There was always the chance that you might bring the police along."

Martin shuddered. "I hate all this. I don't feel safe anymore, not even in the middle of the day, surrounded by people. I always feel as though I'm treading through a minefield, as though I'm being watched all the time."

"Best way to feel," said Keith. "At least you're being careful. And you've been lucky so far. I should think it was you two they came for this afternoon, but when they found you weren't in they had to rethink their plans."

"Well what's to stop them coming back now, while it's dark?" Martin said, alarmed.

Keith shrugged. "Nothing, I suppose. Like I said, it probably depends on how much of a threat Swaney thinks you are. But at least, if they do come back, we'll be ready for them. And the village is swarming with police—they won't get away easily."

"I don't think I'll be able to sleep tonight," Martin said.

"We'll keep alternate watches if you like. I've rung Mags and explained. She wasn't too happy about my being away, but it can't be helped."

"What about your work? Your translating?" said Martin.

"I'll go and get my notes from home tomorrow."

They both turned, alerted by noise and movement from behind them. Kevin, sitting at the kitchen table, had dropped his head into his arms and was sobbing uncontrollably.

"Kev! Kev!" Martin cried, pulling a chair up close to his friend. "Hush Kev, mate. Everything's all right. Don't worry."

Keith put a hand on Martin's arm. "Let him cry," he said. "He's getting rid of it all. Maybe when he's done he'll be ready to talk."

Martin looked bewildered. "Yes, okay. It's just that... well, I've never seen Kev cry like this before. He's usually so... well, I dunno... so restrained. He's not the emotional type."

"We all have our limits," said Keith.

"Son! Son!" Mr. Truscott entered and pushed his way through to Kevin's side. "Hush now, it's all right. Everything's going to be all right." He pulled Kevin to him. Kevin responded to the encircling arms, cramming his face into his father's chest. The sound of his crying became muffled by his father's heavy pullover. Martin looked away, dismayed. Keith began to make another pot of tea.

Kevin lifted his head and looked up into his father's face with red, tearful eyes. "I killed him, Dad. I killed him," he sobbed, gulping back tears.

"Killed? Killed who? Who did you kill?" said Mr. Truscott, confused. He held Kevin by the arms and looked into his face. "What do you mean, son? Who did you kill?"

Kevin tried to answer, but his words were lost in a choking flood of tears. His head lolled. His hair was stringy and lifeless, his face blotchy. Mr. Truscott turned to Keith and Martin.

"What did he mean, 'I killed him'?"

Keith and Martin exchanged troubled glances. They hadn't told Mr. Truscott this part of the story, thinking it would do more harm than good. After a moment's pause Keith said, a little too smoothly, "He probably means nothing, Mr. Truscott. I wouldn't worry about it. The mind often acts in a peculiar way in these situations."

But Mr. Truscott had detected something between the two of them—an evasiveness, a closing of ranks. He looked squarely at Martin. The boy avoided his gaze.

"What did he mean, Martin? You tell me!" he ordered.

Martin squirmed uncomfortably. His face blushed crimson, "I... er... I don't know," he stammered.

"You're lying to me!" Mr. Truscott shouted. He turned from one to the other. "Just what are you hiding?"

"Nothing, Mr. Truscott, really," Keith said. Martin could see Keith willing Mr. Truscott to accept their word.

Whether Mr. Truscott was trembling with rage, distress or confusion was difficult to tell. His voice was quiet and contained, but an icy tremor was detectable somewhere below the surface. "Look, my wife, my son and my daughter, both eight-year-old kids, have been taken from my house in broad daylight. Why or how, I don't know. But what I do know is that something has been happening in this village over the last week. The woods have burned down, people have been murdered, others have disappeared. If you two are hiding something from me, don't you think I'm entitled to know? It's my family, for Christ's sake! Not yours, mine! I have a right!"

He looked wildly from Martin to Keith and then back again. Both looked confused and uncomfortable, but neither of them said anything.

"Right!" Mr. Truscott shouted. "That settles it. I'm calling the police!"

He swept out of the room and made for the phone on the hall table. Keith banged down the milk bottle he had been holding and followed him. He skidded into the hall just as Mr. Truscott picked up the phone.

"Mr. Truscott, don't please," he said, holding out a hand.

Mr. Truscott glanced at him briefly, then put a finger in the nine and turned the dial. Keith dived forward and executed a neat rugby tackle just as the little man poised his finger to dial the second nine. Mr. Truscott, too surprised to let go of the telephone, fell on top of Keith, winding him. Telephone table, a vase of daffodils, and a penholder shaped like a croaking bullfrog crashed down around them. Mr. Truscott tried to struggle free, his face red and furious.

"Let go of me!" he shouted. Keith clung on despite a bloody nose and the crunch of his dislodged spectacles being mangled beneath the weight of his body. Mr. Truscott tried to twist in Keith's grip and use the telephone receiver as a bludgeon. The receiver made an ugly *chunk* as it connected with Keith's head, but Keith managed to squirm down to avoid further blows. He grabbed the thrashing arm and succeeded in pinning it to Mr. Truscott's side. He used his height to his advantage, curling his long legs round Mr. Truscott's considerably stumpier ones to stop him kicking.

They lay there for a moment in the debris, gasping and panting, bodies tied in a human knot. Keith snorted blood into his throat, forced himself to swallow it, and lifted his head, bringing his mouth level with Mr. Truscott's ear.

"I'm sorry, Mr. Truscott," he said. "It's nothing personal believe me, but I really can't let you phone the police. If we involve them your wife and children will be dead. I'm not exaggerating, Mr. Truscott, I'm telling the truth. These people have no conscience whatsoever. Do you understand me?"

Mr. Truscott merely snorted. What it was supposed to mean Keith couldn't tell, but at least it showed he was listening. He continued, "Now, I'm going to let you. go. If I do so, will you promise not to attack me or try to call the police? I'll explain everything to you." There was a pause.

"Do you promise?" Keith said again.

"Yes, yes," snapped Mr. Truscott. "Just bloody let go of me, will you?"

Keith spread his arms and legs, releasing his grip. Mr. Truscott scrambled to his feet and yanked his jacket viciously back into place. There were bright blotches of red high on his cheeks, and his eyes glared behind his spectacles.

"Look what you've done to my house," he stormed, indicating the smashed vase and trampled flowers.

"I'm sorry, Mr. Truscott, I'll clean the place up for you. And I'll repay you for any damage," said Keith humbly. He began to pick up the pieces of broken glass. Martin gathered up the mangled daffodils, deposited them in the plastic bag, and mopped up the water whilst Keith righted the telephone table and put the telephone and pen holder back in position. He picked up his spectacles. One lens was smashed, and the frame was bent. He put them into his pocket and made a mental note to fetch his spare pair from home in the morning. Fortunately, he would be able to drive without them if he was careful.

Kevin was sitting on the settee in the front room, sipping a cup of tea, uninterested in the struggle that had just occurred. When the mess had been cleared up, the others joined him.

"Right," said Mr. Truscott, "what the hell is this all about then?"

Keith sat on the edge of the settee next to Kevin, his lips pursed and his hands crossed between his knees. Martin looked at him. It seemed for a moment as though Keith had turned to stone. Then he spoke.

"Kevin did kill someone this afternoon," he said in a voice that sounded weary. Mr. Truscott butted in immediately, jumping from his seat as though someone had put a firecracker under it.

"Killed someone?... Kevin?... But... but what?... who?"

"If you'll just sit down and let me explain," Keith said.

Mr. Truscott sat, a stunned expression on his face. His eyes blinked behind his spectacles, giving him the look of a startled owl.

"This afternoon," said Keith, "after your wife and children had been taken, the boys here received a phone call."

"A phone call?" Mr. Truscott said. "Why didn't you tell me about this, Martin?"

Martin was about to reply when Keith held up his hand. "Please, Mr. Truscott," he said impatiently, "if you'll just stop interrupting every five seconds, I'll explain."

Silence fell on the room. Satisfied, Keith continued, "The phone call was from the kidnappers who told the boys that unless they went to a deserted farmhouse in Redheath Woods within the hour, your wife and the children would die. Naturally, the boys had to agree with the conditions, but before setting off Martin rang me and told me what had happened. I drove to the woods, found a hiding place, and waited for the boys to arrive. A few minutes later they did so and went into the house. I was deciding whether or not to follow them when a man appeared, a young man with a shotgun. He went into the house and a moment later I heard the shotgun being fired. I went to help and found the boys being threatened by this young man. Luckily, I was able to take the man by surprise, there was a struggle, and in the confusion, Kevin stabbed the man, killing him. Martin and I pulled up some of the old floorboards in one of the downstairs rooms, put the body in there, and replaced the floorboards. We buried the knife underneath a tree, and then between us carried Kevin through the woods to my car and drove here."

Mr. Truscott ran a trembling hand through his thin hair. "My God," he said. He looked into Keith's face. His eyes were confused, searching. "What the hell's going on in this village? It's like there's a curse on the place."

"You're not far from the truth," Keith said quietly.

Kevin had been silent since his brief outburst at the kitchen table, but now they all turned as he began to speak.

"I had to kill him," he said as though trying to convince a jury. "Dad, I had to. He said he was going to... to do... things to Mum and Sam." He shuddered. "He made me kill him, Dad. I didn't know what I was doing. He made me." His voice became high and strained, approaching hysteria. Mr. Truscott went to his son and put an arm round his shoulder.

"Shhh, son. It's okay. Don't worry. It's over now, it's all over."

Martin watched the scene with a sad, hollow emptiness in the pit of his stomach. *I wish it was*, he thought to himself, *I wish to God it was*.

<hr />

"Right, I think it's time we had a tea-break," Sergeant Graham Hopper said, bringing the car to a standstill. He leaned over the back seat and reached for the thermos flask and box of sandwiches his wife, Mabel, had prepared for him.

The other occupant of the car, Constable Richard Sykes, was not as enthusiastic about the idea. "Do we have to, Sarge?

Can't we wait until we get back to the station?"

The burly and bewhiskered sergeant gave the spotty youth a look of acute exasperation, thinking not for the first time that there were too many kids in the police force nowadays.

"Certainly not," he said. "That Inspector Garside is much too keen. He'd spring some paperwork on us or send us to deal with a pub brawl the minute we set foot through the door. Besides, what's wrong with this place? It's nice and peaceful."

"It's bloody creepy," said Sykes, looking nervously out into the darkness. All around them, he could hear the creak of the woods and the *drip-drip* of rain from the dead branches. The stars appeared as tiny lights between spiky limbs, and the moon was little more than a dull glow behind banks of sooty cloud.

Hopper laughed. "Creepy," he scoffed, handing the young man a steaming beaker. "What's creepy about a load of old trees?"

"It's not just the trees, Sarge," said Sykes. "It's all the weird things that have been happening here. They've not caught that murderer yet. Did you see what he did to his victims?"

"Aye, lad, but what you've got to remember is that we're not a couple of kids. We're police officers with police training. Don't you worry, son, we'll be all right."

He peeled off the lid of his Tupperware sandwich box. "Here y'are, lad, have a sandwich. They're egg. I'm not too keen on egg—gives me terrible wind."

"Ta," said Sykes, taking a sandwich and biting into it. He wasn't wild about eggs himself, but anything to escape the sergeant's bowel movements. "I think I preferred the woods a couple of hours ago when all those people were around. At least there was a bit of life then and we were kept busy. Now, it's as if there's something out there—something watching us."

"You what?" exclaimed Hopper. "Look, son, will you shut up about bloody ghosties and ghoulies and things that go bump in the night. You're supposed to be a grown man, not some daft kid."

"Sorry, Sarge," mumbled Sykes, embarrassed. "It's just... oh, I don't know. This place just gives me the willies, that's all."

"There'll be more than this to scare you before you get to my age," said Hopper, biting into a tomato. "You learn to relish quiet moments like this in the police force." He stared out of the window as though images from his past were being played out before him against the background of trees. "I used to work in Huddersfield before I moved down here, y'know. And I'll tell you, it's a lot more frightening walking the beat through a town centre full of alleyways and dark corners at two in the morning than it is sitting in a nice warm car in the middle of a lot of old trees."

Sykes gave Hopper a resigned smile. It was no use trying to explain irrational fears to this man. Hopper was a down-to-earth, practically minded cynic, too full of the bare realities of policing to give any time to a lot of daft, mumbo-jumbo ideas.

They ate and drank in silence, Sykes keeping his eyes averted from the trees that were caught in the headlights of the police car. He could hear them, though, swaying and creaking in the summer squall. It was a lost, hopeless sound.

Between them, the two policemen polished off the egg sandwiches and most of the tea. By the time they'd finished, the rain had stopped. Hopper crumpled the polythene sandwich wrapping into a ball, popped it into the box, and slung the box onto the back seat.

"Well, I suppose we'd better be getting back then," he said. He reached for the ignition key and gave it a sharp twist. The engine turned over.

Hopper took a look behind him. "I'll have to turn around here. That path is too narrow up ahead." He manoeuvred the car awkwardly on the uneven ground. The headlights swept across the trees in a cutting edge of light, revealing each crouching shape for a brief moment before moving on. The harsh, shifting contrast of light and shadow had the effect of giving the trees a jerky, convulsive life.

"There we are," Hopper said when the car was facing back the way they had come. "A neat bit of driving though I say so myself."

They followed the path through the woods carefully, the wheels of the car sliding a little as they tried to gain a grip in the clinging mud.

"Looks like it'll rain again before the night's out," said Hopper, looking through the windscreen at the partially obscured moon.

Sykes nodded. "The farmers'll be happy at any rate."

"I'll be happy," said Hopper. "I've had a hell of a problem trying to keep my flowerbeds from drying up these last few weeks. That's the trouble with this country. Too much of the same sort of weather all at one go. If we're not suffering from a drought, we're snowed in, and if we're not snowed in, we're assessing flood damage. There's somethin' wrong somewhere."

"Look out!" yelled Sykes, his voice a sudden harsh intrusion on the lazy grumblings of his superior.

Hopper, who had been giving only half his attention to the road ahead, looked round to see what had caused the young officer to cry out. He had a brief and jumbled impression of a hulking shape, caught in the glare of the headlights, looming over the windscreen. Then he slammed on the brakes and wrenched the steering wheel over to one side. The car turned sharply, and the figure disappeared from view to be replaced by a clump of shriveled trees and bushes perched on a slight incline. The car came to rest drunkenly, one wheel half up the rise, the front bumper a matter of inches from what had once been a proud oak.

Sykes felt cold, shaken and sweating all at the same time. He expelled a long breath. "What the fuck was that?" he said at last.

Hopper already had the door open and was leaning with one arm on the roof, looking over the car into the trees where the figure had apparently vanished. He stuck his head back into the car.

"Looks like another one. Silly sods, don't they realise how dangerous these woods have become at night? I suppose I'll have to go and have a scout round for him. You wait here. Hand me that flashlight, will you?"

"Shouldn't we both go?" said Sykes nervously. "I mean the Inspector said—"

"Bugger the Inspector. Look, I'll only be gone five minutes. Now, give me that flashlight before he gets away."

Sykes reached under the seat and handed the burly sergeant the torch that was kept there. Hopper turned it on and scanned the ranks of wizened trees. There was no sign of movement. He swore and moved off towards the woods.

"Be careful, Sarge," called Sykes. "He looked like a big bugger."

"Probably just wearing a parka with a hood," called back the sergeant. He slapped his ample but solid belly. "Anyway, I'm no Tinkerbell myself."

He walked off into the trees.

Sykes watched the flashlight beam get smaller and more indistinct as it bobbed away. When it had disappeared altogether, he sat back and waited.

There was a deathly silence now in the woods. Sykes shivered as he felt it press around him, touching him like cold, suffocating hands. In an attempt to shrug off the feeling, he shuffled over to the driver's seat and turned the key in the ignition. He would get the car back onto the path, he decided. That would take his mind off things.

The engine wheezed and coughed a few times before turning over. Sykes kept the revs going for a few seconds to ensure the engine was running smoothly, then reversed cautiously back onto the path. The sound of the engine was warm and soothing, and Sykes lingered before turning it off.

He was reluctant to do so, but he knew the sarge would go mad if he wasted the petrol. He was funny about things like that. He brought the car to a halt and resumed his vigil.

Why was it so bloody quiet? If it had been a peaceful quiet he would not have minded, but this was a hard, cold, hostile quiet, as though something was out there, wide awake and watching. Sykes caught a flicker of movement to his left and looked out of the window, startled. For a moment it had looked like the white, leering face of a tall figure standing beside the car, but now he saw it was only the moon shaking off its veil of cloud.

He began to hum to himself, the sound tuneless and wooden. He kept that up for a little while, then a paranoid worry that his voice might attract something from the woods crept in. He shut up immediately.

What about a read? he thought. *That always passes the time.* He opened the glove compartment and took out his book, wishing he'd brought something more cheerful than a horror story. He read a few pages, but the passage he was reading, where a boy called Danny was trapped in a snow tunnel with something crawling towards him through the darkness, made Sykes even more uncomfortable. He marked his place with a chewing gum wrapper and put the book back in the glove compartment.

His thoughts turned to the sergeant. Where the hell was he? How long had he been gone now? Sykes looked at his watch and was surprised to see that fifteen minutes had passed since he had watched the torchlight wavering away into the darkness. He sat back and sighed, wishing he could see the welcoming glow of the flashlight beam returning.

It was ten minutes later when Sykes decided to pluck up courage and go looking for his senior officer. They should have gone together in the first place, he thought. The Inspector would give them a right bollocking if he ever found out Hopper had gone off into the trees alone. The sarge had been away much too long now, which meant he had either found something, got lost or was in trouble. Whichever it was, he would need some help.

Sykes took a second flashlight from under the seat and turned it on. The beam was a filmy acid-yellow, not as penetrating as the light from Hopper's torch, and Sykes remembered that he had meant to get batteries for it some days ago. He let out a sigh. Oh well, it would just have to do. There was probably enough power left in the batteries for maybe an hour's light. That should easily be enough. He closed and locked the doors of the police car but left the headlights on.

He flashed the torch into the trees. The yellow beam made them look sickly and stunted and forbidding. Sykes gulped and walked unsteadily across the path, the mud sucking and slurping at his boots. He peered into the black, creaking trees. Nothing stirred. His body a mass of bristling goosebumps, he entered the wood.

CHAPTER TWELVE

THE VISITOR

Gnarled faces leered at him and twisted claws snaked out, snagging his clothes, as he stumbled through the wood. His breath whistled through his teeth and his lungs felt cold with fear. Black oily mud plastered his boots and trouser bottoms. He came to a halt and made a brave effort to pull himself together. He was behaving pathetically, like a child scared of the dark. He forced himself to calm down and to breathe more steadily. He shone the flashlight ahead. There were more trees, featureless but somehow threatening.

He looked back and could make out the vague twin glow of the police car headlights. He was surprised; he hadn't come as far as he'd thought.

Gritting his teeth, he strode on, the falling torchlight beam twitching before him. The moon flickered in and out of the dead canopy of branches, almost full but providing no light. It was as though the woods reflected the light away, preferring to live in darkness.

The beam picked out a shape ahead and Sykes jumped back, dropping the torch. It plopped into the mud and went out. Sykes stooped and picked it up, trying to stop the panic bubbling up inside him. He fumbled a handkerchief from his pocket and hastily wiped the slime away from the torch's surface. Then, with a desperate, silent plea, he clicked the switch. To his relief, the torch came back on.

Trembling, he directed the beam at the shape that had frightened him, stepping back subconsciously towards the fragile safety of a stark, withered beech tree.

The thing that he had thought was some sort of creature

about to spring turned out to be a young sapling which had bent like a bow and fallen across the path. Sykes shuddered as he went ahead and moved it to one side with his foot. It reminded him of a burnt body, the back arched in a rictus of pain.

The ground became increasingly marshy as he moved deeper into the woods. Clumps of blackened vine trailed around his feet like decaying seaweed, and he had to keep stopping to disentangle it from his feet and ankles. Gradually, the ground became more liquid than solid, and water seeped into his boots. Sykes stopped, puzzled.

Where the hell was the sarge? Had he wandered off in some other direction? All Sykes could see ahead was the dull gleam of water between the trees. He felt sure the sergeant wouldn't wade through that lot. The only answer, he decided, was that somehow they had missed each other. The sarge was probably back at the car now, fuming over the idiocy of his inferior. Sykes decided to turn back. It wouldn't do to get lost in these woods. He might wander for hours without finding his way out. There were no landmarks to focus on anymore, everything looked so alien. Besides the battery was running low in the torch, the light so feeble as to be almost useless.

Sykes considered shouting Hopper's name, but trepidation dried the words in his throat. At the best of times, a horror film landscape like this would have given him the willies, but in the light of all that had happened, his fear was increased tenfold.

He hurried back the way he had come, anxious to reach the comforting safety of the police car before the torch went out on him altogether. He suddenly felt very alone and very vulnerable. The atmosphere of menace and despair was everywhere, crowding him in. He stumbled through the woods, tripping over roots and stumps of bushes, slipping in the mud. The moon fell away behind him, and he felt that even that, uneasy ally though it had been, had deserted him. Only a pale trickle of light issued from the torch now. He could look directly at the filament without it blinding him. He shook it savagely and the torch flared for a second before dying down again.

Sykes stumbled onwards, hoping he was going the right way. The spavined branches creaked eerily as the wind gathered strength again and weaved ghostly passages through the tree tops.

Over the thin moan of the wind, Sykes suddenly heard another sound: a thick, heavy sound as though something huge was moving through the woods towards him. He stopped perfectly still and listened, trying to work out where the sound was coming from. His hair prickled as though a colony of ants was scampering to and fro across his scalp. He switched off the torch, useless though it was. He felt as though his breathing was reverberating through the trees and his thumping heart was making the ground shudder.

Something appeared ahead of him, blotting out the night sky. Its bulk was enormous, and it shuffled like an animal. It crossed the path ahead and then was gone.

Sykes stood rooted to the spot, listening to the huge sounds fade away into the trees, his eyes wide as saucers in his face. He was horribly aware that if he had been just a few feet further on, his and the thing's paths would have crossed exactly.

He forced his legs to move. They felt stiff, as though giant matchsticks were jammed up inside them. In contrast, his stomach felt as though it had dissolved into slops. He gagged and tasted egg which made him gag again.

"Come on," he muttered to himself. He bent over, one hand steadying himself against a tree, the other on his stomach. After a few moments of deep breathing, the acid settled and he continued on his way.

A few minutes later the car headlights winked into view between the trees. It was a welcome sight. Sykes realised he had strayed a little too far to his left on the journey back and altered course accordingly. He struggled through the mud and the maze of trees, wheezing and gasping, aware of how exhausted he was. Eagerness to reach the car made him push his body to its limits. *Please let the sarge be there,* he thought desperately. *Please, please.*

But the sarge wasn't there. Sykes ran the last few yards to the car and collapsed against it, hugging the bonnet as though it was a much-loved pet. His initial feeling of relief faded, however, when he noticed that the car was empty and all around was silent. Where the hell had the sarge got to? Was he lost? And what about that thing in the woods? What had it been, human or animal? If it had been human, it must have been as big as that bloke in the James Bond films, the one with the metal teeth. Sykes shuddered. He didn't fancy the idea of chasing a big bugger like that through the woods at night. He let himself into the car. It felt so safe after the oppressive threat of the woods.

Sykes wondered whether he ought to use the car horn and decided that if the sergeant was lost that would probably be the best policy. Clenching his teeth, he gave a long blast. The sound echoed through the woods like the bellow of an enormous beast. If there had been wildlife in the woods, it would have run from the sound. Sykes waited a few moments and tried again. The thing to do was to keep giving blasts on the horn at regular intervals, he thought. That way, if the sarge was lost, the sound would lead him back to the car.

Sykes repeated the action for six or seven minutes, giving half-minute blasts on the horn. It was after he pressed the horn for the fifteenth time that he thought he detected movement in the woods. He strained his eyes into the darkness through the side window. Had he been mistaken, or had he really seen something? It had looked like a shadowy figure moving about behind the first line of trees. He had an uncomfortable feeling that the shape had been trying to get as close as possible without being seen.

He watched the spot where he thought he had seen the movement. There was nothing there now. He was just about to sit back and give another blast on the horn when it stepped out from behind the bushes and trees ahead and began to shamble down the road towards the car.

Sykes felt his body go cold as though his heart had turned to ice. He scrambled for the ignition key with fingers that felt big and clumsy, as though encased in cricket gloves. The thing was approaching quickly despite the fact that it was hunched and shuffling. He could see it was huge and certainly not human. It kept its head down and shied away from the full beam of the headlights. Sykes' fingers gripped the key at last and he twisted it hard. The engine coughed and died. Frantically, Sykes twisted it again. The engine almost kicked and then whined to a stop. The thing was almost upon him. Sykes was aware of its pitted black bulk blotting out the side window. He twisted the key once more. The engine turned over and then roared into life. Sykes tried to keep calm, terrified of stalling. He felt a sudden lurch as the thing made impact with the car. He turned briefly and saw a pitted torso, ragged like mud-caked fur. His heart blocked his throat as he heard a dry, irregular scratching sound on the roof and then the screeching rend of metal above his head. He looked up. The roof of the car was peeling slowly back. The thing was opening it up like a sardine tin!

Sykes jammed his foot on the accelerator and the car shot forward, slewing to the left in the mud. He desperately regained control and directed the car along the narrow dirt track road between the trees, praying that there weren't any sharp bends ahead. He was going much too fast. He glanced briefly into his rearview mirror, and just for a moment he saw the thing in silhouette—a huge, vaguely man-shaped form that stood swaying in the roadway before being swallowed up by the blackness and the trees.

Desk sergeant Cyril Prothwell was having a crafty forty winks over a cup of tea. He felt he deserved it after the hectic night they had just had: roadblocks, patrols in the woods, pub brawls involving villagers, journalists and outsiders, not to mention the problems they had already—a murder hunt without clues, all nineteen missing people still unaccounted for, and fifty-three prisoners on the loose somewhere. At the moment the telephone sitting on Prothwell's desk was the thing he hated most of all in the world. It hadn't stopped ringing all night and dozens of people had been in and out of the station. His throat was sore from trying to make himself heard over the phone above the din that had been going on in the background.

Most of the coppers he hadn't even recognised. Grim-faced, no nonsense buggers drafted in from Cranbydale under the command of the keen and humourless Inspector Garside. There was something to be said, thought Prothwell, for small community policing. It may not be as glamourous or exciting as working in the city, but at least you got to know the public, the folk you were dealing with. As far as the city mob were concerned, lawbreakers were lawbreakers; numbers and statistics, not people with personalities. At least in the village you had time to bridge the gap, to get to know the people involved and assess their motives and reasons. It was sad that community policing could not be employed in the big towns and cities. It had been tried in some areas, but it just didn't work. Pity really.

Prothwell's reflections were interrupted by a screech of brakes from outside, a slam and a shudder. He groaned and glanced at the clock. *Here we go again*, he thought to himself, *the happy hour between ten thirty and eleven thirty when the boozers are turned out of the pubs for the night.* Indicating to a constable to take his place at the desk, Prothwell hurried outside.

He was surprised to find, however, that it was no drunk who was sitting behind the steering wheel, bemusedly trying to work out where the lamppost had sprung from. It was one of his own lads, police constable Richard Sykes, who had appeared in a car that looked as though it had just had an encounter with low flying aircraft. The car had mounted the pavement and made short work of a wire litter bin set in a concrete base. Rubbish lay scattered about like confetti.

Prothwell opened the buckled car door with difficulty, reached in and grabbed the young constable. Sykes stirred and his head lolled. He had a gash on his cheekbone where the impact had thrown him forward on to the steering wheel. Prothwell noted that the boy wasn't wearing a seatbelt and was thankful that the accident hadn't been more serious.

"Constable Sykes," he shouted, and then when the young man failed to respond, "Richard, Richard!"

Sykes brought a trembling hand up towards his face. He opened his eyes and Prothwell was shocked at the expression of terror they held. Sykes focused on the looming face of the sergeant and gave a sudden scream. He flailed weakly at the older man.

Prothwell, taken by surprise, jerked back to avoid the blows and cracked his head on the door frame. He swore, and recovering, reached in and caught hold of the thrashing wrists. Sykes began to whimper and cower away like a small child.

"Hey, Richard. Hey, it's me," Prothwell said. "It's Sergeant Prothwell. You're at the station, boy. Don't worry."

A flicker of recognition appeared in Sykes' eyes and he looked around him. "Sarge?" he said.

"That's right, lad, that's right. Come on now. Let's go into the station and you can tell me all about it."

He coaxed Sykes out of the car. Sykes allowed himself to be led into the station. Prothwell propped him against a wall and pulled up a chair. Sykes slumped onto it gratefully.

"Bloody hell, what a state," exclaimed the young PC behind the desk. "What happened, sarge? Has he been kicked in?"

"No, I don't think so," said Prothwell. "He came haring around the corner as though all the demons of Hell were after him. Crashed into the dustbin outside. The car's in a bit of a state."

"Well, it would be," reasoned the constable.

"Hmmm. Funny thing though—part of the roof is peeled back. Almost as though someone's tried to open it with a giant tin opener."

"Probably had another accident earlier."

"Could be," said Prothwell.

"He's not pissed, is he?" piped up Constable Atkins who had been sitting, typing, over the other side of the room. Prothwell glared at him.

"Constable Atkins, if you have nothing useful to contribute, I suggest you shut up," he snapped.

"Huh. Just like being back at school," muttered Atkins with a hangdog expression, and bent back over his typewriter as Prothwell gave him another sharp look.

"Johnny might not have been wrong though, sir," said the young constable whose name was Nuttall. "Do you think he has been drinking?"

"If he has there's no sign of it," said Prothwell. "I can't smell it on his breath."

Atkins gave up his typing and walked over. "Dicky was out with Sergeant Hopper, wasn't he, sir?"

"Yes."

"Well, where's the sarge then?"

"I don't know," said Prothwell, "but as soon as this one can talk, I intend to find out."

"They were out in the woods, weren't they, sir?" said Nuttall. His tone seemed to suggest there was a hidden meaning to his words and made Prothwell look up quickly.

"So?"

Nuttall looked uncomfortable. He reddened slightly and shrugged his shoulders. "Nothing, sir, really. It's just that... well, some funny things have been happening there recently."

Prothwell frowned and didn't answer. He turned his attention to the slumped figure on the chair. "Constable Sykes... Constable Sykes, wake up," he urged. Sykes' reaction was a low moan and a flickering of the eyelids.

"I think he heard you, sir," said Atkins. Prothwell, irritated by the two young constables who were hanging over the desk like medical students examining a particularly interesting case, barked, "Atkins, make us all some tea, and Nuttall, go and get the first aid box. We'd better see to this cut."

"Yessir," they responded smartly and disappeared on their errands while Prothwell made another attempt at reviving the constable.

Suddenly Sykes moaned, opened his eyes wide, and stared straight at Prothwell. Prothwell moved back a little, startled by the ferocity of Sykes' stare. Sykes reached out a hand and gripped Prothwell's lapel.

"It came for me... it tried to get me," he whispered. His hand slid away.

"What tried to get you, Richard? What was it?" said Prothwell.

Sykes shuddered. "Don't know," he muttered. "Something big. Not a man."

"Where was this, Richard? In the woods? Did it happen in the woods?"

Sykes looked at him again, the wildness of remembrance

creeping into his eyes. "In the woods, yes. It was huge." He emphasized the word *huge*, saying it as a child might to impress his friends.

"Was it an animal, Richard?" asked the sergeant gently, coaxing.

"Yes. An animal!" Sykes voice suddenly became strong, almost a shout. Atkins poked his head out from the tiny kitchenette, roused by the noise, and asked, "Everything all right, sir?"

Prothwell waved a hand impatiently for silence. He couldn't afford to lose Sykes' attention now. The boy was obviously under a great deal of stress.

"What sort of animal was it, Richard?"

Sykes' voice became subdued, more coherent. "Dunno," he said. "Something really big. A bear. Or a gorilla."

Prothwell's voice became urgent. "Now are you sure about this, Richard? Are you absolutely certain?"

"Yes, yes."

"And where's Sergeant Hopper?"

Sykes looked confused. "Huh?"

"Hopper, Richard. Sergeant Hopper. He went out with you tonight. Where is he now?"

Sykes shook his head. "Dunno. Couldn't find him. I did look for him, Sarge, but he wasn't there. He wasn't anywhere."

"All right, son, take it easy," said Prothwell, putting a hand on the young constable's shoulder. Sykes slumped back down in the chair, his body becoming slack and relaxed again. Prothwell straightened up and turned to Nuttall who had been hovering uncertainly for several minutes, the white first aid box clutched in his hands.

"See to Constable Sykes, Nuttall," he said. He picked up the telephone and began to dial.

"Who you calling, Sarge?" asked Atkins, coming out of the kitchenette.

"Inspector Garside," replied Prothwell crisply. "I think we've just been given a lead on our murderer."

Keith woke and for a few seconds experienced complete disorientation. Where the hell was he? He was sitting up in a chair, not lying in his bed at home as he had thought. The lines of the room were unfamiliar and what was that heavy breathing he could hear? Then his thoughts settled in his head and he remembered. He was on guard—or rather he was supposed to be.

He must have dozed off. He stretched in the chair, groaning at the cramped stiffness in his neck and back. The heavy breathing came from Martin, stretched out on the settee, a sleeping bag curled around him like a cocoon. Keith shivered despite the warm air and stretched his arms and legs to get his sluggish circulation going again. He looked at his watch. It was a little after six thirty. Yawning, he went into the kitchen, made himself a cup of coffee, and had a wash in the sink, using one of three towels that were spread over the radiator to dry himself. After the wash, he felt much better.

He took his coffee into the sitting room and stood with his back to the mantlepiece, sipping it. For a little while at least, the house was at peace and Keith felt reluctant to break the magic of sleep that hung over it.

A sudden sharp clack made him jump. His coffee slopped in his cup, a few drops abandoning ship and plunging to the carpet. Keith gave a humourless snort of breath through his nose. It was only the letterbox, for God's sake.

For want of something better to do, he strolled to the front door and picked up the mail. The postman delivered early in these parts, he thought idly. He glanced at the letters which were mostly bills and tossed them onto the telephone table. When he had finished his coffee, he put on his jacket and looked around for pen and paper. He found a biro with a chewed end and tore a strip off yesterday's newspaper. He wrote 'Gone back home. The roads should be clear this early in the morning. Back soon. See you. Keith.'

Then he propped the note up on the coffee table where Martin would see it, left the house, got into his car and drove away.

Margaret Francis lay in bed and listened to the sounds coming from Keith's study. She had been woken up just a few minutes ago with what sounded like someone knocking at the front door. However, when the sounds continued, Margaret realised they were coming not from outside, but from inside the house, and somewhere close by at that.

Her first confused thoughts had been that Keith was up and about early, making breakfast for them both. Then she remembered he had not slept at home last night, and she pulled the covers up tight around her, the beginnings of a crawling fear chilling her into immobility.

She tried to convince herself that he had returned that morning and was in his study now, looking for something. But if he had come home, wouldn't he have looked in on her and said hello? Maybe she had been sleeping. Yes, that must be it. She had been asleep and Keith hadn't wanted to wake her. But she couldn't quite believe that. For one thing, it was too early for Keith to come back. It was only 6:55 and he was not renowned for being an early bird (she would have been surprised to learn he was on his way home at that very moment). On the other hand, he had been obsessed with that silly book just recently. Maybe he had got up early just so he could come home and start work.

But there was something about the intensity of the noises that troubled her. The thuds and bumps were loud, no attempt at concealment, as though someone wanted to attract her attention and this was the only method by which they knew how to do so.

She got out of bed, put on slippers and dressing gown, and picked up the half snooker cue that lay along the length of the wall on Keith's side of the bed. She had no idea what it was doing there, but it certainly gave her some reassurance now as she clenched it in her hand.

As soon as she pushed open the bedroom door she heard singing. No, not singing. Chanting. That's what it was. Chanting, coming from behind the study door.

She stood and listened, feeling the flesh on her body creep and the hairs prickle on her neck. It was a man's voice, deep and resonant, yet at the same time quavery, suggesting great age. She strained to hear the words. They sounded jumbled and strange, completely alien.

She felt cold with fear, yet at the same time entranced, soothed. It was a lullaby rhythm, one that floated with you into sleep. Alarmed that she might be falling under some kind of spell, Margaret braced herself and shoved the door open.

The sunlight streaming in through the study window hurt her eyes. She squinted and shielded her face with her hand. After a moment, her eyes became accustomed to the brightness, and as they did so she saw a figure standing by her husband's desk.

It was an old man, a tramp, wearing a dirty, stained overcoat and a wide-brimmed hat. He was standing in a spotlight of sunshine, mumbling to himself like a child reciting a nursery rhyme in a school play. All Margaret could see of his face was his lips moving with shadow and his chin which was heavy with stubble. As she entered the room, he looked up. His face was dark and swarthy, lined like wood, and his eyes glittered a brilliant blue.

It was not the figure himself, but the fact that he was in her house at all that froze Margaret's heart and forced a scream from her throat. The figure seemed to react to her scream. The solidness of flesh and bone seemed to melt away and the figure became vaguely indistinct, as though it was not a real person at all, but a three-dimensional projection.

As Margaret watched, the figure became even more shadowy and intangible. An invisible wind seemed to whip about the frail form, dissolving the hair into smoke and smudging the features from the old man's face. The ghostly form came towards her, stretching out a gnarled brown hand that was fading into shadow, riveting her with blue, blue eyes. The eyes seemed to fill her and Margaret passed out.

And that was how Keith found her, sprawled in the doorway of his study when he arrived home a little under half an hour later.

PART THREE

ICE

CHAPTER THIRTEEN
STORMS

Inspector Garside was pale and thoughtful. "Who found the body?" he asked.

Sergeant Prothwell nodded over to where a willowy young constable was slumped in a police car, his legs dangling out of the open door. The constable's head was hunched down between his shoulders, his chin on his chest, his hands clenched tightly together.

"Young Atkins, sir. It was a bit of a shock for him, I think."

"Yes, well," said Garside, glancing across, "it was a bit of a shock for us all." He spoke loudly to make himself heard above the barrage of rain. Prothwell nodded again, causing water to drip furiously from the peak of his cap.

Garside thrust his hands into the pockets of his overcoat and trudged over to the car. Above him, clouds like filthy shredded sponges rolled across an iron sky. He was faintly irritated by Atkins' failure to acknowledge his approach but tried not to show it. He pulled open the back door and sat down next to the constable, taking care that the oozing mud did not ruin his meticulously polished shoes.

"You all right, son?" he said at length.

Atkins inclined his head briefly. There was another pause before Garside said, "You sure? You don't look it."

Atkins closed his eyes and swallowed before looking up. "I'll be okay, sir," he said in a faint voice. "It's just that I've never seen nothing like... that before."

"There's not many of us have, son," said Garside. "Homicide is always an unpleasant business, but this one... well, it's going a bit far."

Atkins attempted a smile but could manage only a grimace.

"I was talking to Sergeant Hopper only yesterday, sir," he said, "but today... well, if it hadn't been for the uniform I wouldn't have recognised him."

Garside put a hand awkwardly on Atkins' shoulder. "You have a word with Sergeant Prothwell," he said. "Take the rest of the day off. You'll have to pop down to the station, though, before you go. Do you think you're up to it?"

Atkins nodded. "Yes sir."

"Good lad," said Garside and stood up. He squelched back through the mud to his own car, anxious to get away from the dismal scene.

He pulled open the passenger door and got in. Once inside, he let out a long breath and rubbed a hand across his eyes and forehead as though to erase the unpleasantness from his mind.

"Bad one, sir?" enquired Sergeant Freeman, his driver.

"You can say that again," replied Garside. "The poor bugger looked as though he'd had an argument with a combine harvester."

Freeman pulled a face. "Do you think it's true what they reckon, sir? About this being the work of some animal?"

"I just don't know. I laughed when they first came up with that, but after seeing the condition of this body... well, I'd hate to meet any man who could inflict such injuries."

"Don't they reckon it's a grizzly bear doing it?" said Freeman.

"Yes, or something similar," agreed Garside.

Freeman unwrapped a stick of gum and popped it thoughtfully into his mouth. "But what I want to know," he said, "is where something like that could have come from? And more importantly, where does it go to? You'd think someone would've noticed." He offered Garside a stick of gum. Garside waved it away in distaste. It made him think of a dried sliver of brain.

"There's a couple of officers back at the station checking up on all the zoos and circuses in the area," said Garside. "Maybe something's escaped which hasn't been reported."

"Not reported?" said Freeman incredulously. "That's not very likely is it, sir?"

"No," said Garside, "I agree with you. It's not very likely. But what else is there to do under the circumstances?"

Freeman shook his head. "Bloody hell, sir, it's all a bit far-fetched. Like one of them werewolf films on the telly."

Garside snorted. It was the nearest he could get to a laugh. "Come on," he said wearily. "Let's get back to the station. There's nothing more we can do here. Maybe our zoology expert will be able to shed some light."

"Who's that then, sir?"

"Oh, some professor or other, coming over from Leeds to have a look at the body."

"Rather him than me," said Freeman. He manoeuvred the car over the rutted ground between the haphazardly parked police vehicles. An ambulance was sitting at the edge of the little clearing like a sinister ice cream van and, as they passed, Freeman noticed two men in white sliding a stretcher into the open back doors. The stretcher was covered by a red sheet and Freeman shuddered at the outline of the form beneath.

He had seen plenty of murder victims in his eleven years with the force and had never been unduly disturbed by them before. But this one made his skin crawl. As the ambulance doors closed on the stretcher, Freeman thought that perhaps it would have made him feel better if the thing under the sheet had been shaped like a human being.

Celia, the maid at The Shoulder of Mutton, deposited a pile of towels in the laundry basket, then hurried to the door of Room 10. She wiped her hands self-consciously on her apron as she put an ear to the door and listened. Hearing nothing, she rapped hesitantly.

"Who's 'at?" came a voice slurred with sleep.

"It's me, Celia, Mr. Donahue. Please open up. I've got something to tell you." She looked round nervously, expecting the bad-tempered landlady, Edith Carter, to come steaming around the corner at any moment.

"Just a minute," said Donahue.

There was a pause and then the door opened. Donahue was

wearing a red dressing gown which contrasted sharply with his white legs. His hair was wild, and he was unshaven. He scrutinized Celia through bloodshot, heavy-lidded eyes as he tied his dressing gown cord.

"What is it, Celia?" he asked wearily.

"They've found another one, Mr. Donahue. In the woods," Celia blurted out.

"Another one? What do you mean?"

"A body, Mr. Donahue. There's been another murder."

"What?" All traces of sleep fled from Donahue in an instant. He looked around wildly as though uncertain what to do next. "Er... erm... give me ten minutes to get washed and dressed, and then I want you to tell me all you know. Do the others know about this?"

"The others?" Celia was confused.

"The other reporters? The London mob?"

"Oh, I don't know, Mr. Donahue. I suppose they might do. Word gets around."

"Right!" Donahue held up both hands and splayed his fingers. "Ten minutes," he repeated and slammed the door.

Celia nodded at the closed door, a little bemused by Donahue's urgency.

Ten minutes later, Donahue was sitting in the small dining room eating a hasty breakfast and listening to Celia. The bacon and eggs on his plate were as rubbery as joke shop novelties and he forced them down with difficulty, thinking it may be the last chance he would get to eat for some time. It was only seven forty, still too early for most breakfasters, but despite the emptiness of the room, Celia kept her voice low, repeating what she had heard Marjorie Atkins tell Edith that morning with a dark, dramatic reverence.

When she had done, Donahue thanked her and went back to his room for his parka, into the pockets of which he stuffed wallet, notebook and pen. He slipped from his room, descending the back stairs that led out into the carpark unobserved.

The rain was dreary and pitiless. It sidled down the outside of the pub, transforming the windows into streaming eyes and the walls into slabs of dribbling chocolate. The trees behind the pub sighed and hissed as though complaining about the weather. Donahue yanked up his hood and broke into a sprint. The rain drummed around him as he groped for his car keys. He found them at last and opened the car door.

"Miserable crappy weather," he muttered to himself as he slammed the door shut again.

He eased the car out of the carpark and onto the main road. Despite his grumblings, the sound of the rain's muffled clattering on the roof soothed him. The windscreen wipers swept away great swarms of kamikaze raindrops.

The streets of Limefield in the early morning were almost deserted. A flapping, nodding thing on a bike swept past to deliver newspapers. A black bulk with a trilby let itself into the butcher's shop to chop meat. Soon, thought Donahue, the hostilities would start again. Villagers, journalists, sightseers and police, all watchful of each other's movements.

He drove steadily and thoughtfully, the village gradually giving way to the farmland, which swayed and blurred between the wipers. Above the car, the bruised sky bore down oppressively.

Huddled over the wheel, Donahue pondered over the implications of this latest murder and wondered how it would all end. Celia's news that morning had shocked him, but at the same time he had been expecting it, like waiting for news of an elderly relative who is not expected to last out the night. As yet, only the story of the first murders had been covered by the major dailies, but even the ripple of nationwide interest that they had attracted had been enough to unsettle the sedate predictability of village life. Donahue foresaw the likelihood of an even more unpleasant and violent upheaval in the village when the story of "The Winter Tree", as it had been dubbed, reached national newsstands that morning. Limefield would become a household word. Visitors to the village would increase dramatically. More police would be needed to deal with the siege. The media would hover like vultures, picking, probing, dissecting, gnawing at the bones until they were free of flesh.

And, amidst all this confusion, the terror would still be there, lurking insidiously, waiting for the chance to strike again.

Donahue shuddered, shaking off his apprehension. *Getting a bit dramatic aren't we, Philip?* he thought, and smiled grimly.

He was so immersed in his thoughts that he almost didn't notice the fence. He braked sharply, causing the car to waver on the slippery ground. He sat for a moment, then got out and lumbered down the lane.

The fence was hastily erected with rough lengths of timber, but it looked solid enough. Barbed wire coiled, bristling, along the top. The path beyond the fence marked the start of Redheath Woods. In the rain, the tree branches seemed to writhe and squirm like black tentacles, and the ruts in the ground were like soft, putty mouths, drinking thirstily. Donahue caught a glimpse of a skeletal shape from the corner of his eye and heard a hungry bubbling sound. He whirled, but the shape was only a scarecrow drooping forgotten in a field, and the bubbling came from a drainage grille, choked with sludge.

A sign on the gate attracted his attention. **NO TRESPASSING** it said in large red capitals, and then underneath in smaller letters:

By police order, Redheath Woods are out of bounds to the general public until further notice. Anyone found beyond this point will be prosecuted.

- Inspector J.M. Garside, Cranbydale Metropolitan Police Force.

"Charming," muttered Donahue to himself as he lingered, undecided, for a moment. Should he obey the sign and make his way back to the village, or should he ignore the warning and make his way towards the scene of the crime?

It was really no contest. Donahue was, after all, a journalist, even if he didn't possess the ruthlessness of many of his London counterparts. He tugged gingerly at the barbed wire, trying to flatten the lethal coils. When he was satisfied that they couldn't do him any permanent damage, he began to climb.

The fence was only six feet high, but it was tough going. His feet, clad in gripless shoes, kept slipping on the wet wood, and his jeans had a nasty habit of ensnaring themselves on the barbed wire when he was at his most precarious. At last, he struggled to the top and was poised, one foot on either side, ready to swing his leg over when behind him he heard a voice.

"Oy, you, what the hell do you think you're doing?"

"Shit," said Donahue. He swiveled round, almost losing his balance, to see who had shouted. A policeman wearing a blue plastic topcoat was advancing determinedly. Donahue groaned. Further up the lane, nosing its way out of the shelter of a barn-obscured farmyard, was a police car.

The policeman stopped a few yards from the fence and regarded Donahue, his bulk threatening under his layer of clothes. He raised his arm and very deliberately pointed first at Donahue and then at the ground. "Down," he ordered, his face as stormy as the day.

Donahue clambered down with difficulty, reeling like a schoolboy caught in some mischievous act. He wiped his hands together nervously as the policeman took a step forward, and said, "I'm sorry, officer, I—"

"Can't you bloody read?" interrupted the policeman.

Donahue assumed the question was rhetorical, but quickly changed his mind when he realised the man was waiting, hands on hips, for an answer.

"Well, yes of course, but—" he began.

"Then what the bloody hell do you think you're up to? Are you people stupid or something?"

"No. I'm not a sightseer, I'm Philip Donahue," said Donahue, hoping the policeman would recognise the name. He didn't. Donahue groped in his pocket for his press card. "I work for the *Cranbydale Observer*," he said. He produced his card and handed it over. The policeman looked at it, turned it over, and then handed it back, unimpressed.

"I worked on the original murder story," Donahue continued. "I heard there was another murder last night. I was hoping to get down here to talk to someone about it before all the big boys in the village started muscling in."

"Well you won't find anyone in there now," said the policeman, obviously satisfied by the look of disappointment on Donahue's face. "They took the body away at seven o' clock this morning."

"Oh, I see." Donahue thought for a moment. "I don't

suppose you can tell me anything, can you?" he ventured. "I understand the man who died was a sergeant at Limefield station?"

"Sorry, pal."

"Well perhaps you can give me the name of someone to get in touch with, then? It would save me a great deal of time."

The policeman's expression was not encouraging. "I understand Inspector Garside will be giving a press conference in Limefield village hall at eleven o' clock this morning," he said in a bored voice.

"But I was hoping to have a private word," said Donahue. "Look, it's only quarter past eight now. I've got nearly three hours to wait."

"That's your watchout, mate. Now I'm getting very wet here, so I suggest you get into that car of yours and go back the way you've come."

Donahue opened his mouth, then, sighing, shut it again. One look at the policeman's face was enough to convince him it was no use pursuing the argument. He trudged back to his car and unlocked the door. He got in, cringing as his wet jeans squelched on the seat. The policemen sat, watching suspiciously, as he started the car and turned it back up the lane. Donahue waved to them as he jolted past. He got no response.

He decided to go back to The Shoulder, have a bath, change, and make a few phone calls before heading for the press conference in the village hall. He could see it was going to be a long and frustrating day.

⁂

Martin swam lazily upwards through a bubbling green spiral. At his side was a dolphin, and the dolphin was Keith. Only the fact that Keith was a dolphin didn't strike Martin as unusual. It was the most natural thing in the world. They were swimming upwards and upwards, following the bubbles. It was a long way, but where they were going was a good place.

Suddenly, the glowing green light around them dimmed. It became oily and lethargic, and the spinning bubbles started to distort and burst like light bulbs. A voice came to Martin, a dragging, dreamy voice that was indescribably chilling. "Martin, Martin," it repeated over and over, and the sound of his own name seemed to pluck him onwards. The dolphin, Keith, became very agitated.

"We must go back, Martin," the dolphin said. "We must go back. Don't look up."

Martin tried not to look, but his own name became an invisible wire that snared his jaw and wrenched his head back. The soothing green spiral had been replaced by a dark and forbidding landscape. A livid purple sky, striped with red wounds, heaved sluggishly over black earth. And from the earth sprouted hundreds of crosses, all charred and hung with ugly black chains.

Martin tried to backpedal like the dolphin, Keith, had done, but something pulled him onwards. He looked down and saw a gigantic chain wrapped round his waist. He tried to loosen the chain, but it was no use. He felt himself being tugged higher and higher.

He looked up again. In the middle of the black landscape was a huge bent tree. And with a thick and cloying horror Martin saw that the limbs of the tree were moving, working like arms, reeling him in...

"Martin."

Martin awoke. Kevin was leaning over him, shaking him. For a split second, an afterimage of the dream stayed with Martin and threatened to engulf him. Then it slipped away and lost itself, leaving only his tensely pounding heart as a reminder. Martin reached out and gripped Kevin's hand. He shuffled from his sleeping bag and sat up on the settee.

"Phew, I'm glad you woke me up. You've just rescued me from a nightmare," he said. He looked around him. The plump, benign furnishings and soft, familiar colours eased his racing body back to normality. He turned his attention to his friend. Kevin looked pale and washed out, but Martin noted that he seemed calmer, less shocked than the previous night. "You all right?" he asked cautiously.

Kevin shrugged. "I've got used to it a bit I suppose, but I'm still worried sick. I did a lot of thinking last night."

"Do you want to talk about it?"

Kevin looked noncommittal. He began to run his finger abstractedly over the outlines of the speech balloons in one of Jamie's old *Beano*s. "I suppose so. You want any breakfast?"

"Yeah. Hey, I'll get it. You sit down."

"No, it's okay. I'm not an invalid. I've got to do something."

"Well let's both do it," said Martin. "We can talk at the same time."

"Okay."

Martin pushed himself out of the sleeping bag and padded over to the chair where his clothes were. He pulled on his jeans. The sleeping bag crouched on the settee like a fleshy blue worm, its pouting red lips edged with glinting teeth. Martin smoothed out the mounds and rolled the bag up.

"Where's Keith?" Kevin asked suddenly. For a second an image of a dolphin flashed into Martin's mind. He said, "Uh... I don't know. He was sitting there last time I saw him. He must be around somewhere."

"What's this?" Kevin picked up the strip of paper Keith had left. He deciphered the scrawl with difficulty and then read it aloud to Martin.

"Oh well, one less for breakfast anyway," Martin said.

They went into the kitchen. The rain on the window split the street up into shards of black and grey. The slithering glass made Kevin think of something pulsing and jelly-like, enveloping the house.

He fumbled about the kitchen as though unfamiliar with it. Martin said, "So what did you think about last night?"

"What? Oh... this and that, y'know. I was just clearing things up in my own mind. Yesterday I was so confused. Nothing seemed real. And the more I tried to make sense of things, the more confused I became."

Martin nodded sagely, though he couldn't identify with the feeling at all.

"That... man I killed yesterday," Kevin continued, putting Weetabix into a bowl, "it couldn't be helped. I mean, I had no choice. It was either him or us. He was... I don't know, possessed or something. You see that, don't you, Mart?"

"Yeah, course I do," replied Martin. "You did the right thing, Kev. You saved all our lives."

Kevin nodded and his face twitched into a grateful smile. Martin realised it was the first time he had seen his friend smile since the kidnap and he felt strangely moved.

"Don't worry, Kev, we'll be all right. You'll see," he said. "We'll get your mum and the kids back somehow."

Kevin nodded again, more eagerly this time, half-convinced by Martin's resolve. "So... what do we do now?" he said.

"Wait, I suppose, until Keith gets back."

Martin saw Kevin's face fall at the prospect of more waiting and wished he could have followed up his confident assurances with something more positive. They both turned at the clack of the letterbox. Kevin made as if to stand up, but Martin said, "You sit down. I'll go."

Kevin settled himself in his seat again and continued munching his way stolidly through his bowl of Weetabix. The rain thrashing against the window made him shiver, but it was comfortable sitting in the warm kitchen, like having a shield from the world.

"There's a meeting in the village hall this afternoon," said Martin, handing Kevin the soggy handbill that had been delivered. "Everyone in the village is invited to attend to air their views on what's been going on. The police must be getting desperate for ideas."

"That's hardly surprising," said Kevin in a subdued voice.

"It should be worth going to," said Martin. "It'll be interesting to see what the villagers think about all this."

"What about Keith?" said Kevin.

Martin considered. "I'd better give him a ring. He wouldn't want to miss this." He went through to the hall and began to dial Keith's number.

Kevin looked out of the window. The rain seemed to be easing a little. Up above, the sullen clouds picked themselves apart. They reminded Kevin of himself. He gripped the coffee mug as though it was his one link with reality and wondered how long he could hold himself together.

Donahue stood in the rain, getting his second pair of trousers that day soaked through. He jostled bad-temperedly for position on the village hall steps with the other journalists, waiting for Inspector Garside to grace them with his presence.

"C'mon, where the hell's Garside? It's quarter past," shouted a sandy-haired man with bristling eyebrows and sharp elbows. The police constable standing in the alcove at the top of the steps shrugged, obviously enjoying the discomfort of the huddled group.

"Watch what you're doing," snapped Donahue as the spiky rib of an umbrella lunged and jabbed him in the head. He glared at the two people sheltered underneath. The woman was unscrewing the lid of a thermos flask whilst the man held the umbrella. The woman glanced up disinterestedly and gave a short, "Sorry."

Donahue rubbed his head and gasped as yet another elbow caught him in the back. He swung out backwards with his arm and was gratified to feel it make contact with something solid. He heard a muttered "Oof", and then a voice said, "Fucking pillock," which made Donahue grin.

Heads in the crowd turned as though all pulled by the same string as a car sloshed round the corner and drew to a halt, spraying up water for crisp bags to surf on. The door opened unhurriedly and a beefy man with oiled-down hair and a clipped moustache emerged, wearing a grey overcoat. There were a few sarcastic cries of "Hurrah" and "Such punctuality" among the journalists.

"Sorry I'm late," Garside said as he weaved his way through the crowd and up the steps. The constable at the top produced a key and unlocked the door, much to the chagrin of many of the journalists, and Garside hurried inside.

The journalists surged forward, eager to get a prominent seat. Donahue moved forward with the crush.

"One at a time, please, ladies and gentlemen," bellowed the police constable, forcing them back. An elbow made contact painfully with Donahue's forehead, and a foot scraped down the back of his heel, almost pulling off his shoe. *If this is competitive journalism you can forget it*, he thought.

It was like being in the middle of a football crowd.

A few minutes later they were all sitting in the village hall. Overcoats and umbrellas dripped from the backs of chairs.

It was a spacious if rather bare hall. Rows of seats squatted patiently, gazing expectantly up at the stage. The last time Donahue had been here had been to review the Limefield Amateur Dramatics production of *The Mikado* for the Observer. That night the damp patches on the peeling back wall had been obscured by elaborate Chinese drapes, and the shabby trimmings had been skillfully obliterated by lighting. Now the stage reminded him of a faded actor, haggard without the makeup.

Garside ascended the steps at the side of the stage, carrying a chair. He plumped it down in the centre, then peeled off his overcoat and draped it over the back. Already questions were being shouted out, like the swell of catcalls. Garside held up his hands for silence.

"If we could just have a bit of order please, ladies and gentlemen." The hubbub died down. "That's better, thank you. Now, before we start, I'd just like to say a few things. I've called this press conference here this morning for a number of reasons. Number one is to answer any questions you may have concerning the murder which took place in the woods last night, and number two is to inform you that there is a meeting here this afternoon to which everyone is invited. What I want to make clear, however, is that this afternoon's meeting is intended as a platform for the villagers to air their views, and whilst you lot are not actually banned from attending, you will be expected to keep a very low profile. So, if you want to ask anything do it now. It will not be tolerated at this afternoon's meeting. Okay, who wants to start the ball rolling?"

Questions immediately blasted like ammunition. Donahue, somewhat cowed by the aggression of the London reporters, was content just to sit and scribble details in his notebook.

"Could you tell us about the murder?"

"What do you want to know?"

Who was killed for a start?"

"It was a police sergeant from Limefield named Graham Hopper."

"What were the circumstances of his death?"

"He was on night patrol with a colleague in the woods. Apparently, a figure appeared from the bushes and they were forced to swerve the car into a tree to avoid it. Hopper followed the figure into the woods and never returned. His body was found early this morning."

"What was the name of his colleague? Could we talk to him?"

"I'm afraid not. He's on leave. He's not expected back for a few days."

"Where can we find him? Could you tell us his home address?"

"I'm afraid not."

"Why not, Inspector? Has he got something to hide?"

"Certainly not. I just don't want you hounding my men when they are supposed to be on holiday."

"Was the body found near to where the first murders took place?"

"Not especially so. The two areas are approximately a mile and a half apart."

"Can we assume it's the same murderer that killed the first two?"

"Yes, I think I can safely say that we are dealing with one murderer."

"So, you don't think it's a gang killing as has been suggested?"

"I think that is highly unlikely."

"Do you have any suspects?"

"A number of people are helping with enquiries."

"Could you give us any names?"

"No."

"There have been rumours that the murders were committed by a wild animal. Is there any truth in this, Inspector?"

Hesitation. "Every possibility is being explored."

"So, there is some truth in it?"

"As I say, every possibility is being explored."

"What sort of state was the body of the murder victim in, Inspector?"

"It was badly mutilated."

"So, it could very possibly have been the work of an animal?"

"The forensic experts are working on it now."

"But what is your honest opinion, Inspector?"

"I cannot pass opinions without evidence."

"Are any of the events over the last week connected?"

"Which events are those?"

"Well, the fire, the prison breakout, the disappearances, the sheep killing, the murders..."

"There is no evidence to suggest so."

"Oh, but surely there's a connection!"

"As I said, there is no evidence to suggest so."

"So, you are saying that all these events are separate issues?"

"As far as we know, yes."

"Do you think the killer will strike again?"

"That's impossible for me to say."

"Do you hope to make an arrest soon?"

"We are always hopeful."

"How are police investigations in this matter proceeding?"

"Investigations are proceeding satisfactorily."

"How do the police propose to safeguard the lives of the villagers whilst the killer is at large?"

"By stressing the need for caution and co-operation. Much of it is up to the individuals themselves. They cannot expect the police to take responsibility. Having said that, we have taken steps to try and reduce the risk of this sort of thing happening again. The number of police officers in Limefield has been quadrupled over the last week. House calls are regularly being made around the area, and the woods themselves have been cordoned off and declared out of bounds to the public."

"Don't you think that last step is taking the law into your

own hands, rather?"

"Madam, we are the law." Laughter.

"What about the people who live right up on the edge of the woods? The farmers and their families?"

"What about them?"

"Is anything being done for them?"

"Well naturally they are included in our programme of house calls. We do try to make sure each household is checked up on at least once a day, but that's not always possible."

"Is there any possibility of evacuation for these people?"

"No, none whatsoever. If the farmers wish to vacate their premises, then it is entirely up to them."

"Do you have any comment on the so-called winter tree?"

"No."

"So, you don't think it bears any connection to this case?"

"None that I can see."

"There is talk in the village, Inspector, of curses, of witchcraft, of devil-worship... this sort of thing. What would you say to the suggestion that the murders are the result of some form of paranormal activity?"

"Preposterous. We are conducting a murder inquiry, not some supernatural crusade."

"So, you completely disregard the possibility of supernatural influence?"

"Of course. This isn't the Middle Ages."

"Do you believe in the power of the Devil, Inspector?"

"What's that supposed to mean?"

"Well it must be said that the injuries of the first two victims were somewhat... spectacular. Inhuman, some might think."

"Madam, I find this line of questioning rather pointless. All I can say is that whether the murderer is human or otherwise he or she must still abide by the laws of this country. At the end of the day it is still up to us to see that justice, as we know it, is done. And if that means slapping the cuffs on Old Nick himself then so be it."

There was ragged laughter at this. The woman who had asked the question looked furious.

Gradually, the questions became fewer and fewer. One

journalist, apparently from some backstreet minority interest magazine, continued doggedly to pursue the supernatural angle, and it soon became clear that Garside was becoming irritated. It was when the journalist asked how many UFO sightings there had been in the area over the last year that Garside decided it was time to call it a day. He thanked the journalists for their time, retrieved his coat from the back of the chair and left, hurrying along the aisle to the door. A few unanswered questions pursued him, only to settle uneasily as Garside closed the door firmly behind him.

The slam of the door was followed, as if on cue, by a general scraping of chairs. Conversation babbled as the journalists split up into their respective pub-going groups. Donahue stood up, cringing at the clamminess of his jeans. He looked at his watch. Almost lunchtime. He decided to go back to The Shoulder for something to eat and to change his clothes yet again in readiness for the meeting in the village hall that afternoon.

⚬❧❧❧❧⚬

Margaret Francis looked up at the ceiling and wondered why the house suddenly seemed so threatening. Faces appeared to writhe and snarl on the textured surface, but of course when she looked closer it was only the moving shadows of rain from the window.

She shivered. Her little house, her home, had been infiltrated by something inexplicable. And because it was inexplicable, it was frightening. She thought of the old man, of the way he had reached out for her, of the way his blue eyes had seemed to swallow her mind. The thought disturbed her, picked and probed at the organized security of her world. She squirmed lower in her bed as though to evade scrutinous fingers.

The door opened, and Keith entered balancing a breakfast tray. "Come on, Mags, sit up," he ordered cheerfully.

"Put it down there, she said, indicating the bedside table. Keith did so.

"Don't you want anything?" he asked.

Mags shook her head miserably. "My stomach is still too

wobbly. I don't think I could keep anything down."

"Not even a cup of tea?" Keith said enticingly.

Mags considered. "Well, maybe a very small one."

As Keith poured the tea, he said, "Do you feel like talking about it yet?"

"About what?" The casualness of Mags' expression was a little too smooth to be convincing.

"About why you fainted," Keith said firmly.

Mags pretended to preoccupy herself with wiping an invisible mark from the rim of the teacup with her finger.

"I... I just fainted, that's all. People do sometimes. It's nothing to be worried about."

"Rubbish!" snapped Keith. "I know you. You've never fainted before. Are you ill? Shall I call the doctor?"

Mags looked alarmed.

"No, there's no need for the doctor."

"Then tell me why you fainted," Keith persisted. He tried to catch her eye, but she avoided him skillfully, a sure sign that she had something to hide. There was silence for a moment which Keith broke by saying, "Right, I'm calling the doctor."

He jumped up, but Mags grabbed his wrist.

"No, don't," she exclaimed. Her grip slackened and her voice became quieter. "I'll... I'll tell you."

Keith settled himself back on the bed again and crossed his arms. There was an embarrassed pause. The ticking of the rain raced with the ticking of the bedside clock.

Well... I'm waiting," Keith said.

Mags smiled uncertainly. "You'll think I'm going loopy," she said.

"No, I won't," promised Keith. "Come on, Mags. You know you can tell me."

"I saw... a man," she mumbled as though her mouth was packed with cotton wool.

"A man? Here in the house?" Keith's thoughts went back to just two nights ago when he had been certain there was someone in his study. "Was it in the study?" he asked.

Mags looked up. "Yes, how did you know?"

Keith shrugged. "You were lying just inside the study door."

"Oh. Yes. Of course."

"What was he like, this man?" asked Keith, and then, before Mags could answer, another thought came to him and he said, "He didn't hurt you, did he?"

"Oh no, nothing like that," replied Mags. "No, he was an old man. He had an overcoat and... and a big hat... sort of shabby and dirty. He might have been a tramp."

"A tramp?" Keith was bewildered. "Well, what did he do, this tramp?"

"I heard this... this chanting," said Mags, "coming from your study. I went in and there he was. That big book on your desk was open and he seemed to be reading from it."

Keith sat bolt upright in sudden excitement. "My book? You mean the old red one?" Mags nodded. "Can you remember what he was reading?" Keith asked.

Mags shook her head. "I don't know. It sounded like gibberish to me."

"Wait a minute," Keith said. He darted from the room and reappeared a few moments later, holding the book open as though about to recite a sermon from it. He plumped it down on the bed. "This is the section I've been working on," he explained. "Now, Mags, do you recognise any of these words?"

Mags looked down almost fearfully, as though she expected the medieval lettering to leap off the page and cavort around her. After a moment she said, "I don't know."

"Please think, Mags," Keith urged. "It's very important."

Mags sighed and looked again. At last she shook her head. "Keith, I just don't know; I can't remember. It all seems a bit of a blur now. What does all this mean anyway?"

Keith picked up the book, his eyes greedily scanning the lines. "I've no idea," he admitted. "What did this man do then?"

Mags looked uneasy. "He... well, he sort of... vanished," she said.

"Vanished!" echoed Keith.

Mags nodded. "I screamed and he went all hazy like a ghost and came towards me. That's when I fainted." She blushed. "I knew you wouldn't believe me."

"But I do believe you!" Keith cried. Mags looked uncertain.

"Mags, I do, honestly." He put down the book and gripped her arm as though in an attempt to physically convince her of his belief. Her expression was confused, but grateful. Keith jumped up and began to pace the room, hefting the book in one hand like a barbell.

"This is incredible," he enthused. "A visitation right here in my own home. But what can it mean? A warning?... or... or some form of guidance perhaps?"

"Keith, you've lost me. Will you explain what you're on about?"

Keith stopped pacing the room and looked down at his wife's perplexed expression. He realised she knew nothing of the real events in Limefield.

He was being unfair. She needed comforting, not this constant to and fro on his part. Did the fact that the old man had appeared to her and not him mean that now Mags was involved too? He hoped not. Perhaps if he explained everything and took the book away with him, back to Limefield, he could still keep her out of it.

He settled himself on the edge of the bed, and reaching out, touched Mags' cheek gently. She smiled at him, and it was only when her face relaxed that he realised how tightly she had been keeping herself under control, how frightened she had really been. He snuggled closer and kissed her on the forehead.

"I have something to tell you," he said.

❦

"If Keith doesn't get back within the next two minutes we'll just have to leave without him," Martin said that afternoon. "We'll probably be late as it is."

Kevin looked at the kitchen clock for the millionth time that day. It was three twenty-five. In five minutes time, the meeting in the village hall would be due to start.

"I think we should go now," said Kevin. He appeared relaxed, but the meticulously shredded newspaper at his feet betrayed his nervousness. Martin glanced out of the window. The street was grey through a heavy mesh of rain.

"He said he'd be here. Maybe he's been held up in the traffic. I don't think the police are letting people into Limefield at all now."

"It's a free country," said Kevin. "People should be allowed to come and go as they please."

Martin shrugged. "No one's stopping people getting out," he said.

Kevin stood up suddenly as he noticed a streak of yellow invade the greyness outside. "Keith's here," he said. The taxi pulled up in front of the house and an overcoated figure emerged. Keith leaned into the driver's side window and they saw his head bobbing as he conversed with the driver. A moment later he was spattering up the drive. Kevin hurried to open the door.

"We'd almost given you up," said Martin as Keith tumbled through the doorway, bringing part of the rainy day with him.

"Yes, sorry about that, but the bloody police wouldn't let me back into Limefield," said Keith. He unbuttoned his coat, produced the ancient book and placed it on the telephone table. "I'll have to leave that there for the time being," he said. He rebuttoned his coat and continued with his explanations. "Anyway, I had to park outside the village and tramp over acres of muddy field to avoid the police. Eventually I managed to find a phone box and called for a taxi. It's waiting outside for us now, so look sharp."

Kevin and Martin hastily pulled on their coats.

"Dad, we're off to this meeting," shouted Kevin.

Mr. Truscott came downstairs, looking pale and withdrawn. "Yes, yes, all right," he said. A nervous hand fluttered to his head and smoothed down his thin hair.

His moustache puckered, and Martin thought for an alarming second that the little man was going to burst into tears. Then Kevin stepped forward and gave his dad a brief hug, something Martin had never seen him do before.

"We won't be long, Dad," he said. "See you later."

Mr. Truscott looked bewildered, as though his son had suddenly spoken to him in Swahili. His only response was a dismissive waft of his hand and a small, indistinct grunt. Then he turned and wandered slowly away into the kitchen.

Martin noticed the look of anguish that passed over Kevin's face at his father's odd, almost senile behaviour, and he felt furious at Swaney, at the heartlessness of the thing that had brought all this pain on his friend. He put an arm around Kevin's shoulder.

"Don't you worry, Kev," he said. "We'll win, you'll see. We'll find your mum and the kids."

Kevin smiled gratefully.

"Come on, it's half past now," said Keith. He opened the door and the three of them plunged out into the rain.

CHAPTER FOURTEEN

THE BURNING

Donahue watched as the villagers filed into the hall. Most of the men sat silently, looking uncomfortable in their starchy, little-worn suits, their hands and faces scrubbed to a gleaming redness. In contrast, the women gossiped to neighbours, frequently nodding, hairdos stiff with hairspray. It was hot in the hall, and the air smelled of mothballs, cheap scent and sweat.

It seemed as if the whole of Limefield had gathered here this afternoon. There at the front was Arthur Willis, a frail, wheezing figure hunched in a wheelchair. A few rows behind him Donahue recognised Sidney and Rachel Cooper, parents to Macky. They sat stiffly, acknowledging no one—not even each other. To his left, he saw Reginald Carter, landlord of The Shoulder, with a bandaged hand. And over there was the vicar, Desmond Crossthwaite. Oh yes, and there was that old farmer who had shown him the tree. What was his name? Bussey, that was it.

The hall was nearly full now. Shirt-sleeved policemen and pompous officials fetched more chairs, and, regardless of fire regulations, lined them up along the walls. Everyone who came in was closely scrutinised by the notebook and camera wielding journalists at the back. Donahue felt fortunate that he had managed to slip through the crowd unchallenged and find a seat in the middle of the hall. He obviously didn't look like a journalist. He wasn't sure whether to take that as an insult or a compliment.

He glanced up as another straggle of latecomers entered. There were three of them: a tall man with owlish spectacles and a beard, and two boys in their late teens. One of the boys, the shorter one with dark hair, seemed to sense he was being watched and looked up, catching Donahue's eye. He regarded

Donahue curiously for a moment before looking away again.

The three figures shuffled down the aisle. Occasionally, the taller of the two boys, the one with the messy blond hair, would wave or nod at people he knew. Finally, the blond-haired boy spotted a row with three empty seats and veered away towards it. By cajoling the people in the row to perform a clumsy game of musical chairs, he was able to secure three adjoining seats.

"Phew," said Martin as they sat down, "this place is packed out, isn't it?" Keith and Kevin nodded. Martin noticed that Kevin was looking agitated and asked, "You okay, Kev?"

"Yes, course I am," said Kevin unconvincingly. "I just wish the meeting would start, that's all. All this waiting is getting to me a bit."

The chatting died away as Garside walked up the steps onto the stage. His appearance seemed to act as a cue for a woman in the second row to have a coughing fit. He waited patiently until the coughing had subsided before he began.

"Good afternoon, ladies and gentlemen," he said, "and thank you for attending here today. I realise how busy some of you must be, so it's very gratifying to see so many people giving up part of their Friday afternoon to concern themselves with the affairs of their community." As Garside went on to introduce himself and run through the events of the last week, Martin stole a look to his left. The farming stock certainly produced some grim, tough-looking characters. He didn't envy Garside being the centre of attention. The men were nearly all thick-set with weather-hardened faces and hands that rested on their knees like joints of beef. Many of them seemed to swell out of their clothes, the brawn of labour padded out by plenty of good food and strong ale. But it wasn't only the men who were daunting. The women too were fearsome, despite their lacquered hair and carefully applied make-up. Handbags like small, wrinkled animals with snapping, silver mouths rested between pudgy hands on acres of lap. Legs bulged out of shoes that seemed ludicrously small. Martin, glancing back, felt as though he were looking along rows and rows of bobbing red balloons with only the insipid features and spiky purple hair of a punk rocker intruding on the display.

He looked back up at the stage where Garside was nearing the end of his spiel. "Just so the meeting doesn't get out of hand," Garside was saying, "could I suggest that if you want to contribute would you please stand up and I'll point you out. If you feel your contribution is particularly urgent could you put up your hand as well. Brevity would be appreciated. We're hoping to cover a great deal of ground this afternoon." He paused briefly to allow his comments to sink in and then said, "Right, who wants to start?"

It seemed at first that no one did. People looked at their neighbours. Wives whispered fiercely, urging their husbands to stand up and speak. Martin heard a woman behind him hiss, "What's happened to all this 'I'm going to give 'em a piece of my mind' rubbish that you were spouting at home?", and a man's defensive voice reply, "I'll say something, love, don't worry. I'm just giving the meeting a chance to warm up a bit first."

Eventually, reluctantly, one or two people rose from their seats and stood, hovering, uncertain whether or not to remain there. Garside pointed out a small, stout man with a face like a bulldog and a paunch that sagged from his open waistcoat like a badly concealed poacher's sack.

"Me name's Abram Winters from up Redheath way," the man said, "an' I'd just like to ask what exactly the police 'ave bin doin' to catch this bloody nutter? Me wife an' the young lass 'aven't dared go out of the house these last few days."

Garside puffed out his cheeks. "Yes, well... in answer to your question, Mr. Winters, all I can say is that the police are doing their best. The force in Limefield may have been increased to just over a hundred men in the last week, but believe me, those men are still spread very thinly indeed. There are so many areas to cover you see. We have a programme of house to house enquiries in operation. We have to hunt for clues in the woods in the daytime and have patrols in the area at night time. We need officers to man the special information office which has been set up in Limefield police station, and behind the scenes I need men to follow up leads, sift through evidence, and interview suspects. So, you see, Mr. Winters, we are kept very busy. I would love to see this killer behind bars as much as you would."

Abram Winters nodded gravely, and Garside was pleased to note that the farmer seemed suitably impressed by the endeavours of the police force. Perhaps he could win this stubborn audience over after all. He noticed a man flapping his arm impatiently and said, "Yes, the gentleman there with the cream jacket."

The man lowered his arm and glared around the hall as though outraged that he had not been allowed to speak first. From the looks the villagers were giving him, somewhere between curiosity and animosity, it was obvious that he was not from the village. He was a slightly built man, and everything about him—his hair, his clothes, his posture—had a slick, manicured look as though he had just stepped straight from the pages of a hire purchase catalogue. Even his voice seemed neatly clipped.

"My name is Ronald Crouch," he said, "and I'd just like to express my disgust at the ridiculous police decision to cordon off the local woodland. I and many other visitors have spent good money in coming here, and we feel we should be entitled to see what we have come to see, namely the Winter Tree." Crouch sat down amidst a sea of hostile stares and resentful mutterings.

Up on stage, Garside gritted his teeth and reminded himself how important it was not to lose his temper. He counted slowly to ten, and then in a voice unnaturally calm said, "Mr. Crouch, I realise how unpopular the decision to cordon off Redheath Woods has been, but if I may I'd just like to explain the thinking behind this decision.

"Now the woods cover a wide area, which at the best of times is difficult to police, so I'm sure that even you, Mr. Crouch, can appreciate that people tramping in and out all day and all night acts as a great hindrance to efficient policing. It impedes police progress and wastes a great deal of police time. Anyone who is found in the woods after dark must be viewed as a potential suspect and their motives and movements investigated. This, subsequently, puts a drain on manpower and a great burden on scheduling procedure. In order to work in peace, therefore, and to preserve and protect the lives of villagers, journalists and visitors alike, the woods were placed out of bounds."

Garside smiled smugly, pleased with the succinctness of his reply. He could see he had the support of many of the villagers. He felt he had put voice to their quiet resentment; he had put *the visitor* in his place.

But Crouch was not to be outdone. Before Garside had time to point out another contributor, the man in the cream jacket rose from his seat again and said loudly, "If you ask me, it's the police that stir up all this bitterness in the village. We're quite prepared to go quietly about our business, but it's you lot telling us where we should go and what we should do, herding us about like animals, that cause the trouble."

For a moment Garside didn't trust himself to reply. He clenched his teeth until his jaws ached and his hands involuntarily balled into fists. Crouch was quite prepared to continue despite the boos and whistles and cries of "sit down" his outburst was attracting. Finally, with steely patience, Garside said, "Mr. Crouch, without police organisation there would be absolute chaos in this area. It may come as a surprise to you to learn that you people do not own this village, you are simply visitors and as such should show a little respect and understanding. Do I have to spell it out to you? There is a murder inquiry going on here. Three people have been brutally killed over the last week, and if Redheath Woods had not been cordoned off it could very easily have been more. If you want to get killed, that's fine, but don't do it on my patch. I don't want to have to be the one to shovel up your remains."

A ragged burst of applause and a few cheers from the villagers followed Garside's retort. Crouch, still standing, blushed crimson. Making himself heard above the clamour he shouted, "That is just the sort of response I would expect from someone like you. The police are nothing but thugs in uniform who think that just because they have a bit of authority they can—" The rest of his rantings were drowned out by a storm of boos and insults.

Jack Steadman, a hulking farm labourer with more than a trace of Nordic blood in his veins, stood up a row behind Crouch and grabbed a fistful of the expensive cream jacket in one enormous hand.

"Just sit down, mister," he rumbled ominously, "you've had your say."

Crouch's eyes bulged and his face went the colour of the punctured fire bucket that dribbled sand in a corner of the hall.

"I will not sit down!" he yelled, squirming to free himself.

"Oh yes you will. You've said more than enough," said Steadman, and shook Crouch as a cat might shake a rat. Crouch's faultlessly swept-back fringe flopped over his face, and a button, unable to stand the strain any longer, popped off the cream jacket. Steadman gave Crouch one last shake and dumped him unceremoniously onto his chair. "Now stay down or I'll knock you down," he warned. His words were greeted with cries of encouragement. A number of people clenched their fists in the air, evidently eager to do the job themselves.

Crouch fell awkwardly, cracking his knee on the metal strut of his chair. He struggled to his feet, the collar of his cream jacket scrunched out of shape by the force of Steadman's grip. A little nub of vein in his forehead began to throb and the tendons in his neck stretched scrawny and tight like a chicken's.

"I'd like to see you try," he screamed, brandishing his fists like an old-fashioned pugilist. Steadman looked amused.

"Just sit yourself down, mister," he said.

"Oh, backing out now, are we?" sneered Crouch. He lashed out clumsily and made contact with Steadman's chin.

The blow wasn't particularly hard, but it took Steadman by surprise. He had been about to say something when the impact had clacked his jaw shut again on his tongue. Steadman's face tautened and set like concrete. His eyes narrowed and flared with anger.

Crouch took a step back, appalled. He looked round desperately, but there was nowhere to run. Steadman sucked in his cheeks and spat, peppering the cream jacket with blood. The audience clapped and cheered.

"Right, mister, you've asked for this," snarled the farm labourer, and drew back a mighty fist.

"Gentlemen, sit down!"

The audience turned to see Garside perched on the edge of

the stage, glaring down at the two men like a headmaster witnessing a playground brawl,

For a moment time seemed frozen. Then a few cries began to issue from the crowd.

"Hit him, Jack!"

"Cave his bloody head in!"

"Go on, Jack! Hit 'im back."

"This will not be tolerated," shouted Garside. "If you do not sit down immediately, I will give orders for my men to arrest you both."

No one moved. "All right, have it your way." Garside signaled to two constables at the back of the hall who began to make their way towards the two men. Slowly, Steadman lowered his fists and sat down. The blood-speckled Crouch yanked his jacket back into shape and prepared to make as dignified an exit as possible. He shuffled along the row towards the aisle. A waiting police constable took his arm, but Crouch angrily shook him off.

"I can manage, thank you," he muttered tartly, and stomped towards the exit, staring straight ahead, pretending to be oblivious to the jeers and threats that accompanied his departure.

Garside watched Crouch leave. As soon as the door had closed on the cream jacket he turned to the audience. "Now, perhaps we can continue this meeting in a civilised manner," he said.

❦

They stood shoulder to shoulder, silent and motionless like an army of mannequins waiting to be brought to life. They stood on the stairs, in the corridors, in every room of the house. Some spilled out into the garden where they stood like eerie garden ornaments in their sodden clothes, wet hair clinging to their heads like caps of seaweed. Their eyes were blank, reflecting their minds which were waiting to be filled.

Silas moved among them, flickering in and out and between the rows of bodies like a spider perusing its next meal. His movements were unnatural, mechanical, guided by a force that was uneasy in its use of the human shape.

Occasionally Silas would stretch out a convulsive hand and, like a blind man, lightly touch a face before moving on. His body shuddered and spasmed as though in the grip of fever. The skin crawled on his bones—taut, slack, taut, slack—as though breathing by itself, and the whites of his eyes strained horribly from their sockets.

Suddenly his back arched and his clamped jaw sprang open, releasing a drooling flood of spittle. His head thrashed from side to side. Breath rasped stertorously from his burning lungs and up his constricted throat. His heart laboured raggedly. Vast sections of his brain lay dormant, reacting only to the callous, all-embracing will of the dark soul.

Silas lurched and stumbled, falling to his knees. His head lolled and drooped as though all the supportive bone and muscle in his neck had dissolved to pulp. He remained in that position for a full minute, a shrunken, pitiful shell of a man.

Then his body was plucked into motion again. The head came up, the legs unfolded and straightened out. Silas shuffled forwards. He reached out and lightly touched the foreheads of two of the motionless figures.

"Wake," he rasped. The men that had been chosen blinked and swayed as though released from a trance. They regarded Silas sleepily, showing no reaction to his bestial appearance. One was dressed in a grey pin-striped suit, the other as though out for a day's golfing. Silas gripped their faces in his claw-like hands. His mouth opened and saliva oozed down his chin.

"There is something you must do," he grated.

Martin was bored. The meeting had been going for over half an hour now, and in his opinion virtually nothing had been achieved. He found the fact that he knew so much more than those discussing the issue intensely frustrating, and more than once had almost been tempted to stand up and tell them what they were really up against. The suggestion that an escaped wild animal was responsible for the killings had been discussed at length, but this idea had finally been quashed by the observation that, with the exception of Bussey's sheep, only people had been killed; there had been no widespread sheep or cattle worrying, and there was no food left in the woods to eat. The line of arguing had developed from there into the supposition that some maniac was harbouring the wild animal and using it as a murder weapon. This, it was argued, explained how the sheep came to be nailed to the tree—obviously to provide food for the creature.

Martin's mind was wandering. He closed his eyes. The flat, droning voices mingled with the scuttling of the rain. With an effort, he focused his attention back to the stage.

"It's certainly an interesting idea," Garside was saying, "and one which we have considered. At present, I have a zoology expert working on the case and a couple of officers ringing round all the local zoos, circuses and wildlife parks in the area in an attempt to find out whether any animals have escaped or been stolen recently without it being reported. It's a long and time-consuming job and, so far, has produced no positive results. I think that's all I can really say on the matter at present. I'm sorry not to be more positive." He smiled apologetically.

The person who had asked the question, a pasty, acned youth with baggy jeans and a combat jacket, seemed satisfied with Garside's response. He nodded seriously and resumed his seat. Garside scanned the audience.

"Yes, the lady there with the green hat," he said, pointing.

The lady in question looked around at the audience and smiled warmly. She was an ancient, dark-skinned figure with a face so puckered it seemed to be moulded from beaten leather. She was hunched over as though the weight of her thick coat was too much for her frail body.

Garside detected an expectant stirring among the audience and noticed one or two secretive smiles and winks being exchanged. He wondered uncomfortably whether he was the butt of some private village joke. His fears in that direction were allayed, however, when the woman began to speak.

"Friends," she cried, and just for a moment Garside was convinced she was going to add 'Romans and countrymen.' "We are gathered here in the face of God, and He has sent us a sign of His anger. Friends, we have done Him wrong; we have sinned in the face of His Divine Light, and now we must endure His wrath. He has destroyed our land with His fiery breath! He has sent a creature amongst us, an evil creature not of this world—a fallen angel from the Legion of Lucifer himself! Friends, we must repent! Come, get down on your knees and pray for your souls. Come friends, follow my example."

The little old lady lowered herself gingerly onto her knees, clasped her hands in front of her face, closed her eyes and began to pray.

"Oh Lord, deliver us from this evil which thou hast cast down upon our village. We have sinned, Lord, we have wandered from thine good and true path, and thou hast sent a sign to warn us. Lord, we are humbled in thy presence. We beg thy forgiveness." She opened her eyes and waved her arms as though rallying troops. "Come on, everybody, the Lord's Prayer," she shrilled. "Repeat after me... Our Father, Who Art in Heaven, Hallowed Be Thy Name, Thy Kingdom Come..."

"Get that bloody woman out of here," Garside muttered to a constable he had beckoned over. He did not share the audience's humour. The woman, whoever she was, had reduced his meeting to a farce. He noticed that one or two of the villagers were actually joining in with her in reciting the Lord's Prayer, and a group of youths at the back kept yelling out "Hallelujah, Praise de Lord!" and then hooting with laughter at their own stunning wit.

Martin, like the rest of the audience, was craning his neck, amused at the old woman's antics. He thought of what she had said about a creature, a fallen angel, being sent amongst them and turned to Kevin.

"You know, Old Ma Parker may be a bit crackers," he said, "but she's probably got closer to the truth than anyone else here today."

Kevin smiled stiffly in reply.

By now the police constable had reached the old woman. He tapped her self-consciously on the shoulder and began to speak to her in a low voice. The audience laughed and applauded as the old lady shook her head and wafted her hand imperiously in the constable's face. The young policeman glanced at Garside, but the Inspector merely shrugged and shook his head. The constable thought for a minute, then bent down again and said something to the old woman, jerking his head towards the other side of the hall. Immediately, the old woman looked distressed. Aided by the constable, she struggled to her feet and glanced across to where he had indicated. Garside looked too. For the life of him, he couldn't see anything across the hall that might have alarmed her, but without saying another word, the little old lady collected up her brolly, bag and headscarf, and made her arthritic way towards the exit doors, escorted like a dutiful boy scout by the constable. She was given a spirited ovation as she left.

"How the hell did you get her to go?" asked Garside when the audience had resumed their seats.

"I just told her the vicar was annoyed because he thought she was after his job," replied the constable. "That seemed to worry her a bit."

Garside laughed. "I'll bet it did. Incurring the wrath of the Lord's messenger on Earth. Well done, constable."

"Thank you, sir."

⚬ᘓ᛫ᘓᘗ᛫ᘓᘗ

Mr. Truscott trudged slowly downstairs in his dressing gown, one hand holding onto the banister to steady himself. Outside the rain had finally stopped, and he could hear the faulty drain in the back garden gurgling like a baby. He sighed. Even that made him think of Angela. He had promised her two days ago that he would fix it this weekend.

He groaned and rubbed his back. His legs felt stiff, and his skin seemed to weigh down his bones. In one day he felt as though he had acquired all the aches and tiredness of old age. It was the mental pain of anxiety that was bearing him down, crushing him, exhausting him more than any physical effort had ever done. He had just taken a bath, hoping it would wash away some of the dirt and the pain and the sorrow of the day before.

But the pain was still there, eating him up inside like a cancer.

He reached the bottom of the stairs and paused, wondering whether he ought to go into the kitchen and make himself something to eat. He hadn't eaten since breakfast, and then it had been only half a slice of toast. He sighed, angry with himself at his indecision. He tried to convince himself that he should be strong, that moping wasn't going to help anybody. But the words were just words, empty and meaningless. They couldn't change the way he felt.

He took a step towards the kitchen and then changed his mind. He needed to sit down before he did anything else. He felt so tired.

He shuffled towards the sitting room, his slippers swish-swishing like a lonely road sweeper. On the way he passed the hall table and noticed something he never seen before. It was a heavy book, bound in leather. He wondered vaguely where it had come from but wasn't curious enough to look at its contents. Nothing really interested him at present. His mind was filled only with an almost unbearable longing for his wife and children. Leaving the book where it was, Mr. Truscott went into the sitting room.

The meeting was hotting up. The incident with the old woman seemed to have acted as an ice-breaker, and the problem now facing Garside was not whether he could find enough contributors to keep the meeting going, but whether he could fit in everyone who wanted to say something before the meeting's scheduled end at five o' clock.

For the last ten minutes, the topic of conversation had been the prison breakout and the disappearances in the village. Most of the villagers were of the opinion that all the events of the past week were connected, but the problem was trying to discover some pattern, some logical way in which the pieces could be fitted together.

"It stands to reason," said a willowy woman with pale skin, whose feathery grey hair was coaxed into a bun and held in place with hair clips. "I mean Limefield has never known anything remotely like this before. Take it from me, Inspector, as soon as one problem is solved everything else will begin to fall into place."

There was a rumble of agreement.

"I understand your reasoning, Mrs. Scales," Garside replied diplomatically, "but I honestly don't see how a fire in the woods can be connected with a prison breakout, or... or a spate of murders with an ice-covered tree. It just doesn't make sense. Until we do get some evidence to suggest otherwise, these events must be seen as separate incidents."

"I reckon it's nuclear," a man in the audience shouted out. "I reckon the government have been messing about with somethin' nearby an' it's gone wrong. There's been a leak or somethin'. Maybe they've been muckin' about with the weather—that's why there was a fire an' that's why the tree is like it is. And maybe there's some nuclear dust or somethin' still in the air and it's affectin' people's minds—making them turn nasty or just go wanderin' off. Aye, that's what it'll be. Nuclear."

Garside raised his hands as a debate on this latest theory began in the audience. "Please," he said, "shouting out will not be tolerated. The next person to do so will be asked to leave. If you wish to make a contribution, could you please stand up and wait for your turn." Eventually, the audience quietened. "That's better. Thank you. Now does anyone have any comment to make? Yes, the gentlemen over there."

The man Garside had indicated was stout, with sideburns so bushy they threatened to engulf his face. He had dark heavy folds like teabags under his eyes and, as he spoke, he tapped a small briar pipe on the chair in front of him like a gavel.

"It seems to me," he began, "that we're trying to deal with too many problems all at once. It doesn't really matter what caused these things to happen—they've happened an' that's all there is to it. As I see it, the most important thing is to stop them happenin' again, and I reckon if we can catch this murderer, think of some plan between us, our biggest problems will be solved." He sat down amidst a plethora of nodding heads.

"All right then," Garside said. "That seems to be the general consensus. Now does anyone have any ideas?"

Ideas were not in short supply. A dozen more people sprang up from their seats. Garside was not surprised to note that they were all men, all hard-bitten, solid-looking farmers—grim-faced as a hanging jury from an old western. Garside selected one of them at random—a young man with a square, craggy head perched on muscular shoulders.

"I reckon we ought to get the dogs out, hunt the bugger down," the man said in a thick, clogged drawl that suggested adenoidal problems.

"That's all very well, Mr...?"

"Jameson."

"That's all very well, Mr. Jameson," said Garside, "but I hardly think the suggestion is feasible. There have been so many people in the woods recently that dogs would be likely to lead us on a wild goose chase."

"Aye, well, you should've thought o' that before, shouldn't you?" Jameson snorted. "You should've had the dogs out as soon as the bodies were found. Dogs aren't daft y'know. They can follow a scent for miles if it's strong enough. And there's nothin' stronger than the smell o' blood to a dog."

"Yes, I am aware of their value, Mr. Jameson. We do use them quite extensively in the police force."

"Aye, well, just think on in future. A dog'll not let you down."

"Yes, well, thank you, Mr. Jameson, we'll bear your suggestion in mind," said Garside tactfully, and turned away, pointing to a toothless old man with a scarred nose, who looked from his clothes as though he worked the night shift as a scarecrow. "Yes, the gentleman there."

The old man scratched his head vigorously with soil-encrusted fingers.

"My name's Brierly," he said. "I work for Mr. Bates, up yonder by Moor Cross. Now, I can tell you where you can get 'old o' some traps." He winked knowingly. Garside was confused.

"Traps?" he echoed, hoping it would prompt the old man to continue. It did.

"Aye, traps. That's what you need. You put 'em along the

paths in the woods, and then wait. Sooner or later the bugger that's been killin' all these folks'll come along. And when he does—*BANG!*" He smacked his hands together. "We'll have 'im." He grinned round at the audience, glowing with self-esteem.

Garside was both amused and dismayed by the brutal simplicity of the old man's logic "Are you suggesting we lay man traps for the killer?"

"Aye," said the old man.

"But how do you guarantee it will be the murderer who's caught?" said Garside. "What about the danger to other people?"

Brierly thrust out his white-stubbled chin indignantly. "You said yourself that no one was allowed in Redheath now. It's all been fenced off, you said."

"That's as maybe," Garside replied, "but there are still ways and means of entering the wood. We are still arresting perhaps a dozen or more trespassers a day."

"Well, the traps'll save you the trouble of havin' to chase about after 'em then, won't they? All you 'ave to do is go round an' pick 'em all up." Brierly smiled, content in the belief that he had solved everyone's problems.

Garside knew he would joke about Brierly's suggestions over a few drinks with his colleagues afterwards, but for now it dismayed him that he was being called upon to deal with such ridiculous proposals. The meeting was not turning out to be the serious discussion he had been hoping for. It seemed unlikely that they would reach any positive solutions before five o'clock.

"I don't really think mantraps are the answer, Mr. Brierly," he said, trying to be tactful. "For one thing, there would be too many practical difficulties to overcome. Trespassing may be a hindrance, but it doesn't really merit the loss of a foot nowadays. Also, the safety of my own men must be considered. And another danger, of course, would be that rather than catching the murderer, the traps may in fact provide he, she or it with ready prepared victims—unable to move, weak from loss of blood. I'm sorry, Mr. Brierly, but I don't think it would work."

Garside noticed that the vicar, Desmond Crossthwaite, had stood up during the exchange and pointed him out, ignoring the disgruntled murmurs of some of the farmers.

Crossthwaite looked self-conscious, uneasy without the barrier of his pulpit between himself and his congregation. However, he needn't have worried. As soon as he began to speak the audience settled into a respectful silence.

"I would really like to pick up on what Mr. Brierly was saying about traps just now," he began hesitantly. "Whilst I feel that the employment of such devices would be both ill-advised and inhuman, Mr. Brierly's suggestion did spark off an idea of my own." He looked nervously around the hall, noted the attentive faces, and continued more confidently. "Now, the first murders, as we all know, were committed against a young couple in a car, so I thought it would be a good idea if we... er, that is the police, were to re-enact that scene. What I mean is, have two people sitting in a car in the woods, perhaps with the lights on and music playing to attract attention. Hopefully this will act as bait for the murderer who, as soon as he shows his face, will be jumped on from the surrounding bushes by a dozen policemen." Crossthwaite tailed off, looking anxious. A round of excited chattering and nodding demonstrated the popularity of the idea amongst the villagers.

Garside raised his hand for silence once more. When the chatter had died down he said, "We have, in fact, been considering that idea ourselves, Mr. Crossthwaite. The only drawback is having to use people as bait. However, it is an idea worth keeping in mind."

Martin, sitting in the audience, was wondering whether the plan would work, whether a dozen or so policemen could capture the Swaney-thing or even kill it. Detecting movement to his left, he turned and saw Kevin rise from his seat and put his hand in the air. Martin immediately felt a thrill of panic though he couldn't say why. "Kev," he hissed. There was no response. Kevin's body was rigid, his face set and serious. "Kev," Martin repeated, more urgently this time. Still Kevin failed to respond, and now people were starting to turn and look at him. Martin tugged at the sleeve of Kevin's jumper. "Kev, what are you doing?" Kevin shook himself free, but the expression on his face never changed. Before Martin could try again he heard Garside say, "That boy there, the one with the blue jumper."

More heads turned. They seemed, to Martin, to be hostile and accusing. He shrunk low into his seat. Beside him he sensed Kevin's body tense, and then suddenly relax.

"I... have to say something," Kevin stammered.

There was a strained pause which Garside broke by saying, "Well go on, son. That's what we're here for."

For one terrible moment Martin thought his friend was going to faint. He saw Kevin's eyelids flicker and his mouth open and close slowly. Martin looked round at the audience. All eyes in the room were on Kevin. Many looked concerned, others confused, expectant, impatient. As Martin watched, they seemed to merge, to become one creature with rows and rows of unblinking eyes. He felt light-headed, as though he was being hypnotised. A soft, puzzled murmur, like an approaching wave, began to swell about the room.

Then the spell was broken. Martin was jolted back to reality as Kevin, his voice blandly casual, said, "Yesterday my mother, my brother Jamie, and my sister Samantha were kidnapped by the murderers."

⌒⌒⌒⌒

Mr. Truscott looked up tiredly as he heard the front door bang.

"Kevin, is that you?" he called. There was no reply. He tried again, this time a little louder. "Kevin?" Still no reply. He frowned, irritated. He was damned if he was going to sit here shouting himself hoarse. He slumped further into his armchair and wondered why Kevin and his friends had not come in to say hello. They would in time, he supposed.

He sighed for the hundredth time and turned his attention back to the television screen. White figures in padded armour raced from one set of stumps to the other and then back again. A West Indian fielder dived full-length to stop the ball going over the boundary line. Mr. Truscott's eyes were fixed on the screen, but his mind was elsewhere, snatching at memories which were torturing him with sentimentality. He remembered an evening not so long ago when he and Angela had walked hand in hand along the banks of Coniston Water in the Lake District. He remembered how beautiful the sky had been, washed with pinks and reds and crimsons, how the mountains had crouched, stark and awesome in the foreground, and how the dying sun had scattered jagged slivers of light onto the still water. But most of all he remembered the warmth of Angela's hand in his; how he longed to hold that hand now.

His thoughts shifted. This time it was Sam, sitting cross-legged by the side of the Christmas tree, her hair haloed by fairy lights. She was stripping the wrapping paper excitedly from a box almost as large as herself. Crumpled Santa Clauses lay about her in heaps. He could picture now her gasp of delight as the paper came away to reveal the doll's house she'd said she'd wanted, and he'd said was much too big and expensive. "Never mind, Sam, perhaps Santa'll bring you one," he'd told her, and she had nodded, unconvinced.

Dozens of other images, like confused clips from a home movie, tumbled in his head. Sam and Jamie clinging to him as they clanked towards a grinning demon on a Ghost Train ride. Jamie sitting on his shoulders, eating candy floss. Angela kissing and hugging him when he produced the engagement ring from the breast pocket of his jacket. Sitting out on the back lawn sipping lemonade whilst the children splashed happily in a paddling pool with a slow puncture. The results of Angela's pregnancy test finally coming back positive after months of hope and despair.

The door banged again, scattering his thoughts.

"Kevin, is that you?" he shouted. There was no answer. Mr. Truscott groaned and struggled to his feet. He supposed he would just have to go and close the door himself.

He shuffled into the hall. Sure enough, the door was ajar, the wind causing it to waft back and forth. He pushed it to with a click. He went across the hall and into the kitchen, expecting to find Kevin and his friends sitting round the kitchen table, drinking coffee. But they were not there. Upstairs then? He stood at the foot of the stairs and called up. No answer. Strange. He shrugged. Maybe the door hadn't been closed properly in the first place. It had probably just blown open.

But he was frowning as he ambled across the hallway, back towards the sitting room. He had a niggling suspicion that something was not quite right. A vague notion was circling blindly in his mind, trying to push its way through the grief that smothered it. He stopped in the sitting room doorway and stared out into the hall. Something here was wrong, but what was it? As far as he could tell everything was as it should be. He screwed up his eyes and tried to concentrate, but it made no difference. The thought still buzzed like a trapped insect, agonizingly just out of reach.

It was only later, as the West Indies chalked up their eighth wicket, that the thought bubbled its way to the surface.

That book that had been sitting on the hall table had disappeared.

⁕

The village hall was in uproar. Flashbulbs flared like soundless explosions. Journalists remonstrated with police or stood on their chairs to yell questions. Villagers conversed excitedly with their neighbours. Furniture scraped as people tried to see what was going on. Garside shouted and flapped his arms in an effort to restore order. And in the midst of it all, Kevin stood, face impassive, waiting patiently for the furore he had sparked off to die down.

Eventually, a restless peace was restored. The journalists were ushered back to their seats and told to be quiet. Those that refused were escorted unceremoniously out of the hall amidst a chorus of camera shutters and the blazing litter of flashlights.

Martin was sitting back on his chair, blinking into space, not really taking anything in. He felt an almost intoxicating release as though a plug had been pulled on his emotions. He experienced relief, shock and fear, each emotion as hard and separate as rocks in his stomach. Beside him, Keith looked intent, thin hands massaging his knees, troubled eyes swimming and blurring behind thick lenses.

At last Garside was able to resume. "Go on, son," he said to Kevin.

Kevin told his story, in a voice so calm and toneless it was almost chilling. He described how he and Martin had arrived home yesterday afternoon to find the house empty, and about the man who had phoned up with a warning that any mention of the disappearance to the police would result in the imminent deaths of his mum, his brother and his sister.

"But what makes you so sure it's the murderer who is responsible?" asked Garside.

"Murderers," Kevin corrected. "There are a group of them." He looked down at his hands. "My mum told me," he lied. "The man allowed her to speak on the phone and she told me before he could stop her."

"I see." Garside looked thoughtful. "And what made you decide to break your silence and tell us all here today?"

"I... I had to do something... positive, something to help them. This whole thing is... my dad is..." Kevin's voice trailed off for a moment and then picked up again like a dying radio. "I... I think they intend to... to kill Mum and Jamie... and Sam anyway. I think they'd... kill them whether I told the police or not." His voice was choked off by a sob. He pressed an arm to his face as though determined to squeeze back the tears. Apparently unable to do so, he sat down.

Immediately, a speculative buzz of chatter started up again. Powdered faces creased in concern. Garside raised his hand for silence at the same moment that Keith raised his hand for attention.

"Inspector, I have something important to say," Keith shouted, making himself heard above the commotion.

Garside had the uncomfortable feeling that he was beginning to lose control of the proceedings. "Will everyone please be quiet!" he bawled and immediately all noise in the hall stopped, the audience stunned into silence. Garside scanned the rows of surprised faces. When he was satisfied that he had regained the audience's attention once again, he said, "Thank you. Now perhaps we can continue. I believe that gentleman there with the beard would like to say something."

"Thank you, Inspector," said Keith. He looked round at the audience, trying to hide his nervousness and project an air of authority. "My name is Keith Francis," he began. "I teach English at Cranbydale Comprehensive. I'm also something of a scholar in the field of parapsychology. That's, erm, the study of paranormal phenomena—ghosts and suchlike. In the last few days I've been doing some research into the happenings in Redheath Woods and have come up with some very disturbing evidence of my own."

"Is that so?" said Garside. His tone was not encouraging.

"Yes, indeed," said Keith. He took off his spectacles, produced a white handkerchief from his pocket and carefully cleaned the lenses. His movements were calm and assured, but his thoughts were racing, tumbling over one another. What could he say? How could he stress the urgency of the situation without telling the truth? He was uneasily aware that all eyes in the room were fixed on him. He replaced his spectacles, trying to stop his hand from trembling as he did so. *Oh well, here goes*, he thought.

"Yes, I'm afraid my investigations are not as thorough as I would have liked them to be, but in the light of what we have just been told by Kevin here, I felt I ought to warn you."

He paused again. *So far, so good*, he thought. *Now comes the hard bit.*

"Warn us? About what?"

"About the terrible danger to this village." Keith instilled as much earnestness as he could into the words. "I'm afraid we're dealing with the, er..." he remembered something the old lady in the green hat had said and struck at it desperately, "...the Legion of Lucifer."

"Legion of Lucifer?" Garside scoffed. "Just what sort of idiocy is this?"

Keith held up a hand. "Please, Inspector, I understand your scepticism, but I assure you this is a deadly serious business. Of course, Legion of Lucifer is a name by which they are popularly known. In fact, I think it's a name culled from a newspaper headline."

As Keith had hoped, Garside rose to the bait. "Newspaper headline? You mean these people—"

"Yes, indeed, they are a very established group. Surely you

remember the case, Inspector? 1971, I think it was. An entire family slaughtered as a human sacrifice. Of course, they caught those directly responsible, but it was simply scratching the surface. The Legion has hundreds, perhaps thousands of followers."

Keith was talking off the top of his head, surprising himself by his own inventiveness. He only hoped he wouldn't dry up or tie himself in knots. A glance at the faces around him assured him his story was receiving whole-hearted, if horrified, attention. Garside, however, was an altogether tougher nut to crack.

"This Legion of Lucifer," Garside said, and the sarcasm weighed heavy in his words. "How do you know so much about them?"

"I've been researching them for years," Keith said, "and I don't really profess to know that much. Of course, I know more than most people, but that's still very little."

"And what makes you so sure this particular group are responsible for everything that's occurred?"

"I've studied their rituals closely," Keith lied. "I've visited the scene where the sheep was killed and where the murders took place. These people know what they're doing, Inspector. The moon alignments, the zones of power, the temporal link with the summer solstice..." he shrugged, "there's plenty of evidence." Keith could see that his spouting of mystical gobbledygook had impressed the villagers, many of whom were hanging on his every word. He pressed home his advantage. "It is imperative therefore, Inspector, that we act on this situation as soon as possible."

"Is it indeed?" said Garside. "And how do you propose we do that?"

"Everyone must help," said Keith, "I suggest armed patrols in radio contact to make a thorough search of the woods immediately."

"Armed patrols? Radio contact?" spluttered Garside. "Don't be preposterous, man. It's out of the question."

"It's the only way," insisted Keith.

"Is it indeed?" Garside said again. He shook his head. "No,

I don't think so. Police investigations will proceed as normal."

"And meanwhile people will be killed," retorted Keith angrily.

"We have only your word for that," said Garside.

Keith suddenly flared up, losing his self-control. "God, why are you people so... brainless!" he shouted. "All you've done this afternoon is to dismiss suggestion after suggestion just because they haven't fitted in with your way of thinking. Look, Inspector, something must be done now, or believe me, more people are going to die."

Garside pursed his lips. His eyes refused to meet Keith's. "I'm sorry, I can't accept that," he said.

Keith glared at him for a moment as though he would dearly have liked to strangle the man. "Right," he muttered, "in that case we'll just have to deal with this without your help." He turned his back on Garside, stood on his chair, and addressed the villagers. "Now, will all those who would like to help please raise their hands," he said. A good half volunteered immediately. Others looked uncertainly from the long-haired, sloppily-dressed figure on the chair to the thick-set policeman on the stage.

"Arrest that man!" Garside bellowed. A couple of policemen began to make their way over to Keith.

"Now, how many people possess firearms?" Keith was saying. He could see the policemen approaching from the corner of his eye. It reminded him of his student demo days. It struck him that if he didn't pull this one off he could probably wave goodbye to his teaching career—if there was still a career to go back to after all this was over, that is.

"Come on, sir, get down now," said one of the constables politely. Keith snatched his arm away from the hand that reached for him.

"You can't arrest us all, you know, Garside," he said. "The villagers have a right to try and protect what is theirs."

"Come on, sir." The policeman's voice was a little less polite now and the other constable was fast approaching from the other side. A square set man with a crooked nose and pudding basin haircut suddenly stood up.

"I agree wi' the young feller," he said. "We've got to do somethin'. We can't stand around while folk get killed."

"Aye, he's right," another man said, standing up.

"Aye," said another, and then another, and another. Soon Keith had perhaps fifty or sixty supporters. The hand that had been trying to tug Keith from his makeshift platform fell away. Keith regained his balance and turned to Garside.

"You see, Inspector," he said, gesturing around him, "a majority decision."

Garside expelled a long breath. For a moment he said nothing. Then, finally, he nodded, accepting defeat. "All right," he muttered. "All right, but this is to be a police operation with police planning. I'm not having people in the woods unless they're going to be controlled and monitored."

"Oh of course," said Keith. "I wouldn't suggest it any other way."

Garside frowned, unsure whether or not he was being mocked. He regarded Keith closely, but the young teacher's face was set and serious.

"What about radio contact?" said Keith. "It's important to keep in touch with one another."

Garside gave him a look, but grudgingly said, "Radio contact is easy enough. As long as each group is accompanied by a police officer, we can use standard issue police walkie-talkies."

"Okay, fine," said Keith. "And what about guns? Each group must be armed."

Garside puffed out his cheeks. "I'm not sure that's really necessary."

"Of course it's necessary," snapped Keith. "As many people as possible should be armed."

"No," said Garside, "that's an idea I'm not keen on. I could never justify the distribution of firearms to civilians."

"You won't have to distribute them, Inspector. Most of the farmers have their own weapons."

Garside shook his head again. "No, absolutely not. Guns are out. It's too dangerous."

"It will be a damn sight more dangerous if we're not armed!" retorted Keith, his voice wavering. He felt angry, almost fighting angry, and it came from the guilt that churned deep in his gut. He knew he was talking these people into a horribly dangerous situation. Even with guns, things would be bad, but without them it would be suicidal.

"Look, Inspector, these people we're dealing with, they're not cranks, they are dangerous—very, very dangerous. We must be armed."

Garside still looked unsure. Keith turned and addressed the audience again. "How many people here have their own weapons?" Most of them put up their hands. "And how many of you agree with me, that we should be armed?"

It was an almost unanimous decision.

"There you see, Inspector. You don't have the authority to prevent the use of licensed firearms."

Garside looked smug. "I'm afraid that's where you're wrong," he said. "The guns that these farmers possess are licensed for sporting purposes—shooting game, not shooting people, not even in self defence. What you're suggesting is that I give my permission for these people to commit illegal acts. Well, I'm afraid that's just not on. I have neither the authority nor the desire to encourage criminal activity."

Keith was almost tearing his hair out. "But we must be armed," he repeated. "What about your own men? Surely, they are allowed guns?"

Garside looked around him, intimidated by the accusing eyes. At last, reluctantly, he said, "Yes, my men are allowed guns in certain situations."

"Situations such as this?" Keith said.

Garside shrugged. "Maybe."

"Please try, Inspector," Keith said. "It's our only chance. Believe me, we must have some means of protecting ourselves."

Garside considered, and at last, grudgingly, he nodded his head. "All right," he said wearily, "all right, I'll see what I can do. But I insist that no farmers are to bring firearms with them; those that do so will not be allowed into the woods. Also, this is to be a well-disciplined police operation, not some bloodthirsty man-hunt."

"Agreed," said Keith with a satisfied nod.

"Okay then." Garside looked at his watch. "Will all those wishing to volunteer for this operation meet back here at—what? Eight thirty?" He glanced at Keith for confirmation.

Keith nodded and said, "Yes. I doubt if there'll be anything to see before dark."

"Okay, eight thirty it is," said Garside. "In the meantime, I'll arrange everything. Well, if no one has got anything more to add..." he paused. No one had. "I shall declare this meeting closed. See you all later."

Silas had awoken from a nightmare only to find it was part of his waking life. He sat quietly, slim hands clasped between his knees, bleary eyes set deep in grey, sallow features. He looked like a man who was very, very ill.

Figures stood around him like jailers, their eyes glazed over, many of them dressed in rough, dull-blue clothes. Silas wondered who they were, what they were doing here. He had only a vague recollection of the last few days, a dream-like image of struggling against something stronger than himself, of gradually being forced to give way, to give up control of his body.

He shifted slightly in his seat and winced at the pain it caused him. He felt bruised and tender, his muscles pulped by some inner decay. He flexed his fingers experimentally and winced again. He had woken over an hour ago, but only now was his body beginning to feel like his again. Only now did he feel he could attempt to stand up, but before he could try there was a knock on the door.

Immediately Silas felt the dark cloud enveloping him again, pushing him back and back, to become a prisoner in his own mind. He managed to whisper one word, "please," before the darkness hemmed him in completely.

Silas changed. His eyeballs rolled up into his head. His face became sharper, leaner. His hands hooked into bony claws. He opened his mouth and saliva frothed into his beard. Breath began to rasp and rattle in his throat. His head raised slowly as the two figures entered, and a thick, grating voice said, "The book."

The man in the pin-stripe suit took the book from his jacket and held it out. Silas leaped up, snatching the book with a hiss of triumph. "Come," he said and, followed by the two men, he shuffled between the ranks of figures and out into the back garden.

The rain had stopped. A listless sun was emerging from convalescence and trying to squeeze its way through clouds that looked solid as tanks. Water dripped solemnly from trees. Silas pointed to a rusty oil drum, brimming with mushy weeds.

"Bring that," he said.

Obediently, the two men lifted the drum and wrestled it to the centre of the lawn. They set it down and stepped back, palms slimy with rust.

Silas shuffled forward, the book held before him like a sacred relic. Suddenly he laughed, an obscene, raucous sound, and tossed the book onto the bed of compost as though it was something nauseous, like maggot-riddled meat or a putrid cabbage. The book came to rest like a sinking boat in a thick, oily sea. Spiders and woodlice emerged and scuttled mindlessly over the ancient leather. Silas continued to snigger and snort. His white eyes jerked and trembled excitedly as though about to burst from their sockets. He stretched out his arms and cupped his hands, like Oliver asking for more. Suddenly a flash, a fork of flame, seemed to dance in his palm, and then a ball of fire appeared from nowhere. It sat in his hands, burning in a rough sphere, spitting and crackling with a furious hunger. Silas cradled the flame, appearing not to feel its heat. Then, almost affectionately, he tossed the fire into the oil drum. He stepped back to watch, something like insane rapture on his face.

The fire took hold immediately, steadily devouring the contents of the oil drum and giving off a biting black smoke. The book was engulfed and consumed in seconds. Parts of the oil drum started to warp and char. It lost its wet sheen, and acquired a dry, brittle look, its surface glowing faintly from the fire that raged in its belly. A minute later, it was all over. All that remained was a heap of smouldering ashes.

Silas stepped forward and, ignoring the fire which still

popped and belched like a satisfied diner, thrust his hand deep into the blackened contents of the drum. He withdrew, his hand full of flaky ashes. He clenched his fist, allowing the ashes to dribble through his fingers like treasure. Delving into the oil drum again, he scooped out great handfuls of ashes and began to scatter them, like seed, over the sodden ground. The ashes, stirred by the wind, rolled and separated and crumbled away, lost forever like the last vestiges of hope.

CHAPTER FIFTEEN

THE HUNTERS

By eight fifteen, the sun was as hot as ever, so hot it seemed almost to buzz overhead. It had banished the rain clouds and was now sucking the streets dry, leaving only a few reminders of the storm behind; patches of wet that lurked around gutter openings; gardens that gleamed as though varnished; water that drummed on a sagging drainpipe like a Morse code message.

But in a while even this legacy would be gone. Already, clothes were starting to appear magically on washing lines, and old ladies were drifting out from indoors to see what damage had been done to their dahlias and sweetpeas.

On and around the steps of the village hall, the crowds were beginning to gather. Shirt-sleeved, they milled about, some looking lost, others determined, others laughing and joking as though in readiness for a summer outing. Rucksacks were in evidence, perched on backs like babies. Makeshift weapons such as clubs and cricket stumps leaned against walls or hung from belts. Beer cans were drained, crumpled in fists, and fed to the plastic litterbin that hung from a nearby lamp-post.

Halfway up the steps sat Keith, Kevin, Martin and Mr. Truscott. Keith was hunched over, smoking, worrying about the theft of his book. Glumly, he watched as the crowds thickened below. He estimated there were perhaps seventy or eighty people here already. A ramshackle farm wagon drew up with maybe a dozen farmhands crouched in the back. As the men climbed down, a few of the people on the steps began to clap and cheer. One of the farmhands, a wiry man with slightly pop-eyes, grinned and raised his arms aloft like a homecoming war hero.

This air of expectancy, of hope, of resolution, only dismayed Keith all the more. He felt guilty and responsible, sick with worry. Because of him, some of these people might die tonight. They didn't really know what they were up against. What good were clubs and sticks against Swaney? They might as well take a peashooter to try and kill an elephant.

He kept trying to convince himself that he had done the right thing, that it was better to strike now whilst there was still the chance that Swaney might be vulnerable. He told himself that by putting lives at risk more would be saved in the long run, and that if Kevin's family were to be found alive then there could be no more delay in going to look for them. However, it was no use. Whatever he told himself he still felt guilty.

Martin, unaware of Keith's dilemma, peeled off his t-shirt and wafted himself with it. "Hot," he said, turning to Kevin. He puffed out his cheeks and stuck out his tongue to emphasize just how hot it was.

Kevin nodded, "Yeah," and swiped at the flies that hovered above his head like discarded thoughts. Martin swiveled round further and said,

"You okay, Mr. T?"

Mr. Truscott sat just behind Kevin, looking pale, eyes deep in his sockets, his hand clenched tightly round the sawn-off barrel of an old shotgun he had insisted on bringing. His head jerked up at the sound of his name. He gave a short nod and a muttered, "Yes."

Heads turned to the end of the street. Those who had been sitting began to stand up, shielding their eyes to follow the pointing fingers. Martin stood up too and strained to see.

"The police are here," he announced. Hastily, Mr. Truscott concealed his shotgun in the special pocket he had sewn into his overcoat. He was just in time, for a moment later Garside's silver Rover drew up with three Black Marias in tow. The back doors opened and policemen piled out. The walkie talkies attached to their belts made it look as though they ran on batteries. Keith went forward to greet Garside, and the two men shook hands awkwardly.

They made an odd pair, Keith with his straggly beard, his

spectacles, his cheesecloth shirt tucked unevenly into faded jeans, and Garside with his slick, oiled-down hair, his craggy features, his clipped moustache and his smart suit. It looked from the start as though it was going to be an uneasy collaboration.

And so it proved. Garside, a stickler for discipline and efficiency, was anxious to compare numbers (forty policemen, close on one hundred and fifty villagers), and begin arranging them immediately into groups of three and four. Keith, however, wanted to get down to the woods and, once there, let the groups sort themselves out—as long as each group was armed and equipped with a radio it didn't really matter who went with who as far as he was concerned. Garside, naturally, was horrified at such a free and easy attitude, and, predictably enough, within a few minutes the two men were at loggerheads.

"Come on, Francis, pull your bloody finger out," snarled Garside. "Go and deal with that lot there." He gestured over to where a dozen or so men were standing around, talking and drinking beer. Keith glanced idly across but made no move to obey Garside's order. He didn't even take his hands out of his jeans pockets which irritated Garside even more.

"Oh, they'll peel off easily into three or four groups once we get to the woods," he said airily.

"Never mind all this 'when we get to the woods' crap," retorted Garside. "It's now that we want to sort them out." Sweat stood out in beads on his forehead. He pulled off his jacket and loosened the knot of his tie, and, just for a second, Keith had the silly idea that he was squaring up for a fight.

But Garside merely slung the jacket over his shoulder, his white shirt glaring like a washing powder commercial.

"Look, there's no need for all this sergeant-major stuff," Keith said mildly. "It won't impress anybody. The sensible thing to do is to wait until we get down to the woods and then sort things out. It's pointless doing it here. People have already been swapping themselves around."

Garside couldn't believe his ears. "And you mean you just stood by and watched them do it?"

"Yes, why not?"

"Why not? I'll tell you why not," stormed Garside, a deep flush of anger reddening his face. "This is supposed to be a well-ordered, well-disciplined police operation. I am responsible for the people here. I don't want the finger to be pointed at me if some idiot wanders off and gets himself killed. Because that's what'll happen if we don't plan things properly."

Keith held up his hands. "Yes, okay, agreed. I'm just as concerned about safety as you are. All I'm saying is that I don't see the point in sorting it all out here. It's no good throwing your weight about. That just makes for bad feeling. These people aren't stupid. You've got to give them some credit. They're not going to go scampering off like children as soon as they come in sight of the trees, you know."

Garside whipped a handkerchief out of his pocket and dabbed ruthlessly at his face with it. "Look, Francis, you don't have to tell me how to do my job. I know how to deal with the public, thank you very much, but I just think it's important that we get a balance here."

"A balance?" Keith exclaimed. "What the hell's that supposed to mean? This is a search party, not a gymnastics display."

"You know what I mean," Garside retaliated, stung by Keith's sarcasm. He noticed a few heads turning their way, attracted by the raised voices, and took a step closer to Keith. He kept his voice steady with difficulty, biting off his words and spitting them out like bullets. "Some of these men," he said, "have been drinking heavily from the looks of it, and I personally don't think it's a good idea to have drunks staggering about. This is a serious situation, and I don't agree with people who want to get pissed and treat it as a laugh."

Now it was Keith's turn to get angry. "Oh, come on, Garside. Don't you think you're over-reacting a bit?"

"Am I? What about all the cans piled up in the litter bin, on the steps, in the gutters? It looks as though there's been a party here."

Keith shrugged. "A few cans, that's all. I don't see anyone falling around. These people appreciate the seriousness of this situation as much as you and I, you know."

"Do they? I doubt that."

"Oh, don't be a bigger fool than you are, Garside! This is their village, and it's their families that could be in danger. Who fucking cares if some people have a couple of beers before they set off. With all that's happened in the last week, you can hardly blame them. In fact, I could do with a drink myself."

"Well, I don't like it," Garside said through gritted teeth. "It's not the way I would run things."

"No, if you had your way, we'd all be lining up like schoolchildren and marching down to the woods in fours, holding hands."

"Don't be such a fucking moron, Francis!" Garside's eyes were blazing, and his face had flushed a deep, mottled red.

"You're the moron, not me," Keith retorted. He raised a finger threateningly. "You're the one on a fucking power trip. There's no wonder the police have such a bad name with pillocks like you running things."

"Now just you listen to me!" Garside yelled. He took a step forward, trembling with fury.

"I've been listening to you long enough!" Keith yelled back. "And I've heard nothing but shit coming out of your mouth."

Up on the steps, Martin groaned as the voices carried over to him. The argument was attracting great attention by now. Some of the villagers looked amused, but many more seemed unsettled by the dispute.

"Come on, Kev," Martin said. "We'd better do something, or they might start fighting in a minute."

The two boys made their way down the steps and through the mass of people. Martin pushed his way between the two men like a boxing referee and, drawing a deep breath, screamed, *"Quiiieet!"*

Immediately, the two men were shocked into silence.

Martin smiled and said, "That's better. You two should be ashamed of yourselves. There are lives at stake here, you know. It's Kevin's family that's important, not your stupid little squabbles." He gestured around at the muttering groups of villagers. "As you can see, you've hardly set an example for friendship and cooperation."

Both men looked suitably shamefaced. Despite the situation, Kevin couldn't help smiling. It was typical of Martin to take charge like this. There was something very satisfying in seeing a school teacher and a police inspector put in their place by a seventeen-year-old boy.

A moment later, Keith was smiling, too. He put his hand out to Garside. "You're right, Martin," he said. "Sorry, Inspector."

Garside scowled at the proffered hand for a moment, then grudgingly shook it. "Yes, I'm sorry too," he mumbled. The words sounded clumsy, tripping over themselves in their haste to get out in the open.

"I shouldn't have said what I did," Keith said. Garside muttered something unintelligible in reply.

There was a pregnant silence, which Martin broke by saying, "Can we leave you now? I mean you're not going to start fighting as soon as our backs are turned?"

Keith laughed. "No, I don't think so. At least I hope not." He looked at Garside for confirmation.

"I'm sure we can settle things amicably," Garside said.

"Okay then. Come on, Kev." The two boys made their way back towards the village hall steps and sat down.

"What was all that about?" Mr. Truscott said.

"Oh, I don't know," replied Kevin. "They're like big kids."

Martin lay back and closed his eyes, enjoying the warmth of the sun on his face and the drone of conversation below. A hundred horrors and anxieties lurked below the surface of his mind, but for the moment he tried to blot them out, refused to face them. In an hour from now, it would be dark and he would be in the woods, but for now it was warm and sunny and he was safe.

He opened his eyes as the orange glow was suddenly obscured by black, thinking that darkness had crept up on him unawares. A man stood over him, his hair flaming with a halo of sun. He was a thin man with a pale, rather sulky expression. He extended a hand over Martin's body to Kevin.

"Hello," he said, "I wonder if I might just have a word."

Kevin looked at the hand but didn't take it. He squinted up at the man suspiciously. "Do I know you?" he said.

The man squatted down on the steps, causing the sun to shine once more into Martin's face. Martin shielded his eyes and sat up.

"Not exactly," the man said in answer to Kevin's question. "My name's Philip Donahue. I'm a journalist. I work for the *Cranbydale Observer*."

Martin sensed Kevin tense beside him. "What do you want?" Kevin said, frightened.

"I just want to ask a few questions. That's all."

"Aren't you the one who's been covering the murders and everything?" asked Martin.

Donahue seemed pleased that his name had been recognised. "Yes, that's right," he said.

"We don't want to talk to you," a voice said suddenly from behind them. They turned to see Mr. Truscott, his face rigid, hands clenched tightly into fists. Donahue looked questioningly at Martin.

"Mr. Truscott, Kev's dad," Martin explained.

"Look, Mr. Truscott," said Donahue, "I'm only here to help. I'm joining the search like everyone else. I was hoping maybe we could talk later—when we've found your family."

"Not to you. We don't want to talk to you," Mr. Truscott repeated. His tone was threatening, his body stiff as a ramrod.

Donahue opened his mouth to reply, but Martin put a hand on his arm and gave the tiniest shake of his head. "Maybe if you ask again later, Mr. Donahue, when we've seen how this all works out. Kevin and his dad have got a bit too much on their minds at the moment."

"Yes, okay," said Donahue, admitting defeat. "I just thought I'd come over, you know."

"Yeah, that's okay."

"Well I suppose I'll see you later," Donahue said, putting out his hand again. Martin took it. "And good luck."

"Yeah, you too, Mr. Donahue," he said as Donahue left.

"Bloody journalists! All they care about is getting a good story. No respect for anyone else," Mr. Truscott snarled, watching Donahue saunter away.

"Oh, he's only doing his job, Mr. T," said Martin. "He didn't seem too bad. At least he's helping in the search."

Mr. Truscott harrumphed. "Bloody journalists," he repeated, and slumped back into inertia again, muttering to himself.

Looking at him, Martin felt a sudden overwhelming sadness, and behind it a cold, tensile fury. It was all so unfair, he thought. A family he had known for years, a family who had always been so kind and cheerful and happy, had been devastated, uncaringly torn apart in just a couple of days. Why? Why had it happened? Martin looked again at Mr. Truscott. He looked like an old man. His skin seemed to have jaded, to have become yellow and slack, and deep lines of worry had etched themselves around his eyes. It was a frightening transformation. Martin found it hard to believe that this was the man who had beaten him at swing-ball just over a week ago. His gaze shifted and found Kevin's face—the pale, waxen expression, the haunted, tired eyes. He felt like weeping. There was a hollow in his stomach, fragile as an egg, in which he was storing his tears. He swallowed. Now wasn't the time for tears, not while there was still that thin membrane of hope to keep the egg from breaking.

"All ready to go?" said Keith, coming up the steps.

Martin nodded slowly. "I suppose so. Ready as we'll ever be, anyway."

Keith sat down, leaned back, and let out a long, heartfelt sigh. Martin looked at him. "You okay?"

"Yes, it's just bloody Garside. He gets to me. He's so pig-headed."

Martin sniggered. "You'd better not tell him that. He'd probably take it the wrong way."

"What do you—oh, yes... I see what you mean." Keith smiled stiffly and lay back with a groan.

"So, what did you finally decide?" said Martin.

Keith lit up and took a long pull at his cigarette before answering, "Oh, Garside's got it all planned out. We're all to be divided into groups, given a number—one to thirty—and issued with maps. And yes, before you say anything, Garside does have thirty maps with him."

"He's very thorough," said Martin.

"Painfully so," agreed Keith. "Between us, we've managed to divide the woods up so that each group has its own little section to explore. Garside's got half a dozen men working away now with pens and rulers, dividing the maps up into sections. Naturally enough, each section is numbered to coincide with the particular group that's allocated to search it. If any group finds anything they just quote the number of the section and all the other groups make their way there."

Martin nodded, impressed. "It's a good idea."

"Yes, he's not short of brains. It's just the pompous way he goes about it that annoys me."

"So what number are we?"

"Thirty. We're the last group to go, which means Garside will be the policeman to come with us,"

Martin smiled. "Should be fun. Who's in our group? Me, you, Kev, Garside and Mr. T?"

Keith shook his head. "We thought it would be better if Kevin and his father were kept apart—too much emotional interest. Mr. Truscott will be sent off with an earlier group."

"What about guns?" asked Martin. "I haven't seen any sign of any yet."

"No, Garside's keeping them under lock and key until the last possible moment. I don't think he even trusts his own men to be careful with them. He assures me, though, that each police officer will be issued with a handgun, and there are even one or two rifles knocking about for the higher-ranking officers."

Martin nodded sombrely. "Hmmm... So, when do we set off?"

"As soon as the maps have been done and Garside's taken all the names and worked out who's going with who. Probably about another twenty minutes or so."

Martin looked up. The sun had lost some of its radiance now and the pastel blue of the sky was imperceptibly deepening. Night was on its way.

"It'll soon be dark," said Martin.

Keith nodded and followed Martin's gaze. "Let's hope," he said, "that when morning comes all this will be over."

"Amen to that," Martin said quietly.

The feeling of utter helplessness was the worst thing of all, but Angela Truscott felt she had to be strong for the children. She had awoken she didn't know how long ago to find herself smothered in hot, itchy darkness. After the initial panic, she realised she had a piece of rough sacking stretched tight over her head and tied at the neck. The sacking smelled dryly of soil and scratched her face like sandpaper every time she moved.

She had been lying awkwardly on her back with her hands tied behind her, so that when she finally managed to struggle into a sitting position, a spasm of pain shot from her head to the small of her back and ricocheted like a pinball machine. Finally, it had settled into a dull ache that coiled around her spine like a spring.

She had awoken to crying, though that hadn't registered at first. When it did, she called out, "Jamie, Sam," and almost choked on a mouthful of dust that tasted of dry potatoes. Her children had crawled towards her, Sam first calling out, "Mummy," in relief, which made Angela realise they must have thought she was dead. She had nuzzled up to them as best she could, like a mother seal with her pups, and had spoken softly to them until Sam stopped crying. They had sat, huddled together in their own separate darknesses for a long time, Angela reluctant to leave them though she knew she had to explore.

Eventually she had said, "Stay here. I'll be back in a minute," and had shuffled painfully across the stone floor, expecting at any moment to crash into a wall or a sharp corner. She almost crawled head-first into a coal pile, and a stray leg kicked over what she supposed to be a stool, which tottered and crashed to the floor. But, apart from that, their prison seemed relatively empty.

At last she had collided with something unidentifiable, something which appeared to be sprawled across the floor ahead of her. She had thought it to be a piece of furniture, a collapsed sofa perhaps, and had nuzzled curiously against it in an attempt to nudge it out of the way.

And that was when the smell hit her. It appeared that moving the object had released the smell, though she had been vaguely aware of an odour before then. The smell had caused her to recoil, gagging and heaving. It was a cloying, rich, cheesy-sweet smell, greasy like rotting meat. Angela had propelled herself back to her children, scraping her elbows, suddenly terrified of the object which had released the smell. She found them at last and lay, shivering, for a long time, eyes wide open though she could see nothing.

Since then, the smell had grown steadily worse. Angela imagined it creeping across the floor like mist, infiltrating the walls and the ceiling. She had refused to name the smell, though in her heart of hearts she knew what it was. They had been lying here for what seemed like days now, hearing nothing, growing hungrier and hungrier. The children had cried a lot, but Angela had managed to curb their panic by telling them stories. She had told them the story of 'Charlie and the Chocolate Factory' from beginning to end, stopping only briefly when the dust and her own hot breath had become too much for her. A number of times she had felt hysteria and panic rising within her but, so far, she had managed to keep it under control. Sooner or later, someone will find us, she kept thinking, sooner or later. She tried not to think about why they were here, or who their captors were; she tried not to think of the murders and the disappearances in the village. All she thought about was Alan and Kevin, and though that caused her pain it gave her hope too.

They would find her; they would be searching even now. It was only a matter of time.

When she heard the door open somewhere above and in front of her she stiffened, her thoughts frozen. Who was this? Captor or rescuer? She listened to the slow, measured footsteps getting lower and lower, obviously descending a flight of steps. Her hearing had become so acute, so well-tuned, that she knew when they reached the bottom step and began walking across the stone floor. She nuzzled tightly into Sam and Jamie, her first instinct to protect her children. The footsteps came closer, closer, closer, stopped. There was a long silence. The cheesy smell seemed to clog Angela's nostrils. Finally, unable to bear the suspense any longer, she whispered, "Who are you? What do you want?"

And a bony hand whipped out and grabbed her face, and a high, mad, sing-song voice said, "Feeding time."

⁂

"Good luck, Dad," Kevin said. He moved forward and hugged his father. Mr. Truscott responded, holding Kevin to him as though he never wanted to let him go.

"You too, son," he whispered. They broke apart. Mr. Truscott reached out and smoothed Kevin's fringe over to one side. "I'll see you later," he said. Then he was gone, plodding into the trees with the other members of group twenty-two. Kevin watched his father until he had been swallowed up by the shadows. When he turned away, there was something like agony on his face.

Keith was perched on a wooden fence, smoking a cigarette, knees hunched up to his chin, peering over his spectacles like a wise old leprechaun. He caught Kevin's eye and gave a *c'mere.*

Keith patted the fence beside him.

"Care for a seat?"

Kevin climbed up to join him. His movements were slow and listless. When he had settled, Keith said, "You okay?"

Kevin shrugged. "I suppose so. A bit nervous."

"Don't you worry, we'll be okay," promised Keith. Kevin gave him a strange look.

"What about everyone else?"

"What do you mean?"

"Why did you suggest this, Keith? These people don't know What they're up against. I'm scared some of them are going to get killed."

Keith was silent for a long moment. He drew on his cigarette. The tip glowed, illuminating his worried expression and emphasising how dark it had become in the last half hour.

"I felt it was the only way," he said at last. His tone suggested that he was trying to convince himself as much as anything. "Once the news of the kidnap was out in the open I felt there was nothing else to lose. Alone, we were ineffective, there was nothing we could do. I know I've endangered lives, but at least now we may have a chance, there may still be time to do something. And the people are prepared. I mean they're in groups, they have guns, radios..." His voice tailed off. It wasn't a pleasant task to have to justify his actions. He felt he had launched a badly-made boat in the hope that by paddling furiously they could get to the other side before it sank.

"I suppose you're right," said Kevin. He looked across to where the black, jagged silhouette of land met the sky. Only a few more brush strokes and it would be full night. "I'm scared," he said.

"Me too," admitted Keith. "Bloody terrified as a matter of fact." He tossed the butt of his cigarette into a roadside puddle where it bobbed and then sank without trace as though pulled under.

"There's that journalist," said Kevin, nodding across to where Donahue and three other men were standing, talking to Garside. They saw Donahue nod and gesture into the woods, and then Garside and the men Donahue were with laughed. This seemed to act as a cue for the discussion to break up. Donahue's group turned and, raising their hands briefly in farewell, trudged away into the woods. Kevin and Keith watched until their silhouettes had merged into the trees and disappeared.

"Group twenty-seven," Keith said. "Soon be us."

Kevin made no reply.

Donahue had never known a place that could arouse such fear as he felt now. It was a fear that seemed to loom over him like something vast and unseen. He could feel it tugging at his nerves, embedding its roots in the deepest, most vulnerable part of his subconscious.

He looked around and the fear was there in everything he saw; in the clutching, nightmarish trees; in the cold, dead slate of sky overhead; in the crouching, lumpy vegetation; in the bobbing shapes that seemed to lurk in the shadows just beyond the range of his torchlight. The fear was in all these things, pulsating and directionless.

He looked at his companions and he saw that the fear was in them too; he saw it in their eyes, in the tension of their bodies, in the way they walked with soft, cautious steps. Even Tom Nixon, six feet five inches in height and two hundred and thirty pounds of solid muscle, looked frightened.

Donahue could see the fear curling and flickering in Tom's vapid blue eyes like a small, slow flame, and he could see Tom's hand gripping the handle of a cricket bat so hard it looked as though it might crack and warp under the strain.

They followed the path for a mile before anyone spoke. Donahue, a little ahead of the others, came to a point where the main path split into three and meandered away through the trees in different directions. He looked along each path in turn and shuddered. They all looked equally murky and uninviting. Tangled black weeds stretched across the narrow passageways like waiting snakes, and the trees craned over in an attempt to blot out the sky.

"Which way now?" Donahue said as the others caught up.

"Let's have a look," replied Dick Johnstone, the young policeman who had been assigned to the group. He took out the map Garside had given him and propped it against a convenient tree stump. He shone his torch onto the map, the beam lighting up his red hair which glowed like fire above his long, serious, heavily-freckled face.

The others watched over his shoulder as he began to trace their route with a finger. Titus Rowe took a hip flask from the inside pocket of his threadbare tweed jacket and solemnly passed it round. Donahue took a long and grateful swig. The brandy slid down his throat and sat glowing in the pit of his stomach.

Titus cackled, "Y'look as if y'enjoyed that, son."

"I did, Mr. Rowe," said Donahue, handing back the flask. "Thank you very much."

Titus nodded and took a swig of the brandy himself. When he had done, he patted the bottle as though it was an old and faithful friend and slipped it back into his pocket. "Aye, there's nothin' like a spot o' brandy to calm the nerves," he said.

Looking at the little farmer, Donahue thought how healthy and satisfying the farming life must be. Titus was an old man, a whippet-thin septuagenarian with a face like a crumpled brown paper bag, but he had a physique that belied his years. His muscles were hard and tight like knotted rope, his back straight, and his capacity for strenuous physical exercise unquestionable. Both he and Tom Nixon carried *weapons*—Tom a cricket bat, Titus an iron bar.

"This is where we are at the moment," said Dick, his finger resting on the map. The others crowded round to look. "Now," he continued, "we take the left-hand path here, and then again here. After that, it's a sharp right and that should take us up into our area."

"Looks easy enough," said Donahue.

"Mmmm... we'll have to watch out for the ground, though. It's likely to be very boggy in parts."

"Wonderful," Donahue murmured. Titus turned to Tom, hefting his iron bar in one gnarled hand.

"I hope we're the ones to catch these buggers," he said. "I'll soon show 'em what's for."

"No, you won't," snapped Dick. "Those weapons are only to be used in self-defence." The retort was a little harsher than necessary, and Donahue suspected that Dick was using bluster to try to overcome his uncertainty and his inferior years. It was clear, however, that Titus didn't take kindly to the reprimand. He said nothing, but the way his lips pursed and his eyes narrowed into slits made the message clear—copper or no copper, no young upstart was going to tell him what to do.

For a moment, the two men stared at each other. Dick's discomfort was obvious, but he held Titus's gaze defiantly. In an attempt to clear the air, Donahue said, "Well, shall we carry on?"

Dick nodded, and Donahue moved forward to pick up the map, positioning his body between the two men so that their uncomfortable contact could be broken. He folded up the map slowly and handed it to Dick. Dick's expression was grateful. "Thanks," he said.

With the young policeman leading, the four of them

continued on their way. The path was narrow, allowing only single file, and the ground was slippery, almost oily in its texture, and strewn with chunks of burnt wood and a debris of vegetation. Daggers of dim moonlight spiked down through the trees and gleamed like metal on the ground ahead.

Donahue thought how desolate it all was, how silent. Yes, that was the worst—the silence. No birds, no insects, no animals, no rustling of wind in treetops; just a yawning, waiting, empty silence. He shuddered, his mouth suddenly very dry. He needed someone to talk to. Just ahead of him, Tom Nixon was blundering through the woods, but Donahue made no attempt to catch him up. Tom was not the most enthralling conversationalist. Instead he waited for Titus, who was a little way behind, to catch up. Titus's face was still set in a thin-lipped frown.

"You all right, Mr. Rowe?" Donahue said. Titus glanced up.

"Aye. Why shouldn't I be?"

"Oh, no reason. I was just asking, that's all."

"Aye, well, I'm fine, thank you, young man."

"Good, good." Donahue allowed Titus to pass and then fell into step behind him. "Are you er... are you a farmer, Mr. Rowe?"

"Aye." Titus's tone was not encouraging, but Donahue stuck to his guns with determination.

"Anywhere nearby?"

"Over yonder," Titus said, jerking his head to the right.

"Close to the woods?"

"About two miles."

"Any family?"

Titus stopped so suddenly that Donahue almost walked into the back of him. The old farmer turned and looked at Donahue for a moment, eyes shrewd and suspicious.

"What is this?" he said quietly. "Why y'askin' me all these questions?"

Donahue found himself unable to hold Titus's steadily searching gaze, and his eyes flitted away, fastening themselves on Tom's broad back.

He shrugged. "Oh, I don't know, Mr. Rowe. I'm just curious, that's all. It's my nature, I suppose. I have to ask a lot of questions in my job."

"Goin' to write one of your stories about me, are you?"

Donahue detected something in Titus's voice and glanced up. He was relieved to see a twinkle of humour in the old man's eye.

"I might just do that, Mr. Rowe, when all this is done," he smiled.

"Well you just make sure you spell me name right, that's all." Titus pointed along the path where Tom was just disappearing round a corner.

"We're droppin' behind, lad. Come on."

They trudged on. Titus produced his hip flask again and they shared a companionable swig. Donahue decided to try and smooth over the rift that had opened between Titus and Dick. Probing tentatively, he said, "Do you know Dick and Tom very well, Mr. Rowe? Are they from the village?"

"Call me Titus. There's only me bank manager calls me Mr. Rowe," Titus said.

Donahue smiled "Okay then. Titus."

"Aye, that's better. Now, what was it you wanted to know?" Donahue repeated his question.

"I know young Tom," answered Titus.

"What's he like?" said Donahue

"Oh, he's a nice enough lad. Trouble is, he's not all there, if you see what I mean." Titus tapped the side of his head. "They say his mam dropped him down a flight o' stairs when he was a baby."

Donahue plunged in. "What about Dick? Is he a local?"

"Naw," said Titus contemptuously. "He's one o' these know-it-alls from Cranbydale. Big head to match his big feet."

"Oh, he's okay really," said Donahue. "He's just following orders, doing what he thinks is best."

Titus grunted, unconvinced. Donahue opened his mouth to argue further, but at that moment Titus pointed ahead. "What's wrong with young Tom? What's he stopped for?"

Donahue looked up. Tom was standing still in the middle of the path, head cocked to one side as though listening. When they got closer, Donahue was alarmed to see the fear on Tom's face.

His eyes were wide, almost comically scared, flickering to right and left as though he expected ambushing warriors to erupt from the bushes at any moment.

"What's up, Tom?" said Titus.

Tom's head turned slowly to look at them. At first, it seemed as though he hadn't understood the question. Then, in a hushed voice, he said, "I 'eard somethin'."

"What do you mean? What did you hear?" said Donahue.

"Don't know. Like someone movin' about. Through there." He jabbed a meaty finger into the trees at the right of the path. Donahue shone his torch where Tom had indicated, but all it revealed was a dense army of twisted black tree trunks, each no more than two or three feet apart, their topmost branches writhing together to form a canopy.

"What's going on?" said Dick Johnstone, strolling back down the path.

"Tom heard something."

"Like what?"

Donahue was still directing his torch into the trees, moving it slightly from side to side. "He said it sounded like someone moving about. Here, give me a hand, Dick. If we both shine our torches in together we might be able to see a bit better. My beam just seems to bounce off trees all the time."

Together, the two men directed their torches into the dense woodland. In the combined beams, the trees looked harsh, almost white, like teeth, and they seemed to crawl and sway with a ghastly pseudo-life. But the torchlight succeeded only in making the surrounding woodland blacker than ever, and alive with moving shadows.

"I can't see anything," said Dick. "What exactly did you hear, Tom?"

"Dunno. Sounded like people."

"You mean there was more than one of them?"

Tom looked confused. "Dunno. Might have been one or more than one. It was like things movin'. Bushes and... things."

"I see." Dick looked thoughtful. He turned to Donahue and Titus. "What do you think?"

Donahue glanced at Titus, but it was obvious the old man

still held his grudge. His mouth had clamped into a terse line and he was giving Dick the same hostile, slanted look as before. Fortunately, Dick had either not noticed the old man's expression or he was choosing to ignore it.

"I suppose we'd better check it out," said Donahue. "Titus?"

Titus gave a brief nod of his head. "Aye."

"Come on, then," said Dick.

He moved forward, drawing his gun from its holster. Donahue and Titus were about to fall into step behind him when Tom said, "I'm not goin'."

Dick paused, unsure of how to handle this new situation. He said, "You must come, Tom. We've got to stick together. We can't leave you here."

Tom shook his head adamantly. "I'm not goin'. Not in there." He jerked his head towards the trees. Dick looked flustered.

"Me and Titus'll go if you like," said Donahue. "You stay here with Tom."

"But you're not armed," said Dick. "All you've got is that." He indicated the iron bar.

"Aw, we'll be all right," Titus said impatiently.

"We won't take any risks," added Donahue.

Dick hesitated, then said, "Okay, but don't go too far. Keep within shouting distance."

"Don't worry, we will."

Donahue smiled with a confidence he did not feel, then he and Titus plunged into the trees. They moved forward, Donahue's torch beam probing cautiously, seeking out hiding places. The darkness skittered away from the light then closed in again, settling like mist. Donahue found his breaths coming sharp and quick, as though shadows were filling his lungs, suffocating him. He felt sweat on his forehead and wiped it away with his sleeve.

"It's hot in here," Titus whispered. Donahue nodded.

A slippery, gnarled root snagged Donahue's ankle, pulling him up sharp and causing him to look down with a small cry of fear. He put out a hand to steady himself. The tree he touched was warm and damp, almost flesh-like, and he withdrew with a distasteful shudder.

Now Titus moved ahead, Donahue just behind him, lighting his way. After some minutes of aimless weaving, Titus said, "Aw, there's nothin' in here. We might as well turn back."

"I think you're right," said Donahue. He turned and shouted, "Dick!"

Dick's voice came back through the trees, faint and ghostly. "Yes, I'm here. Are you two all right?"

"Yes, we're fine. Look, we haven't found anything. We're coming back."

"Okay."

They started back, Titus in front, pushing his way between the trees, prodding aside clumps of black undergrowth with his iron bar.

The trees crowded in, jostling, their roots impeding progress like outstretched feet. Donahue gasped as a tree clutched at his hair. He instinctively ducked, causing the torch beam to dip and swoop like a wounded bird. Titus turned back and was relieved to find Donahue still intact, sitting on a tree stump, extracting bits of ashen wood from his hair.

"Y'all right, son?"

"Yes, I'm okay. I walked into a tree branch, that's all."

"I wondered what had happened, the torch beam movin' like that," said the old man. "I thought somethin' had jumped out on you an' grabbed hold."

Donahue chuckled. "Nothing so dramatic, I'm afraid."

Titus sat down beside Donahue. He looked about as though seeing his surroundings for the first time. His eyes were dark like black buttons.

"This is a bad place," he said. The statement was simple but, coming from the lips of the hard-bitten Yorkshireman, it seemed to hold great weight. Donahue shivered, and the hairs on the back of his neck quilled, itching like week-old stubble.

He raised his torch which had been pointing at the ground and swept it in a wide arc. The trees appeared to move in the torchlight, to hem them in like the bars of a cage. Beside him, Donahue heard Titus suddenly draw in breath.

"What—" he began.

"Quick, quick," urged the old man. "Back over there. Shine your torch back over there."

Donahue did as he was asked. Trees stared back at them. Titus looked agitated, straining his eyes into the darkness.

"What's up?" said Donahue.

Titus's voice was strangely hoarse. "I... saw somethin'," he said. "A shape. A shadow. A man. He was standin' just there."

Donahue felt a fear he had not experienced since childhood. Any moment now, he thought, he was going to run screaming through the woods as though all the demons of Hell were after him.

Titus stood up shakily, raising his iron bar to shoulder level. "Keep the beam steady," he said. "Keep the beam steady on that spot. I'm goin' to take a look."

Titus, no. The word formed in Donahue's mind, but he was too terrified to translate them into sound. He simply did as he was told, holding the torch beam as steady as his trembling hands would allow.

Titus seemed to move in slow motion. Donahue saw him walk, step by step, up to the trees, iron bar held before him like an extension of his arm.

He saw Titus's fingers coil around the dull metal. He saw him prod the bushes cautiously aside. He saw him peer into the trees. He heard Titus's voice, "Well, there's no one here now," saw Titus half-turn towards him.

And that was when the hand clamped down on Donahue's shoulder.

CHAPTER SIXTEEN

VOICES

Donahue turned, his heart threatening to hammer its way out of his chest. The trees revolved silently about him like a macabre roundabout. The torch, still clutched in his hand, picked out a face—the eyes and mouth black pits, the skin a ghastly yellow. Vaguely, he heard Titus's voice. "Who are you lot?"

The mouth yawned. The face shifted. A voice said, "Group twenty-three. Sorry if we startled you. Look, would you mind not shining that torch in my face?"

Donahue lowered the torch, his fear subsiding like the aftermath of a stormy nightmare. He swallowed and licked his lips, his tongue like paper.

"Thank you. That's better," said the man who had put his hand on Donahue's shoulder. He was tall with a pockmarked, moustached face and he wore the uniform of a police officer. The three stripes on his sleeve boasted his sergeant's rank.

Another man came forward, enormously fat with bulging toad eyes, yellow hair poking like straw from beneath his cap.

"Y'all right, young man?"

Donahue opened his mouth to reply, but the words jammed in his throat like rocks. The toad-man regarded him curiously, slack mouth drooling open to reveal yellow teeth and a pulpy greyish tongue.

"Yes... I... I'm all right," Donahue managed at last. The words seemed to release an obstruction. Saliva came squeezing back. "You just gave me a fright, that's all."

The toad-man grinned, like the successful perpetrator of a practical joke. He turned to his mates, standing in the shadows like hulking garden gnomes.

Titus said, "Why were you followin' us?"

"Because we don't know who you are," said the sergeant.

"Group twenty-seven," explained Donahue.

The sergeant looked sceptical. "Then why are there only two of you?"

"There's two more of us through there," said Titus, gesturing back the way they had come.

The sergeant frowned. "You're not supposed to split up, you know. The idea is to stay together."

"One of our number heard something. We came to look."

The sergeant raised his eyes heavenwards and shook his head. "That's all the more reason to stay together then, isn't it?" he said cuttingly. "Who's your assigned police officer?"

Donahue thought of Dick Johnstone—young, fresh-faced, nervous of the responsibility he had been given. "I can't remember his name offhand," he lied.

The sergeant sighed. "Well I'll just have to look it up later. Group twenty-seven you say?"

"We had no option but to split up," blurted Donahue. "The other member of our group slipped and hurt his ankle. Di— er, the constable stayed with him."

The sergeant looked long and hard at Donahue. "Is this true?" he said, turning to Titus. Titus nodded mutely.

The sergeant considered. "Go on, then," he said at last, "I'll let you off this time. But remember, stick together in future. This bloke who hurt his ankle, is he all right to carry on?"

"Oh... oh yes," said Donahue. "I'm sure he'll be fine. He just needed to rest it for a few minutes, that's all."

"Hmmm. Well get along then, you've still got a way to walk."

"Yes, your Highness," Titus muttered sarcastically.

Donahue was alarmed to see the tight, resentful look creeping over the old man's face again. Hastily he said, "Well, thank you very much for solving our mystery for us. As you say, we'd better get back. We'll no doubt see you gentlemen later. Goodbye."

He raised his hand to the group. They nodded and 'cheerioed' back at him.

"Bloody towny," Titus grumbled a few minutes later. "Who does he think he is? Thinks he bloody owns the place." The old man's face was crumpled into a crab-apple scowl, his lips puckered, his eyes small and black and glittering with indignation.

"Oh, he was only doing his job," said Donahue, finding himself once again defending the law. "At least he believed our story and let us go."

"Aw, he knew who we were straight away," Titus said.

"What do you mean? How do you know?"

"I knew all them blokes in that group, bar the copper. They're drinkin' pals o' mine. That big 'un was Trevor Buckle and two o' them others were Frank and Jimmy MacIvenny. That copper must've told 'em to say nothin'. He wanted to make us sweat."

Donahue thought that Titus might very well be right, but stubbornly he said, "Why would he want to do that?"

Titus looked at him with something like contempt, or perhaps it was pity for Donahue's ignorance. "Because we'd broken the rules, our group had split up, we weren't armed. He wanted to make us look daft. If he really didn't think we were tellin' the truth, he would've called up that Inspector on his radio and got him to read out the names of everyone in group twenty-seven. D'you think he would've let us go if he had the slightest suspicion about us?"

This time Donahue made no reply, and the two men trudged the rest of the way in silence, retracing their steps through the ravaged woodland as best they could. It was five minutes later when Donahue noticed that the trees were beginning to thin out. Beyond the trees, his torch beam picked out a nebulous, orangey-grey area. He pointed. "That must be the path."

Thirty seconds later, both men were standing on the path, looking up and down its length, confused.

"Where are the silly buggers?" Titus wanted to know.

Donahue shrugged. Uneasy thoughts were squirming, half-formed, in his mind, but he tried to keep his voice light. "We've probably just strayed a little off course. Maybe they're up ahead,"

"Or back yonder," said Titus, pointing in the other direction.

"Hmmm." Donahue looked for landmarks but could see nothing he recognised. "Dick," he yelled, "Tom." There was no reply.

"Heads or tails?" said Titus.

"What?"

"Heads or tails? Heads, we go on, tails, we turn back. All right?"

"Yes, okay."

The coin spun, a glittering light in the air. Titus fielded it neatly, slapped it down onto the back of his hand and revealed it.

"Heads. We go on."

Donahue looked uncertainly down the path for a moment, then he shrugged and nodded. "Why not. It's as good a way as any."

They started walking, the path unwinding grimly before them. Occasionally, Donahue would see something huddled on the ground ahead and his heart would leap. Then the torch beam would spear the shape, only to reveal it as a crumbling tree branch or the remains of a bush, slumped in death.

The further they walked, the more fearful and apprehensive Donahue became. The muscles of his stomach seemed clenched, gripping a fear that was setting and curdling like sour jelly. He had a paranoid, almost overwhelming impression that they were going nowhere, that the trees, like the path, were simply winding round and round on an endless reel, trapping them in a nightmare from which they would never escape. It was, as Titus had said, a bad place.

"This is hopeless," Donahue said after they had been walking for some fifteen minutes. "They're never as far ahead as this. We'll have to turn back."

Titus scanned the path ahead. "Aye," he said. "I think you're right. But let's stop for a minute first an' have a bit of a drink."

He sat down on what must once have been a gently sloping, grassy bank, propped his iron bar between his knees and produced his hip flask. Reluctantly, Donahue sat beside him. He would have liked to have set off back down the path straight away, but there was no budging Titus when his mind was made up.

"We'd better not be very long," Donahue said. "Dick and Tom'll be wondering where we've got to. I hope they don't go off into the trees looking for us. If they do, we might never find them, and they've got the gun and the map and the radio."

"Well, there's nothing to be solved through worryin' about it," said Titus. "Here, 'ave a drink o' this." He handed over the flask. Donahue took it and drank. The brandy was very welcome. Between them, Donahue and Titus finished off the remains of the hip flask and started on another which Titus had taped to his belt. Normally, Donahue's alcohol threshold was very low, but this time he was too anxious to think about getting drunk. He was relieved when Titus finally screwed the top back on the flask and replaced it in his pocket.

"Come on, then," said the old man, clambering to his feet with an agility that made mockery of his seventy-two years. Donahue stood up and again the two of them began to retrace their steps.

Donahue's fear continued to increase. He found himself wishing desperately that the group had stayed together. Now he and Titus were cut off with no means of communication. He looked around him. How he hated these woods! Even now he couldn't recognize any landmarks and they had only passed this way moments before. The trees were all so horribly alike—faceless, characterless, yet somehow alive, incarnate with menace. They seemed to strain inwards, their branches drawing a serrated criss-cross pattern against the sky. It was like walking along an immense jawbone between rows of jagged teeth.

"What's that?" Titus said, fragmenting Donahue's thoughts. Donahue looked. Something was gleaming dully ahead, reflected in the torchlight.

"Just something someone's thrown away," said Donahue.

"No, no, it's not." Titus's voice was strangely urgent. "I... I think it's Dick's torch."

It was Dick's torch. Donahue picked it up. Apart from the hairline crack on its glass face, it was the twin of his own torch.

He flicked the switch. Nothing happened. He held the torch to his ear and shook it. Something tinkled inside.

"It's broken," he said heavily.

"Dick must've dropped it," said Titus.

"Yes," said Donahue, but neither of them believed it. Both men knew that Dick and Tom would never have left the torch and gone wandering off without any source of light. They would have sat tight and waited, or alternatively called for assistance on the radio. Donahue toyed with the broken torch, fearing the worst.

"Well, what do we do now?" Titus said. "Carry on goin' back?"

Donahue considered. "I suppose so. We've been forward." Defeat washed over him. "Oh shit, if only we had the radio."

"Come on," said Titus.

They walked on. With each step, hope dwindled, sliding gradually into black despair. Occasionally, they called out, but the trees and the darkness and the oppression acted like a blanket, swamping their cries.

They came to a fork in the path. Donahue looked at it in frustration. "This shouldn't be here," he said. "We've come the right way, haven't we? We've been following the path?"

"Aye, I think so," said Titus, puzzled.

"Then what the fuck's this?" Donahue said. He sank down onto his haunches and buried his head in his hands. He could feel his mind trying to pluck his shredded thoughts into some semblance of order. Eventually he straightened up. Titus was leaning against a tree, looking glumly at the two paths which snaked ahead in different directions.

"We've got to think this through calmly and logically," said Donahue. "We went off into the trees to investigate a sound we heard. On returning through the trees to the path we had been following, we were unable to find our companions. We followed the path forwards with no result, and then backwards where we came across a broken torch. We continued to follow the path backwards under the impression that eventually it would widen out and merge with the main path. However, this has not proved to be the case. Instead of widening out, it has in fact forked, and now leads God knows where. So, what do we assume from that?"

"We're lost," said Titus.

Donahue ignored the comment. He was thinking hard. An idea began to form in his mind, bringing with it a trace of hope. "I think," he said slowly, "I think I can guess what's happened. I think we went the wrong way coming back through the woods. I don't think this is our path at all. This may be a parallel one, or one nearby."

Titus looked sceptical. "What about the torch?" he said.

Donahue was ready with the answer. "Well obviously it wasn't Dick's torch at all. It must have belonged to another group. Remember, we were all issued with torches and they were all the same kind. It wouldn't be so unusual for a group with two or three torches between them to just throw one away if it got damaged. That must be the answer. There's no other explanation."

Titus pursed his lips, mulling over the idea. "I think you're probably right," he said at last. "So, if we carry on walkin', we're bound to come across another group eventually."

"Yes, and then they can radio through to Dick and Tom and tell them we're all right."

"Aye, that's the best idea. Well, which path is it to be? Right or left?"

"Let's toss for it again."

They did. It came out heads and they took the right-hand path. It was a tight squeeze, little more than a narrowly winding passageway which snaked through the crowding ranks of trees. Thorny branches, stretched across the path in places, scratched at their faces, trying to hold them back, and amorphous clumps of vine and weed coiled round their feet, trailing like muddy shoelaces.

Donahue felt at times that he was being overwhelmed by the vegetation. The smoky smell, ever-present in the woods, clung to everything like a thick layer of dust, greying the torch beam like a filter. He had to bend almost double as a branch met him at chest height and called a warning back to Titus. As he straightened up, he saw that the torch beam had picked out something in the treetops above. He looked closer. It appeared to be something round and black and pulpy. It adhered to the tree like a fungus, but as he shone his torch onto it, it began to move. He managed to track it with the torch as it slithered down the trunk towards them. Then it struck a protruding branch and bounced off into mid-air and Donahue lost sight of it.

The next thing he was aware of was when something wet and slimy struck the side of his head and oozed onto his shoulder. He screamed and dropped the torch, plunging himself into darkness. Frantically he clawed at the thing; pieces of it came away and stuck to his hands. Revolting images pulsed in his head—grubs, brains, decomposition.

Tree branches jerked, tearing at his face. Vines tightened around his ankle in an attempt to drag him down.

He was trapped in gnashing, rending darkness.

Then he felt strong hands grip his arms, iron fingers bruising the flesh. A voice: "Hold still, hold still. How can I help you if you keep jumpin' about?" The thing was plucked from his shoulder. Titus's face came into view as a dim orange shadow, his hand holding the torch. Donahue looked at the black, dripping mass in Titus's hand. Incredibly the old man was grinning.

"It's a bird's nest," he said. The words seeped, one by one, into Donahue's brain, like separate items being chalked up on a cash register. As the last one chinged through, realisation dawned. He looked again. It was indeed a bird's nest, burnt out and wringing wet. He must have disturbed the tree, bumped against it, caused the nest to drop from its perch and dive-bomb onto his head. The thought caused a surge in his stomach like the release of a safety valve. His face muscles stretched wide and within seconds he was laughing, high and helplessly, the tension and fear being carried away with the sound. He laughed and laughed until his ribs hurt and his jaw ached. He laughed until he couldn't laugh anymore. And when it was over he knelt on the ground, head bowed, arms hugging his ribs, feeling weak and drained.

"Better?" said Titus.

Donahue nodded. The simple act seemed to require great strength. He stood up with difficulty, legs trembling. His throat felt as though it had been scoured with Brillo pads.

"Just rest a minute," said Titus. "Have another drink." He produced his trusty hip flask and handed it over. Donahue took a long swig. The brandy danced in his head, filling the empty spaces, sparkling behind his eyes. Gradually he felt his body relax. He handed back the flask.

"Thanks. I feel a lot better now."

In point of fact he felt a bit foolish. Titus wasn't saying anything and his expression gave nothing away, but he was sure the old man must be thinking of him as paranoid and childish. "I... I'm sorry about... this," he stammered inadequately. Titus patted him on the shoulder.

"Nay, lad, there's nothin' to be sorry about. I would've had the screaming abdabs just like you if that bloody thing had landed on my shoulder."

Donahue was grateful for the kind words, but he knew the old man was only saying it to make him feel better. "I suppose I shouldn't—" he began, but Titus suddenly tensed, held up his arm and said, "Shhhhh!"

"What is—"

"Shhhhh!"

Donahue shushed. Titus was standing, head cocked, listening. The seconds stretched out, became a minute, and Donahue said, "What is it?"

Titus's body relaxed. "I thought I 'eard somethin'." He smiled. "I'm gettin' as bad as Tom, hearin' things."

"What did you hear?" asked Donahue.

"Dunno. Sounded like a voice."

"Another group?"

"Could be."

Donahue cupped his hands around his mouth. "Hello. Anyone there?" he shouted. There was no reply. He tried again. "Hello?" Silence. "Well if it is a group they don't seem to be nearby. Perhaps it—"

"There it is again."

This time both men stood stock still, listening. The woods were silent—so silent that Donahue fancied he could hear the stars twinkling in the sky. After a moment he said, "Well I can't hear any-"

"Shhhhh!" Titus butted in. "Listen."

Donahue heard it now—the soft, low murmur of a human voice. It came floating through the trees and dissipated even before his senses had had time to fully latch onto and identify the sound.

"Did you hear it?" Titus said.

"Yes," replied Donahue. "What was it?"

"Ghosts?" suggested Titus. The word, spoken only partly in jest, seemed to whisper and echo eerily in the treetops. Donahue shivered.

"Think we ought to go and investigate?"

Titus nodded doubtfully. "Aye, I reckon so."

"I think it came from this direction," said Donahue, pointing ahead.

As if to verify his words they suddenly heard another voice, a woman's, that shouted, "Let me go," before being abruptly cut off,

"Did you hear that?" said Donahue, unaware of the fact that his own voice had sunk to a whisper.

"Aye, someone's in trouble," said Titus.

Donahue felt as if pancakes were being flipped in his stomach, but he forced his legs to move forward. As they progressed, the path became narrower and narrower, and the two men found that they were having to crouch, sometimes walking bent over double. The woods became even blacker, tighter, denser, in some places forming an almost impenetrable wall of blackness like the inside of a mineshaft. Donahue had never been troubled by claustrophobia, but he understood now how confined spaces could terrify people. Even the torch beam seemed to be narrowing, producing the illusion that the walls were closing in.

At last they could go no further. The walls of trees came together, producing a dead end of thickly tangled tree trunks and gaps plugged up with vines and bushes.

"Shit!" said Donahue. He kicked out angrily at a tree. The bark splintered and crumbled away into powdery ashes. Titus moved forward to examine the 'wall', sliding his hands into crevices, looking for a way through. Halfway along he stopped, rested his palms flat on the knotted timber, and laid his cheek against a tree trunk.

"What are you doing?" asked Donahue.

"I'm listenin'."

"Listening? What for?"

Titus crooked a finger. "Come 'ere." Donahue came. "Now, have a listen an' tell me what you hear."

Donahue put his ear to the wood, feeling a little self-conscious. "I've never stood cheek to cheek with a tree before."

Titus gave a slight smile. "Just listen."

Donahue settled down to listen. At first, he heard nothing but the faint roaring in his own ears, then after a while he began to pick out other sounds—creaks, rustles, the slurp of mud, the crunch of dead branches.

He felt uncomfortable; it was almost as though the wood itself was breathing or shifting in its sleep.

"Hear anything?" said Titus.

"I think so," replied Donahue. He listened again. "It sounds like... like movement. Soft and stealthy."

"Aye," said Titus, "that's what I thought."

"You don't think it's another group, do you?" Donahue said hopefully.

"Naw," said Titus. "There sounds to be too many of 'em. Besides, remember the voice—a woman's voice. I think we've probably found what we came here to look for."

Donahue nodded gravely. "I think you're right. We'd better be careful."

"Help me find a gap," said Titus. "See if we can see anythin'."

The two men examined the wall of trees thoroughly, searching for a suitable cavity. It was a dirty job. Every crevice was packed full of dust and ashes, and the trees themselves were like giant charcoal sticks, covering them with sooty stains. Finally, however, they found what they were looking for. Close to the ground, Donahue noticed a bush sprouting between a small arch produced by two leaning trees. He squatted down and pulled at the bush, trying to release it from its moorings. He soon found that although the roots of the bush were secure, its black coat of foliage was as flimsy as sodden paper, and he set to work picking it to pieces. It came away in clumps, slick and greasy like entrails.

A few moments later, all that remained was a bare, sorry-looking skeleton. Donahue peered into the gap he had made.

"See anythin'?" said Titus.

"There seems to be another couple of trees there," said Donahue, "but it looks as though I might be able to wriggle through between them." He dropped down onto his stomach and, using his elbows for leverage, started to shuffle forward.

"Be careful," said Titus.

"Don't worry," replied Donahue, "I will be. I'm not the sort of person who takes unnecessary risks."

He eased himself forward through the oily mud, which sucked and slurped at him, occasionally exposing a sharp stone or a piece of wood to jab him with. How he longed to soak in a hot bath. The image of a bathroom—white-tiled, harsh electric lighting—seemed like paradise. He paused to scratch his head. His hair and body itched with filth and dust and sweat.

He looked back. Titus must only be able to see his feet by now. He skirted round a bush with difficulty, swearing as the thorny twigs snatched at his jacket and drew a snick of blood from his ear.

He stopped for a moment, breathing heavily, and listened. He could hear nothing now, and somehow that was worse than ever. It meant the murderers—if that was what they were—had stopped. Perhaps they had heard him and were crouching in ambush somewhere nearby. Before he could stop himself, Donahue recalled a film he had once been sent to review by *The Observer*—a charming little piece entitled *The Axeman of Cemetery Lane*. One scene had been of a man, wounded by the axeman, who had escaped into a nearby graveyard and crawled behind a gravestone. For a while, the man had sat there, panting and gasping, sharing his relief with the audience. At last he had stirred and, feeling brave, had peeked around the edge of the gravestone. And then - close-up of swooping blade—*THWACK!* Off with his head.

Donahue closed his eyes. His body tingled. He felt a sudden absurd desire to sink into the mud and sleep until morning. He forced his head up and eased himself forward. The slopping of the mud as he moved through it seemed abysmally loud. Surely they would hear him? Hadn't he better turn back? But a terrible, morbid curiosity drove him on.

Ahead, the trees appeared to be thinning out. Beyond them, Donahue detected a black space and a wide bowl of sky, snippets of which hovered in the trees, plugging up the spaces between the branches like jeweled cloth. The black space was a clearing. If the murderers had stopped, this would be the likely place for them to have done so. All he had to do was round the last line of trees, which loomed like finishing posts. He shuffled forward, creasing his face as though that would quieten the mud, and made for the tree. When he reached it, he stopped, panting, feeling just like the man behind the gravestone. Bracing himself, he peered around the edge of the tree.

His insides leapfrogged into his throat, his fingers jammed hard into the earth. "Jesus Christ," he whispered. "Oh, Jesus Christ!"

There were hundreds of them, literally hundreds. That was what Donahue couldn't believe. He had expected maybe a dozen, certainly no more than twenty or thirty, but there was a whole army of them here, all lined up, row after silent row, like clones...

After the initial shock, his mind began to take in details. It was a huge clearing, very possibly man-made judging by the blackened remains of picnic tables and chairs. At one end, a picnic table, looking charred but sturdy, formed a kind of altar, and it was to this that Donahue's eye was drawn.

The man on the table was hunched and bearded, and even from this distance Donahue could see there was something peculiar about his eyes. He seemed frantic with energy, scuttling from one end of the table to the other like a caged monkey. His face appeared to be fluttering and jerking, stretching like a mask, but perhaps that was the effect of shadow.

For a long time Donahue watched the man, fascinated and terrified. There was something horribly wrong with him. Perhaps he was on drugs or having a fit. It took a great effort for

Donahue to tear his eyes away and turn his attention to the audience.

In a way, they were even worse. They were so silent, so still. Donahue shivered. They reminded him of walking corpses—zombies. The nearest person to him was a woman about six feet away. She was middle-aged and dumpy, an archetypal grocer's wife. Her dress hung heavily as though damp, and her legs were splattered with mud. What Donahue found most chilling was that one foot was clad in a fluffy white slipper, the pom-pom like a drowned rat, and the other foot was bare. He couldn't see her face. It was tilted away from him, hidden in shadow, but looking around he could see other faces and they were all the same—blank and dead, the skin somehow heavy-looking, the eyes glazed over. He shuddered again, feeling he had come to a morgue.

As his eyes became fully accustomed to the gloom of the clearing, Donahue noticed that a large number of the men were wearing uniforms. Not military uniforms, simply rough work-clothes—identical jackets, trousers, boots. Donahue was puzzled. The uniforms reminded him of something. They sparked a memory that he couldn't quite grasp. Then, as though drawn into focus, the memory crystallized.

Of course! They were prison clothes. Then... these men must be the escaped prisoners!

Now Donahue was even more confused. He remembered what Keith Francis had said in the village hall. What had he called the cult? The Legion of Lucifer or some such rubbish? Donahue suspected that Francis had been lying, masking the truth for some reason, though from all that had happened in the village he was prepared to swallow the notion that a group, rather than a single individual, was behind everything. But why were all these prisoners here?

He couldn't believe that over fifty inmates had been members of the same cult. What then? Were they hypnotised? Drugged? Had something been slipped into their food at the prison? And all these other people. They looked so normal, so ordinary. Donahue could not believe they were members of the cult either. Then who were they? The answer came quickly. The missing villagers, of course.

Donahue's mind was in a turmoil. His discovery had answered many questions but had raised even more. He decided to wriggle back and tell Titus what he had found.

But suddenly he froze. He could detect movement amongst the rows of figures, an almost imperceptible ripple like a wave on the sea. What was happening now? He craned his neck to look.

The bearded man on the table was going frantic, performing an epileptic dance. Donahue heard him say something, but he couldn't make out the words.

The voice was low, rasping, little more than a growl. A bald prisoner suddenly broke rank and made his way out to the front. What was that in his hand? A rope? A chain? A dog lead? He certainly seemed to be leading something.

A wave of pity and horror and disbelief washed over Donahue, because now he could see what was on the other end of the chain. They were people, people being led like animals. There were three of them, and as they stumbled into view his horror and his anger and his disgust heightened to an almost unbearable peak. He could see that one of the figures was a woman and the other two were just children.

Donahue's eyes burned with tears. His mind spun helplessly, unable to conceive of such depravity. How could human beings treat other human beings like this? Even from this distance Donahue could see their torn, mud-streaked clothes, the rough sacks which obscured their faces, pulled tight at the necks. Worst of all he could hear their pain, their pathetic, terrified whimpers. It was the saddest, most hopeless sound he had ever heard.

The bald prisoner suddenly yanked on the chain, drawing it taut. The cries of the woman and the children cut out as the chain tightened on their throats, and they fell, sprawling, before the table. Donahue had seen enough. If he watched any longer, he knew that blind fury would take him over. He mashed his fingers hard into the ground and pushed himself backwards. He felt wretched, disgusted with himself for abandoning them, but he knew it was the only way. He had no chance on his own. The best he and Titus could do was to find help. If only Dick and Tom were still with them. If only they still had the radio.

All his frustration, his horror, his loathing, suddenly overwhelmed him, and he began to cry, the tears hard and sharp and endless. He was still crying when he rejoined Titus. The old man pulled Donahue the last few feet by his legs and sat him against a tree trunk.

"Now then, now then," he murmured. "What's the matter? What's wrong?"

Donahue tried to reply, but something hard and bitter-tasting seemed to be lodged in his throat which produced only tears, not words. Titus saw him struggling for speech and placed a finger on his lips.

"Nay, lad. Don't force yourself. Take your time."

Donahue closed his eyes and gave himself up to his tears. Gradually, they ran their course. The crying became sobbing, the sobbing weeping, and the weeping finally trailed to silence. When he was done he lay back, breathing heavily, feeling drained and exhausted.

"Now," said Titus in a voice that was surprisingly gentle, "can you tell me what you saw?"

Donahue told him, in a voice so quiet it was almost a whisper. Titus listened attentively, his face grim. When Donahue was done he said, "Christ Allbloodymighty." His legs seemed to give way and he sat down with a thump.

"We've got to get help," said Donahue. "We've got to start now, straight away."

Titus looked up. "Aye, you're right. Come on." He clambered to his feet, and this time the action was slow and stiff and painful, the weary action of an old man whose age was beginning to tell.

Donahue moved forward to help him up, and the two men began yet again to retrace their steps. They felt beaten, in dire need of rest, their clothes and faces caked in mud and soot. They walked mechanically, almost mindlessly, not talking. They paid little heed to the twigs and branches that clawed at their bodies.

They had been walking for only a few minutes when Donahue saw the light up ahead. He stopped, clicked off his own torch, and waited for Titus to catch up. "Look there," he said.

Titus looked. About thirty or forty yards up, the path was a disc of dazzling light, obviously a torch pointed in their direction. By shielding the light from their eyes, they could just make out a shadowy figure holding the torch.

"Hello?" said Donahue. "Which group are you with?"

There was no reply, just the flat, intense circle of light, like an eye staring them down. Donahue took a step closer.

"Hello, can you hear me?" he said. "Look, we need your help."

Abruptly the light went out. By the time Donahue had recovered his wits sufficiently to switch on his own torch and shine it along the path, the figure had disappeared.

"I don't like this," he said uneasily.

"Nor me," replied Titus.

"Who do you think it was?"

"I don't know. I don't even think I want to take a guess."

"We'd better carry on. The sooner we get out of here, the better."

Titus nodded, and the two men started forward again.

"Maybe it'd be better if you switched off your torch," Titus suggested. "Then we wouldn't draw attention to ourselves."

Donahue hesitated, then agreed. Titus was probably right. He could always hold the torch in his hand and keep his thumb on the button. He pressed down and their world disappeared.

"Just wait a minute," Donahue whispered. "Stay here until we get used to it."

They stood for a few minutes, aware of nothing but their breathing. Then, bit by bit, dark, ill-defined outlines of trees and bushes eased into sight, providing the vaguest blueprint of the way ahead.

"Ready to go on?" Donahue hissed. He saw the dark blob that was Titus's head move in the blackness.

"Yes."

"Come on then but be very careful. Take it slowly."

They crept forward, hands held out like blind men to ward off obstructions. In the darkness Donahue imagined he could feel fingers prodding him, hands brushing across his head.

They're only branches, his mind kept saying, *nothing to worry about*. But whenever he put out his hand to grip the branch as a reassurance, there was never anything there.

Beneath his feet, things popped and crunched like the skulls of animals. *Just dead wood*, he thought. If the torch was on, he wouldn't even notice. Nevertheless, he squatted briefly to touch the ground. His hand met something warm and soft that squirmed beneath his fingers. He snatched it back as though the thing had bitten him, then, cautiously, touched the spot again. Nothing. Just mud and a stringy carpet of dead vegetation.

He shivered and turned his attention to other things. He wondered who the flashlight bearer was. His mind groped for the most comforting explanation. He was obviously a member of another group. Maybe he had heard them in the woods and had come to investigate. Maybe, at this very moment, he was telling the rest of his group what he had come across—two wild-looking guys, covered in mud, one of them wielding a metal bar.

It was only natural that he hadn't wanted to tackle them on his own. Maybe, and here his heart soared for a brief second, maybe the group would be just around the next corner, ready to rescue them from this nightmare.

They plodded on, Donahue trying to convince his turbulent mind that all was well, Titus stoic and silent, channeling his thoughts into the single task of going forward.

It was when they saw the light for the second time that Donahue felt his mind bend. It was a terrifying sensation. He had heard of minds snapping, of people reaching their breaking point, and now he knew what that phrase meant. His mind hadn't snapped, but it had come close to it.

The light was further away this time and to their right, as though the person with the torch had run ahead and veered off the path. The light flickered as it moved between the trees, like a searching, one-eyed beast. Donahue felt his throat freeze up, and alarmingly a tear ran down his face, as though that part of his mind which controlled his emotions had been thrown into chaos.

"See it?" Titus said.

"Yes." The word trickled out as a tiny whisper.

"Think we ought to shout?"

"No." Donahue heard the panic in his own voice and imagined the old man in the dark, looking at him curiously.

There was a long pause, then Titus said, "Righto. Let's just wait here awhile then, an' see what that light does."

So, they waited and watched. For a time, the light continued to hover in the trees like a firefly, staying in much the same place. Then, quite suddenly, it began to move forward, away from them.

"Quick," said Titus, "follow it. Don't let it out of sight."

They blundered along the path, trying to keep one eye on the light and one eye on the way ahead. The light moved swiftly, skimming along four feet from the ground as though the dense woodland created no problems for the torchbearer.

"It's no good," panted Donahue, "we're losing it."

"No," said Titus, "it's stoppin'. Look, it's startin' to come towards us."

He was right. The circle of light had halted in the trees as though getting its bearings, and now it was moving across at a right angle, weaving between the tree trunks, on a route that would bring it out on the path ahead.

"Think we ought to go an' meet it?" said Titus.

"No," croaked Donahue. He had a bad feeling about this, as though the light was something supernatural, perhaps a presage of death. "Let's wait here and see what happens."

"Aye, all right."

They watched as the light bobbed casually along through the trees. Donahue had the unpleasant impression that it was controlling their actions, that it knew exactly what it was doing. He peered closely at the light itself. It was just a torchlight, there was nothing weird about it at all. Yet he couldn't shake off the feeling that there was something wrong, something they had overlooked. And then he realised what it was.

All the time they had been following the torchlight it had appeared as a dazzling white circle, a mini-moon, casting only a slight aura around itself. Never once had they seen a break in the circle as the torch was turned to one side, and never once had they seen the actual torch beam cleaving through the trees. That could only mean that the torch had been turned their way, pointing directly at them all the time. It was a disturbing thought. Their attempt at secrecy had failed. There was no doubt now in Donahue's mind that they had been led here. But for what purpose? Perhaps they were about to find out.

The disc of light broke from its cover of trees and emerged onto the path ahead. It was about twenty yards away, swaying from side to side like a waltzing ghost. Without warning, it stopped and hung in the air for a moment, immobile. Then, slowly, it began to turn. For the first time they saw its beam, picking out objects with a flat, orange light. It swept over the ground ahead, momentarily lifting stones and bushes into focus before allowing them to slip back into shadow. When it had travelled perhaps ten yards, halving the distance between itself and the two men, it stopped and rested, concentrated for a long moment on something on the path ahead... then clicked off.

Donahue became aware that he had been holding his breath. He exhaled and switched on his own torch. Nothing. The path ahead was empty. Or rather... not quite empty. There was still the thing there, the thing that the other torch beam had alighted upon before going out.

Donahue now shone his own torch in that direction, trying to make out the object's shape. But it appeared to have no shape. It was large and bulky, slumped against a tree like a bag of laundry.

"What is it?" said Titus.

Donahue shrugged. "Let's take a look."

They crept forward as quietly as possible, half-afraid that the shape might suddenly rear up. It was certainly a curious thing, thought Donahue. It appeared to have four legs.

Behind him he suddenly heard Titus suck in a hissing breath, and the old man murmured three words, "Oh God... no," in a peculiar, halting voice. What was wrong with him, Donahue wondered. Then he saw what the shape was.

It was Dick and Tom. They were sitting against the tree, legs out before them, and they were grinning. Donahue was about to say hello when it struck him that something was wrong. Why did they each have two mouths? And why were they staring like that? And then he realised.

Their throats were cut, slashed cleanly from ear to ear, producing long, wide, bloody smiles. Donahue smiled back uncertainly. And then—*SNAP!*—his mind went.

"Nooooo!" he screamed. He raised his head. "Nooooo!" It was an anguished, animal sound. Titus stepped forward and put a hand on Donahue's arm.

"Son, don't—"

Donahue whirled, wrenched his arm from the old man's grip, and swung out wildly with the torch. It caught Titus on the head with a vicious clunk, and the old man crumpled to the ground.

Donahue dropped the torch and ran. *Away, away,* his shattered mind screamed, *away, away, away.* He ran and ran, ignoring the tree branches that clubbed his body and scratched his face. One branch crunched into his mouth, splintering teeth, another drew a long strip of flesh from his scalp. But Donahue ran on, oblivious.

Then, ahead, he saw a tree move. Immediately his mind closed up, blotting out the sight. He continued to run forward. The tree lumbered across his path, blocking his way. Donahue saw its face hut he couldn't stop. His legs were acting independently. He ran on...

And in his last moment of life he felt the arms of the thing closing around him.

※

"Cigarette?"

Garside looked distastefully at the grubby packet Keith was holding out to him, but he managed to keep his voice polite. "No, thank you."

Keith shrugged, popped a cigarette into his mouth, lit up, then stuffed packet and lighter into the back pocket of his jeans. The smoke formed a fragile blue wreath around his head which he flapped at and broke apart. He strolled over to where Kevin and Martin were sitting on sheets of newspaper, talking.

"You two okay?"

The boys looked up. Keith's eyes were invisible, his

spectacles like flat, silver coins reflecting the light of the moon. As Kevin watched a cloud moved across, making it look as though Keith's eyes were turning to vapour.

Martin nodded. "Yes, I suppose so."

Keith squatted down, his long legs crossing over like the slats on a deck-chair. "What do you mean 'I suppose so'? What's wrong?"

"What's wrong is we're not doing anything," said Kevin. "We're just sitting here."

Keith looked around as though searching for inspiration. They were in a natural clearing within a circle of trees. It was the first place they had found where the moonlight could penetrate, where they didn't feel quite so hemmed in and threatened.

"We've done all we can for the moment," said Keith. "We've explored our area. What else do you suggest we do?"

Kevin shrugged. "Oh, I don't know. Keep looking I suppose. Go over the same ground again."

"We will, just as soon as we've had a breather."

Kevin pulled a face. "I know, it's just... well, I feel so guilty just sitting here. Anything could be happening to Mum and the twins while we're sitting around."

Keith looked at Kevin, concerned. "Okay," he said, standing up, "I suppose we've had a long enough rest. I'll just have a word with Garside and we'll be off again, all right?"

Kevin nodded. "Yeah, thanks Keith. I'm sorry to be so... I dunno... impatient."

Keith waved away the apology. "You know what they say," he said, grinning, "impatience is a virtue." He strolled across the clearing to where Garside was looking at the map. Cigarette smoke trailed him like a lost child.

"You all right to carry on?" he said.

Garside looked up, irritated. "Already? Why?"

There was something about Garside, his superior manner, that got Keith's back up. However, he kept his voice calm.

"It's Kevin. He's anxious about his mum. I think it would be best for him if we kept moving."

Garside glanced across. "He looks all right to me."

Keith's voice hardened just a touch. "Well, he's not. I've

been talking to him. I think we should move on."

Garside tutted, but began to fold up the map. "All right, if it'll make him happy."

"Thank you, Inspector," Keith said sweetly. "Okay," he called across to Kevin and Martin, "get your stuff together. We'll carry on."

The boys scrambled to their feet. Kevin scrunched up the sheets of newspaper, Martin searched through his jacket pockets for his torch.

"I think it might be an idea to go and have a look at that... what do they call it?... winter tree," said Keith.

"Why?" Garside replied, picking up the rifle he had been carrying and slinging it over his shoulder.

Keith shrugged. "Oh, I don't know. I've just got a feeling about it, that's all. Maybe it'll tell us something."

Garside gave Keith a strange look and said, "It's not in our area."

Keith sighed. "I know, but it's not far away. It wouldn't take us long to get there."

Garside looked unconvinced.

"Come on, Inspector," Keith persisted, "what harm is it going to do? If it had been up to you, we'd still be sitting round here for God knows how long."

Garside shook his head. "I don't think so."

"Please, Inspector, let's just go and have a quick look," said Martin.

He felt a strange excitement at the prospect of visiting the scene of the crime. Garside admitted defeat. "Oh, all right then. But we'd better not be too long."

They set off, Garside in front, Keith second, and Martin and Kevin together, bringing up the rear. Keith lit another cigarette. He was a heavy smoker at the best of times, but that evening he had surpassed himself, chain-smoking his way through one and a half packs of twenty. He counted his supply. Only another nine cigarettes left. Wistfully, he touched the bulge in the breast pocket of his denim jacket, the tin which contained his quarter ounce of grass. How he longed to smoke it, but he didn't think Garside would take too favourable a view.

The going here was easy. The ground was still hard, not too muddy, and the path was wide. The trees seemed to stand back, watchful. Martin wiped sweat from his forehead.

"Phew, it's like an oven," he said to Kevin. "I could murder a pint."

Kevin nodded and smiled though he hadn't noticed the heat. He had been preoccupied thinking about his family.

Five minutes later, they stood at the edge of the valley. Martin pointed across to the other side. "The tree's over there and a bit further along the path," he said.

Garside gave him a strange look, half-questioning, half-suspicious. "How do you know?"

Martin felt his face burn as it blushed red and was glad of the dark. "I've seen the map," he blustered. "The place is ringed. We've come here since we were kids."

Garside opened his mouth to reply, but before he could do so, Keith said, "Come on. Let's go and have a look at it."

They scaled the wall and began to trudge down the side of the valley towards the stream at the bottom. The ground here was little more than muddy ashes, and their feet sank up to their ankles with every step.

"Bloody stuff gets everywhere," said Keith, spitting ash from his mouth. It left a smoky taste, worse than cigarettes.

"The fire started around this area," Garside said. "The heat was at its most intense here."

"I envy the first lot of groups." Keith said. "Their section of the woods isn't burnt at all."

"No, but they had to walk through all this lot to get there," said Garside. "And when we've done for the night, they'll have to walk through it all again to get back."

"True."

Kevin and Martin were a little way ahead. Martin nudged Kevin and pointed up to the other side of the valley. "Look, Kev, there's our old den again."

Kevin looked. The den loomed above them like a huge, empty face, blank and featureless, its shape traced against the night sky. Martin played his torch over its pitted surface. Shadows retreated from the light, shrinking into hollows like timid sea-creatures.

"It looks so different now," Kevin whispered. "Sort of... spooky."

Martin nodded. "It does, doesn't it?" His torch beam left the den and straggled down the hillside, returning to them. They had reached the valley floor by now. Despite the heavy rain, all that was left of the stream was a runnel of marshy leaves, and rocks half-submerged in mud.

"I wonder where the water's gone," said Kevin sadly. "Water can't burn, can it?"

"Evaporated," said Martin wisely.

The two boys crossed the stream and trudged up the other side of the valley. By stooping forward and digging their toes into the soft ground, they found it was just like climbing stairs. Kevin reached out for the ear-trumpet shaped root that jutted from the main body of the den with the intention of pulling himself up the last couple of feet, but the root mouldered away at his touch. Caught by surprise, he lost his footing and slipped back down the hillside, arms flailing like a frenzied scarecrow. Halfway down, he managed to regain his balance. He stood, panting, while dust and ash billowed around him. Up above, Martin was laughing.

"You should have seen yourself," Martin hooted. "You looked so funny."

"Fuck off," Kevin said amiably. He climbed again to the top. Keith and Garside had overtaken him and were now standing with Martin. All three were grinning, but Kevin didn't mind. He was just pleased to be doing something. To him, being out in the woods was better than moping round the house all day. Keith held out a hand. Kevin took it and was hauled up over the edge.

They trudged along the top of the valley. Kevin took one last look back at the den and shuddered. The roots made him think of blackened, shriveled arms, reaching out to him entreatingly.

A few minutes later, Keith stopped and pointed, "My God, look at that," he breathed.

Ahead of them, they saw a glittering, twinkling radiance spiking the darkness. They moved towards it almost reverently. Martin felt his foot skid away from under him and he looked down. The ground was covered with a thin layer of ice. He jabbed down with his heel. The ice cracked, and black, muddy water oozed out like blood.

"Be careful," he said. "The ground is slippery."

They could see the tree now. It reared towards the night sky, white and gleaming. The ice was like skin, transparent, placental. Beneath it they could see the outline of the original tree, like something trapped.

"It's fantastic," breathed Keith. He shuffled over the blanket of ice, holding out his arms for balance. At last, he reached the tree and touched it. As he did so, Kevin shivered.

"I don't like it," he said, keeping his voice low as though the tree might hear him. "It's... creepy."

The tree was like something half-formed, like a foetus that was even now growing and developing. Stumps were sprouting like arms, ridges in the trunk seemed to be slowly changing, acquiring human characteristics. And way up on the bark, a bump between two hollows; surely the beginnings of a face?

"Look at the other trees," said Kevin. "They're going the same way."

Martin looked. He hadn't noticed it before, but Kevin was right. The ice was crawling like a fungus, slowly smothering everything around it. The trees nearest to the centre were almost covered already, and he could see trees twenty feet beyond that with tell-tale signs of frost collecting on their trunks like cold handprints.

"God, what is it? What's making it happen?"

"Swaney," Kevin whispered.

Martin looked around fearfully, as though mention of the name might act as an invocation. He pondered Kevin's answer. "No," he said finally. "No, we did this!"

Kevin looked at the ground, his face troubled. Martin clutched his arm.

"Kev, we did this! We're responsible for everything!"

Kevin wrenched his arm away and rounded on his friend. "I know," he said, his face suddenly furious. Keith and Garside turned at the loudness of his voice. "I know we are! But there's nothing we can do now! It was an accident, wasn't it?"

Martin didn't answer. His eyes were wide and appalled as

though the realisation had only just struck him, the true scale of the blame that could be laid at his and Kevin's door.

Garside's voice was dark and heavy with suspicion. "What was an accident?" he demanded. "'What are you talking about?'"

"Nothing," muttered Kevin. "Martin was blaming himself for the kidnap. He left the back door unlocked. I told him it was an accident." His look was defiant, challenging Garside to pursue the matter.

Garside looked at the two boys for a long moment, then turned away. He would let the matter drop for the time being, but suspicion, his sixth sense, told him there was something wrong, something the boys were not disclosing. He sensed their guilt, had seen them whispering secretively when they thought themselves unobserved. Yes, there was definitely something... he would just have to bide his time.

"What was all that about?" Keith asked, a trifle too glibly Garside thought.

"Oh, nothing." Garside mustered a smile. "I just think the boys are feeling the tension a little."

"I see." Keith looked as though he was about to say more but changed his mind. Instead he walked back to the tree. "You know, this is incredible. The ice just seems to form from nothing."

"Is that so?" Garside tried to sound interested, but he was listening out for Kevin and Martin, trying to overhear their conversation. It was no good, they were too far away. Perhaps if he moved closer...

"Why did you have to go and shout like that?" Martin hissed.

"It was your fault, grabbing my arm, going on at me. Mart, I know what we've done. You don't have to go on about it."

Martin looked weary, the shadows dark as bruises beneath his eyes. "I've just never really thought about it before though," he said. "It's never really struck me that way. I'm not saying I'm stupid. I mean, of course I realized... it's just...well, I suppose I've been blotting it out." His voice took on a note almost of wonderment. "Kev, all this..." he gestured around him, "is our fault. We're responsible for the fire, for Swaney, for the murders, for the meeting in the village hall, for the journalists, for the police... everything."

"I know," Kevin said dully.

Martin's voice held a note of desperation. "So, what do we do? How can we stop it?"

Kevin shrugged. "Kill Swaney again?"

Martin was about to reply, but Kevin noticed Garside sidling closer.

"Can we go back now, Inspector?" he said loudly.

"Er... yes, if Mr. Francis is ready."

"I'm ready," said Keith. He took one last look at the winter tree. "Amazing," he said. "It's almost beautiful."

They began to head back along the valley top. Martin trailed at the rear, for once silent and withdrawn. Try as he might, he couldn't shake an image from his mind. The image of the Earth, hanging in space, completely coated in ice.

⚬⌒⌒⌒⚬

Angela Truscott was dragged, kicking and screaming, up to the table.

"Mummy," sobbed Samantha, her voice muffled through the sacking hood. The figure holding the children captive cuffed the little girl casually on the head, knocking her down. She lay there, sniveling.

"Bring her to me," croaked Silas.

"No!" howled Angela. She renewed her efforts to escape, but it was no use. She felt her body come into contact with crumbling wood; she was dragged across it and laid flat. Weights were crushing down unbearably on her arms, so much so that she thought her shoulders would strain out of their sockets. She squirmed slightly and the pain in her arms intensified, wrenching a gasp from her throat.

Slowly, Silas raised his hand. Moonlight gleamed on the knife he held. His face twisted into a horrible parody of amusement, and from his mouth came a throaty, pig-like sound that might have been a chuckle. He pressed his face close to Angela's. She flinched back. Even through her sacking hood, his breath smelled like the thing in the cellar. In her ear a voice whispered lovingly,

"Feed me."

Titus struggled into wakefulness. The top of his head seemed to be bulging outwards as if his brain were swelling. His lips felt tacky, and someone had poured treacle down his neck. He touched it. No, it wasn't treacle; it was blood. His hand went to the top of his head as memory throbbed back. *Donahue. Where was Donahue?* His thoughts were veiled, muffled as if by fog. He felt his mind groping, trying to clear itself.

Bit by bit, shards of memory began to float back, like pieces of a smashed mirror reassembling itself. The woods. Dick and Tom dead. Donahue. The torch. He had been hit with the torch. He sat up and his head swam with pain. He fished a handkerchief from his pocket and dabbed at his head. The handkerchief came away covered in blood.

Beside him, Dick and Tom lolled like drunks. He looked away. The almost surgical neatness of their slashed throats sickened him. But the sight spawned another thought. It almost bubbled to the surface then fell back, swamped. Then, unexpectedly, it came to him again. *The radio!*

He turned back, trying to avoid looking at Dick's throat. The radio was still there, clipped to the dead policeman's belt. Titus removed it, plucking the body into brief motion. The nausea rose in him again, his saliva juicy and metallic. He had seen hundreds of sheep and cattle and pigs with their throats cut, had even slaughtered some of them himself, but none of that could compare to this. He tried to put the thought aside and turned to the radio. Now, how did the bloody thing work? He examined it for a moment, then switched to *transmit* and said, "Hello, hello, can anyone hear me?"

There was a tinny buzz of static, then a voice. "Receiving you loud and clear. What seems to be the problem?"

Titus felt his head spin again. He struggled to stay conscious. His words came, clogged and thick. "I'm Titus Rowe.

Group twenty-seven. We've found the buggers. They've... got that... woman and her kids with 'em."

This time there was a babble of voices. They cut out and one asserted itself. "What is your present position?"

Titus looked round, bewildered. "I... I'm not sure. We got lost. But... but look for a clearin' near area twenty-seven. That's where they are... please hurry."

Again, the tinny voice, this time urgent. "Look, can I speak to your appointed officer? We need exact details."

Titus looked at Dick, at the red, wide, oozing grin, and a small sound escaped him. "Dead... they're all dead... I'm the only one left..."

He felt his eyes revolve and cloud over. The voice over the radio, frantic, insistent, spun away, echoing down a long tunnel. Then something cast a blanket over his mind and dragged him down into unconsciousness.

꩜

"Hello! Hello! Answer me! Please answer!"

Mr. Truscott's voice became frantic. The policeman from whom Mr. Truscott had snatched the radio put a hand on his arm to calm him down.

"Please, Mr. Truscott. He obviously can't answer or he would have done so. It's an open line."

Mr. Truscott swung round, and his eyes were so desperate, so enraged, that the policeman took a nervous step backwards.

"This is my wife, my children. We've got to go to them now."

"Mr. Truscott, I appreciate the urgency of the situation—"

"Now!" Mr. Truscott shouted.

Morgan Rice, a large, bald-headed West Indian who was better known in the wrestling ring as Morgan the Mauler, interposed his body between Mr. Truscott and the police constable, Steven Morelli.

"Now, come on, sir," he rumbled, "don't get excited. I'm sure the constable knows what to do."

Mr. Truscott seemed to calm down. He handed back the radio. "Yes... yes, of course. But please, we must hurry."

Morelli was already unfolding his map. "He said a clearing in area twenty-seven." His finger jabbed at the map. "That must be here." He quickly worked out the route, all the time aware of Mr. Truscott hovering agitatedly at his shoulder.

"How long will it take to get there?" Mr. Truscott asked.

"Fifteen minutes," estimated Morelli.

"Will all the other groups have received the message?"

"Yes, they should have done."

"Come on, then, let's go."

"That's Mum! They've found Mum!" Kevin shouted. He listened, breathless, as Titus's voice came over the radio. When it trailed away he looked up, panic-stricken. "What's happened? Why has he gone off? Try and get him back." Unconsciously imitating his father's actions, he made a snatch for the radio. Garside held it away from him.

"Something must have happened to him," Garside said.

"You mean... he was killed?" Kevin's voice was strained.

Garside and Keith exchanged a glance, so quick it was more of a ricochet.

"No, no, it sounds as if he passed out."

"But he said he was the only one left. He said they were all dead."

"Who was in group twenty-seven?" Keith asked.

Garside drew a list from his pocket and began to unfold it. In that moment, Kevin hated them both. "What does it fucking matter who was in it?" he said, his voice trembling. "We've got to go to Mum and... the kids... they might still... be alive." His voice finally cracked, was overtaken by sobs. Martin put an arm round his shoulder.

Garside handed the list hastily to Keith and, looking almost shamefaced, took the map from his other pocket and spread it out on the ground.

"Now, let's see," he said, "area twenty-seven."

"Donahue," said Keith.

"What?"

"That journalist, Donahue. He was in twenty-seven."

"Poor sods," said Martin. "I wonder what happened to them."

"Here," said Garside, pointing at the map. "That must be the clearing the old man meant. It's not far. Only twenty minutes away."

"We'd better get going then," said Keith.

They got going. Together with twenty-eight other groups they began to converge on the clearing.

Death whispered on the air.

Swaney felt its power deep in the woods, feeding, nurturing, strengthening. The vast bulk, the makeshift form, stood motionless, its hunger gorging the mind of Silas, filling the puny flesh.

Through Silas's eyes, Swaney saw the knife, saw the claw-like hands tighten around its hilt.

It made the puppet speak, the words thick and ravenous, each syllable a spasm of power.

"*Feeeeeeeed meeeeeeeeeee.*"

The knife flashed down.

Swaney was fulfilled.

CHAPTER SEVENTEEN

THE FEAST

11:42 PM - REPORT FROM GROUP THIRTEEN:

"...heading towards the area from the north side, sir. We've met up with groups fifteen and sixteen, so there's thirteen of us altogether now."

11:45 PM. REPORT FROM GROUP TWENTY-SIX:

"...we should be there in about five or ten minutes now, sir, although the going here's pretty tough. One of our lot, Bob Becker, thought he saw a light up ahead, but it's gone now..."

11:47 PM. REPORT FROM GROUP TWENTY-NINE:

"...by rights we should be at the clearing now, sir, but we seem to have come to a dead end. We'll try and get through, but I think we're going to have to double back and try again..."

11:52 PM. REPORT FROM GROUP TWENTY-SIX:

"...still not there, sir. Can't be much further now, though. Bob Becker reckons he's seen something big moving in the trees up ahead. The lads are pulling his leg about it, but... er... well, you are sure those gorilla stories aren't true?"

꧁ꕥ꧂

Titus groped his way, once again, into consciousness. His mind was moving restlessly between the two worlds, focusing in, then fading out, like the zoom lens on a camera. He groaned as reality set around him—the cold, the pain, the despair. Why couldn't he just sleep? That was all he wanted to do, sleep it all away. But something inside him kept prodding him awake, kept telling him it was important he didn't sleep for too long. He tried, but couldn't quite grasp why. His thoughts were dulled, muffled as though wrapped in grey cotton wool. Vague, aimless shapes floated before his eyes. Maybe his thoughts escaping. He closed his eyes and the shapes were still there. Their anonymity soothed him.

Once again, he jerked awake. The suddenness of the action seemed to tug at the lips of his wound, causing the pain to poke and prod in his head. He put his hand up, stretching his fingers as though in an attempt to hold the shattered skull together. As before, his hand came away drenched in blood and a watery seepage.

I might die, Titus thought suddenly, and was surprised to find the thought didn't alarm him at all. He closed his eyes, feeling he never wanted to open them again...

...and jerked awake once more, this time with a dreamy certainty that something had woken him. He had been woken by... by... He tried to clutch at the thought as it wavered on the edge of consciousness, but it slipped away, unrecognised.

He sensed movement to his left. He looked and saw his brother strolling along the path towards him. And who was that hobbling along behind? Titus gasped. It was his mum. His brother and his mum. He could see them both plainly, and yet it was a very strange thing, because both of them had been dead for a long, long time. Ah well, thought Titus, they were here now, that was all that mattered. Soon he would be home. He closed his eyes.

Bob Becker's strangled squawk made them all jump. In his hand, the torch beam tottered drunkenly.

"For God's sake," hissed Sergeant Lee. "What is it this time?"

Becker's trembling lips made the words quiver. "There... Look... Dead bodies!"

Sergeant Lee sighed. He was about to deliver a crushing

rejoinder when he saw what the erratic torch beam revealed, and the words dried in his throat.

For a moment the group could only stand, gaping. Then someone behind Lee breathed, "Jesus God," which seemed to break the spell. Lee hurried forward, towards the huddle of bloodstained figures caught in the wavering pool of torchlight. They appeared to mouth at him as he approached, their faces animated by shadows as black as bats.

"Bring that bloody torch over here, can't you?" he shouted. "And hold it steady, for Christ's sake!"

"Here, let me." Roger Irwin, manager of Limefield's only supermarket, prised the torch out of the transfixed Bob Becker's hand and joined the sergeant.

Lee glanced up with a muttered, "Thanks."

Irwin held the torch as steady as he could and tried not to look at the bodies as Lee examined them. He looked instead at the trees, which seemed to hover like outlines cut from the darkness. He blinked as one of the trees suddenly detached itself and moved away. It made him think of a Disney film that had given him nightmares as a child, where trees with evil, gnarled faces had uprooted themselves from the ground. He smiled and rubbed his aching eyes. He was getting as bad as Becker, imagining things. Nevertheless, he didn't look into the trees again. He glanced down at Lee and met the gaze of the dead men. They regarded him with blank hostility. He closed his eyes, but could still feel their stares on him, marking him. "Jesus Christ," Irwin heard one of the dead men say. He opened his eyes to see which it had been, but of course it had been Lee.

"Are they all dead?" Irwin croaked.

"I'm afraid so," Lee said. He was squatting over an old man whose head was covered with blood, feeling for a pulse. Suddenly he started. "No, wait a minute! I think this one's still alive!" Carefully he examined the cap of dried blood and hair on the old man's head. "I don't know how much longer he'll last though," he said. "I think his skull's fractured. He needs urgent medical help, but I daren't move him."

"Isn't there anything we can do?" said Irwin, anguished. It was worse somehow that the old man was still alive.

Lee considered for a moment, then reached for the radio at his belt. Turning it to transmit, he said, "This is Sergeant Lee, group twenty-six, calling Inspector Garside. Are you there, Inspector? Over."

There was a short silence, a fuzz of static, and then a voice said, "This is Garside. What is it, Sergeant?"

"Bad news, I'm afraid, sir. We've found three men, two dead, one badly injured with a suspected fractured skull. I think it must be group twenty-seven. What should we do, sir? All stay here or split up?"

Garside's voice, shocked and angry, asked, "How did the men die, sergeant?"

Lee sounded almost apologetic. "Their throats were cut, sir."

The radio made a choked sound, followed by a muttered word that sounded like "bastards". The silence lingered before Garside said, "Do you think the injured man can be moved at all, Sergeant?"

"I wouldn't like to risk it, sir."

There was another muttered oath, then Garside's voice faded away as though he had turned to talk to someone. "Well, look, sergeant," he resumed, "the only thing I can suggest is that you all stay there with him until we can get some help to you. What is your present position?"

Lee consulted the map and told him.

"Right, any takers out there?" said Garside, addressing every group.

The radio crackled as though clearing its throat. There was a brief silence, then another crackle, then the hint of a voice abruptly cut off.

"Why doesn't anybody answer?" Irwin said.

"They're trying to," explained Lee. "The radios often cut out like that when the channels are overloaded. Don't worry, they'll sort themselves out in a minute."

After a long and particularly savage burst of static, a tinny voice said, "Hello, group twenty-six? Sergeant Lee, are you receiving?"

"Yes, loud and clear."

"This is Constable Parker, Sarge. Group twenty. We're heading your way. Should be there in a few minutes."

"Okay, thanks."

They were promised assistance from three more nearby groups should they need it, and group nineteen, who were closest to the original starting point, were ordered by Garside to leave the woods and fetch an ambulance.

Lee peeled off his jacket and draped it over the faces of the two dead men. He felt a little better now that he knew help was on the way but tried not to think how long it might be before they eventually got the old man into hospital. He busied himself trying to devise some sort of stretcher which would give the old man's head some support.

Beside him, Irwin was having very different thoughts. He couldn't quite convince himself that the moving tree had been his imagination. In that case, what had it been? The murderer? He shivered, remembering the reports in the paper, the talk of mutilation. He looked at the shapeless bulge of Sergeant Lee's jacket and shuddered at the thought of what it covered—the bloodless, empty expressions, the frozen eyeballs that wouldn't close, the neat red slits which stretched like smiles across their throats. Beneath the jacket, the legs of the two men stuck out grotesquely, stiff and lifeless like the legs of Guy Fawkes dummies. Irwin stared at those legs and, as he did so, he couldn't help thinking that somewhere, out in the woods, whoever was responsible for it all was waiting... and watching them.

~ ~ ~

They were finding it difficult to keep up with Kevin who was forging ahead, anxious to get to the clearing.

"Hey, whoa! Stop!" Keith gasped finally. He bent double, sure he was going to be sick.

"Wait a minute, Kev," Martin shouted.

Kevin turned and came back. "What's wrong?"

Martin jerked a thumb at Keith. "It's the old man here. He can't stand the pace."

Kevin looked dispassionately at Keith. "You shouldn't

smoke so much," he said.

Keith struggled for a reply, but his breath was too precious to allow for the luxury of speech. He felt as though all the tar he had inhaled had coagulated into a sticky lump that was hardening around his lungs. Eventually, he managed to straighten up and meet Kevin's impatient stare.

"I know, I know," he wheezed. "You don't have to tell me."

Garside was taking advantage of the impromptu break to get a few up to date progress reports. He was speaking into the transmitter, his voice low as though whispering intimate secrets. Kevin looked from Keith to Garside and back again.

"Ready to go on now?" he said. His eagerness to get to the clearing had had the effect of bringing him out of himself, and Keith couldn't help grinning.

"Yes sir," he said, raising his hand in mock salute. Kevin looked hard at him as though unable to ascertain whether or not he was being ridiculed. At last he muttered, "Come on, then," and turned away. Keith and Martin exchanged a shrug and a sigh, and followed, with Garside, still talking into the receiver, bringing up the rear.

As they got closer to the clearing, the path began to narrow, the trees squeezing together as though to keep out intruders. Instinctively their pace slowed, and they began to look warily about them, all experiencing the first crawlings of real fear. Keith swallowed, and his saliva tasted like rubbery smoke. Martin felt a desperate urge to relieve himself but dreaded the thought of having to go behind a tree to do so. Even Garside's voice dropped an octave as he spoke into his radio. To break the creaking silence, Keith said, "What's new then, Inspector? Anything to report?"

"Groups twenty and twenty-one have both reached the group with the injured man now," Garside said, "and group nineteen says there's an ambulance on the way."

Keith nodded. "That's good." He wanted to prolong the conversation but could think of nothing further to say. He was still trying to think a minute later when Garside stopped dead, his face intent.

"What is it?" Keith whispered, fear ballooning in him.

Garside waved him to silence and said, "Group twenty-nine have reached the clearing. Come and listen."

They all crowded round as the voice scraped through, heavy with static. Although addressed to Garside, the officer in charge, the report was really intended for everyone to hear.

The first thing Keith heard was, "Jesus Christ, sir, you wouldn't believe it. There must be hundreds of them, all lined up in rows, not saying anything. All the escaped prisoners seem to be here, sir, and a couple of the lads with me have recognised some of the people as those that were reported missing in the village. It's incredible, sir, you ought to see it. They must be on drugs or something - everyone looks so spaced out. At one end there's this looney, standing on a table, waving a knife about. He's the only person I can see moving."

The voice paused for breath. Kevin opened his mouth to speak, but Garside was already asking his unspoken question. "Can you see Mrs. Truscott or the children, Constable?"

"No, sir, I—Oh, fucking hell! Yes, I can now. Sir, the bastards have laid Mrs. Truscott out on the table just as if she was a bloody chicken. I can't see the kids, though. There's too many of these other buggers in the way."

Kevin flinched at the news. His voice was strained as he said, "Is she still alive? Ask him, Inspector. Ask him if she's still alive."

When Garside didn't make an immediate move, Kevin screamed, "Ask him!"

"Hey, Kev, keep calm," said Martin quietly.

"Yes, sorry," said Kevin, his voice suddenly low and subdued.

"I have... er... Kevin Truscott here," said Garside. "Mrs. Truscott's son. He wants to know whether his mother is... er... all right."

"How do you mean, sir?"

"Is she still alive?"

"Oh, I see." There was a long, agonizing pause which Kevin thought would never end. He was about to scream into the transmitter when at last the voice said, "I'm not really sure, sir. I can't see her moving, but she could just be drugged or unconscious. We've come in from the back, you see. We must have walked all the way around without realising it... Sir?"

"Yes."

"What should we do if that nutter makes a move with the knife? I mean, there's hundreds of them, sir, and I don't think we..."

"You do have a gun, I assume, Constable?"

"Well, yes, sir."

"Good. Now, do you think you would be able to hit the man with the knife from where you are without giving away your position?"

"Well, maybe, sir, but I don't think-"

"Then be prepared to do it, constable."

"But sir, I can't gun him down. I mean I've never-"

"Look, constable," said Garside, "this isn't the time for pussyfooting around. This is a desperate situation. Just do as I say."

"Yes, sir," said the constable unhappily.

"Don't sound so worried," Garside said. "Look, there should be enough of us there anyway in about five minutes to move in and arrest them. They aren't armed, are they?"

"I don't think so, sir, except for that one with the knife. I can't really tell."

"All right then, constable. Well, keep me informed. I should be there in a few minutes."

"Yes sir. Over and out." The radio fuzzed and cut off.

"You okay, Kev?" said Martin.

"He said she wasn't moving," Kevin murmured, his voice heavy with grief.

"He also said she might be drugged or unconscious," Martin said, trying to sound encouraging.

Kevin nodded, but Martin noticed that tears had pricked his friend's eyes and made them glisten.

"They've found them, Kev," he said, his voice suddenly quiet. "At least they've found them. At least now there's a chance."

Kevin nodded again. His throat felt swollen. "Yes," he said.

꧁꧂

"How long now?" Mr. Truscott asked for what Morelli estimated was about the hundredth time. Morelli was about to give the answer he had given for the past ten minutes, "Nearly there," when they rounded a final corner and found themselves at their destination.

"Does that answer your question?" he said. There was a narrow corridor of trees ahead which curved like the shattered frame of a burnt-out ship. Beyond them they could just make out a wide, dark, treeless area.

"The clearing," Morgan Rice said, his voice hushed with awe and dread.

"Yes, the clearing," said Mr. Truscott. His voice, by contrast, was determined and hateful, and his face grim. He strode forward as though he wished to have it out with the kidnappers there and then. Morelli went after him and caught hold of his arm.

Mr. Truscott turned, but before he could open his mouth Morelli said, "Let's not do anything hasty, Mr. Truscott, shall we? Going in with fists bared won't solve anything, will it?"

To Morelli's relief, the mask of hatred on Mr. Truscott's face slipped.

"I... I'm sorry," he stammered. "I don't know what I was thinking for a moment there."

"That's okay, Mr. Truscott. I understand," said Morelli. What he didn't understand was why Mr. Truscott had been allowed to join the search party in the first place. The strain was obviously getting too much for him.

They crept forward along the corridor of trees, lured by the moonlight which could be seen flickering in the treetops. There were five in the group altogether. As well as Morelli, Morgan Rice and Mr. Truscott, there was Jock Greening, a balding, toothless farmer with a wart like an extra sightless eyeball on his forehead, and Gerard Sparetty, a thin, nervous, bespectacled boy in his late teens who, Morelli suspected, had been shamed into coming by either his father or his friends.

"Better switch off the torches," Morelli hissed, switching off his own. Morgan Rice switched off the one he was carrying, and after a moment's hesitation, Gerard Sparetty's pocket torch clicked off too. Now, the only light came from the dim, silvery glow of the moon. Morelli put out both his hands for balance and touched trees on either side like ribs. He felt like Jonah walking through the black belly of the whale. He looked ahead, and at first couldn't work out what the tide of darkness beyond the trees was. He had almost blundered forward to investigate before he realised it was people, row upon row of them, standing silent and immobile. He ducked behind the mangled bole of a tree, turned and put a finger to his lips to warn the others. All he could see of them were black, hunched shapes on a black surface and he hoped they had seen him. Apparently they had, for all at once the largest of the black shapes assumed the form of Mr. Truscott and dropped down beside him.

"What's up?"

"Ssshhh. Look."

Mr. Truscott looked, and gave a gasp as though someone had punched him in the stomach. The lenses of his spectacles glinted silver-white, making his eyes look blind yet somehow angry. Morelli grabbed his arm.

"I don't believe it," Mr. Truscott said. He turned, and Morelli could see his eyes once more. They didn't look angry, just confused.

"Me neither," said Morelli. He had been warning himself to expect this, to expect all these people, but to actually see them lined up and waiting had still come as a shock.

Morgan Rice had joined them now, slithering forward on his knees as though his legs had given way.

"Jesus," he breathed.

Jock Greening muttered, "Bloody 'ell," and Gerard Sparetty merely whimpered and looked as though he was about to wet his pants.

"So, what do we do now?" rumbled Morgan Rice. "I mean, even with all the groups here they must outnumber us by two to one."

"Yes, but we're armed remember," Morelli said, patting the holstered gun at his side. "If everything goes to plan it should be a simple case of surrounding and arresting them."

"Arresting them?" said Rice. "But the constable on the radio said a lot of them were missing villagers. Surely none of them could have done anything wrong?"

Morelli shrugged. "Then why are they here? Anyway, it's easier to arrest first and ask questions later."

"Yeah, I suppose you're right," said Rice.

"Where's my wife?" Mr. Truscott wanted to know. His voice rose angrily. "And that bastard with the knife, where's he?"

"Ssshhh. For God's sake, keep your voice down!" hissed Morelli. "I've told you, you'll achieve nothing by making a scene."

Mr. Truscott did not apologize this time. He simply glared at Morelli and stood up slowly to get a better view. In the darkness he looked like some strange squat plant rising from the ground.

"See anything?" asked Morgan Rice.

"Just about," said Mr. Truscott. "I can see the cunt with the knife." He watched for a few seconds more, then suddenly emitted a low, agonised groan that made them all jump.

"What is it?" asked Morgan Rice. Morelli instinctively clutched at Mr. Truscott's jacket. In his opinion, Truscott was not beyond giving away their hiding place in a sudden burst of blind rage.

Mr. Truscott groaned again, like a pained animal, and then in a hollow voice said, "I can see my wife. Oh God, what have they done to her?"

"Here, let me see," said Morelli. He felt nervous, exposed without the full cover of the trees. Nevertheless, he stood on tiptoe and peered over the heads of the silent audience.

His first impression of the scene was so shocking it seemed to freeze in his brain like a cold, mental photograph. They've cut off her head, he thought, and each word seemed hard and huge as though carved in granite.

Then, gradually, he realised that that was not in fact the case. They hadn't cut off her head at all, she merely had something dark wrapped around it—a sack or a binding of some sort. She was lying, stretched out, on the remains of a wooden table, and even from this distance Morelli could see that her clothes were tom and filthy.

He groped for consoling words but could think of nothing adequate. The revulsion, the horror he felt was too overpowering to express. He felt impotent, helpless with fury. He was still struggling for expression when Mr. Truscott said, "Where's Jamie and Sam? I can't see them."

Morelli looked, not knowing who he was looking for. Then he realised that Mr. Truscott was referring to his children.

"No," Morelli said, and his words felt dry and cracked. "No, I can't see them either." He detached the radio from his belt and waited for a break in transmission. Many more groups had reached the edge of the clearing now and muted reports were coming in every couple of minutes. Morelli looked again at the scene in the clearing, past the rows of figures to the black line of trees beyond. It was comforting to know that they had allies there, hiding in the bushes like themselves, waiting for the order to move in. When the line was clear, he gave his own brief report and clipped the radio back onto his belt.

"Hey, look," Morgan Rice said suddenly. "Something's happening."

Morelli looked, and felt Mr. Truscott tense beside him. Something was indeed happening. The figure on the table was leaning forwards as though beckoning the audience, using the knife like a carrot to entice a donkey. Morelli shivered at the dead, inhuman grin on the man's face, the gleaming, bulging eyes which seemed to be always moving, always active, slithering wetly.

A small figure was handed up to the man. At first, Morelli took it to be a dummy made of sacking, then he saw its legs kicking and he almost retched. The man took the child, lifted it above his head in one hand like a trophy.

Morelli was so horribly bewitched by the scene that he didn't notice Mr. Truscott unbuttoning his overcoat. He didn't even notice when Mr. Truscott extracted the shotgun he had concealed there. Only when Mr. Truscott began to scramble through the trees at the edge of the clearing did he finally realise, and by then it was too late. He made a grab for the flapping overcoat, but it was a useless gesture. "Stop him!" he implored, turning to Morgan Rice. "He's got a gun!"

Shaken, Morgan Rice made a half-hearted grab for Mr. Truscott. His enormous hand closed on the tail of Mr. Truscott's coat, but was not strong enough to secure a hold. With an almost manic fury, the coat was wrenched from Rice's grasping fingers, and Mr. Truscott spun round, his eyes huge and furious.

"Leave me!" he yelled, froth spraying from his mouth. "Just fucking leave me alone."

Morelli shrank back, terrified, as figures began to turn blandly towards them. Their movements were slow and hesitant, their faces blank, their eyes white and crawling. It was like a morgue stirring into life.

Three of the figures, two prisoners and a young man naked but for a pair of shorts, broke rank and took a few jerky steps towards Mr. Truscott. He whirled to face them, his fury making him fearless.

"Bastards!" he screamed and, raising the shotgun, fired at one of the prisoners. The man collapsed, his middle blown open.

Before anyone could react, Mr. Truscott was running towards Silas.

"Hold on," said Lee, and shifted his grip to wipe the stinging sweat from his eyes. Constable Parker, at the other end of the makeshift stretcher, looked back.

"You okay, Sarge?"

Lee flexed his aching arm. "Yes, I'm fine." He renewed his grip on the stretcher. "Okay."

They moved forward again, progressing slowly and painfully. The need to keep the stretcher steady as they stumbled over the uneven ground made the muscles in their arms and backs throb with tension. One slip, one jolt, and the old man could be a goner. Mind you, thought Lee, looking down at him, he wasn't far from that now. His face was pale and mask-like, his body still. He was obviously in a state of deep coma.

It was a grim little procession that wound its way through the woods. There were two of Constable Parker's group at the front, one carrying a hefty-looking club, the other with a torch to light the way, then came Parker and Lee carrying the stretcher, and bringing up the rear was another man from Parker's group and Bob Becker with a torch. The rest of their thirteen-strong contingent had gone the other way, towards the clearing.

They were listening to the reports which were flooding in over the radio, all telling the same story of zombie-like figures and maniacs with knives.

"I've never known anything like this," Parker said, bemused. "I didn't think this sort of thing really went on."

"It's television what does it," came a voice from the back. "Television and drugs, that's what it is."

"Shhh," said Lee. "I want to listen."

He recognised the voice that was giving the latest report. It belonged to Constable Nuttall, the latest teenaged addition to the Limefield constabulary. The voice sounded very young, and as bewildered as Lee felt. Parker was not the only one who couldn't believe what was happening.

Listening to the reports, Lee felt that the situation was poised, that the climax was about to begin. He was glad to be out of it.

⌘

Kevin held up a hand, "Listen."

"What is it?" said Martin.

"I thought I heard something."

They all stood and listened for a moment, but the woods were as still as ever. Eventually Kevin relaxed. "It must have been my imagination."

"I wish you wouldn't do that, Kev," Martin said. "You're giving me the willies."

"What did you hear?" asked Keith.

Kevin shrugged. "Oh, I dunno. Movement. Rustling."

"We must be near the clearing now," Garside said, consulting the map. "Be very quiet, and careful as we go."

They crept forward again, like hunters through the trees. Martin kept his eyes on the way ahead, refusing to acknowledge the shadows that crept along with them. He almost leaped out of his skin when an explosion blasted the stillness apart. Kevin grabbed his arm, and even Garside, in front, jumped.

"What was that?" Kevin hissed.

"Shooting," said Garside. "Something must be happening. Come on."

They moved at a faster pace now. Trees appeared to lunge forward, then recoil as they passed. Suddenly Garside stopped.

"Shh," he said. "I think we're here." He pointed ahead to where the trees thinned out, forming an almost natural doorway. Moonlight glared harshly like an invitation or a dare.

"Be very careful," Garside said, and led the way forward.

The moonlight seemed to expand as they approached. Martin felt exposed, like an actor on a stage, and was glad of the shield of Garside's body. Garside half-turned and indicated they should move off the path, into the trees on their left. They did so, slipping into shadows that seemed to stretch between the trees like dense cobwebs.

They came to the last line of trees. Garside unslung his rifle and checked it, then peered around the tree he was leaning against.

"Jesus," he said quietly. "Would you look at that."

The others pressed forward to see. Martin thought that the people in the clearing were almost like a continuation of the trees they were so silent. But even as he watched they began to spasm into motion, moving hands or heads, stepping forward, bumping against one another. It was like a forest coming to life.

Suddenly Kevin pointed. "Look," he hissed. "There's Dad!"

⁘⁘⁘⁘⁘

Mr. Truscott was only forty yards away from Silas now, close enough to see that the thing holding his kicking daughter was not human. He saw the Silas-thing turn towards him, saw it open its mouth impossibly wide and gnash down. When it next opened its mouth blood bubbled out, accompanied by an oozing, red, slug-like thing that Mr. Truscott recognised as a piece of tongue. The Silas-thing laughed, and its eyes, though white, seemed to flare with hate and madness. *"Kill,"* it crooned in a silky-dead voice. *"Kiiiilll."*

The zombie-figures began to lurch towards Mr. Truscott. With revulsion he saw that some of them were slavering like babies. Others had snot dribbling from their noses. All had white, gleaming eyes.

With a mixture of hate, panic and disgust, he raised the shotgun and fired. Another figure collapsed. Undeterred, the others continued to shuffle forwards. Unable to reload, Mr. Truscott began to swing the shotgun like a club. Whenever any of the zombies came too close he battered them down.

"Stop! You're all under arrest!"

The order came from the other side of the clearing. The Silas-thing's head turned like a snake's. It opened its mouth and the remains of its bloodied tongue twitched.

"Feeeeed," it crooned. *"Feeeeeeed."*

Remorselessly the zombie-figures advanced.

"You must give yourselves up," Garside shouted desperately. "My men are armed. They have orders to shoot in self-defence."

But his words went unheeded. The zombie-things continued to advance, raising their arms, hooking their fingers into claws.

"I must get to my dad," Kevin shouted, and took a step forward. Martin grabbed his arm.

"You've got no chance, Kev. Not across the clearing. Let's go around the outside, through the trees."

After a moment's hesitation, Kevin nodded, and the two boys ran back into the trees.

Keith and Garside stood side by side, ready to do battle with the relentlessly advancing army. Keith had a half-charred branch in his hand, Garside was holding his rifle to his shoulder, though for once he looked hesitant, as though loathe to use it. Police and villagers were emerging from the trees on all sides of them and forming into a tight knot.

"Try not to kill them," Keith shouted. "They're not evil. They don't know what they're doing. Try to knock them out."

An old man to Keith's left suddenly broke rank and

stumbled forward. "Emily," he said, "Emily, where have you been?"

"Get back," yelled Garside, making a grab for the old man. He missed, and the old man rushed forward, holding out his arms to a thin, grey-haired woman in a pinafore whose eyes were yellowy-white and whose false teeth were loose and clattering in her mouth.

Without breaking her stride, the old woman grabbed the man's face, dug in and wrenched back. The old man fell, screaming, to the ground.

It was at this point that Garside lost control of the proceedings.

Some of the villagers, horrified by the attack, began to charge. After a moment, policemen followed them, and like rival football fans the two sides clashed.

Gun reports rent the air. Arms wielding weapons were raised and brought down. Fists flew. Slow, deliberate fingers, lethal as fistfuls of knives, ripped and pulled and gouged.

Within minutes the clearing was littered with bodies. Keith turned away, sickened, as a man fell heavily against his legs, blood spurting in a fountain from a torn jugular vein. A moment later, he clubbed down a prisoner who lunged at him, blood dripping from his outstretched hands.

⁂

Fifty yards away, Mr. Truscott was still swinging his shotgun, screaming defiance. But now the figures were closing in, herding him back, overwhelming him with sheer numbers. All at once, Mr. Truscott felt the shotgun stop in mid-swing, and a moment later it was plucked from his hands. He lashed out with his fists but was quickly overpowered. He went down under a wave of bodies, glimpsing shadowy faces, nightmarishly bland, smelling stale urine and unwashed flesh.

A pallid, hooked hand swooped towards him. He cringed away, closed his eyes. A moment later he opened them again, realising he was not dead. A white-eyed man in a torn Hawaiian shirt loomed over him, mouth open as though yawning. But even as Mr. Truscott watched, the man keeled over, clubbed down from behind. He saw the moon.

The next thing he knew, strong hands were pulling him up. Real faces, not blank masks, were looking at him.

"All right, mate?" said a voice. It belonged to an unshaven man with a tomato nose. Mr. Truscott put a hand to his stinging face.

"I think so." His fingers came away, speckled with blood.

"Just a scratch," the man said.

Mr. Truscott pulled his shotgun from beneath the sprawled body of a prisoner.

"Is that yours?" the man said.

Mr. Truscott nodded. "I'm going to get that bastard up there." He indicated Silas.

"You know you weren't supposed to bring them things, don't you?"

"You going to stop me?" Mr. Truscott's voice was suddenly low and dangerous.

"No, mate, no," the man said hastily. "Good luck to you, I say." He turned away.

Mr. Truscott reloaded his shotgun, looking at the scene around him. It was utter carnage. Bodies were strewn about, many of them bearing horrific injuries. Some were still alive, moving weakly like stranded fish, trying to make their pleas for help heard above the clamour.

Mr. Truscott looked up at Silas. The thing was crouched over, hungrily observing the scene in the clearing, drinking in the pain and the violence. He felt disgusted, but at the same time he felt relieved. Garside's intervention and the ensuing battle meant that, for the moment, Sam and Jamie were forgotten, though Sam's feebly struggling body still dangled from Silas's left hand.

Grimly, Mr. Truscott moved forward again, avoiding the battling groups, stepping over dead bodies. One body he stepped over suddenly reached out and grabbed his ankle. Mr. Truscott cried out in pain as the hand tightened its grip, obviously intending to grind his bones to powder. Instinctively, he pointed the shotgun and fired. The hand parted from the wrist in a shower of gore, but still it clung on. Mr. Truscott shuddered, kicking out his leg, and the hand spun away like a crab, trailing blood.

He stumbled on, his body screaming for rest. At last he came to within six feet of the table. He raised his shotgun and aimed it at the ravaged, bearded face of Silas.

And it was then that Silas turned to look at him.

Mr. Truscott was suddenly transfixed as though every nerve, every cell, every muscle in his body had been frozen. He couldn't move, couldn't speak, couldn't even blink. The Silas-thing leaned forward and grinned at him, its teeth yellow, its mangled tongue seething in its mouth. Slowly, lovingly, the Silas-thing began to remove Sam's hood with the knife, cutting the cords at the neck, plucking the sacking from the little girl's head.

As the hood came free, Mr. Truscott could see Sam's face, rigid with terror, tear-reddened eyes fixed on the knife which wavered before her like a snake about to strike. She was dirty, one cheek bruised, and her blond hair stood up in knotted strands. The Silas-thing twisted its fingers into her hair and pulled back her head to expose her throat. Gently he touched it with the point of the knife. *"Nooowwww,"* he purred, and the sightless eyes widened.

Suddenly he bucked and staggered backwards, releasing Sam. The knife dropped from his hand. Mr. Truscott looked on in wonder, believing for a moment that he had witnessed a miracle. Then he saw the mess of blood and brains frothing from the place where Silas's ear had been. He turned and saw Morgan Rice, frozen in tableau, a wisp of blue smoke curling from the barrel of the police rifle he held. Silas seemed to spin in slow motion. His legs gave way and he fell from the table. Mr. Truscott watched as Silas's pupils rolled slowly back. For a second Silas looked up and his eyes found Mr. Truscott's. Mr. Truscott saw an appeal in them, or perhaps gratitude. Then the life went out of them forever.

Mr. Truscott dropped the shotgun and stumbled towards the table, his legs like rubber, to be with his children. Sam saw him coming, screamed, "Daddy!" and burst into floods of tears.

Mr. Truscott reached Jamie first. He pulled off the hood with trembling hands and kissed and hugged his bemused son.

He pulled Sam to him and kissed and hugged her too. For a moment he just stayed there, nestling in the warmth of his children, thanking God that they were safe. Eventually he said, "Where's Mummy?"

Sam's face crumbled into new tears. "Oh, Daddy," she sobbed.

Mr. Truscott felt panic grip him. "Where is she, Sam? Do you know where she is?"

Sam nodded through her sobs and pointed behind the table. Mr. Truscott let go of his children and scrabbled along the ground, grazing his knees.

Angela's body was sprawled in the mud, her arms and legs beneath her, giving her the look of a broken rag doll. Even with the sack covering her face Mr. Truscott knew it was her. He crawled on spent legs and cradled the body in his arms. The sack-obscured head lolled back. When he saw what had been done to her, Mr. Truscott began to cry.

⌒⌒⌒⌒⌒⌒

Kevin and Martin were moving swiftly through the trees, the sounds of battle somewhere on their left. Martin's lungs felt choked with smoke-dust, but he ran on, anxious not to let Kevin out of his sight.

"Kev," he gasped, "Kev, wait a minute."

Kevin looked round. "Come on, Mart," he urged, and ran ahead again. Martin looked up, and a huge shadow seemed suddenly to loom in the trees to his right. He stopped dead.

"Kev," he said nervously.

Kevin stopped. "What now?" he said, annoyed.

"There's something there." Martin jerked his head towards the blackness of the trees.

"Where? I can't see anything."

Martin pointed. "It was just th—"

His words dried up as Swaney stepped from the darkness. For a moment the two boys could only stand and stare. The monstrous bulk seemed to pulse and throb with life, gnarled frame grooved with shadow. It stood, silently watching, motionless as a tree. Then, with a creaking and a rustling, it began to shuffle forward.

Kevin turned to run but found he couldn't move. His legs were paralysed through sheer terror. He looked at the dark soul again, at the hellish frame growing larger and larger as it advanced. Just for a second, it passed into a shaft of moonlight, and Kevin saw the shriveled features of Russell Swaney—the dead, chilling eyes, the cavernous mouth. He screamed, and the scream released his limbs.

He and Martin ran through the trees, arms held up to protect their faces Behind them trees crashed and splintered, bulldozed aside.

Suddenly they burst into the clearing, and Kevin staggered, blinded by moonlight, limbs shaking with terror. The fighting had now split up into pockets and it seemed as though the police and villagers were at last getting the upper hand. Kevin looked up and saw Garside and Keith hurrying towards him. From the looks on their faces, Swaney was close behind.

"For God's sake, boy, move, get out of the way," Garside shouted. He planted himself firmly in Swaney's path, rifle at his shoulder. Kevin almost laughed. The length of cold steel now seemed so flimsy and useless.

He tried to tell Garside it was no good, tried to grab him as he stumbled past. But Garside seemed determined to play the hero. Shoving Kevin out of the way, he raised the rifle and fired. The blast echoed and re-echoed, ringing through the trees, but the thing kept on coming. Garside muttered "What the fuck—", then the rifle was plucked from his hands by a monstrous limb and dashed to the ground. Garside dived for it, but too late. A tangle of roots and knobbly growths that might have been a foot smashed down, mangling the rifle as effectively as a steamroller. Garside looked up and screamed as the bulk of the thing overwhelmed him. He felt his bowels evacuate as he was swept up and smashed to the ground. He hit his head and mercifully lost consciousness.

The dark soul continued its remorseless advance. People

scattered before it, but the massive, creaking form ignored them all. Martin looked up, exhausted, as someone grabbed his arm. It was Keith.

"Come on, Mart," Keith urged. "Run. Run. It's you it wants. It's not interested in them." He tugged at Martin's arm, attempted to drag him along.

Martin tried to comply, tried to run, but his legs felt incredibly heavy and the ground seemed to be melting into slops and sludge beneath him. It was like being pursued in a dream, wading through glue as the nameless thing got closer and closer. He was dimly aware that Kevin was suffering the same experience.

"I can't move!" Kevin screamed hysterically. "I can't move!"

"It's Swaney," Keith shouted, trying to urge them along. "Try and fight it."

But it was no use. Their bodies were dragging them down. It felt as though gravity was trying to suck them into the earth.

Kevin risked a look back. Swaney loomed behind him, so close he could see each ridge and groove in the 'skin' quite plainly. He tried to scream. Last time it had helped him to move. But this time all that emerged was a soft and pitiful sigh. He tried again, and his throat felt as though his vocal cords had snapped. A smell touched his nostrils of something fetid and crawling. A twig that might have been a finger snagged in his hair. Another began to apply pressure to the back of his neck. A rustling, creaking sound seemed to overwhelm his senses.

And then...

Something happened.

Just what happened Kevin was not sure. All at once his eyes seemed full of stars or lights. He saw Martin and Keith by his side as flat, two-dimensional figures, and his surroundings seemed to melt away, become mist.

A man appeared.

An old man with a shabby overcoat and a broad-brimmed hat and a face that was brown and stubbled. Kevin thought he asked, "Who are you?" but the man merely smiled and said nothing. The only clear thing was his eyes. As blue as water.

The man walked up to Keith and went into him.

Kevin still couldn't move, but now it didn't matter. He felt somewhere else, on another plane where nothing could hurt him. He watched as Keith turned and began to walk slowly towards Swaney. Kevin was struck by how blue Keith's eyes were.

As Keith walked past him, Kevin realised he could move again. He retreated a few paces and turned. At his elbow, he was vaguely aware of Martin.

The two boys watched as Keith walked calmly up to the dark soul and held out a hand. "Come to me," he whispered. The dark soul was immobile, a grotesque tree drenched in moonlight. Keith opened his arms wide, wide, wide, and embraced the dark soul. He grew and smothered it. His mouth opened, and a voice came out. A gentle old man's voice which spoke strange, soothing, hypnotic words, words to calm a wayward child or a timid dog.

The dark soul began to rock and shudder in Keith's grip, tormented by the words. But Keith with the blue eyes and the old man's voice never let go. Indeed, his grip strengthened. And from the mist of the woods, the boys saw people come to help. People who also embraced the dark soul. People they recognised.

They saw Kevin's mother and Macky Cooper and Sharon Stewart and big Sergeant Hopper and Philip Donahue, and other people they didn't know, some of them insubstantial, little more than suggestions of form. Ghosts.

Silently the battlefield rose. The boys saw dead people leave their bodies and stand up. They seemed out of sync, not quite there, blurred projections. Colourless, effortless, they moved across the ground.

And all these people embraced the dark soul. And the words of the old man went on. And on. And on.

And then...

Keith began to change.

His skin turned dark and mottled. His arms extended, entwined, merged like branches. His feet extended, grew from his legs, and took root in the ground. His face disappeared. His body disappeared. He became Swaney's prison.

The woods sighed and settled. The words faded away like a

distant echo. The mist dispersed, taking the people with it. And Kevin found he could talk again.

"What happened?" he said.

Martin gave him a strange look and said nothing.

Kevin looked at the tree in the centre of the clearing. Its healthy bark and broad green leaves contrasted sharply with the black, wasted frames of its neighbours. Around him people were blinking and shaking their heads as though woken from a collective dream. Some were sitting on the ground, shivering or crying. Bemused prisoners were raising their arms as police surrounded them. The air was heavy with the coppery smell of blood and a lingering sense of decay. Kevin looked up as he heard someone call his name.

And suddenly he was running over the battlefield towards his father.

THE END

ABOUT THE AUTHOR

Mark Morris has written over twenty-five novels, among which are **Toady**, **Stitch**, **The Immaculate**, **The Secret of Anatomy**, **Fiddleback**, **The Deluge** and four books in the popular **Doctor Who** range. He is the author of three short story collections, **Close to the Bone** (Piatkus), **Long Shadows, Nightmare Light** (PS Publishing) and **Wrapped In Skin** (ChiZine Publications) and several novellas.

His short fiction, articles and reviews have appeared in a wide variety of anthologies and magazines, and he is editor of **Cinema Macabre**, for which he won the 2007 British Fantasy Award, its follow-up **Cinema Futura**, two volumes of **The Spectral Book of Horror Stories**, **New Fears** and **New Fears 2** (Titan Books).

His script work includes audio dramas for Big Finish Productions' **Doctor Who** and **Jago & Litefoot** ranges, and also for Bafflegab's **Hammer Chillers** series.

His recently published work includes the official movie tie-in novelisations of **Noah** and **The Great Wall**, the novellas **It Sustains** (Earthling Publications) and **Albion Fay** (Snowbooks), and his **Obsidian Heart** trilogy, **The Wolves of London, The Society of Blood** and **The Wraiths of War** (Titan Books). Most recently, his audio adaptation of the classic British folk-horror movie **Blood on Satan's Claw** was the Gold Winner for Best Drama Special at the 2018 New York Festival's International Radio Awards

ALSO FROM
BLOODSHOT BOOKS

When Adam was 15, a terrible thing happened. So terrible that he and his father ran away in an attempt to put it behind them. But the past is not so easy to shake off. And a new start does not necessarily mean a better start. Who is the figure at the top of the stairs? Whose is the face in the mirror? What is the thing in the pond? And why does Adam often feel he is being followed, only for his pursuers to dissolve into shadow when he turns to confront them?

When Adam was 15, a terrible thing happened. So terrible that he believed it to be the worst thing of all. But he is about to find out that there are far worse things waiting out there....

Available in paperback or Kindle on Amazon.com

http://bit.ly/Sustains

From a crater lake on an island off the coast of Bronze Age Estonia...

To a crippled Viking warrior's conquest of England ...

To the bloody temple of an Aztec god of death and resurrection...

Their presence has shaped our world. They are the Riders.

One month ago, an urban explorer was drawn to an abandoned asylum in the mountains of northern Massachusetts. There he discovered a large specimen jar, containing something organic, unnatural and possibly alive.

Now, he and a group of unsuspecting individuals have discovered one of history's most horrific secrets. Whether they want to or not, they are caught in the middle of a millennia-old war and the latest battle is about to begin.

Available in paperback or Kindle on Amazon.com

http://amzn.to/1peMAjz

Welcome to the small Midwestern town of Belford, Ohio. It's summer vacation and fourteen-year-old Toby Fairchild is looking forward to spending a lazy, carefree summer playing basketball, staying up late watching monster movies, and camping out in his backyard with his best friend, Frankie.

But then tragedy strikes. And out of this tragedy an unlikely friendship develops between Toby and the local bogeyman, a strange old man across the street named Mr. Joseph. Over the course of a tumultuous summer, Toby will be faced with pain and death, the excitement of his first love, and the underlying racism of the townsfolk, all while learning about the value of freedom at the hands of a kind but cursed old man.

Every town has a dark side. And in Belford, the local bogeyman has a story to tell.

Available in paperback or Kindle on Amazon.com

http://bit.ly/AWAKEpb

HOW MUCH DO YOU HATE?
Eddie Brinkburn's doing time for a botched garage job that left Sheraton's brother very badly burned.

HOW MUCH DO YOU HATE?
When Sheraton's gang burn his wife and kids to death, Eddie soon learns the meaning of hate.

HOW MUCH DO YOU HATE?
And that's how the prison psycho transfers his awesome power to Eddie. A power that Eddie reckons he can control. A power that will enable Eddie to put the frighteners on Sheraton...

Available in paperback or Kindle on Amazon.com

http://bit.ly/FrightPB

ON THE HORIZON FROM
BLOODSHOT BOOKS

2018*

Killer Chronicles – Somer Canon
The Special – James Newman & Mark Steensland
Victoria (What Hides Within #2) – Jason Parent

2019-20*

Bleed Away the Sky – Brian Fatah Steele
The Devil Virus – Chris DiLeo
The October Boys – Adam Millard
The Cryptids – Elana Gomel
What Sleeps Beneath – John Quick
Dead Sea Chronicles – Tim Curran
Blood Mother: A Novel of Terror – Pete Kahle
Not Your Average Monster – World Tour
The Abomination (The Riders Saga #2) – Pete Kahle
The Horsemen (The Riders Saga #3) – Pete Kahle

* other titles to be added when confirmed

BLOODSHOT BOOKS

READ UNTIL YOU BLEED!